PHILLIP THOMAS DUCK

PLAYING WITH
DESTINY

sepia
★BET
BOOKS

BET Publications, LLC
http://www.bet.com

SEPIA BOOKS are published by

BET Publications, LLC
c/o BET BOOKS
One BET Plaza
1900 W Place NE
Washington, DC 20018-1211

All KensingtonTitles, Imprints, and Distributed Lines are available at special quantity discounts for bulk purchases for sales promotions, premiums, fund-raising, and educational or institutional use. Special book excerpts or customized printings can also be created to fit specific needs. For details, write or phone the office of the Kensington special sales manager: Kensington Publishing Corp., 850 Third Avenue, New York, NY 10022, attn: Special Sales Department, Phone: 1-800-221-2647.

BET Books is a trademark of Black Entertainment Television, Inc. SEPIA and the SEPIA logo are trademarks of BET Books and the BET BOOKS logo is a registered trademark.

ISBN 1-58314-524-9

First Printing: April 2005
10 9 8 7 6 5 4 3 2 1

Printed in the United States of America

PLAYING WITH
DESTINY

BACK IN THE DAY (CIRCA 1989)

Dreams of an R&B Chick

Kim Parker was on the second floor of her family's Brooklyn brownstone when the level below burst into flames. She sat at the vanity in her bedroom, staring at herself in the mirror, rubbing her hand over her growing belly, and singing in her angelic voice—determined that this pregnancy wouldn't derail her from her ultimate dream of one day being like Whitney Houston.

Kim hadn't heard the glass shatter on the bottom floor, hadn't heard the crackle of burning wood. She had yet to smell the smoke, so she kept singing and rubbing her belly.

The flames ate through the kitchen, embracing the recently shellacked cabinets, charring the linoleum flooring. The cheap kitchen table set went quickly. The flames climbed the walls and licked the curtains, swallowing them in a hot orange and blue rage. With determination, the flames moved on, traveling out beyond the kitchen and heading for the room at the end of the hall where Kim's parents now slept.

Kim continued singing and rubbing her swollen belly, studying her reflection in the mirror. There was the fleck of a light birthmark on her nut-brown-colored neck. A rose growing through the concrete of this ghetto, that's what she was. Her look was complemented by spandex shorts and door-knocker earrings, sporting the image of Salt from Salt-N-Pepa like the majority of her other female classmates. But unlike the other girls at George Westinghouse

High School, Kim's voice trailed off and her cheeks turned brighter than the colors on her leather 8-ball jacket when that song *Push It* came on the radio. She never could form her mouth to say the words—*Push it reeeeaaaal good*. She was more R&B than rap. Soft like a flower, not hardened like the other girls. Kim rubbed her belly. She was going to make sure her child was the same way, soft and delicate.

The fire downstairs continued to roar and grow, eating away at the magazine rack in the hallway and Kim's brother's Big Wheel.

The surprise pregnancy had already made Kim's father slump in his wheelchair, shaking and crying so hard she had feared he would fall to the floor and injure himself. It had already made her mother cut back on Sunday church service and weeknight Bible study, and had already made her little peanut-head, six-year-old brother ask her questions she was too embarrassed to answer. And her baby's daddy, shoot, he didn't want a thing to do with Kim anymore. He'd gotten all he wanted from Kim—to push it real good—and that was that. He was a boy himself.

Still, Kim was determined that this child be loved, nurtured. She'd never utter the word "accident" to this baby. She was fifteen and pregnant, but far from a statistic, no proof of an epidemic.

Kim stopped singing, frowned, and turned in her seat.

The smoke finally caught her nose—at the same time as the other chaos broke out. The fire alarm hit a high note and held it. Someone banged at the backyard door. Sirens wailed in the distance.

Kim threw on her robe and moved into the hall to check what was happening.

The thick smoke stung her eyes and quickly filled her lungs. She coughed and blinked her way through the grayish fog, moving in the direction of her brother's bedroom. She prayed the entire way that her parents were okay on the first floor, that her mother was able to get her father to his wheelchair without incident. She found her brother's door ajar, Jason's bed empty. He likely had that nightmare about Oscar the Grouch again and went downstairs to sleep in the crawl space between his parents.

Kim backed out into the hall again, feeling along the walls, pushing through the grayish fog, coughing violently now.

"Kim! Fire, Kim! Kim!"

It was the stern voice of her father coming from downstairs.

She could imagine him in his wheelchair, devastated that he couldn't climb those stairs and rescue his little girl. She took a few more steps forward, the smoke getting thicker with each step.

"Kim, come down, sweetie! We have Jason! Fire, Kim!" he yelled.

She could also hear her mother's pleading voice now, no doubt speaking to Jesus again, no longer too embarrassed to face Him after the humiliation of her teen daughter's unexpected pregnancy.

Kim made it to the stairs. Through the grayish fog, she could see hot orange flames waiting for her at the bottom of the stairwell. It was a stunning sight. She swallowed and squint her eyes. The sound of her parents' voices had changed now to the thud of trampling feet. The sirens that had been in the distance now pressed down on her. Firefighters had come to save Kim, her parents, brother, and their home. Kim wondered if it were too late for her, because her legs felt heavy as sand sacks, and she could barely catch a breath. She wanted to drop right there and let the fire have its way with her, but then she thought about her swollen belly and pressed on. In this short time, her lungs had filled with smoke and caused a hard ache in her chest. She felt for the handrail and made her way down.

The red flash of lights and sirens became more prominent. Kim made it to the base of the steps and turned to her right. One of the firefighters reached her as her legs were about to turn into *Play-Doh*. She straightened up and felt for his hand. The firefighter rushed her outside. The neighbors, most of them in pajamas, lined the sidewalk for the entire block.

Next door to the Parkers' burning brownstone, a mother proudly caressed the shoulders of her teenage son as he sat on the stoop between her legs. He had a blanket draped over him and sweat glistened on his forehead. He looked as if he'd been in the belly of the fire himself. "Good thing you woke up and seen the smoke, Colin," his mother said. "Good thing. They'll be fine, because of you. You're a hero."

Colin leaned against his mother's chest, his younger brother, Courtney, standing off behind them in the doorway. Courtney had seen everything, too, and couldn't figure out why his mother was rubbing Colin's shoulders and telling him he was a hero. Maybe she had knowledge that a nine-year-old didn't understand.

Outside the Parker residence, Kim loosened her grip on the firefighter and searched for her family. Once she found them huddled together by the curb, she allowed the black mask hovering above her to come down and shade her eyes. She collapsed on the slice of lawn in front of her family's brownstone.

Colin gasped, went to stand, but his legs pushed him back to his seat instead. His mother placed a hand to her mouth. They both watched, tight with anticipation. Courtney, in the doorway, looked at Colin, studying Colin's reaction to Kim falling.

The paramedics worked on Kim Parker, her pregnant belly exposed through her robe for all the neighbors to see. It would be the gossip for a long time to come. That's why she was walking around, no matter what the temperature, wearing those bulky sweatshirts, they'd say.

Colin blinked back tears as the paramedics hoisted Kim on a stretcher. Kim's eyes were closed, her beautiful, nut-brown-colored skin marred by charcoal-black soot. Colin preferred the old Kim, flat-stomach Kim, whom he always could beat in a foot-race to Bagley's corner store. *Why you read so many books, Colin?* Nosy Kim. Kim, the first girl he ever kissed. Now, he silently chastised himself for not being worthy of that kiss. Kim deserved better than he gave her.

As the doors of the ambulance closed, Colin could hold the tears off no longer. They came, warm and wet, racing down his face. His mother continued rubbing his shoulders, praising him, telling him everything was going to be okay because he was a hero. *You banged on their back door, Colin. You came and woke me up, baby, had me dial for an ambulance.* Colin loved his mother, but now, hated the caress of her hands, the grating sound of her voice.

The ambulance drove off and the crowd immediately withdrew. Colin remained on the stoop, eyeing the charred house next door, thoughts of that first kiss with Kim Parker lingering like the scent of smoke in the air. His mother brought him a glass of lemonade, but he shrugged it off. After about ten minutes, Colin eased back into the house and headed straight for his bedroom.

His brother Courtney lay spread across his own bed, looking up at the ceiling. Colin entered the bedroom, slump-shouldered. "Hey," Courtney said, sitting up.

Colin moved into the room and took off his sweat-soaked T-shirt. "Go to sleep, Court."

"Can't," Courtney replied.

"Try," Colin said as he removed his sneakers and tossed them to a corner.

"You think Kim's gonna be okay?" Courtney asked.

"Don't know," Colin barked. "Now go to sleep."

Courtney nodded and lay back on his pillows. Colin did the same on his bed.

"Hey, Colin," Courtney called out.

"What!"

"I hope she's all right, 'cause she got that belly with that baby inside her. I hope so for you, too."

The tenderness of his little brother took the bite out of Colin. "You know she's pregnant? What you know about babies, Court?" At fifteen, Colin was just learning about sex; he couldn't believe his nine-year-old brother was so far ahead of him, always far ahead of him in the things kids considered cool and of interest.

Courtney answered, "I know how they get made. I know I hope she's okay."

"I hope so, too, Court. I hope so, too," Colin said, softly.

The next day, Colin would find out that Kim Parker had lost the baby, and drifted into a sad silence no one could break through. He cried for Kim that day. He'd spend the rest of his life crying for Kim, her unborn baby . . . and himself.

1

MAY 6, 2002

*O*ver my dead body.

Colin Sheffield tapped out the four words on his computer screen, paused for a moment to take them in, as a wine taster swirling a vintage on his tongue would do, then hit the backspace key to erase them. The flicker of light from his computer monitor shone off his face. The tight expression around his eyes, in his forehead, meant only one thing. The words weren't flowing with the ease he'd become accustomed to. Perhaps it was the hour, early morning, when the darkness of the predawn sky covered the sunroof above the loft like a coat of black paint. He could count on one hand the number of times he'd written after the sun slept. He did most of his writing early in the day. Or it was the story itself. Never before had he written a novel so close to his own reality. The characters were all pieces of people he knew; the main protagonist, a skewed replica of himself.

He leaned back in his leather recliner and massaged the soreness from his overworked fingers. That his fingers hurt didn't bother him, that what they'd produced wasn't usable, did. He'd done a thorough sketch of all his characters before he wrote one word on this latest novel—yet here he was, up to his knees in mud.

"Come on sweetheart," he commanded of the woman inside his monitor, talking to her with tenderness, this woman inside his imagination. "What's going on in that head of yours? Think of what he asked you, how are you going to respond? Angry? No, no, no, maybe you brush it aside—he wants you to be angry." He almost pulled the file with his character sketches aside, so he could read over it again to get a tighter feel for how she'd play this scene, but the scattered disorganization of his desk made the task an afterthought.

The sound of slippers scratching across the linoleum flooring on the lower level of the condominium took him from his novel-in-progress. He followed the soft swishing sound, like medium-grade sandpaper chiseling something glorious out of wood. His wife made her way through the pitch black of their home. He listened to her but kept his gaze on the computer monitor.

"Smile that heartbreaking smile of yours and walk away. That'll kill him," Colin said aloud as he decided on his sassy female character's action.

After a few beats the kitchen light came on. The sink turned on, shut off, and then turned on again. Colin could hear paper being torn. He rose from his desk and went to the rail of the loft so he could sneak a look at his wife, Liza. He touched his abdomen as he took in her dark chocolate legs, still feminine despite their muscularity. The teal-colored silk of her pajama top hung off her thin shoulders, opened through the middle so her full stomach could breathe. His jaw muscles tensed as he eyed the round belly. Could he deal with fatherhood? Was he ready? Was Liza?

Liza had a deep erotic presence, stronger than at any other time he could remember, her skin glowing like a florescent bulb. She moved about with ease, unaware of his eyes on her. If she had looked up and seen him watching, her ease would have dissipated quicker than the words he had typed and backspaced away a few moments before. He watched her a few moments more. Oh, how badly he wanted them to regain the closeness they once had. Their fight from earlier still hung in the air, unresolved. He looked at Liza's full belly again. It was criminal to bring a child into this mess. He sighed and returned to his chair.

He took the lukewarm cup of coffee from his desk, swallowed the concoction, and washed his tongue with the milk and extra sugar that would make a serious coffee drinker cringe with disgust. He was prepared to return to his story when the loud screeching sound, metal on metal, halted him. He glanced at the clock and frowned.

Kraaaaaa. Kraaaaaaa.

He saved his file and rushed down the steps that led from his loft to the living room and then to the kitchen.

"Mrs. Sheffield, you know what time it is?" he asked his wife as he appeared in the kitchen. Liza released a button on the blender, stopped the machine.

"What?" she asked.

She still seemed peeved from their earlier disagreement, Colin noted, and so he lowered his voice to ask, "It's late, Liza, what are you doing?"

There was a pan on the countertop with little postage-stamp-size blocks of scrap paper submerged in water. The blender looked like it had a batch of the same paper scraps filling the glass container.

"I'm making paper to sketch on," Liza answered.

"Making paper?" Colin's face turned up, bewildered. "Why didn't you get some from the art supply store?" He had many failings as a husband, but not when it came to Liza's creative endeavors. He knew too well about the yearning to create.

"Didn't want to have to ask you for anything," Liza replied. Her tone was embittered. "I used to do this all time when I was studying at FIT," she added. "Broke college student, you know the drill."

"I've never noticed you doing this before."

Liza pursed her lips, said, "A lot you haven't noticed," and then pressed the blender back into action.

Enough was enough. Brave soul that he was, Colin moved closer to his wife and wrapped his arms around her waist. It made his stomach somersault when his hands touched her pregnant belly, but he held firm with his embrace. Liza's skin was warm and giving, a perfect complement to his hands, which were cold and taking. Colin moved Liza to a rhythm that played in his head only, a music that only he heard. She swayed with him. Colin's tight grip on her hips made her sway, not some shared melody of love in the air.

"Ask me how my book is coming," he sang in her ear, talking as if the fight earlier that evening had never happened.

"Ask me what I'm sketching," she replied. Liza turned her head to Colin, her eyes bore into him, intense enough to see through steel. "Better yet, ask me about the baby. Ask me if you can feel for a kick."

Colin released the hold on his wife. "Okay, Liza. What are you sketching?"

She shook her head, her eyes held captive by sadness. "Noah's Ark."

"Really? That's cool."

Liza continued looking deeply at Colin. "You remember the significance of that, of what I told you?" It was obvious from his expression he didn't. "The nursery," she answered for him.

"Nursery?"

"Remember, I told you me and Mama picked out the Noah's Ark theme for the baby's room? The wallpaper, the crib linens, all of it is Noah's Ark."

"Oh, yeah, yeah," Colin replied. He tapped the side of his head with a long finger. "That's right, and you're going to hang the picture in there when you finish it, by the door or something?" He smiled.

"In that special frame," Liza said.

"Jog my memory; what special frame?"

Liza sighed and returned to her papermaking. Why did Colin have to be so detached when it came to their unborn child? A genuine smile every now and then would have sufficed. He was present during this entire nine months, attending childbirth classes and the like, but not once did his eyes light up like they did when he talked about his writing. He had talked on countless occasions about children before her pregnancy and then—when nature had done its part with his sperm and her egg—he'd shut down on her. Was this attitude a precursor to what lie ahead? Was he expecting her to raise this child all by herself—that he could be the wallet, and she would be the caregiver, the nurturer, the disciplinarian, the teacher?

Liza poured the pulpy mixture from the blender in an empty milk carton. She placed a piece of felt flat on the countertop, covered the felt with an eight-and-a-half-by-eleven-inch picture frame. She turned up the milk carton and poured the pulp over the felt within the frame.

"Liza, about earlier . . ." Colin's voice trailed off as he thought of how to explain himself further, how to shorten this gulf that separated them.

"Don't begin with your explanations," Liza said, raising her hand to ward him off. "Heard them all before and I'm not into sequels."

"I need your support is all I was going to say," Colin responded. "You know Langston Campbell's new book is coming out soon, and I have to make sure my tour is a home run. I've gotta squelch the love I'm sure he's going to get so that it doesn't automatically doom my book. I've got about a four-week float to make my mark in the marketplace before his shit comes to bludgeon everything in sight. I worked hard on this joint, baby, and it's better than anything he could ever imagine writing. I need my mind clear, my focus tight. I need you in my corner, Boo."

Liza turned to face her husband, the empty milk carton in her slender fingers. "I've always been in your corner, Colin; that's a given. How 'bout if you were in mine, too?"

Colin stood in place, leaning casually against the countertop next to her, gazing. He perused the contours of her rounded belly, wiry frame, and the sexy hairline that ran up her stomach and looked like the crease of a book. She watched him back, the silence between them deafening. "Okay, I'm in your corner, Liza. I'll do better," he said, after a moment. Even in anger, Liza was hostage to his retreat. His dimpled smile made her smile against her will. That's how it had been between them for some time. He dictated, she followed, sometimes with hesitation, but she always followed.

"So," Liza said, trying to move forward. "What's Langston's new book about?"

That was the last question Colin wanted to hear. He blew out an air of frustration. "Same shit. Boy meets girl. Girl's caramel-colored skin and pearly white smile works boy up in a frenzy. Boy screws girl over somehow—or maybe she screws him over—and then they spend two hundred fifty pages avoiding each other, not returning calls. Just to be—" He paused in contempt. "Just to be united somehow in the end."

"Oh," Liza said. "Another bestseller in other words."

A painful half smile appeared on Colin's face. "In other words," he admitted. He was peaceful in surrender to the truth.

"You need to put serious thought into writing something a little . . ." Liza stopped.

"Less heady? Fluff? You can go ahead and say it, Liza."

"Lighter," she replied.

Colin shook his head. "I gotta feed my black folks, Liza. I can't be giving them Chinese food, knowing they'll be hungry again as soon as they finish. Baldwin didn't do it, Ellison didn't do it. Toni Morrison doesn't do it."

"Look, I'm just the wife of a novelist, and I don't like to read myself," Liza said. "I tried to read *The Bluest Eye* because of Oprah, and I couldn't finish the damn thing—and don't look at me in judgment. But I know you're an excellent writer, and your books are admirable in the fact that they tackle issues that a lot of the others don't look at, but if you truly want to accomplish what you say you do, then you need a broader audience. To get that audience you need the right mixture of fun and seriousness in your writing."

Colin stood in contemplation. Everyone, from his agent to his publicist, had always nudged at him to make a complete crossover. Never had anyone made the suggestion Liza did. "Balance is what you're saying?"

"That's it," Liza said as she averted her eyes, ran them across the spare countertop. Her hands stopped moving, immobilized by her thoughts. *Balance.*

Colin moved closer, took her chin in his fingers, and looked deep into her eyes. "I like the idea of balance. So simple and yet none of us ever thought of it. Haven't you heard about the yin and yang? Every yin needs a yang. You're my yang."

Liza smiled from the warmth of his fingers. In the midst of all the madness, they could still have these moments, straight off a Hallmark commercial. "You would give me the uglier of the two words. How about I'm your yin and you're my yang?"

Colin shrugged. "Whatever's clever, Boo."

Liza cleared her throat. "Since we're in this sharing mode . . ."

Colin swallowed, forced a half smile. "Go 'head."

Liza looked at him, deep again, deeper than he ever wanted any person to look at him. "You were kicking and flailing earlier. Damn near punched me in the belly. I need you to talk to me about the nightmares."

Colin frowned, shook his head. "Nothing to talk about, Liza," he lied. He'd had another dream about Kim Parker. He didn't talk about Kim Parker with anyone, and had practically convinced himself it didn't happen all those years ago.

Liza rubbed her stomach, shook her head in return. "I think there is."

Colin shook his head, yet again. "Nothing, trust me." He kissed two fingers and placed them gently on her forehead. "I'm going back to write."

Liza watched Colin climb the stairs. She bit back tears as she continued rubbing her belly. *Just you and me, little one to be,* she thought. *Just you and me. As much as I'd like otherwise . . . it's just you and me.*

Courtney Sheffield paused at the top of the key—by the free-throw line—his hands down on his knees. His lungs were being pushed to their breaking point. The burning in his chest prodded him on, a physical marker of what it took to reach the highest pinnacle in the game Michael Jordan had dominated. The game that Michael artistically left an imprint on, as Picasso had with a paintbrush in his hands. Since he was a young kid, Courtney wanted to be like someone else—Michael one moment, his older brother, Colin, the next. Tonight, in the shadows of this outdoor court, he only wanted to be himself. He could hear the crowd's roar in his ears, could imagine the packed stands off in the distance. The college basketball season was over, and he was alone on this court, but he could feel the thrill of competition running through his veins as if the season had never ended. As if the kid from Wake Forrest hadn't thrown up that Hail Mary shot at the buzzer, prematurely ending another of Courtney's runs at March Madness. Hail Mary shot or not, Courtney was on notice. He'd dropped thirty-seven points on Wake Forrest and had the Red Storm fans of St. John's University cheering his every move. This was his world.

He ran his fingers over the leather of the ball, caressing it like the curves of a beautiful woman. Dribbled to the far left corner, stopped on a dime, and jumped high into the air. He cocked the ball at the apex of his jump and then released it. It spiraled ahead on course for the rim and found its way through the hoop. Courtney chased down the ball, cupped it in his large hands, rose in one swift motion, and took another shot.

The shot missed.

So he ran the length of the court in the other direction and bounced off the chain-link fence at the other end. Lungs burning, he took a quick inhale of the night air and then ran back toward the ball. Missed shots meant he had to run the court, so he was determined to make more than he missed.

The air held the scent of impending rain. He prayed it would come soon, wash away the horrible May humidity and the salty sweat that ran down his face and settled on his lips. A patrol car passed by, slowing to see who was out this time of morning. When the campus security saw Courtney Sheffield shooting baskets, they flashed their headlights and serenaded him with a toot of the horn. This was indeed his world.

The lights around the perimeter of the courts didn't offer much but it didn't matter. Courtney had mastered all the nuances of this game, this court. He could shoot with his eyes closed, like Michael had done that one time during an actual NBA game. Courtney crossed the faded line that was the half-court marker, dribbling easily. Then, as he neared the basket, he took one long stride and bounded toward the hoop for a soaring dunk. He could hear Marv Albert hollering his trademark "Yes!" as he executed the move. He could see them standing at the Garden or other famous arena, cheering his name, mesmerized by his every move. *Court-ney Sheffield. Court-ney Shef-field*, the rabid fans screamed, emphasizing every syllable in his name. Inner-city kids emulating how he walked, how he chewed gum, how he styled his cornrows. Surely, a packed arena screaming his name had more of an impact than his name written in bold purple letters on the cover of a book. Tell that to his mother and Nana.

"According to anonymous sources, Courtney Sheffield out of St. John's University has been mulling over a decision regarding his final year of college eligibility. NBA scouts project him as an early first-round lottery pick if he forgoes his final year and declares himself for the draft. He has a week left before the May 13 deadline for declaration. With the draft only a month away, one can only imagine the dilemma this young man is facing."

The news story had broken earlier that evening. The unlisted phone in his off-campus room had been ringing ever since. The endless chime had chased him outside, to solitude on this court. The nets were torn down, the backboard shaky, the lines of the court fading, but she was his best friend. He didn't just play basketball. He orchestrated the tempo and rhythm of a game. He made love to the court. He'd explored every one of her inches, had mastered all the moves that made her buckle under his spell. And every time he touched her, he left her satisfied. Unlike everyone else in his life, she didn't betray him, leave him, or undervalue him.

"Who do you think would draft me?" Courtney had asked one of the sports agents that courted him of late.

"My guess is Atlanta," the agent replied. "They're picking fifth and they need a quick, smooth-scoring guard like you in the worst way."

"What kind of money we talkin' with the fifth pick?"

"One point five, at a minimum," the agent had said. "Trust me, Courtney. You'll be seeing Oprah-Winfrey money if you follow my course. You're what's known as a 'can't-miss,' son. Why go back to school and risk blowing out a knee or something? That college degree might get you a decent job, but it's not going to get you one point five million dollars."

Courtney stood tall, asked all the right questions. "Suppose the experts are wrong and I end up not getting drafted that early, or not at all? Then what? I pissed away my last year of college for nothing?"

"You know the rules, son. You can go back as long as you don't sign with an agent before the draft."

"But that's it," Courtney said. "If I declare early, then that's it. I can't ever go back." Courtney knew you couldn't take back any done deed in life.

The agent smiled. "If you declare early, you won't have to. Trust me."

Courtney dropped the ball on the concrete and started running his laps around the court. His mind was focused on the decision that laid ahead, all the people who wanted a piece of him. Were they telling him the truth? Was he good enough to be the player they all said he'd be? He could think of at least a dozen other talented players that had come up before him, players bigger, stronger, and more skilled. None of them had made it to the pros. School-yard legends that dominated the asphalt courts and nothing more. Sadness clutched his heart when he thought about one of those legends, "Prime," dunking on everybody in sight one moment, in a back alley shooting up the next. Prime was the best player Courtney had ever witnessed. Another one of his heroes. If Prime couldn't make it, Courtney didn't see how he could.

"New York City has a rich tradition of breeding talented guards. Nate 'Tiny' Archibald during the sixties. Mark Jackson, Kenny Smith, and Dwayne 'Pearl' Washington in the eighties. Kenny Anderson and Stephon Marbury in the nineties. Courtney Sheffield has a chance to surpass them all. He combines Archibald's quickness with Jackson's uncanny passing ability, and Marbury's explosiveness. All in one tidy package. If he declares for the draft, the team that gets him will have itself a future superstar."

Courtney paused at the water fountain, allowed himself a quick swallow. The cool water soothed his chest and took the numbness from his weary legs. The NBA had been his dream for as long as he could remember. This decision shouldn't be so hard. But it was. He knew his mother and his Nana would be disappointed. They didn't understand the opportunity that pro ball presented. They always threw the fall of neighborhood legend Prime in Courtney's face whenever the topic of basketball came up. Be more like your brother Colin, they told him. Stop chasing after this foolish dream.

Turning pro would be Courtney's greatest achievement in life, and yet it would still place him a notch below Colin. For his mother and Nana, the purple block letters on the cover of Colin's books were the apex. The packed stadium screaming Courtney's name—that was okay. On the one hand, you had a professional basketball star, on the other, a successful novelist with a college degree. To most, there wasn't any doubt the sports star was the sexier of the two, but Courtney's mother and Nana couldn't see it. That one point five million that the agents assured Courtney of sounded mighty good, but was it enough to cover the pain of Colin upstaging him again, in his finest hour?

"He combines Archibald's quickness with Jackson's uncanny passing ability, and Marbury's explosiveness. All in one tidy package. When he declares for the draft, the team that gets him will have itself a future superstar."

Yeah, he'd be a superstar. He'd have the money, the glamour, and yet Colin would still be the prize of the Sheffield family. The thought stung more than Courtney's lungs. He sat on his basketball, his back pressed against the chain-link fence. For as long as he could remember he'd operated from the shadows. He couldn't stand it. Only six years separated the two brothers, but the gap had always felt wider. Colin had their hearts. Colin had their respect. They read Colin's books with pride. As if he was friggin' Ralph Ellison or Maya Angelou. Courtney wanted to shake his mother and Nana back to reality. "Colin writes books, yes, but he hasn't cracked the *New York Times* best-seller list since the first book. Dude's career is nose-diving, can't you see that? Do you know how many times the *New York Times* has covered me? More times than I can count, that's how many. My stock rises. Meanwhile, Colin is going down, fast."

His mother and Nana were so in the dark. They thought Colin was so kindhearted and so generous. They thought he cared so much about the people around him. They thought he was a role model, novelist, family man, and child of God. It was like someone died when Colin got married and moved to Jersey. His mother and Nana were proud as can be, happy for Colin, but they missed him with an emotion akin to grief. The brownstone in Brooklyn was always quieter than a funeral home now. Every day cast as the night before Christmas. As far as Courtney was concerned, his big brother was nothing but a fraud. He had them all fooled, but he wasn't fooling him. He knew the truth. He knew the secrets that Colin guarded with his life. Colin didn't deserve half of what he had. He didn't deserve Liza.

Courtney's cell phone buzzed. He quickly scanned the screen. It was another call from his ex-girlfriend, Chante. She was the other thorn in his side. Courtney shut off his phone's ringer and tossed the phone on the grass.

Courtney had something Prime didn't have—motivation. He had a brother to outshine and an ex-girlfriend that he wanted to remind, with every basket he scored in the NBA, what she'd thrown away.

2

MAY 6

Colin and Liza had separated from their early-morning encounter in the kitchen, hours before, and each fell into the warm arms of his or her creative haven. Colin entering the darkest places of his soul—working on this newest novel—in his writing loft. Liza, in her drawing studio, sketching Noah's Ark, wishing the ark could keep her from drowning in her own tears.

The drawing studio was perfect for her artistic endeavors, with north-facing light, good ventilation, and cotton drapes lessening the harshness of light that dared sneak in through the windows. The sparseness of the room fit her personality. Liza was without pretense, without glitter, a former model whose idea of makeup was a splash of lipstick that would disappear after one kiss. In the center of her room was a large storage table—next to it, an easel. Along the left wall, drawings hung from what looked like an indoor clothesline. On the storage table, in the center of the room, were three jars—one holding pencils, one holding crayons, and a third holding charcoal sticks. There was no chair, no couch, and no other tables in the room. That was it. That was Liza's room.

Colin's writing loft was a bit more extravagant. A large oak desk held his laptop computer, his fax/copier/scanner, and his telephone with all the new features—though he seldom had the ringer on and rarely accepted calls. All the techno gizmos of this talented writer swam amongst crumpled scrap sheets with notes jotted at odd angles and books of the writers he adored. James Baldwin's *Go Tell It On the Mountain,* Ellison's *Invisible Man,* a bunch of Elmore Leonard novels for fun reading, with tight plots and too-real dialogue.

Colin's chair was a leather recliner with all the correct ergonomic features so he didn't come away with a stiff neck. His room had a plush couch, a coffee table, bookshelves stuffed with texts. He had a stereo system for playing mood music while he wrote. He had a television set for goofing off during his infrequent downtime. None of the gadgets and odds and ends would put together the words for Colin's book, though. None of those gadgets and odds and ends would help make this newest novel a success. And that's what Colin needed, as much as Liza needed snuggling and reassurance; Colin needed a success, a best-seller.

After hours of writing, Colin had settled into bed, had allowed sleep to overcome him when Liza stormed into their bedroom, anxious, out of breath.

"Colin! Colin!"

He shook aside the voice, turned over on his side. He could hear her calling, like from the bottom of a well, but he couldn't open his eyes, couldn't answer, his body no longer under his control. The soft mattress was too comfortable, sleep too dominant. His new novel had stolen his slumber, and now that his prolific spirit had allowed him to shut down the computer and settle into bed, Liza was in his ear. Whatever she had on her mind would have to wait until the sun rose in a few hours.

Liza persisted, shaking his shoulder this time. The charcoal on her fingertips drifted to his nostrils. "Colin, baby, wake up please! I thought it was something I ate at first, but now . . . I think I'm having contractions."

Colin yawned, stretched his dormant muscles and turned back facing his wife. Tired as he was, it was evident Liza wasn't going away. Had he heard her say something about contractions? "What's that you say?"

Liza turned the bedside lamp on, the light shot out like claps of fireballs. Colin covered his face, turned his head aside. He blinked his eyes and tried to focus his vision. "I think I'm going into labor, baby. I'm having contractions," Liza repeated. There had been six weeks of childbirth preparation, where they'd gone over at least a half-dozen different ways to relax, and Liza could barely speak through her labored breaths. It was as if she'd been daydreaming, doodling in her notebook during the entire six weeks. What happened to the *hee . . . hee . . . hoo . . . hoo . . .* deep-breath calmness that the instructor had assured them would make the contractions easier to tackle?

Colin thought through what he'd learned in the class, about the different stages of labor. "How far apart are they?"

"I don't know." Liza looked at the clock. "Ten minutes or so."

In one motion Colin took his wife by the shoulder, directed her into the bed next to him, and leaned across her and turned the lamp off. His voice was scratchier than his overused copy of Michael Jackson's *Thriller* album. "Early labor," he calmly told her. "Get rest, you're gonna need it later."

Liza struggled to rise, but Colin's arm held her firm. She attempted to slide under his embrace, to no avail. "Colin," she fumed. "What the hell is this?"

Colin's eyes were shut and he'd reclaimed his comfortable position on the bed. "Go to sleep, Liza. When they get five minutes apart we'll call the doctor and start preparing for the hospital. You've got the bag packed already, right?"

"Yeah, it's packed." Her emotions were a roller coaster; she wanted to scream, curse, cry a river, laugh, smile, and bounce this little one-to-be on her knee.

"Good," Colin said. "Now seriously get some rest." He leaned over and kissed her cheek. "I know you're thinking I'm the devil incarnate right about now, but this is just the beginning. We've got a long way to go before this baby gets here. Remember what we learned in class."

Liza eased back against her pillow, comforted by Colin's calm and the fact that he'd said, "We've got a long way to go." She couldn't remember at any other point during this pregnancy it being a "we" thing. Ever since she flowed on that little stick in their bathroom, it had always been a "she" thing. But in spite of all those nights she left class feeling depressed because he hadn't uttered a word or acknowledged the learning, he must have been listening and learning after all, because here he was referencing the classes. Maybe the divide between them wasn't as wide as she had calculated. Maybe the man she had married was back—the man who rubbed her feet at night, the aspiring writer who wrote her dozens of original short stories with a glamorous heroine named Liza, before Amazon.com book sales rankings and best-seller lists mattered. Before the days of make-or-break reviews, before the quest for blurbs of recommendation from other authors, and before agents, publicists, and editors, it had been Colin and Liza. Maybe they could get back there, to that wonderful place, and still have their individual and collective dreams come true.

"Hey, baby," Colin called to her from the darkness of their bedroom.

"Yes?"

"Your timing is impeccable. You know the tour starts in a few weeks, and if you'd gone on your due date that would have put us a couple days before. Now I can hit the road with peace of mind, and what I'm sure of will be a beautiful addition to our family. That's if this baby takes after its mama."

It wasn't a bouquet of roses, and couldn't make up for the loneliness she'd felt these past thirty-eight weeks, but it was a start. Of course his books would always matter. In a perverse way they would always be more important to him than anything else life offered. He'd worked so hard to get his name on those book spines, to get those covers in prime position with booksellers across the country. He developed ulcers when the sales went poorly, and had Catholic school posture when the reviews spoke highly of his work. Those books were his babies.

"Thanks, baby," Liza said, as if she'd had any say when her body was ready to tumble forth with the new life. "You know I aim to please."

Again, Colin leaned toward her, this time kissing her shoulder like her husband of old. "*Thank you*, Liza. Love you. Now get that rest."

"We're going to have a baby," she said.

Colin closed his eyes, tried to chase away the vision of a fire, a pregnant girl falling to the ground on the lawn out front of her burning brownstone. He was going to be a father. It both thrilled and nauseated him.

Courtney's legs hung over the side of his bed like a cast net combing through murky salt water for shrimp. At six feet five inches tall, he had one inch on anyone else in his family, three inches on Colin. It was as if God decided that basketball would be his saving grace, the court his paper, the ball his pen. His trademark cornrows were shucked, his hair loosened into an unwieldy Afro. Tamika, his main girl during this past school year, was behind him. Her thighs wrapped around his torso like a tunic, as she busily re-established Courtney's cool cornrow design, one strand at a time.

"When's the last time you washed this mess, Courtney?" she asked. Her fingers struggled through the tangles of mane, and she brushed aside a few flakes of dandruff that hung to his ends like cobwebs.

Courtney smiled in response. "Tamika, you start with that, *you're* gonna end up washing it. I let you off the hook by just having you braid. You got to learn to appreciate a nigga's kindness."

"Nuh-uh, Courtney. You listen to me, nee-grow," she said. "I'm not about to have you talkin' that crap to me like I'm a chicken-head." She held a plot of hair in her right hand, leaned in over Courtney's left shoulder and let him see the seriousness of her expression. She had practically hitchhiked her way from Long Island after Courtney called in the middle of the night. And here she was now expecting Courtney's respect.

"Oh, my bad," Courtney replied, undeterred. "I keep getting it twisted. You just taste like chicken." He licked his lips and diverted his eyes to her spot down below.

"Crazy ass," Tamika said. "It's hard to believe you could have a brother writing books. Silly as your ass is." She stopped a touch, reflecting. "By the way, you know my book club's reading his—"

"What's up with Kenya?" Courtney cut her off. "Did she get that situation with Renaldo fixed?"

"Renard," Tamika corrected. "And, yes, she did."

"Good," Courtney said. "I was hoping I wouldn't have to put one in ol' dude, ya know? Twisting caps ain't my cup right now. I'm a lover, ya know, not a fighter."

Tamika stopped again. The process always took forever with her because of her frequent pauses. That was the one condition Courtney had accepted with having Tamika braid his hair. "Can I ask you a question, Courtney?" Her voice had softened, her posture shifted backwards like she was ducking a boxing punch.

"What, you want me to eat that chicken again?" Courtney said, while winding his hips like a male exotic dancer against the inside of her thighs. "You're getting greedy on me, Tamika?"

Tamika tapped his shoulder. "You gotta always be nasty, don't you? Seriously, Courtney, I want to ask you something."

"Fire away."

Tamika cleared her throat. "You . . . you don't like your brother much, do you?"

The air left Courtney's dorm room. He looked over his shoulder at her with eyes she'd never before seen, the usual golden-brown tint of his irises looked to her now flame-red. He slid from between her thighs, as if nothing had changed between them, stood and picked up his basketball from his study desk. He tossed the ball between his hands, keeping his focus on the ball as it moved from side to side. Tamika wasn't sure what to do. She looked at his door, noticed the latch. Oddly, she felt nervous all of a sudden.

"Me and dude are brothers, but we ain't friends," Courtney said after awhile. "And you're best to leave it at that. Your little book club wants to read his books, cool, do your thing." His eyes were on Tamika again. He didn't blink. "But don't ever ask any questions about me and him again. Aiight?"

Tamika swallowed and nodded.

It was around eight thirty in the morning, and Liza's contractions were coming five minutes apart. Colin rose at that point without complaint, dialed the doctor's office, and let his wife speak into the receiver, so the doctor could determine from Liza's voice if it was indeed time for her to prepare for the hospital.

"You sound like you're close to getting ready to go, Mrs. Sheffield," the doctor said.

"How many years of college was it for you to get that medical degree?" Liza snapped.

"Mrs. Sheffield, I'll meet you and your husband at the hospital in two hours, okay?"

Liza sighed. "Okay." She turned and faced Colin. "We're to meet her at the hospital in two hours."

Colin flipped his wrist and checked the time.

"I'm going to shave my face and head," he told Liza. "Why don't you take a warm bath to get yourself stimulated, then I'll take a quick shower, and—" He cupped his wife's face in his hands. "We'll be headed down the road to parenthood."

"Colin, we don't have time for all that."

"Liza, just do it." His jaw muscles clenched. "Trust me."

Liza brushed aside the thought and went to run the bathwater.

They prepared for the hospital in their own little worlds, but in the same bathroom. Liza bathed in a soft pool of bubbles and fragrance. Colin shaved at the sink. He ran the electric razor across his head and then his face, taking the time and care he did back when he first started dating Liza.

"Can you believe we're going to be parents?" Liza said to him above the buzz of his clippers.

Colin ran the razor along the left side of his face, cleaning away the stubble. "It's scary when you think about it."

"How so?" she asked.

Colin stopped shaving and turned to her. "I'm scared I won't be a good father, that I'll turn out like my old man." He then resumed his shaving, not mentioning his other worry, about the bad karma he was afraid would come to pay him for his past bad deeds.

"Your father made a choice, Colin. Most of the men do. It isn't that they don't have the skills to be good fathers; they choose not to. They run instead of staying and dealing with all the challenges. The choice is yours."

"You make life sound so simple."

"It is." She gazed away from him. "People make it tougher than it has to be."

Colin placed his razor in the sink and sat on the toilet next to Liza. "I know you said you didn't want to talk about our argument yesterday." He thought for a moment. "I won't ever put my hands on you like that again."

Liza waded through the water with her fingers, couldn't keep herself still as she thought about the course of their lives, the ugliness that had come between them. "It's not like you hit me or anything, and I know that's your point," she said. "And I agree, I guess. But you grabbed my wrist pretty hard—I was honestly scared. You know how you get when you're angry. But most of all, I was upset because you weren't thinking about anything, not me, not the baby. You were in one of your moods. You've got to stop bottling all these feelings inside and then exploding. I know the writing is pressure. I know this book, if it doesn't do well, could set you back. You need to learn how to open up. God." She closed her eyes, smiled, then reopened them and looked at Colin. "I sound like Dr. Phil or somebody."

"One thing my old man did teach me—men are supposed to be strong. He never said anything about opening up and all that New Age jazz. Certain things are better left unsaid sometimes."

"Expressing yourself doesn't make you weak, Colin; snatching your pregnant wife up does, though."

Colin shifted on the toilet. "I thought you had erased that file. I think this is my best work. I freaked." He shook his head.

Liza tried to lighten the mood. "I'm staying away from your computer, Colin. Don't worry. You scarred me for life with anything electronic. I can't even use the television remote anymore."

Colin smiled, feeling better. "It's just that I know I've got another best-seller in me. I want to make you proud."

"I'm proud, Colin."

"These publishers are bloodsuckers, Liza. And the reading public doesn't know any better than to gobble up anything marketed to them. Half of what sells is garbage. I'm absolutely obsessed with this and it's making me crazy. When I read that article yesterday and they quoted Langston like he's an authority on writing . . . it set me off. I was waiting for an excuse to go off on someone, and then when you closed the computer down without saving the file . . ." He laughed to keep from crying. "I'm sorry. I know you're tired of it all. But this is my livelihood and it's killing me. It's killing us."

Liza touched his fingers with her wet, soapy hand. "Like I said before, you can write well *and* write popular, too. I don't know how, but I know you can do it. That's what your challenge is—to figure out how."

"Where would I be without you?"

"I shudder to imagine," she said. "But you need to go on and finish getting ready. I just had another contraction, and they're getting closer."

Colin furrowed his brow. "I didn't notice. You're getting so calm with them."

Liza placed his hand on her slippery belly. For once, he didn't pull it away. "What does not break me, makes me stronger," she said.

Colin thought about the burning brownstone, Kim Parker, his baby-to-be. He nodded at Liza. *What does not break me makes me stronger, indeed.*

* * *

On the other side of the makeshift curtain, which the Red Storm's basketball trainer had erected, was a throng of eager reporters, pencils tucked behind their ears, tape recorders ready, and writing pads close by. Courtney parted the green curtain and snuck a quick scan of the room. His agent passed by, his hand brushing over Courtney's right and left shoulder in one quick sweep. Courtney had made his decision in the wee hours of the morning as Tamika parted and braided his hair. He called the agent that made the biggest impression on him, on his cell, as soon as the sun rose. The agent had a press conference set up in less than an hour.

"Wonderful turnout, baby boy," the agent said, moving like a man who'd won the lottery. "This early start makes you the lead story of the day."

Courtney turned his head to the blur of his agent's voice. Matt Dresden III, the white man charged with molding Courtney's career, skip-walked up the tunnel, tapping one hand against his leg as he moved, cell phone pressed to his ear by the other hand.

Courtney turned back from the curtain. His coach leaned against the concrete wall across the hall, lost in his thoughts. Courtney moved over to him.

"So, this is it, Coach D?"

"What?" Coach Delancey's deep thought had blocked out Courtney's words. Crow's feet walked from the corner of his eyes as he forced a smile. He'd shaved away his usual five o'clock shadow and put on a tie especially for the occasion. With his slight crossed eyes and dumpy build, he put folks in mind of that seemingly dim television detective, Columbo. And like Columbo, he had a brilliant mind that made the complex offensive schemes he implemented for his team the envy of most of the top coaches in the game.

"I said this is it," Courtney said.

Coach nodded. "Bittersweet moment for me, Court, I must admit. I still remember the day I first came out to your mother's place to recruit you. How you sat back in the corner watching me, and I tried my hardest to get an expression from you. You looked at me without blinking. You were tough. I told you you'd start right away—no response. Said, 'We'll build the offense around you.'" Coach laughed at the memory. "I got nothing from you. If it hadn't been for your mother asking all those questions about academics the only sound in the room would have been my shaky voice. I was sure when I left that you'd commit somewhere else. Boy, that was a sad car ride."

"I figured it was my opportunity to make the white man sweat for a change," Courtney replied with a smile.

"Sweat I did."

"Seriously, though," Courtney said, "you think I'm making the right decision here?"

Coach sighed, pursed his lips. "I've always said if one of my players has the chance to be among the top ten picks in the draft that he has to seriously consider it. College is about opening doors, presenting you with opportunities. Is graduating with your degree in communications going to give you more opportunity than the NBA? College allowed you to showcase your talent—and now you're going to get employment based on that talent. Way I see it, that makes you no different than the senior accounting major by-passing job interviews to stay with the firm he interned with."

"I need to have you speak with my mother."

"Yeah, I'd imagine she wouldn't trust this."

Courtney lowered his voice so no one could eavesdrop on the conversation. "I begged her to come today; she wouldn't have it. She hung up the phone on me, Coach D."

"She only wants the best for you."

"Support is what I need."

"She'll support you plenty, Court. Once you sign a contract and she sees that you're making something out of yourself, she'll come around. She's been through a lot. She's scared of the unknown. Scared what this opportunity will do to you."

"I'm not him," Courtney said.

Coach smiled. "No, you're not."

"So why does she treat me like I am?"

"Your father's missteps," the coach said, carefully choosing his words, "worry her, Court. But as you said, you're not him. She'll see that eventually."

Courtney pursed his lips. "I hope you're right. It all makes me nervous, though, Coach D. Things always look bright for me and somehow, someway, the brightness fades. Maybe she's right to be worried."

Coach placed his hand on Courtney's shoulder. "Listen, son. I spoke with the scout, Blake; he told me teams were trying to trade up with hopes of landing you. The big Chinese kid is obviously the top pick—you can't teach seven feet two inches, you know. The kid from Duke has the pedigree for success. The two other seven-footers, the one from Wake Forrest and Bridges from Georgetown, they're the other top four picks, and then there's you. Atlanta's hot on you, Court. Blake told me they've gotten offers of All-Star players to trade away that pick and they haven't budged. They want to keep the pick—they want you. You're gonna do fine, son, and yes," Coach looked off wistfully, "though it puts our program in the rebuilding stage, I think you're making the right decision."

Courtney's agent came striding up the hall, not talking on his cell for a change. He wore a gray blazer covering a black turtleneck sweater. He was a bit on the chunky side, and his brown hair had thinned so much that he cut it into a close-fitting buzz cut that made the little wisps of hair look red. He complemented what he thought was a hip look with a neatly trimmed goatee of mixed brown and gray, and though he hadn't done anything resembling physical activity in twenty years, his forehead glistened with sweat—always glistened with sweat.

"They're panting like dogs out there for you, C-rock," Dresden said. Everything he said came out sounding like a radio disk jockey's audition tape.

"I was having a word with Coach," Courtney told him.

"Understandable, understandable," the agent said, nodding. "But don't be too long. You're about to make hysteri. Spelled like hysteria, baby, but without the *a* on the end."

Courtney's coach patted him on the back. "Your public awaits you, Court. Better get out there."

Courtney nodded and rubbed his hands together. "Let's go do this."

Colin could feel his wife's discomfort as he steered the car. The contractions were no longer of the grin-and-bear-it variety. "So," he said. "Did you finish the Noah's Ark sketch?"

"Nope," she managed.

"How far did you get?"

"Couple planks. *Hee . . . hee . . . hoo.* Screw it . . . let 'em . . . whew! Let 'em all drown."

She was cranky, but looking at it with a positive spin. Colin realized it could have been worse.

"How about your new book?" she asked. "You get any more writing done on it?"

Colin shifted his view from the road for a moment, looked at her. "I'm having a tough time with the female character. I can't get her voice as true as I want it," he said. "I thought I knew her like the back of my hand, but writing from a woman's perspective isn't one of my strong points. I don't want her coming off cardboard like one of the characters in Langston's books. I want her to have depth, and for her voice to ring true. You got any suggestions that might help me strengthen those creative muscles?"

"Yeah," Liza said. She paused to reach forward and clutch the dashboard, her fingernails digging into the material. "Damn! Sorry, that was a big one. These contractions are starting to kick my ass. Now, what did you ask me?"

"Writing from a woman's point of view," Colin said. He applied his brakes and eased the car into a turn.

"Oh, yeah." Liza took a deep breath with her eyes closed. "I'm sorry, baby. I'm no good at this kind of stuff. I don't know. Kill that bitch off or something, then you won't have to worry about her." Colin looked over at his wife, searching for the frost of a smile. Her eyes were shut and she was deep in concentration. He thought of what she'd said. Maybe, in her tensed state, she'd come up with the answer. He needed to develop a killer instinct. He thought of it as they approached the hospital, as the staff checked them into their room, as the nurses hooked his wife up to monitors. He had a wife, a baby soon to come. He had family that he needed to provide for. Writing books that the critics loved and readers avoided like a call from the bill collectors wouldn't cut it anymore. Every time he thought of his books, Langston's image flashed before him. That cocky grin. That carefree attitude. Writing his garbage and calling them novels. Cashing those royalty checks—which Langston joked were so big his publisher had to put him on layaway—for that drivel he put out once a year. Yeah, Colin needed a killer instinct. He needed this next book to catapult him to Langston's level. Then he could have the cocky smile. He could cash those huge royalty checks. He could be a star.

The thoughts lingered with him up until the time his wife came down to the final stretch of delivery. Then, like a light switch, his demeanor and attitude changed. It was all about the baby.

"Okay, get ready to push, Boo. One . . . two . . . three . . . four . . . five . . . six . . . seven . . . eight . . . nine . . . ten. Aaargh!" Colin screamed as if the fetus was passing through him.

"You see it yet?" Liza asked, between labored breaths. "You see my baby yet?"

"Dime of her head, baby. It looks as if she has a lot of hair."

"Why you keep saying her and she? How do you know it's not him or he?"

Colin stroked his wife's ankle with the softness of a Luther ballad. "Because," he started, then struggled to finish, "I've been praying for a girl. I know how troubling boys can be. Plus, I want her to be beautiful like you."

Emotions tumbled from him after all these months of throwing himself into work, using words and the shaping of his novel as a diversion from the paranoid thoughts that his faith in God couldn't conquer: What if there truly was bad karma? He thought about the burning brownstone of his nightmares. What if the baby was born without a lung, or with some other serious ailment? Every paranoid thought imaginable entered his mind.

Colin cleared his throat. "You know, I uh . . . ." He looked at the delivery nurse, paused, and then pressed on. "I never shared it with you, and I know I should have, but I'm happy about this baby, Liza."

The nurse interrupted his moment, asking Liza to press down hard, give it a good push. "One . . . two . . . three . . ." Liza raced along with the nurse and her husband to ten. She wanted to expand on Colin's last statement, to pick his brain here, like she'd been unable to do at home.

"Whew!" Liza struggled again for her breath. After she caught her breath, she turned her attention back to what Colin had said. "You are? You're happy about this baby?"

"Yeah, I am," he answered. "I'm at peace."

"Glad you're at peace, baby," Liza said, " 'cause this epidural is wearing off. I'm starting to feel these con-trac-tions. Damn!

Honey, hit the button. Shoot me more pain killer." Liza shot up in the bed and grabbed a hold of Colin's arm. "When's the doctor coming in again? I want that bitch—"

"Liza!"

"—to explain to me why this shit is hurting so much."

The nurse laughed. "You're doing excellent, Mrs. Sheffield," she said. "Hold on to your husband. Keep talking when you can. Continue breathing, and push like you've been doing when we ask. The doctor will be in shortly."

Colin took his wife's hand, rubbed the side of her face. She was a good woman, he thought to himself. Like Kim Parker so many years ago, Liza deserved a great deal better than he'd given her.

Liza closed her eyes and continued her tight hold on Colin. The doctor arrived, more than half of the way through delivery. Liza's cramps had worked their way to her back, but Colin kept her calm, stroking her head with the same unhesitant motion; no more than a second between each stroke. In a flash he'd gone from husband to super-husband.

"This next push should do it," the doctor said after awhile. "Make it a good one."

And, sure enough, the next push did it.

The time of delivery was officially recorded as 6:49 P.M. Colin would tell people later that it was "six forty-nine and twenty-eight seconds."

"Say hello to your new baby girl," the nurse said. The doctor first flushed the baby's nostrils and mouth. The staff performed an *Apgar test*—graded the newborn in the areas of color and appearance, pulse rate, reflexes, muscle tone, and respiration. After coming up with a healthy evaluation, they handed Colin his cleaned baby for the first time.

"Look, Liza!" Colin said. "Our baby girl—I told you. Look, she, she—she has my cleft chin. Full head of hair, too. She's perfect."

It was a moment that words couldn't describe. Seeing life manifest was one of those events that flowery language and vivid descriptions could never truly capture, no matter how skilled the wordsmith. Baldwin, in all his imaginative glory couldn't describe that first cry. Ellison couldn't tap into the psyche of emotions new parents felt when the medical staff handed them their bundle of creation for the first time. Maya Angelou, who could make words bend and obey with the stroke of her pen, couldn't manipulate a couplet that would give justice to the miracle God brought forth. Colin Sheffield, man of words, stood, dumbfounded by the joy and exhilaration of the moment. Images flashed before his eyes, movement happening all around him, but his focus remained on his beautiful infant daughter. Daddy's little girl. Her head full of tight black curls. Her eyes, large like silver dollar coins. Her skin, softer than a kitten's steps, cream-colored. She had small fingers, but he could see them as miniature versions of Liza's hands. She had Liza's eyes, too. Her nose, lips, her bushy eyebrows, that chin—they were all Colin. The perfect blend of both her parents' traits. She was more perfect than a top-rated diamond stone.

"What's her name?" one of the medical staff asked.

Without turning in the direction of the query, Colin stuck out his chest with pride and said, "Lyric Erica Sheffield." He placed the baby closer to Liza. "And she's *perfect.*"

3

MAY 6

Colin lost himself in the small world encumbered by the walls of the hospital gift shop. There were too many options, too many choices in a cramped corner of space. There were greeting cards, some left blank so personal messages could be penned, and some sprinkled with generic thoughts of love, friendship, and the like. To the left of the cashier was a stand with an assortment of balloons, each one waiting to be stuffed with helium. There were flowers—single-stemmed, arranged in vases, or arranged in pots; candy, chocolate—either white or dark—mint drops, butterscotch balls; and books by authors Colin only envied when he received his royalty checks. Colin, of course, chose the blank greeting card and composed a line of love to Liza before the cashier rang it up. The few minutes he'd been away from his daughter and wife challenged his patience like reading through Langston Campbell's drivel.

Colin twisted the security bracelet the nursing staff had placed around his left wrist. He looked again at the small lettering that identified him as Lyric's father. In writing, being pigeonholed was his biggest fear. He didn't want to be "that clever African American novelist," or "that black male writer." Colin lived his life by contouring to his environment like liquid in a solid container. Never would he allow himself to be characterized as anything. If he felt like writing a mystery, then Walter Mosley, hold tight. If he wanted to write sci-fi, then Octavia Butler, hold on. His act was constantly changing, constantly evolving. However, with the security bracelet, he'd found the one tag that he would hold like a bloodstained banner, displaying it with the pride of the black power fist of the sixties: Lyric's father. The joy of it all surprised him. In a span of a few hours, his life had changed three hundred and sixty degrees.

Colin left the gift shop and passed by the cafeteria. The smell of burgers and French fries caught his nose. His stomach growled, but his mind was too full for food, his adrenaline too high for him to attempt sitting still long enough to gulp down a greasy burger.

One of the other fathers he'd seen during the course of the day was exiting the cafeteria as Colin passed. "Hey, how's it going?" the smallish, brown man asked him. "Any baby yet?"

"Not just *any* baby," Colin beamed, "a beautiful little girl, seven pounds, one ounce."

"Congrats, man," the smallish man said, offering his hand.

"What about you? Any baby yet?"

"Not yet, my wife got her epidural so I snuck down here for a quick bite while the waters were calm."

"Well, good luck to you," Colin said, and prepared to move on.

"Hey," the guy called after Colin. "What did you name her?"

Colin smiled. "Lyric Erica Sheffield." He knew he'd be saying that name a lot over the next few days to come, and each time it rolled off his tongue like one of those butterscotch candy drops he'd seen in the gift shop.

The smallish man nodded, wide smile covering the expanse of his face. You could see the twinkle of his own expectancy dancing in his eyes. "Beautiful name, beautiful name. Good luck to you."

"You too," Colin said as he moved on.

Colin had one more thing to do. A quick pit stop in the lobby so he could call his mother and Nana on his cell. He couldn't wait to tell them the good news.

A couple was in the lobby.

The wife sat in a wheelchair with her feet propped on the footrests and her back cushioned by a thick pillow.

Her husband stood guard over her, with their newborn strapped in a child seat.

A nurse at their heels gave the new parents a dose of last-minute instructions.

"Okay, daddy," the nurse said, her voice echoing off the glass. "If you'll pull your car up to the front and let me check that you install your child seat correctly, then you two can go."

Colin smiled at the scene, pulled his cell from his pocket and hit the power button. He had one new message. He dialed the number for message retrieval and punched in his access code.

"Colin, this is your mother. Oh, I hate talking to these things. I feel so stupid talking to a machine. Please call me as soon as possible. I don't want to alarm you, but we've got a slight situation. Tell Liza hello. She must be begging God to get that baby out of her by now. God bless! Call me back soon, okay? Love you." The message stamp indicated that she'd called early this morning.

Colin hurried to call back. "Mama," he said, when she picked up after what felt like the hundredth ring. "I got your message; what's wrong? Did something happen with Nana? Uncle Carl?" His heart raced as he waited for her answer.

"Hey, sweetie," his mother said. "I'm sorry; I didn't mean to upset you none. I called your place and got no answer. Nana's fine and Carl is his usual self. Your brother's what's wrong."

Colin's heart regained its normal pace. So Courtney was still causing them heartache.

"What did he do now?" Colin asked.

"He's dropping out of school," Lena Merkerson announced. "Hooked up with a slick white guy down in Atlanta that has him convinced he's gonna be the next Magic Jordan."

"You mean Magic Johnson," Colin corrected her.

"Whatever. I haven't told your Nana yet, I'm 'fraid of what it'll do to her blood pressure. She was so hoping he'd finish school. Quitting school to run around in shorts big enough to fit him and me both. I don't understand it. I've been getting calls all day, too, from newspapers. It's a darn circus. I'm so mad. Courtney wanted me to come to his press conference and sit next to him with a fake smile on my face—I couldn't do it. You didn't see the press conference?"

Colin could picture her hand on her forehead. "No, I missed the conference, but Courtney's good, Mama," he admitted. "Great, in fact. I did see this feature on ESPN the other day, though. They predicted Atlanta would take him with the fifth pick if he came out. It's not like he was in any danger of blazing any new academic trails, you know. The NBA's going to set him up for life if he handles his money right."

"Colin, what's Courtney gonna do but get himself into all kind of trouble in Atlanta? Those hoochies that chase down the ballplayers will end up sucking his money away, you mark my words. Chante has already called here twice today whining about she's getting a paternity test done on Destiny, and that Courtney better be prepared to handle his responsibility. I fear for him, Colin; I truly do."

"He's not Prime, Mama," Colin offered.

Lena's voice lowered. "Nobody said nothing 'bout no Prime."

"I'm saying—"

"Leave it be, Colin," his mother cut him off.

Colin switched gears. "Listen, Mama, you don't need to be worrying yourself about what your grown son does, or doesn't do." He smiled, though she couldn't see it. "You're a grandmother now."

"I'm gonna worry about you boys until—did you say I'm a grandmother?"

"Sure did," Colin replied. "That's why I called. Liza gave birth to a beautiful girl about an hour ago."

"Oh, precious Lord! Why didn't you call me earlier? Oh, my, and I'm here all worked up over Courtney while my grandbaby's being born. She's healthy?"

"Baby and mother are both doing fine."

"What did you name her? I've been so uninvolved in this whole thing . . ." Her voice trailed off as she considered things. "I wish you all lived closer. If I hadn't seen Liza's belly when you came for Nana's birthday, I would hardly have known she was pregnant."

"I know," Colin said. "It's hard on me, too, but with all the writing and all I don't get to see you like I wish I did. And like you said, it's not like we live right up the street."

"I know, baby," Lena assured him. "So what did you name my grandbaby?"

"Lyric Erica Sheffield is my precious angel's name."

"Lyric?" Lena said. "Well, you and I will have to discuss that one at a later date. No wonder you two were so secretive." She teased him with a snicker. "I'm joking; I like the name. Oh, my precious Lord, Colin sweetie. I bet she's adorable."

"Beautiful isn't strong enough a word, Mama. She has a full head of hair and big eyes."

"Praise be," Lena said. "Listen, I'm gonna put Nana on the phone. I'll let you tell her the news."

"Okay, Mama. And, look, I've got to make a couple appearances in Brooklyn for the new book in a couple of weeks. I'll stop and see you all. And once Liza gets settled, we'll bring the baby up, too. In the meantime, don't worry yourself too much over Courtney, he's doing what's best for him. This is a big move for him. It'll work out fine. Trust me. You got two celebrity boys now." He couldn't help think about how much brighter Courtney's star was about to shine. There was no way Colin's novels could compete with a dunk.

"I can't believe running up and down playing a game makes you a celebrity nowadays," Lena mused. "When I was coming up, our celebrities were folks with agendas, like Martin Luther King, for one. Musicians, maybe. A couple of actors. God, I thought Sidney Poitier could do no wrong. Writers. Zora Neal Hurston, Richard Wright. It scares me how times change, and always for the worse."

Colin forced himself to put aside the feelings of envy that had him thinking about something other than his daughter for the first time since she'd been born. "We'll see if you're still singing that tune when Courtney buys you a beautiful house in Atlanta."

"I don't need any house in Atlanta," Lena growled. "Brooklyn's been good to me. I learned a long time ago—with your father—that less is sometimes more. Courtney thinks about Courtney. You of all people should know that. After all you did for him growing up, and he up and decides one day that he's tired of *living in your shadow*. Brothers don't cast shadows on each other. Brothers love and help one another."

Colin wished that were true, that brothers didn't cast shadows.

He thought about the things Courtney knew about him, things that if ever revealed would forever alter his world. How heartbroken and disenchanted would his family be to realize the demons that Colin carried with him, demons that visited him nightly, in his dreams?

"Courtney's better than you guys give him credit for," Colin said, more so to reassure himself than anything.

"Oh, yeah, there's a lot of good in him. I wish we didn't have to work so hard to pull it out of him. But never mind that, I'm going to put Nana on now. She's gonna be thrilled. Love you."

"Love you, too, Mama."

Colin could hear a great deal of shuffling in the background. It was always a task to get Nana settled so she could take calls. She had so many tubes and wires that had to be placed aside, one by one, so they didn't tangle, and she always had the television blaring loud enough to drown out any voices.

"Hello," she said after awhile.

"Nana," Colin said. "How are you doing?"

"Colin, that you? Lawd, have mercy. I was just thinking about you. I seen't a boy on that Jerry Springra today that looked like you. He went off and married one of them, transvestors. I thought it was you until they brought that—man, woman, whatever she is—out. Liza's belly is plum out to here, so I knew it weren't y'all."

Colin laughed. "Nana, you've got to stop watching *Jerry Springer*, they've got wild stuff on there."

"You chirren act a fool nowadays, Colin. I like to keeps up on what's happening. So how's Liza?"

"She's doing well. And her belly isn't plum out to anywhere anymore. I was calling to let you know you're a great-grand-mother now."

"Good googlie mooglie," Carolina Merkerson said into the receiver. "Y'all chirren done had the baby, has you?"

"Sure have, Nana. A healthy little seven-pound-one-ounce girl."

"Seven pounds! I know Liza's stuff must be hurtin'. Girl ain't hardly got no meat on her bones. Childbearin' women got to have cushioning."

"Liza's doing fine, Nana," Colin laughed.

"What y'all name the child? I hope nothin' foolish. You chirren namin' your kids after appliances and cars nowadays is crazy."

"Her name's Spam Emailia Sheffield," Colin deadpanned.

"Says what," Nana said. She started wheezing right away.

Colin quickly said, "I was kidding, Nana. Her name's Lyric Erica Sheffield. You okay?"

"Lyric? Well, I guess that ain't too terrible. You liked to give me a conniption, boy."

"Sorry, Nana," Colin apologized.

"So when are you coming to see us? We've been missing you

something terrible. You know your fool brother done decided to play that ball in the NBC. Soon he'll be running around with tattoos and his hair all twisted up like a sissy. Earrings, tattoos, twisty-headed naps. And the poor girls chasin' behind these boys sniffin' 'em like flies on sh—"

"Nana," Colin cut her off. "How did you know about Courtney? Mama didn't want to tell you; she was afraid it would upset you."

"Shoot, your Mama is slow on the uptake, boy," Nana told Colin. "I learned about this hours ago. I get that ESP on cable."

Antonio "Star" Redman held the paper bag in his hand, chasing the blood from his fingers until his tips turned a pinkish white. His thick, leathery fingers engulfed the top of the package, wrapped like a vise around the neck of the bottle concealed under the brown paper. He tapped the glass security wall that protected the cashier from would-be robbers and nodded his thanks as his change came through the slot. He exited the store and looked both ways as he stood outside the door. He hurried up the block, scuffing the sidewalk with his battered wingtip shoes, walking his usual crooked bop. One side flap of his shirt hung from his pants, a French-fry oil stain spread across the pocket that covered his heart—outfits his daddy had left when he ran out on his moms. She'd stopped ironing them this year, figuring after thirteen years the old man wasn't coming back. When Star took the clothes off the hanger, back from his latest bid upstate, his moms looked as if her aneurysm was starting to act up again. She didn't say anything, though. She knew what a hard time Star was having getting acclimated to the outside, knew the boy had to have something to wear.

Every few seconds Star peered over his shoulder like a driver switching lanes and surveyed the area around him. He'd erected an invisible barrier of about ten feet around himself—years ago—that was off limits to anyone on nights like this one, nights when his stomach ached for food but had to settle for a warm liquid burn instead, until he could make the ends to pick up something at the Chinese joint.

At just over six feet, and closer to two hundred twenty pounds than two hundred, he was an imposing figure. Factor in his stubbly head, not quite bald, his purplish lips, and teeth sharper than broken glass, and it was no wonder that the invisible barrier he'd set had never been crossed. To that, add his sporadic twists and jerks—his mother called them undiagnosed bouts of Tourette's— and you could see why he was, for the most part, a loner.

He was scuttling along, clacking the sidewalk with those out-dated shoes, when he passed a familiar face. They both stopped and turned back at the same time.

"Yo! What's up, player?" the familiar face said.

Star slowed down outside the entrance to one of the block's many bodegas. "Courtney? Shef? What's going on, b?"

Courtney approached him, gave him dap and a street hug. "Star, damn dawg. Wussup with you?"

"Hustlin' and bustlin', baby." He looked in both directions up the street, tapped the side pockets of the light army jacket that clashed with the rest of his attire. "You know the routine. Makin' that cream. Breakin' young girl's dreams. So, I hear you makin' the jump, huh, son? NBA baller and whatnot."

"Yeah," Courtney said. "Got to take the skills up a notch, ya know? Got tired of dropping thirty on them college fools every night and not getting anything for it. The university got phat pockets and I'm up there scrounging pizza money off my girl. Poli-tricks at its finest. Shit's crazy."

"I hear ya. Life is a beeitch." Star shook his head and smiled. Envy was in his eyes. "NBA . . . damn. Make us proud, son. Represent Brook-lyn. You know Brooklyn's in the da house wherever there's people. You could go over to Istanbul and find someone from Brooklyn. Half the muhfukas would rise if they said, Brooklyn stand up. Rep us good my nigga. Aiight?"

"No doubt," Courtney said. "I plan on hitting the NBA like Marbury did. Maybe harder, ya know?"

Star laughed. "Get us a couple dunks every now and then, get yourself a gang of fat-butt hoochies, and don't forget niggas like me that was with you back in the day." He smiled and tapped Courtney in the ribs. "Nah, though, you ain't gotta be the next Marbury or nothing. Don't be putting that kind of pressure on yourself."

"Been dealing with pressure for as long as I can remember," Courtney said. "I ain't shying away from it."

"Yo," Star said, smiling, his hand balled in a fist and pressed up to his mouth. "Your brother still writing them faggoty-assed books and shit?"

Courtney shifted his weight from left leg to right. "Yeah, he's still doing his thing."

"My Moms swears by that nigga," Star said. He looked down. "I was in the belly for a minute and she used to send me his books to read. I tried to explain to her that reading wasn't what I needed, but . . ." He shook his head. "I can't see it, but hey, all I know is you two have done well by yourselves. Two of BK's finest. That's peace man. These streets are brutal as a muhfuh. You don't want to be out here slangin' and bangin'."

"We're all eating," Courtney said. "That's what matters. You look like you put on weight, kid."

"Jailhouse pounds, dawg."

Courtney nodded.

"So," Star said. "I heard you got a seed."

"Who told you that?" Courtney asked.

"What's her name . . . ? Chick that fucked all them dudes up in Lefrak that time, then accused them of raping her."

"Stacey Kimble?"

Star nodded. "True. She said you had a seed with a light-skinned girl live around her way."

Courtney, despite himself, shook his head. "Not me, dawg." It hurt his insides to say it, opened up old wounds.

A Volkswagen with tinted windows and a passenger side dent slowed in front of the store and then pulled up the block. The misguided owner had invested in custom rims—"twinkies" they called them in the hood—instead of an insurance policy. Star watched the car like a broker looking at the stock ticker and then returned his gaze and thoughts back to Courtney.

"Yeah, though, let me go handle this. Make paper."

Courtney nodded. "Aiight, do your thing. You still in the same spot?"

"No doubt, come check me sometime."

Courtney reached in his pocket and pulled out a small business card. "Hit me up sometime, Star. This is my cell number."

Star took the rectangle of paper and fingered it as if it were a big-busted girl's bra straps. "I'ma do that." He embraced Courtney and gave him dap. "Eat well, my nigga," he said, and headed up the street.

Courtney stood by the bodega door, watching as Star's strut led him to the vehicle. Star looked over his shoulder again, pulled out a Ziploc package of weed, then leaned down and stuck his hand through the car window. He removed his hand, a fistful of dollars in his grasp, and moved quickly on up the block. The car paused for a brief moment, then did a U-turn and headed in the opposite direction of Star. Courtney watched Star moving up the block, looked at the car as it passed by again. "I'm gonna do that," he said, under his breath. "I'm gonna eat well. Get the hell out of here."

Courtney moved inside the bodega, thinking about Prime and the mistakes he'd made that prevented him from ever turning pro. Drugs, women—a familiar refrain. Courtney was determined to eat well, determined to do what Prime had been unable to do—finish what he started.

Liza had the baby in her arms, rocking her with a mother's care, singing to the swaddled newborn when Colin entered the room.

"Aw, man," Colin said. "I wish I hadn't forgotten my camera. Man, I should have bought one in the gift shop. This would be a wonderful picture."

Liza looked up and smiled. "You called your family?"

"Yeah, Mama and Nana both congratulate you and wish you the best. I told Mama we'd get up to see them as soon as you were able. She said she wished she could get down and see us, but it's kind of hard with Nana being pretty much bedridden and the home health lady only able to work until four."

"I understand. Tell her don't worry about it when you speak to her again."

Colin took a seat close to his wife, squeezing himself onto the tiny hospital bed. "I have an appearance in Brooklyn in a couple weeks, but I think I might go up there this weekend and check on them after your mother gets here. Courtney has Mama all out of sorts."

Liza stopped rocking the baby, looked up at Colin. "Courtney? What did he do?"

"He dropped out of school. He's going pro."

Liza smiled. "So he went through with it? And your Mama's not happy? Doesn't she know how hard it is to make it to the pros? Not too many people have enough talent to do that."

Colin frowned. "She'd like Courtney to get his college degree," he answered.

"What about you?" Liza queried. "How do you feel about all this? You excited?"

"I'm happy for my brother, if that's what you mean," Colin said. "But you know how it is with us. It's not like he's going to be sending me free tickets to games or anything." He smirked and reached a finger out and poked the underside of Lyric's chin. "But enough about Courtney; he's hogged up enough of my day. It's all about my beautiful little girl here." He reached for his daughter and pried her loose from Liza's arm. They needed two Lyrics, one for each of them.

"She had her eyes open the whole time I was gone?" Colin asked.

Liza stuck out her lips. "No. She closed them when you left and opened them again when you came back. I can see already she's going to be a daddy's little girl."

"What else is there to be?" Colin rubbed noses with little Lyric. "Ain't that right, sweetie. What else is there to be but daddy's little girl? Because daddy loves you, *mmmmm*." He kissed her cheek. "*So much.*"

"How about mommy?" Liza asked. "Does daddy have any sugar left for her? After all, I did do all the work."

"Oh, yeah," Colin said. He leaned over and met lips with his beautiful wife. "I got plenty to go around."

Liza ran her fingers over Colin's bald head, traced the perfect roundness from the nape of his neck to the top of his forehead. It would be a month and a half at least before they could be intimate. "Nothing in there for six weeks," was how the nurse had put it as she explained to Liza the procedure for taking a soothing sitz bath. "Your body has been through a great deal and it needs all the time it can get to heal." At the time, with her bottom on fire, lovemaking was the furthest thing on Liza's mind, but now, as she caressed her sexy chocolate warrior husband—well, she could see the six weeks being a slight problem. She hadn't felt this close to Colin in who knew how long. See, she knew a baby would bring them closer.

"What are you thinking?" Colin asked. He could see a look in Liza's eyes.

"Nothing," she lied. "Well, actually I was thinking how grateful I am for you and the baby. I might be the luckiest woman in the entire world."

"Since you're in a mushy mood," Colin said, "Here." He handed her the card he'd picked up in the gift shop.

"For me?" Liza asked.

"Open it."

It read: *If you're reading this, then it means Colin Irving Sheffield is totally, head-over-heels in love with you.*

PS: Be thankful, be very thankful.

Liza smiled. "You had me until I got to that PS. You be thankful too, mister."

"Oh, I am." He touched his heart, flashed his wife the dimples that resonated like one of his lines of vivid prose.

"I'll ask now, while you're in good spirits," Liza said. "Did you call my mother?"

"Why you ask me like that? You know I love Mama Brashear."

"So you called her?"

"As a matter of fact, I did," Colin answered. "I told her I'm looking forward to her staying with us. Told her I was thinking about making a quick run to Brooklyn after she gets here."

"What she say?"

Colin shrugged. "Said okay."

"I'm going to need her help," Liza said.

Colin cleared his throat. "I called your father, too, but he wasn't in."

"So much involved in taking care of a baby," Liza said, as if she hadn't heard Colin. "I've read all the books, but this is the real thing. I'm nervous."

"You heard me, Liza?"

"Did you ever read that book I gave you on fatherhood?" Liza asked him, ignoring his question.

Colin nodded. "Speaking of fathers—"

"Let's not," Liza said. She touched Colin softly. "Okay?"

Colin looked into her eyes, those pretty brown eyes. "Okay."

She smiled. "So you're going to Brooklyn this weekend."

"Probably."

"Colin, don't go starting any problems with Courtney," she said. She had reclaimed the baby, was rocking her again. "You've got your life, and it's a blessing. He's got his."

"Hey, I'm going to check on my folks. Stop by and see Uncle Carl. Besides, I don't have a problem with Courtney. He has a problem with me."

"You two have to always try to one-up each other when you get together," Liza said. "I hate for you two to end up bumping chests during what should be happy times for the both of you."

Colin leaned into his wife, looked up and into her eyes. "Courtney wants to have his foolish, immature, jealousy thing, let him. I have no hard feelings toward him. We've got our own life to live and we're gonna live it. Okay? I'm beyond this nonsense. I'm letting it rest. Besides, I might not see him. He's busy with the NBA thing. I'm doing my thing. Bygones are bygones as far as I'm concerned."

Liza looked at Colin, tried to find the truth in his words. There was none. She wondered if bygones would ever be bygones between the two brothers. She thought about her part in their problems and reprimanded herself for wondering.

4

MAY 10

The record shop held the scent of Phillies Blunt cigar smoke. The wonderful melody of a blues record played over the static of the dilapidated sound system. Milk crates lined one of the aisles, each crate stuffed with records. The shopping bins were made of wood, good wood, marked with scuffs and scratches from years of wear, but sturdy. The gate that led behind the cash register hung from its hinge. The curtain behind the register that led to the back office was frayed and no longer purple to the visible eye. Still, Carl's Records was the place to go in Brooklyn if you wanted that good ole funky, foot-tapping blues. Like Sylvia's Restaurant in Harlem, it was a cultural landmark.

The sun kissed the front of the building, contributing another day of yellowing tint to the handwritten storefront sign that Carl had written once. The trees from outside cast shadows inside that etched the walls, shadows that eased from one corner of the wall to the next as the day progressed. Whenever a customer entered the record shop, the bells on the front door would jingle, and Carl himself would rise from his seat behind the counter and force his replacement hip to propel him toward the sales floor. Carl believed in personal service, never forgot a name or a face, and his business thrived because of it. The blues records were wonderful, but Carl, no doubt smoking on one of his cigars, was more revered than drums, guitar licks, and horns could ever be.

Bing, bing, bing, bing, bing.

Another soon-to-be-satisfied customer was summoned by the lure of the shop. It was another opportunity for Carl to serve 'em that cut-to-the-bone lovin' he always spoke of.

"Stay down, old man," this customer shouted as he ducked his head and entered the shop. "It's me, Unc. Save that hip." His distinctive cornrows and the large platinum-and-diamond-encrusted "Jesus Piece" medallion made him a sight to behold. Like Carl, he had a personality that pulled like a tow-truck.

Carl rose anyway, came to greet his nephew. "Who you callin' old man?"

Courtney towered over his uncle but there was no mistaking the family connection. Carl had the same walnut shell–colored skin and confident demeanor that had the marketing reps at the major sneaker companies drooling for Courtney's John Hancock on an endorsement contract.

"My bad," Courtney said as they exchanged hugs. "What's the politically correct term? Age-challenged? That better?"

"You younguns thank you smart, yes suh." Carl turned, feigned walking off on his nephew. His gold eagle ring with the onyx stone sparkled just as Courtney's hip-hop jewelry did. "The NBA can have you." He turned back, laughing. *Hay, hay, hay*—with the inevitable cough at the end. Carl loved to smile, flash his white and even teeth. His high cheekbones always pressed under his eyes.

"You see the press conference?"

"Sure did, young snapper, yes suh." He shifted his weight from his right side to his left. "You were cooler than water, boy. Reminded me of Eddy 'The Chief' Clearwater. God almighty if his shows ain't the biggest joy this side of a warm bed, and a hot woman. He's famous for his showmanship, yes suh." Carl did a quick dance step, all upper torso. "Lean, lanky fella like yourself. Folks compare him to Chuck Berry, you know?"

Courtney smiled, nodded. He loved how his uncle's eyes would shine like two polished coal rocks whenever he got to talking about the blues. Even Carl's right lazy eye yawned itself awake when the old man started reminiscing on the Eddy Clearwaters of the world.

"Yes suh, 'The Chief,' young snapper. You don't know anything about that there. Delta blues, rock 'n' roll, gospel, country, all mixed into one. Now, I don't mind this hippity hoppity stuff you into, but blues is good stuff, boy, yes suh. Musical gumbo. Clearwater recorded the song 'Cool Water' back in '61. I had to put that record on after I watched your TV thang the other day. Cooler than water you were, yes suh."

Courtney reached forward and offered his uncle an arm for support. "I hope I made the right decision, Unc. Ma and Nana aren't too happy about it. Ma cried, and Nana . . . Nana told me I better not dye my hair, get tattoos, and be waggin' my tail behind none of those white girls with the fake titties. I tried to explain to her that I wasn't that type, but she blew me off."

"They confused by all the hype over this, Courtney. We're simple folks. Method, North Carolina, ain't big as this block. We still got a lot of that country in us. Goin' on thirty-five years we been here in Brooklyn, and I still got my country ways." He winced. Courtney rose off the balls of his feet, ready to aid his uncle if need be. "You cain't blame them for wanting you to finish school, boy. I do, too, but I look mighty forward to watching you running up and down them courts. What team you thank gone pick you?"

"My agent thinks Atlanta. They asked me to come out for a pre-draft workout."

"Atlanta, huh? You ready to go south?"

"Yeah, I'm ready for *Hotlanta*. It's metropolitan, so I'm with it. It's like the new cultural Black Mecca. My agent lives down there during part of the year, and he says the city is dying for an athlete of my stature. The fans down there are clamoring for excitement. They're still watching highlights of Dominique Wilkins and Spud Webb."

"Is that right?" Carl asked him.

"Yeah, Unc, you said it yourself. The kid is cooler than water."

Hay, hay, hay. He coughed again. "You boys are something else. Colin writing his books. You with your basketball. Your knuckle-headed daddy'd be mighty proud, mighty proud. I can't help but think about what could have been for him."

Courtney's jaw muscles tensed. "Could have, should have," he said. "Life's about choices, Unc. My old man—he crapped out, ya know? But that's okay, never needed him anyway."

"That's hogwash, Courtney. Now I know I was there for you

boys, but a boy needs his father to show him how to be a man. This store took so much of my time. I never got to spend as much time nurturing you boys as I would have liked."

"I never wanted for anything, Unc. I never missed a beat by not having my father around."

"You was his shadow for those early years, and then he was gone. That had to hurt."

"Never missed a beat," Courtney repeated.

"Maybe, so," Carl said, "maybe so." The old man struggled to turn and get back to his seat, his hip starting to flame up on him. "Colin kind of took over. He always had you with him. Not many older brothers would have dragged you around as he did. We used to call him *Big Colin* and you *Li'l Colin*. You remember that? I swear, anything Colin did, you did."

Courtney moved over by the counter. He ran his fingers along the countertop, his head down, eyes diverted. Wherever he went, and whomever he dealt with, somehow the artery of thought always led to Colin. Frustration grew in the pit of his stomach, stung like an ulcer. Colin hadn't wanted him around, he'd forced himself on his older brother, attached himself to Colin like a limb. And what had he gained from it? Ask his family and they'd say a role model. But the truth, all he'd gained was confusion. The things Colin did were . . . were things a role model didn't do. Leave it at that.

"You plan on getting down to Jersey to see that new baby? You an uncle yourself, now."

"One of these days, Unc. Soon, I promise."

"Don't let this thing between you and Colin make you foolish, boy. Like I said, Colin was good to you. Whatever happened between y'all, you need to nip it in the bud." Carl looked up to see if his words were registering. Courtney was still looking down. "I hear that baby is a sight to behold. Thick black hair and big ole eyes. I cain't wait to see her myself, yes suh."

Courtney nodded. "Hey, Unc. You got that 'Cool Water' record you were talking about? Maybe I'll make that my theme song or something."

Carl watched him for a moment, a huge smile crossed his lips and he nodded, multiple times. "Cool Water, yes suh." He winced as he pointed with his head toward the windowsill on the side of the store. "I keep a couple copies of that record in that crate right over there. Go on and pull yourself one out."

Courtney walked over by the window, bent his long frame and reached into the crate. "Jesus, Unc," he sang out. "How many copies you need of this record?"

"One of my favorite records, boy. You ain't the only one to make that record your theme song."

Courtney smiled. "Oh, so you already claimed dibs on this one, huh, Unc?"

Carl shook his head and smiled yet again. "Nah, son. I ain't got the cool water flow anymore."

"Who then?" Courtney asked as he fingered the spine of the record, examining the jacket like a woman's rounded buttocks.

"Colin," Carl answered. "He said the same thing you just said when I first told him about the record. 'I need to make that my theme song, Unc.' Word for word. Now ain't that something?"

The record slipped from Courtney's fingers and landed at his feet.

Colin walked up the pathway to his house, deep in conversation with himself.

"Milford, Connecticut. Milford, Connecticut." He tapped his shoes on the edge of the porch, checked the mailbox. His early morning writing had been going well until he reached a point in his novel where he needed information regarding Bic headquarters. It was at that point that he questioned his decision to cancel his AOL service. He'd found himself distracted from actual writing, reading over Langston Campbell's Web log, surfing other authors' Web sites, checking his sales at the online book retailers multiple times per day. Liza, as it turned out, had been right when she said he'd regret the decision to cancel the AOL. He hadn't factored in the research capabilities the Internet provided.

"You're going to find yourself one day," Liza told him at the time, "wanting a trivial piece of information for one of your novels, and instead of the answer being a keystroke away . . ."

The answer would require an early morning drive to the drugstore to check out a bottle of *Wite-Out*, so he could strain his eyes reading the fine print on the back of the bottle to find out that the Bic Corporation's headquarters were in Milford, Connecticut. To most writers the detail wouldn't have mattered, but Colin had to be precise, his fiction had to ring true down to the minutest detail. When he decided to have one of his characters interview for a position with the Bic Corporation, well, the location of the company became as vital to his story as oxygen to a human.

That conversation with Liza, the mother wit she possessed, rang in his ears.

"You know that you're gonna get hung up on that little trivial piece of information, whatever it might be, Colin, and the words are going to leave you. Instead of making a mark and coming back to it later—oh, no, Mr. Perfectionist is going to stop cold. You're going to end up messing up your *flow*." Liza had said it as he would. "Trust me, baby, keep the service." Colin thought of her famous last words as he opened the front door. As always, his wife was on the mark when it came to their lives. He needed to pay more heed to her insight. That, and reconnect his AOL service.

There were bags of luggage hugging the wall in the foyer as Colin entered. The darkened condominium that he'd left a short while before now glimmered with light. His stereo system had been shut off—Nas's lyrical raps banished with the electrical current. Colin turned over his wrist and consulted his watch. It was Thursday and not noon yet. He hadn't expected the blinding light, silenced sound system, and heavy luggage until late tomorrow evening.

I'm ev-ver-ry wo-man. I'mmm ev-ver-ry wo-man.

Colin closed his eyes and leaned against the wall in the foyer for strength. The voice from the kitchen grated his ears like fingernails dancing across a chalkboard. He took a deep breath and, after a brief moment, prepared himself for his mother-in-law. The walk to the kitchen felt like a stroll toward a boxing ring to fight an opponent the Las Vegas odds makers considered a heavy favorite. He could feel that old knee injury in his left leg acting up. Every fiber of his being was on alert.

"Mama Brashear," he said as he entered the kitchen with a politician's smile on his face. "It's so nice to see you."

Liza's mother turned toward him. "Zennifer, Colin, Zennifer," she said. "I keep telling you that *Mama Brashear* mess makes me feel old. And, I am too supple to be feeling old." She turned her head to the side, motioned for him to kiss her cheek. Colin leaned down as directed and twisted his head to avoid the brim of her black rhinestone hat as he kissed her.

"Of course, Zennifer," Colin responded after the kiss. "I apologize. I keep letting my manners impede on your wishes. It won't happen again. Rudeness is my new modus operandi."

"Good Lord," Zennifer said, smiling. "Talk down to us ordinary folks, son-in-law. That's precisely why I haven't read any of those books of yours. I don't care to feel stupid. Now, Iyanla, that girl can throw down. And Terry, oh my gosh. The only vacation I've taken in ten years came after I read her book. You know Zennifer booked herself a trip to Jamaica quick fast and in a hurry to get her groove back. And damned if I didn't get it." She noticed Colin looking at her with wide-eyed interest and changed the subject. "You better not have my granddaughter talking like that either. Using those high ciddity words. One of you in the family is enough."

Colin moved to the countertop and started peeking in pans. "So what do you think of the baby?"

"I think she's a precious little angel. Beautiful. She reached back two generations and took my divineness."

"Divineness? Now, I hope you don't have her talking like you either, Ma—Zennifer." Colin lifted a corner of aluminum foil from one of Zennifer's pots. "So where are mother and child?"

"I put them to rest. They've both been through a lot," Mama Brashear said. "Did you know I almost died giving birth to Liza? Childbearing isn't easy, that's why God put it on us women."

"Did you? You almost died."

"Yes." She shooed Colin away from her pans. "You're messing up my presentations, son-in-law. Go ahead and grab yourself a plate, and I'll warm you food in the microwave."

Colin pulled a plate from the cupboard. One thing for sure, Mama Brashear could put together a meal. Her catering business, and the Jaguar she drove because of it, could attest to her acumen in the kitchen. "You were saying you almost died giving birth?" Colin asked.

"Yeah, and Liza's no-account father wasn't there. I shudder to think about dying all alone on that table with my legs spread."

"Men didn't do the delivery-room thing back in them days, huh?"

"Colin, if you don't stop talking like I'm some old hag, I swear. It was 1974, not 1947 for chrissakes! Liza's father was, and is, a louse. I'm telling you, Colin, you love that little girl with all your heart and give her support and encouragement. Teach her to respect herself and how to make wise choices in life. Daughters need their fathers. I know sons do, too, but I believe that girls especially are in need of a father. Liza has turned out to be a wonderful young woman, and I'm extremely proud of my baby girl, but the road to this point was rocky. Rocky!"

Colin thought about the period when he first started dating Liza. She was still modeling at the time, with a steady stream of work. Yet, to her, the big eyes everyone else coveted were too big. The silky, long, black hair was actually more comfortable tangled around the teeth of her comb. The muscular shoulders and arms were "manly." When Liza looked in the mirror, she didn't see the beauty others saw.

Until this moment, until Mama Brashear made the connection between father and daughter, Colin had never considered the source of Liza's problems. He thought about Lyric. Not only must he keep her safe and provide for her, not only must he guide and discipline her, he also had to aid in building her self-esteem as a young adult woman. Could he handle all of this?

"That smells wonderful," Colin said as the food in the microwave filled the air. "What is it?"

"Lemon chicken," Mama Brashear announced with pride. "The key is the basil, not the lemon. That's saffron rice, a Spanish dish. And that is broccoli rabe. And I'll be highly upset if you don't eat it. Liza tells me that you always leave the vegetables that she cooks on your plate, and then complain all the time that you don't have the right energy because you don't get enough vegetables."

Colin wondered what other information his wife shared with her mother. How much did Mama Brashear know about Colin and Liza's free-falling life before Lyric came along? Did she know the day before her granddaughter was born that their marriage almost collapsed?

"I eat my vegetables," Colin said, shaking aside the thoughts.

"You need your leafy greens, too, Colin, not just corn."

"Cabbage, collards, spinach. I eat my vegetables, Ma—Zennifer."

"Good, son-in-law, then you'll have no problem finishing off that broccoli. Is that what you're telling me?"

Colin sighed. "Yes, Ma'am."

"Now you're with the Ma'am." Mama Brashear sighed, shook her head. "Making me feel old."

"Sorry."

"Um hmm. So how does your family feel now that the baby's here?"

Colin swallowed a mouthful of food. "They're excited. My mother and uncle are so upset about not being able to come; it's hard because of Nana. Liza's adamant about following the doctor's recommendation that we don't take Lyric out for two months; otherwise, I would bring her with me when I go."

Mama Brashear took a seat on the stool next to Colin. "Liza spoke with your brother while you were out. He offered his best wishes."

Colin put on a pleasant face. He concentrated on not grinding his teeth together. "Did she? That's good. I haven't spoken with him yet. He's all wrapped up with getting ready for the NBA draft right now. When everything settles for him, after the draft in June, I'll reach out to him. Courtney always talked about how happy he'd be when I had children so he could be an uncle. Matter of fact, back when I was in high school he wanted me to have a kid. My brother has always been good with children. The young kids idolize him in our old neighborhood."

Mama Brashear smiled without opening her mouth. "Good with kids, is he? Is that so?"

5

MAY II

Keep your distance, fucker! Eyes are watching.
Courtney rolled his jaw and strode forward without missing a beat as he closed the flip of his cell phone. Two messages already today. Three—identical to today's messages—yesterday. After five stabs at it he still couldn't figure out what the messages meant, who'd left them, and why he was being targeted. The voice had that ghetto bravado to it, but was unfamiliar. Eyes were watching him for what? Could it be local fools trying to shake him down now that it was common knowledge that his bank account was about to hatch zeros. That was the problem of being black and in the inner city. One crab tried to crawl from the barrel; the other crabs would expend all their energy trying to pull him back in. It didn't matter though. This was his world, and only he would remain at the end. In fact, against his family's wishes, he'd been contemplating having *E pluribus unum*—"out of many, one"—tattooed on his arm. *See, it's starting already*, his Nana had said. He had no intention of going overboard with the tats like Rodham or Iverson. That one would do. But before he made that permanent and bold statement, he had to make sure he had his big guns.

He entered the Barnes and Noble Bookseller on Sixth Avenue and 22nd Street, the grand store with the New York Life Building a gaze away. It felt good to be out of Brooklyn, felt good to be away from campus, making his way through Manhattan's overcrowded streets. It felt good to be recognized every so often and to make mouths smile and hearts flutter with a handshake or a pound. Wait until he made a decision and signed one of the sneaker endorsement deals that were on the table. The commercials would make him more famous than he could have ever imagined when he first picked up a basketball. Wait until he put on that NBA uniform, Atlanta's colors. Flame red and sunny yellow—hot colors for a hot player. Wait until he came to Madison Square Garden and dropped thirty points. The entire city would be proud of their homegrown hero. Then he would have his big guns. Then he could proclaim *E pluribus unum* with full confidence.

Courtney stopped for a split second at the enormous magazine rack at the entrance of the store. He counted no fewer than ten sports-themed periodicals. He could imagine his face plastered across the cover of each of them. Today was the start.

The café was centered in the store. Courtney sauntered up to the cashier, ordered a hot chocolate and a croissant, and found a seat along the front. It had been years since he'd been in a bookstore, longer since he'd purchased a book. He couldn't believe the demand. Couldn't believe how engrossed the people were that sat on chairs and benches reading. How seriously the buyers strolled up and down the aisles perusing the different titles. When he first walked in, he'd been tempted to browse the *Fiction and Literature* aisle, of the authors whose last name began with *S*, but he hadn't.

"Excuse me," a voice cut into Courtney's people-watching, "Are you Courtney Sheffield?"

Courtney nodded at the young brother wearing a Grambling State sweatshirt.

"Cool, bro," the young man said, extending his hand. "I'm Langston Campbell."

"Oh!" Courtney extended his hand to meet Langston's. "Damn, yo. I apologize. I didn't recognize you. I thought you were taller. Have a seat. Or grab yourself something first. I know you writers are into your lattes and so forth. I already got myself something when I came in."

"I'm good, thanks." Langston pulled out a chair and sat. His hair was cut close to his scalp. His eyes drooped as if they were in a race for his mouth. "Langston Campbell isn't like these other writers, Courtney. I dance to my own drum, bro. This game I'm in, much like the game you're in, is too competitive for me to do things like the other writers. I got my own style, my own way about this. No one does it like Langston Campbell."

"Don't I know it—I specifically asked for you to write this article because I knew no one could write it like you, my man." It was a lie. He'd asked for Langston Campbell to get back at his brother. Colin had the nerve to leave a voice message on Courtney's cell phone yesterday that still made Courtney's nostrils flare.

You need to concentrate on doing the right thing with your life, Courtney. This is your opportunity. Don't blow it. Stop upsetting Mama and Nana. Chill with the secret conversations with my wife. You should focus on making sure you see this NBA thing through. Don't be another Prime.

Some people needed putting down, like a horse with a broken leg. Colin, Courtney surmised, was one such person. Dude had serious nerve. He needed checking.

"I appreciate the love," Langston told Courtney. "Truly appreciate it."

Courtney swayed while he talked, flowing with the wave of voices and activity that buzzed around them. "I read that article you did on Method Man for *The Source*. That shit was magical, man. You had me out in Staten Island—*Shaolin*—smokin' weed, talkin' shit like I was right there with the cat, you know." He had in fact read that piece and enjoyed it.

Langston fingered the shadow of goatee that framed his lips. Every time a critic blasted him for his oversized ego and undersized writing talent, he thought of the countless souls who'd been touched by his writing. Sure there was an ironclad formula that he used to write all his books. Sure he wasn't as gifted with words as that other Langston that came many years before him. Yet, you couldn't talk publishing without mentioning Langston Campbell. He had the hit books, the large advances, and the sales to prove it. And during his off-season, when he wasn't working on a novel or out promoting one on the road, he penned these magazine articles and collected obscene fees that his agent didn't get a fifteen-percent cut from.

"You ever read any of my books?"

Courtney scrunched his face. "Nah, man. I don't get into the books. No offense."

"None taken," Langston assured him. "But I'm surprised. I

would've thought you read a lot, having an accomplished brother like Colin."

"Colin?" Courtney smirked. "Even if I read, I wouldn't read his books."

Langston nodded as if he agreed. "Interesting."

"Not really. I'm like most people in that regard."

"What do you mean?"

"Not looking to read any book with Colin Sheffield on the spine," Courtney said. "I haven't seen his name on the *New York Times* list lately, with you, my man."

Despite himself, Langston smiled. "Maybe this new one will do it for him. The advance reviews have been favorable, as always. Couple of folks in the industry I've spoken with said he raised the bar on this one. I don't know. Everybody can't be a best-seller, bro. There's only a few Langston Campbells, so I feel blessed. I hope Colin breaks through, personally. I've always respected his talent. In the beginning he was like my marker, my gauge. You know his first book dropped the same year mine did?"

"I didn't know that."

Langston nodded. "It sold well, too. Better than the latest books. And every year since, we've been battling each other, if you want to call it battling. Him in May, with me following in June. Like clockwork."

Courtney smirked. "Everybody knows June is the hotter month."

"Dang, bro," Langston said. "I need to be writing this stuff down. You're better than my publicist."

"I call it how I see it, that's all."

"Pardon me." Both men looked up as a voluptuous sister moved in. Her pleasant scent hung in the air like Christmas mistletoe, commanding lips to pucker. "Aren't you Langston Campbell?" she asked.

Langston had known from the moment she walked up that he was the object of her desire. In his mind, all the sisters wanted him. "In the flesh," he answered.

"I knew it. I picked up another copy of your book, *Word of Mouth*. You mind signing it for me?"

Langston leaned back in his seat, making no attempt to hide his exploration of her outrageous curves. "Let me ask you something," he said. "You know the new book is dropping in June. Have you reserved your copy yet?"

"No," she gushed. "But I know it'll be available on the 9th—I just had them check their system—and I'll be here first thing to pick it up."

"Then I guess you're a fan, and it's my duty to sign." He nodded and directed her with his fingers to hand him the book.

"Yes," she said as she placed the book on the table. "I swear. I'm a big fan of yours."

"I don't mean to interrupt," Courtney said. "But, you read a lot of books?"

"I'm an avid reader of African American authors," the curvy sister said.

"How do you feel about Colin Sheffield?"

"He's cool. My girlfriend loves him, but then she went to college and I didn't. Most of the time I borrow her copy."

"So you don't buy them?" Courtney said, smiling. He looked at Langston and winked. "I mean, you wouldn't come rushing out to buy his books like you would for my man here?"

The sister pursed her lips, eyed Langston. "No," she said. "I only *come* rushing for Langston."

Langston shot up in his seat. "Damn, baby. You said that sexy as hell. You're inspiring a brother right about now. What's your name?"

"Sonya."

"Well, Sonya, don't be surprised if a sexy-ass sister named Sonya happens to be in my next book." Courtney couldn't help but smile and nod, liking this brother's style.

"I should give you my number, then," Sonya said, "for research purposes of course."

Langston lifted Courtney's cup of hot chocolate, slid out the napkin, and handed it to Sonya. "Sign this, and I'll sign your book. Then I got to get back to work, finish interviewing this brother."

"You're famous?" the sister asked Courtney.

"Is he ever," Langston said. "This is *the* Courtney Sheffield, baby. Basketball superstar. This brother is about to tear the NBA to shreds. He's the more famous of the Sheffield brothers." Langston looked at Courtney and winked.

* * *

Before Lyric's birth, Colin would return home from his nine A.M. walk and head straight for his writing loft, but since her first day home he'd been making a left once he came in the door—heading toward the nursery. In fact, he'd been timing his walk to coincide with his daughter's first feeding of the day, waking up a half hour later than usual so it would all match up. The late start shifted his writing forward, but he accomplished more. The sentences came in magnificent flourishes.

He smiled this morning as he entered the nursery, noticing the sketching of Noah's Ark hanging by the door. "You finished it," he said to his wife, pointing at the sketch. He removed his shoes and walked toward his wife and child.

"Why didn't you ever tell me you played basketball?" was Liza's response.

Colin leaned over and kissed mother and child. His eyes were glued to his daughter, suckling away at a bottle nipple. "What's this about basketball?"

"You played all through high school. Set school records that stood until Courtney came along. Colleges recruited you. Why did you never tell me any of this?"

Colin nuzzled noses with Lyric, stuck out his finger so she could clamp her surprisingly strong grip on the tip. "Colleges recruited me, yes," Colin said, "but I never played a lick of college basketball. Talking about your glory days of sports on the high school level is kind of—I don't know—I don't think about it much."

"So why didn't you continue playing if you were so good?"

Colin frowned. "Liza, what's up with all this? Why are you so stuck on this basketball thing? I hurt my knee during the summer before college. Luckily my grades were strong or I might have never gotten to go to Columbia. I played basketball, yes, but I didn't live and breathe it like Courtney does. I wasn't going to the NBA or nothing like that."

Liza swayed in the rocking chair, her eyes riveted to Colin. Lyric continued to suck at the nipple, oblivious to the conversation, the storm rising, happening between her parents.

"I don't understand in all of our conversations why you never mentioned the basketball? What else have you kept from me?"

Colin stood and moved to the arm of the chair across from her.

He leaned forward in his explanation pose with his elbows resting on his knees and his hands up like he had her hips in his grip. "Kept from you? Look, Liza, I hurt my knee and that was the end of basketball, okay? By the time we hooked up, I hadn't picked up a basketball in years." He cocked his head to the side, stretched his jaw muscles. "Tell me something? How did you find out about the basketball? I left all my trophies and stuff at Mama's, packed away in the basement."

Liza looked down, patted away a touch of formula from Lyric's chin with the burp cloth. "I got a call."

"A call?" Colin asked. "Call from whom?"

"Langston Campbell."

"Lang—what?" His posture on the chair changed, tensed, he almost toppled over the side. "What kind of a call?"

"Apparently he's writing this major article for *Ebony* magazine and he called here wanting to ask you questions. He got to talking to me about the article and it escalated from there."

"Escalated." Colin stood again, came over toward Liza and looked down upon her and Lyric. "Where's your mother?" he whispered.

"She made a quick run to the store."

Colin nodded, raised his voice. "Now what did you mean *escalated*?"

"We got to talking, Colin. He's not at all like you described him. He was polite, and genuine in his support of your writing and your career. He talked about how messed up publishing is. How could a writer with your skills still be largely unrecognized? That sort of stuff. He was polite. I didn't get any hint of the legendary ego you always talk about."

"It's there," Colin said. "He was bullshitting you. He does that with the ladies. So, he's writing an article and he calls here wanting to talk to me. Then, he tells you I played ball in high school. Which, I don't know how he knows. He's checking up on me or something. I still don't get it. What's the article about? Did he say?"

Liza nodded.

"Well?"

"Promise not to get mad," she said.

"Liza, what the—"

"You're getting mad already, Colin, and I haven't told you yet."

She rocked Lyric gently and honed in on Colin with her big eyes. "Promise."

"If this turns out to be something that paints me in a bad light, or something along those lines, I sweartoGod." Colin took a deep breath, sat himself down again on the chair arm. "Okay, I promise. Go ahead."

"He's writing an article about Courtney."

Colin slid from the arm of the chair and sat square on the seat. He rubbed his palms over his scalp, stretched his jaw muscles again, fighting to keep his composure. "An article on Courtney? How did he come to do this article on Courtney?" Colin asked, his voice an open wound that he tried without success to dress with ambivalence. "Did he say?"

The air humidifier was the only sound in the room.

"Well?" Colin asked, breaking the monotony of the humidifier buzz.

"Courtney requested that he write it," Liza said. "Langston thought that was strange and he asked me straight out if you two had a problem with each other."

"What did you say?"

Liza's silence spoke with more clarity than any words she might have chosen.

"If anything, I mean *anything*," Colin said, staring at his wife with menacing eyes, "comes out in that article that makes me look bad, I'm holding you personally responsible. Don't ever take a call from Langston Campbell again. Don't ever answer another question from that man. I don't care how *polite* you think he is. You understand?"

"Yes," she said. "But can I ask you one more thing?"

Colin rose. "I'm done talking."

Liza reached forward and caught a hold of his wrist. "One more question."

Colin escaped her shackle around his wrist and prepared to move from the room.

"What are you running from?" Liza called after Colin.

Colin stopped in the doorway. His frame filled the opening. Liza could see the tension in his back muscles.

She added, "Something's haunting you, Colin, what is it?"

"You know what haunts people," Colin said, "ghosts." And then his figure moved from Liza's view. Out in the hall, he clenched his hand in a fist. So, Courtney wanted this to be ugly. Ugly it would be.

Courtney dribbled the ball the length of the court at half speed, then turned and dribbled back to the other end at full speed. Kept the routine alive, with his lungs burning, for an entire ten minutes. When he finished, his mouth was full of salty saliva, his stomach threatening to empty itself on the concrete. This was how he cleared his head, on this court, in this world where he was regarded like royalty.

Langston Campbell hadn't been at all like he expected. The brother was actually picking up "book hoochies" at a Barnes and Noble.

Courtney laid the ball on the court and retired to the grassy border. He sat on a plot of green and started his stretching.

How would Colin take this slight? How would he feel seeing Langston get the byline for the article? Would he feel? Would Colin be foolish enough to try and challenge him?

Courtney rose and started running in place. His heart rate had steadied, and now he needed to get it pumping again, faster, stronger. The NBA was the big league and he needed to be in tip-top shape.

How could Liza put up with the situation? How could she continue lying to herself? Colin didn't love her. Colin loved that people respected him because it *appeared* he loved her. Everything with Colin was about appearances. He fumed to everyone in earshot about his frustration with the publishing industry. He fumed about wanting to write insightful books and not fluff. Truthfully, Colin didn't have the imaginative creativity to come up with the kind of books Langston wrote. Colin couldn't conjure up the wave of action that Langston wrote about with ease. Colin couldn't detail the drama of everyday lives like Langston could. Otherwise, he would have.

The key to success is sincerity, and if you can fake that you've got it made.

Hadn't Colin said that to Courtney, back when they were still close? He'd said it as a joke, but Courtney knew—it was no joke. There was nothing sincere about Colin. Hadn't he promised to watch over Courtney forever when their father left? Hadn't he told his family he would always be there when they needed him? Hadn't he told Liza that he would never hurt her, that he would always be her backbone? All lies.

He'd abandoned Courtney during his most trying period in life—during his adolescence. "Time for you to take wings and fly on your own, little bro," is how he had put it. He'd stepped out on the family to form his own family, and had mucked that new family up in the process.

Courtney picked the ball up again and started his routine from the beginning. Run half speed one way, then full speed the other way. "Your world," he kept reminding himself when the air threatened to leave him, when his legs offered little support. "You got your wings, Court. Now fly."

6

MAY 12

Henry Marshall rolled up the sleeves of his burgundy flannel shirt and knelt in place. He closed one of his grayish-blue eyes, made a line with an upraised arm, and mouthed a few words of encouragement to himself. Then he stood, tightened his grip on his club, and putted. The miniature golf ball traveled across the green carpet in a straight line, and then, cruelly, as it approached the hole, it veered to the right.

"Sonovabitch!" His stocky shoulders slouched in defeat and for a moment he stood gritting his teeth. The salty, white area around the temples of his forehead moved up and down like faulty window shades, and, as was his habit, he ran his thick hands through his hair, smoothing out the mane, placing every hair back in its rightful position. He eyed the hole. He sneered at the small golf ball resting on the edge of the green carpet.

"Another L," Colin's voice called from over Marshall's shoulder. After pausing to steady himself, Marshall turned to face the music. Colin was all smiles.

"Damn golf club is too short," Marshall said. "I played with a handicap that entire game. I'm kicking myself now for letting you off the hook so easy."

"And so many times, too," Colin said. "What was that, three games? Or was it four?"

"Two. The first one never counts, a warm-up." Marshall flipped his club and held it by the bottom as he made his way off the carpet and headed for the cashier. He brushed past Colin and bumped shoulders without apology. The gesture made Colin laugh all the more.

It was the "take no prisoners" approach, the competitive drive that enamored Marshall to Colin. Few, if any, literary agents could have secured the three-book deal with Beale Street Publishers that Marshall had collared for him. At the time, Colin was twenty-four, a stone's throw from college, up to his ears in newlywed bliss, and had only a short story published in an obscure literary magazine to his writing credit. Marshall secured his deal with only the first fifty pages of Colin's manuscript. "A drop of cyanide can kill you, and a drop of sperm can create life," Marshall had said to the publishers at the time. "This kid has talent to burn, and you guys will be kicking yourselves if you don't scoop him up before someone else does."

Marshall ripped his miniature golf scorecard and tossed it in the wastebasket beside the cashier counter. He handed the young girl his club and his ball and made a quick trip to the restroom, while Colin paid for the three games. Colin was waiting for him by the exit doors, still smiling.

"Henry, my man, you have to face facts. The times are changing," Colin said as he placed a comforting hand on Marshall's shoulder. "African American dominance is a phenomenon. Best golfer in the world is black. Golf, all the major sports, we dominate them. Shit, even publishing. Black books are the only growing segment right now. We're a serious people, Henry. We're here to take over. We're here to conquer."

"It's okay," Marshall allowed Colin. "Because the best rapper is white."

Colin's eyes furrowed and he stopped walking.

"Oh, don't give me that," Marshall said. "Dylan and Katie keep their old man up to date. You know Eminem is the truth."

"You're one crazy cat, Henry."

"Like a fox."

The two of them reached their cars, parked side by side, and leaned against the back of Marshall's late model Saab. Marshall made it a point to get together with each of the authors he represented at least four times a year, and during these face-to-face meetings, he always saved the last few moments before they separated to discuss business.

"I have a bit of news for you, Colin."

"Don't tell me you and your ex-wife are reconciling," Colin joked.

"You ever put the words ex-wife and reconciling together in the same sentence together again and I'm going to have to stop telling people what a wordsmith you are. Ex-wife and money-grubber, ex-wife and migraine headache—now those are much better choices." Marshall had been through a bitter divorce a few years back and ever since any talk of his ex-wife contained nothing but disdain. It got to the point that the people closest to him teased him about the situation, and he'd found that poking fun made the monthly checks he signed over to his ex easier to write. The only good that came out of the marriage, in his opinion, were his two kids.

"Seriously, what's the news?"

"You're not going to like it."

"Book business stuff?"

"Of course," Marshall said.

Colin's voice teetered. "Beale Street doesn't like the new manuscript. They don't want to re-up with me?"

"No, no, in fact Angelo's only half through reviewing it and he said it's your best writing ever. He's been all over me about when you're gonna finish the second part."

"Then what is it?" Colin asked.

Marshall grimaced as he'd done when his golf ball veered from that last hole. "Langston Campbell's coming over to *Beale Street*. He's switching publishers. I got wind of his deal and I called Angelo immediately. It's substantially more than what you signed for, and I wanted Angelo to know we expected more for this new deal. I understand that Campbell outsells you, but your books have helped Beale Street in other ways. The fine qualities of your writing and the positive reviews you've always gotten have given them a credibility they didn't have before. Campbell wouldn't have thought of jumping houses and signing with them if not for that."

Colin shook his head. This Campbell cat was getting too close for comfort, crowding his space. He could feel him on his skin like a sweater. "I can't see myself sharing the ball with Campbell."

"Come on Colin," Marshall said. "Sprewell and Houston can do it, you and Langston can coexist. Having him over there might give a boost to your sales."

"What about marketing and promotions, Marshall? You know those dollars they would give me are gonna go to Langston. I think we should shop the new manuscript at one of the other houses."

Marshall tapped the trunk of his car like a drum. "Angelo has this vision of presenting you two, as a package. A black literary Brat Pack, like Bret Easton Ellis and Jay McInerney. Only without the controversies that always follow those two. I like it, Colin."

"I suppose Angelo wants me to write sickening, grotesque novels that get the critics all riled up, too. Wants me to write something that'll make people hate me and burn my books live on the news in protest."

Now Marshall offered his hand in comfort, rubbing the tensed area at the nape of Colin's neck. "Not at all, Colin. I told you; he loves the new manuscript." He finished his sentence, punctuating his thought with yet another drum tap on his car's trunk.

Colin canvassed the lot, his teeth grinding his face into a painful grin. Who could you truly trust in this cutthroat publishing business? At one time he considered Angelo Hayes, his editor at Beale Street, an ally, but lately the vibe between the two of them was shaky at best. Colin had liked Angelo from the beginning, impressed that a black man could take the industry by storm. Angelo Hayes was a new-school hero of sorts, championing African American fiction, particularly fiction penned by African American males. Searching the universe for a 1990s Ellison, Baldwin, and Wright. His intensity when it came to books was legendary. His penchant for self-promotion, oftentimes at the expense of his own authors, equally chronicled. It had taken Colin's fluid and assured prose, exposed in those mere fifty pages, for Angelo to find a vehicle he'd promote with the same passion and energy as he did himself. He'd found his Baldwin. But now, three critically acclaimed, but all, except the first, commercially disappointing books later, Colin feared the worst. Langston Campbell wasn't just a nemesis anymore; he was now a dangerously close nemesis. They'd be placed side by side, each of their successes or failures judged against the other. Colin could afford that about as much as he could to lose readers.

"I have to think this thing over," Colin said. "But, I need you to do me a favor, Henry."

"Fire away."

Colin spoke evenly, as if his heart weren't racing in his chest, and his adrenaline wasn't threatening to topple him over like building blocks. "This freaking Langston." He blew out an air of disgust, shook his head, and composed himself. "Langston's writing a piece for *Ebony* about my brother Courtney. See if you can get an advance look at it. I'm interested in what he wrote."

"I'll see what I can do," Marshall said. He turned his head to the side, looked over his shoulder with unease. "Let me ask you a question?"

"Fire away," Colin responded, forcing a smile.

"You say Langston wrote the piece on your brother. Why didn't you write it? That bit of pub could have helped with the new book."

Millions of contrasting thoughts like the varied colors of a kaleidoscope ran through Colin's mind. The day his mother came home with Courtney—how puffy his brother's cheeks were, how swollen his left eye was. The time he threatened a kid in the neighborhood who was making Courtney's walk to school a torturous experience. The wide-eyed embarrassment, then curiosity, on Courtney's face that time he walked in on Colin watching a porno flick. How Courtney couldn't say please when he was younger—how it always came out '*feeze*'.

Colin shook the thoughts aside. He looked off in the distance, his eyes slatted under the brightness of the midday sun. He ran his tongue over the dry flesh of his lips. The bitter saltiness of his mouth clung to his taste buds. He could feel Marshall watching him, waiting for a reply.

"I would have loved to have written that piece," he said finally as he fished his car keys from his pocket. "But I wasn't asked."

Hush little buttercup, don't you cry . . . hmm, hmm, hmm, hmm . . . I'll tell you why. And if that mockingbird don't sing . . . hmm, hmm, hmm, hmm, hmm, hmm, hmm.

"Damn, give me my child. You couldn't possibly mangle a song more than that. Not if you tried."

Courtney hesitated to let little Destiny go from the cradle of his arms. Surprisingly, she felt natural there. "At least I'm trying. A lot of dudes wouldn't be here, Chante."

Chante took the child and placed her in the crib. "She's getting so big, so fast. I can't keep up with her." Courtney moved over by Chante's side, looked down in the crib. Destiny had almond-shaped eyes and an extra-pointy chin. Destiny's skin was many shades lighter than his shade. He would have called it eggshell if she was a wall, but he didn't know what to call the color as skin. He touched her closed eyelids and rubbed his hand over her little tummy. *God, she felt so natural.* The curvature of her belly felt like the rounded edges of a basketball. He pulled back and walked over by the window. Chante's eyes followed him until he reached the window, and then she looked back down at the child, afraid that he'd see her eyes upon him in the window glass.

"She looks so much like you. Creepy. A mini you," Courtney said.

Chante didn't reply. She knew that his words meant that Destiny looked nothing like him. Revisiting the issue of paternity was too painful, though. She'd threatened him about it countless times. Usually by a message routed through his mother. But Courtney knew that Chante would never subject Destiny or themselves through a DNA test. The answer in those squiggly strands could prove too hurtful.

Courtney watched a group of youngsters throw a brick through a car windshield. The alarm sounded and one of the teens snatched the radio from the interior before they all scurried up the block like hamsters off the wheel. Across the street a second car was parked with its windshield battered, though that second car's windshield looked as if it had succumbed to bullets instead of brick. Courtney turned from the window. "You need to get out of this neighborhood, Chante. This is no place to raise a child."

"I'd love to," she said, facing him, leaning against the crib with her arms crossed. "Are you offering to help me?"

Courtney almost said something smart but he thought of the little girl in the crib and his tongue settled. "Not exactly," he said. "I'm not ready to commit to that." The birth of his niece, whom he'd yet to see, also weighed heavily on his mind.

Chante searched his face, trying to excavate any emotion, an answer to all the questions in her head. Courtney's eyes were vacant, his mouth turned neither up nor down. His only gesture was a quick rub on the tip of his nose with his thumb and forefinger. Her questions, it appeared, would remain unanswered. At least he was here, though. Third, maybe fourth time he'd darkened her doorway in the past year.

"Thanks," she said, as the joy of the moment came to her.

"Thanks for what?"

"Thanks for coming by, for trying to sing to Destiny. Your voice soothed her."

"I figure she's innocent in all this," Courtney said. "Our mistakes—*your* mistake—shouldn't have any bearing on that beautiful, little girl." He moved from the window, past Chante, and peered down in the crib again. Destiny's chest rose with her breaths. Chante flanked Courtney, watching him watch Destiny. After a moment, Chante's eyes pooled the wetness of hurt that lived inside her, the part of herself that she once would have called a soul.

"You hate me?" she asked Courtney.

Courtney forced his ears shut, continued watching Destiny's chest rise and fall like a dolphin swimming, breaking the water surface then returning below grade as it moved forward. Competition had taught him one thing. Never allow your opponent to dictate tempo because then the game was out of your hands and you were at their mercy. He wouldn't allow Chante to dictate tempo ever again.

"Courtney, please. Answer me."

"Chante, we've been through this."

She slid in between Courtney and the crib, forcing his eyes from Destiny. "We've been through this, but we never resolved anything. I need to know. Do you hate me?"

"Should I? I mean, if this thing was switched, shoe on the other foot and all that jazz, how would you feel? Hate? Something less? Something more?" Courtney moved away from her, his back facing her. He closed his eyes, intent on remaining the maestro of the moment. He could feel the tempo moving faster than he wanted it to. She was controlling the game yet again. Controlling the game, as she'd done that wicked night when the question of hate first surfaced between them.

Mmmm. Yeah, baby. Yeah.

Her soft voice had polluted the air. Her wails of ecstasy stalled the engine that pumped Courtney's contented heart. He'd been so happy in love. He moved down the hallway toward her that night, his stomach churning, his mouth salting over with nausea. He used his fingers as a guide through the darkness of the hall, fingering the surface like a blind man, a blind man about to see the light.

Mmmm. Yeah, baby. Yeah. Give it to me. Give it to me good.

Talking like a prostitute in her breathy, throaty, naughty tone. Using phrases defined by desire, but not bound by love. Phrases he'd never heard screech past her full lips before. Her words violated and betrayed him as much as her sexual actions.

Oh baby, yes. Touch me, baby. Push harder baby.

Darkness and his own tears blinded him by the time he reached the bedroom. He gagged on his tongue. Bile threatened to burst from his windpipe. Her voice tortured his ears like a record played backward, the beautiful and natural harmony distorted by this most unnatural act. The light crept from under the door. Making love with the lights on. There was no way for her to characterize this as anything other than a premeditated act of betrayal. He balled his fist in anticipation. His heart raced as his mind moved forward three or four frames. He'd rush in and surprise her, and this lover. He'd show her a violent surge she never knew existed in him. Bash this lover in the face and then rip her from his thieving arms, by her long, silky hair. The same hair he twirled during their tender moments would now be the umbilical cord, cut, separating their lives. Then he opened the door and . . .

"You're thinking about it again, aren't you?" Chante asked, taking him by his wrist and returning him to the present. Her fingers, hot to the touch, rubbed across his skin.

"Can't shake that moment," Courtney said. He removed her hand from his wrist, tenderly loosening each finger. "We were solid, or so I thought, until that moment. I don't know how I could have been so dumb. I should've seen it."

"*I* didn't see it," Chante said, "No way you could."

Courtney smirked. He thought of that night, the light from the nightstand cascading off her creamy skin. The shadows dancing on the wall. Her gutter mouth, prodding her lover to continue prodding. No way could she chalk that night up to naiveté. She knew full well what she was doing. She knew the risk she was taking, and yet, she'd taken it. Anger warmed Courtney's chest as he remembered.

"Bitches always say stupid shit like that when they get caught with their asses out," Courtney said now, his anger growing stronger with each word. "But let a dude say shit like that and you'd be ready to pop him in the mouth."

"I deserved that," Chante answered, her voice absent of the buoyancy it had held minutes before when he suggested that he might be willing to care for her and Destiny. "And truth be told, you're right. I would have flipped if it had been you."

Courtney shook his head, blew through his nose, and turned his mouth upward. "I give you credit, you know how to shake a brother up, Chante. I never had a boring moment with you. That first date—shit, you had a brother ready to propose marriage. I never was into the light-skinned chicks until you. Then, we had this straight-out-of-a-book romance thing happening. Wearing matching outfits and all that other cutesy bullshit that makes me sick as I think about it today. Then, that night . . . and Destiny." He sighed. "Never a boring moment."

"Destiny's yours, Courtney. I know it in my heart."

"Maybe so, but then again, maybe not. Knowing it in your heart ain't knowing it with a certainty. How I look with a woman who tells me she knows in her heart that the child is mine? What if she ain't?"

"She is."

Courtney looked in the crib again. "Doesn't matter. You tore apart my entire life that night, Chante, and I don't think I'll ever get back what you robbed from me. You were about games, and at the time I wasn't. Let me ask you something?"

"Yes."

"I've been getting these strange messages on my cell. You have something to do with that?"

She looked at him, puzzled. "No, me? What kind of messages?"

"Don't matter. I thought it might be another one of your games."

"I made one mistake, Courtney. You're gonna hold that against me for the rest of my life?"

"Yeah, one *big* mistake," he answered. "Don't make this out like you fell asleep with the stove on and burned my dinner. You can't scrape the burned part off this and push it under my nose as if it's good to go. You fucked around on me, and then got pregnant. You can't look me in the eye with one hundred percent certainty and tell me this little baby girl is mine. That makes you stupid and a slut."

Courtney moved from the crib and started walking for the door. Chante chased him down from behind. Desperation was in her eyes and posture.

"Please, Courtney. Don't walk out now. We're talking finally. You've never been as open as you are right now. This is still an open wound . . . for the both of us. You owe it to what we shared. What you're saying is painful, but I can deal with the pain as long as you're talking to me. It's something." She nodded toward Destiny's room. "That little girl in there, you owe it to her to at least try and work with me on this. I'd apologize to you a million times if it would get us back to where we were."

"I don't owe you anything," Courtney fumed. "I don't know why I came here today. It was stupid of me, plain stupid. You're dead to me, Chante. You could have . . ." He pounded his fist on the door above her head. She flinched in surprise. "How could you? *Colin* of all people—my brother. A married man, for chrissakes. Damn! You know how many lives you were affecting, you dumb bitch? How could you?"

7

MAY 12

Colin ran his fingers across the notes taped to the top border of his computer monitor. The writing reminders had helped him with his three previous novels. *Symbolism, emotions, senses, clues* was scrawled on one of the notes. *Symbolism* was the pepper that added that extra spice to his scenes. *Emotions,* the salt, the key ingredient that made his characters come to life. Every time he sat at his computer, his fingers typing out the melody of word, it was his goal to tap into the *senses* of those characters. Peppering his stories with *clues* that hopefully added to the tension and suspense readers craved, the wondering of what was to come on the pages to follow.

The Langston Campbells of the world didn't care about the multi-hued blueness of ocean waves. They didn't care about the gritty feel of sand crawling between flexed toes. The soft murmur of wind as it whistled nature's songs. The pinch of lips as the tongue engulfed the sweet bitterness of plantains. Colin did, and the readers who experienced his words were all the better because he did. His writing was sensual, his prose vivid, his characters real enough to touch.

Colin reached across his desk and turned the volume up a notch on his stereo, allowing Nas to ooze through his speakers. Lately, he'd been in a hip-hop mood when he wrote and Nas had been his rapper of choice. The drumbeat soothed him, the spoken-word poetry preparing him for his own writing task.

"You're a blonde," Colin said aloud, getting a revelation. He looked at the computer monitor as if it was a floor length mirror and her naked body caught in the reflection. "A sassy sistah with blond curls and an arm full of bracelets. Chew gum, pop bubbles, and the whole nine yards." His character was coming to life before him. "Smart as hell, though. Got to keep that in mind. You wouldn't be standing for this crap. I've got to give you a reason to be here. Sassy . . ." Writing was excavation, digging for bones and then putting meat on those bones.

He tapped out a few lines of dialogue, jotted down a couple of quick notes, and decided to call it a day. As much as he tried to convince himself that Courtney's snub and Liza's stupidity didn't bother him, he couldn't. He couldn't give writing his full attention. He saved his program and clicked it shut, pushed the keyboard roller under his desk, and sat back in his chair. He rubbed his hands together like it was the dead of winter and he was stuck outside without a coat or gloves. The snow-capped mountains background of his monitor screen stared at him until he blinked. He reached forward and shut off the monitor.

This situation with Courtney needed resolution. Too many questions arose because of their divide. Questions Colin couldn't bare the thought of ever having to answer. Then there was the matter of Langston Campbell. And, Liza.

"Freaking *Ebony* magazine," Colin barked. He threw a light punch at the front of his desk.

Liza's voice came from over his shoulder. "One of those days?" she asked.

Colin turned toward the query that had come like a breeze.

"Afraid so," he answered. He looked at his computer again as if he was still working and Liza's presence was an interruption. "What's up with you? Thought you were going to sketch?"

Liza cleared a spot on the edge of his desk and made herself a seat. Colin's eyes followed the books she'd brushed aside as if they were worthless. "We need to check the ventilation in this place," she said as she ran the fingers of her right hand up her left arm. "All the creativity is seeping out."

"When's Mama Brashear getting back with Lyric?"

Liza touched her bare wrist and then looked at the clock on Colin's desk.

"In about—"

"Wait, wait . . ." He leaned forward and ripped a sheet of paper from his pad, scribbled down a thought and then placed the sheet in his idea folder. Seeing Liza before him made Colin decide his main female character wouldn't hold down her man, wouldn't have the common sense to know when she was deeply wounding him.

"They'll be back soon," Liza answered as Colin leaned back in his chair and his eyes reclaimed her. "They were going to the park. Mama wants Lyric to be an outdoorsy type. She said she can't stand the thought of her cooped up inside all the time like her parents, either doodling or typing."

Colin gave his wife the crumb of a smile for the first time since she'd entered the loft. There wasn't any joy behind the smile. "I can't say that I blame your mother. Writing is a lonely thing. Not that I'm complaining, I've been going at it *alone* for some time." That symbolism he searched for, his words carrying multiple layers of meaning.

Liza picked it up. "I am sorry about the thing with Langston Campbell. I thought about it some more, and I can see why you'd be upset."

Colin fidgeted with the pen and pencil organizer on his desk—twisting and turning it like a kid playing with toy cars. With his gaze far off like his thoughts, he said, "Henry let me in on something. Langston's leaving his publisher and moving over to Beale Street. So, now I can have a more constant reminder of the disparity in our careers. I swear, Liza," as he shook his head, "something about that cat rubs me the wrong way. I feel like he's making a concerted effort to get under my skin. Maybe, before, it was me being paranoid, but lately, nah, it's real."

Liza reached for Colin's hand. "Stop worrying about him. You've got to do you, baby. You've always said he didn't have half your talent. Well now is the time to put up. You're ready for this. I know it. It's time to turn the corner and confront this thing."

Colin looked up with that killer instinct she'd alluded to the day she gave birth. "You know," he said, "I keep telling myself that, keep trying to push myself for the inevitable. I know of course that you're right. Langston and I are headed for a confrontation." Colin left Liza and moved within himself, alone with his thoughts. "Confrontation might be what the doctor ordered." Confrontation . . . the only question was, of those who'd wronged him, who would be first? There were so many: Courtney, Langston, and—he looked at his wife—Liza.

"Bitches ain't shit, you just figuring that out?" Star asked.

Courtney shook his head. "Chante was cool for a minute."

"Then she started showing her true colors, though, right?"

Courtney couldn't help nodding. "Guess you're right."

"Guess?" Star said. "Ain't no guessing in that shit, son. She went all Michael Jackson's Billie Jean on you. You don't know if it's your seed or not. Come on, son."

Courtney quieted. It didn't make sense for him to be sharing so much of his personal situation, looking to Star for guidance. Some things you had to figure out on your own.

Two knocks came to the basement door. Star turned, frowned, got up eventually and went to open the door. Two Rocawear-garbed dudes stepped in, out of breath.

"Black is seriously looking for you, Star," one of the two told him. "The streets are buzzing about the shit."

Star waved his hand. "I ain't worried about Black."

"How much you get him for?" the second of the two asked him.

Star barked, "Don't be coming up in here with that shit. Don't you see I got my man over here chilling? We 'bout to celebrate this muhfucka making the jump to the NBA. Not talk about Black's black ass. You got the stuff?"

"I was just saying, Star, Black ain't—"

"Fuck Black," Star barked.

Courtney could feel the tension in the room. He made a move to leave. "I'm gonna bounce, Star."

Star shook his head. "Nah, son. Don't let these two fools mess up the vibe. We 'bout to smoke to bitches not being shit and the NBA being on your dick." Star was a frustrated rapper in his heart.

Courtney hesitated at first, but eased back into his seat on the couch as Star went to work on a cigar, splitting it and filling it with weed.

"You cut the cake and eat the first slice," Star told Courtney as he handed him the cigar.

Again Courtney hesitated, stared at the cigar with the same curiosity and mixed feelings as he'd had with Destiny earlier in the day. Star held the cigar steady, not budging. After a moment, Courtney reached for it. "Okay, I'll take a hit. Got a twinge in my knee; this might help."

Star nodded. "Fuck an Ace Wrap, right?"

Courtney looked at Star, smirked, shook his head.

"Chief it," Star egged him on.

Courtney puffed on the cigar tip, inhaling the marijuana. As it filled his lungs he noticed how cramped Star's basement was, with Star's mother's laundry machine and several of her boxes taking up most of the floor space, and the couch Star slept on taking up the rest. One light bulb lit the entire room. The radio was playing, on low for them, and kept cutting in and out from static to station because the hanger antennae wouldn't stay propped up correctly. A haze of smoke dusted the room, and if not for the illegal activity taking place, it could have been Uncle Carl's record shop, with Eddy Clearwater serenading the young men with Colin's theme song. Yes, suh.

Courtney sucked on the cigar, his cheeks hollowing and then filling out again. He could feel his frustration with Colin and his anger at Chante oozing away with each puff.

"I thought they did piss tests on the ballers? This ain't gonna mess you up, I hope?" Star asked, all concerned now after he'd already showed Courtney to the ledge.

"Nah," Courtney said, shaking his head. "My system will be clean as a whistle by the time camp starts. And they don't check you during pre-draft workouts."

"Whoa, baby, easy on that. Pass back off," Star joked. "We don't need you Len Biasing on us." The ex-Maryland player had his dreams deferred in one foolish moment. Right after Boston drafted him, at a party, Bias sniffed those dreams away. And by all accounts Bias had been a druggie virgin that night. Instead of his cherry, had his heart popped.

Courtney smiled, his eyes, two stray marbles, headed off in different directions, the weed hitting him hard. Unlike Bias, he wasn't a first-timer at this, but he wasn't promiscuous, peeking under Mary Jane's skirt all the time either. "This shit is top-heavy, bro."

Star smiled, nodded at the two others in the room. "You heard of a love jones? Well you're under a *Star Jones,* how you like the view?" It was a line from one of his street corner raps, one of his favorite lines, in fact.

Courtney tried to stand and go fix that damn stereo, but he fell back against the couch cushions.

"Yo, Star," one of the two dudes called out, "Look at son, yo? His legs are getting wobbly and shit. He ain't gone be dunking shit for awhile." They all laughed as Courtney tried to refocus his vision, get the walls to hold steady. No freaking way the belly of this blunt only held marijuana. There was heavier stuff in that cigar.

Courtney's temples throbbed, sharp pains shooting from behind his eyelids.

"Yeah, Court," Star said, "I'm mighty proud of what you about to do with the NBA. I hope you don't forget a nigga."

"I got your back, Star, you know that."

"I'm gonna hold you to that. As a matter of fact, I might need your help on—"

The basement door opened again. All of their heads shot around as one big dude walked right in.

Star was the only one to speak, his voice unsteady like Courtney's legs and vision. "Black, what's . . . what's up, man?"

Black looked through Star and over at Courtney, and narrowed his eyes.

It was waiting for Colin when he returned to his office for his late evening writing session. Six pages lay in his fax machine's paper tray. He scooped up the sheets and sat back in his chair.

We met for the interview at a Barnes and Noble bookseller, a fitting choice of venue considering that Courtney Sheffield's older brother happens to be the novelist, Colin Sheffield.

Colin hunched to the side, scanned further down the first page. Paragraph upon paragraph passed him by, like highway vehicles as he stood on the margins of the road with his thumb extended. Then, at the bottom of the first page came the words that exposed the rift between them, words he'd expected but hoped against.

"Everybody knows June is the hotter month," Courtney Sheffield told me. I was surprised to say the least.

They leapt out at Colin, scratched and clawed at his flesh. The corners of his eyes tightened and his skin burned. Courtney had said it, and Langston printed it. The lines had been drawn. It was without question now: two versus one.

Colin tossed the sheets on his desktop and sat back in his chair with his fingers entwined. He felt the urge to run downstairs, find Liza, and shake her like a bag of chicken and flour. Lucky for her she was down there trying to coax their little angel to sleep. Instead, he picked up his phone and started tapping out numbers.

The voice that picked up the other end chimed, "You've reached the Marshall residence."

"Katie, it's me, Colin. Is your dad in?"

"Hi, Colin, yes he is. I'll get him for you."

Before he could settle his thoughts Marshall was on the line. "Colin, to what do I owe this pleasure?"

"I wanted to thank you. I got the article."

"Article?'

"The *Ebony* article Campbell did on my brother."

"I wasn't able to get my hands on that, Colin. What are you talking about?"

"I've got it right here." Colin retrieved the papers from his desk and shuffled to the last page. Written in ink were the words: *What do you think?* The familiar and hateful *LC* insignia that braced the back cover of all Langston Campbell books was scribbled like a physician's prescription across the bottom. "Never mind, Henry," Colin said. "I'll give you a call back."

"Colin, are you okay?" Henry asked him.

"I'm good, Henry. Everything is clear to me now."

8

MAY 12 AND 13

The haze of the cigar's belly swirled in Courtney's head. He lay back on the couch in an awkward and uncomfortable position. Black kept his gaze on Courtney, lust in his eyes.

The side door in the basement opened again. Two dudes, a touch smaller than Black, walked in. The bottom of the door scraped the concrete surface because of its bad hinge. You had to lift up and push at the same time to open it, or otherwise the friction would prevent entry. These new visitors performed the procedure, as Black had, without any problem.

"Black," Star said, his voice trembling more by the minute, "I hope you don't make this more serious than it needs to be."

This Black character didn't answer. He had dusty dreadlocks that hung past his shoulders. His wild locks dangled like Gaboon Viper snakes at ease in the thick arms of an oak tree. Two half-moon eyes peered out from the mass of hair. His eyes were beyond red—he'd been smoking, too.

Star turned to his boys. "You want a hit of this, Black? Y'all, pass that to Black."

One of them made a move toward Black with the cigar in hand, but Black shook him off. Star's boy dropped back to the couch with his hand shaking like a plane going through turbulence. Star looked on the verge of vomiting. Courtney continued trying to gain a clearer focus with his eyes.

Black noticed the fear in the room. He smiled and told them, "Gwon witcha rec-cre-ayshun." He leaned against the wall, tanned from its normal white by constant smoke. He was dressed in all black, with purple-black skin, giving him the appearance of a giant ink spot. He nodded to the soft radio sounds. The two dudes with him stood by impassively.

Courtney sensed the doom to follow. No one said a word. Star was especially quiet. Courtney tried to gather Star's eyes but they avoided him. He'd never seen Star as shaken as he now appeared to be. This Black character must be the real deal. Courtney decided the hour had come for him to leave, and he attempted to rise and do that, but Black shook his head. "Gwon, sit." Courtney did.

"Bumboclot," Black said, looking directly at Star, after endless moments of staring around the room. "You tink you clever, nuh? Steal fe mi. So is this the big bawl player you spoke of?"

Star hesitated to talk at first, until Black inched from the wall. "Yeah, Black, man. This Courtney Sheffield. We grew up together. He's 'bout to terrorize the NBA."

"Terror bwoy, nuh?" White foamy spit sat on Black's lip. He moved toward the couch and studied Courtney as if he, Black, was the judge in a beauty pageant and Courtney had long legs, a thin waist, and big breasts.

Star shifted, his voice had lost most of its masculine heft. "Black, uh, Courtney's gonna help me out. You'll get your money back. Give me a couple days . . ."

Black shook his head. "Lessons, clot. Lessons. Time fe mi teach you and ya bwoy here a serious lesson." He looked at Courtney. "Mi folk told yah eyes were watching. Tawk straight to yah chelly phone."

Courtney's stomach dropped as he realized that these had been the dudes leaving him those voice messages.

Black moved toward Courtney with a purpose. When he reached the couch, he held out his hand and gestured to Courtney's Jesus Piece medallion. "Run the chains, bawl bwoy."

"Colin, Colin."

Colin's eyes sprang open. He sat up in his bed with a start, his breathing ragged. Liza sat propped next to him on the bed, her hand resting on his shoulder. He wiped slobber from the corner of his mouth and tested his hand against his hard-beating chest. He blinked his eyes and looked through the darkness of the bedroom. He felt comforted that more than ten years removed him from the awful moment of his nightmare. Comforted that the horrible mistake he made was just a memory stained into his conscience. That he'd moved on from that time, and had become so much more, so much better.

And he had, right?

"You okay?" Liza asked when Colin didn't speak.

"What's up?"

"Dreaming again," she said. "Your daily nightmare."

"Was I?"

"Yes, and you called out your brother's name, kept calling it, in fact."

"Courtney?" Colin said, hesitating.

"Only brother you have, right?"

Colin fumbled to turn on the lamp from the nightstand. He sat up on the side of the bed and stretched. His muscles ached and his fingers itched for activity. Fingers itched for the keyboard in his writing loft.

Liza ran her hands over his shoulder. "The way you kick and flail, I'm afraid of getting hurt."

Colin rose to his feet, plucked a wrinkled T-shirt off his side of the floor and put it on. "I'm going to go write." He had to channel the emotion from his dream state, use it to his benefit. That's how brilliant novels came to be—the writer digging into the deepest tunnels of his soul, brushing the dirt off whatever he found, using that fossil for fuel.

The light from the bedside lamp cast a glow on Liza's face. "Why does your new book have to be so dark? It's affecting you in so many ways." She shivered as if a draft walked in the room. "You worry me, Colin."

"The whole book isn't dark, just parts of it are," he reasoned.

"You started having these nightmares when you started this book."

That was the downside of art. Sometimes it took the artist to places he wasn't fond of going to create it.

"Coincidence," Colin lied. "I'll be in the loft. Don't disturb me."

Liza sighed at the words from the familiar refrain. "Go on to your loft. Go run off and write the elusive best-seller. God knows that's the most important thing in the world." She sighed, and under her breath said, "I should have gotten pointers for you from Langston Campbell, made it a lot easier for you."

Colin heard her and turned back. "What did you say?" he asked.

"Nothing," she lied.

"You can be a real bitch," Colin said, waving her off dismissively as he passed through their bedroom door. It was to the point that it wasn't worth his effort to care about what Liza did and said. It was obvious she wasn't in his corner.

Liza wasn't having it, though. She struggled to rise from the bed, followed him down the hall. "Don't be flipping me off and calling me names, Colin. I don't play that shit. It's disrespectful."

Colin kept his pace. Liza's voice, her presence in the hall with him was no more than an annoyance.

"I said it to try and get something from you, something other than your silence. Stop and talk to me," she pleaded.

Colin continued to ignore her. As they reached the end of the hall, where the turn was, he put his arm out and brushed her aside as if she were a dressing room curtain. This infuriated her. "Stop and talk to me," she repeated. "You can't keep walking around here barely talking to me because you're angry I spoke with Langston Campbell. We have a baby to worry about now. Not just about us anymore. I said I was sorry."

Colin stopped. "Sorry doesn't cut it."

"All I have," Liza told him.

"Well it's—" Colin stopped, craned his neck. "That the baby crying?"

Liza listened, too.

The sound grew louder as Lyric awakened.

Liza said, "Damn you!" and balled her hand in a fist. She hit Colin in his left shoulder.

Colin grabbed her by the wrist, his eyes still as the ocean of the night. "What's up with you?" he asked.

"Let me go. You're hurting me," she said.

Colin loosened his grip a bit. Liza pulled free from his shackle.

"You're a fuck-up, Colin," she said as she stormed off up the hall.

Colin watched her. Regret kept him company as he considered the mess into which they'd brought Lyric. With each passing day, he and Liza grew farther apart. His world was coming unraveled and he didn't know how to begin fixing it.

After struggling to dial for help with his cell phone, struggling to decide in his fragmented mind which quick-dial button to push, Courtney had punched in the key for his agent. Matt Dresden III had his local associates have Courtney checked into the hospital under a fictitious name. Dresden didn't want to jeopardize the upcoming sneaker deal.

Courtney's eyes weren't what you'd call glazed over. No, for that effect you had to see the pupils. Courtney's eyes remained barely open. His jewelry had been taken from him. His face scratched by his own chain and medallion, which had been wrapped around a fist—like a tourniquet—and used to punch a tattoo of indignity across his skin. The little money he had in his pocket was gone. His height hadn't saved him. His athleticism hadn't revoked the punishment. His soon-to-be fame hadn't conquered the attackers. If anything, it had all led to his falling. What goes up, must come down.

"Who did this to you?"

Courtney glanced at his mother, shifted his weight on the table trying to find warmth on the cool surface. The concrete walls and bright lights of the hospital ER obviously weren't conveyors of heat. He couldn't stop shivering.

"I said, who did this thing? Courtney!" His mother was near tears.

He looked up again, thinking about the episode in Star's basement. "Don't know."

"Don't know? Or won't tell?"

Lena Merkerson processed his silence as the latter. "Don't think I'm a fool," she said. "I've been hearing from people about you hanging around these unsavory souls you call friends. Now don't you feel stupid?" She sighed. "Some friends."

"Ma, you mind letting up a bit. I don't need this, aiight?"

"You don't need—" Lena put her hands on her hips, huffed, turned, and huffed again. "You don't need this? You think I do? You think I like being awakened in the middle of the night to come down here for this? Not knowing if when I got here I was going to find a tag on your toe. Not knowing if you'd gotten your head split clean wide open. Hearing about this from that agent of yours—that slickster, talks like those drug dealers in the neighborhood I worked so hard to keep you boys from. How you think I felt in the ride over? Worrying myself sick about you. What about Nana? I haven't seen that woman cry in God knows how many years, that is, until today. Carl—he looked like he swallowed poison. He wanted to come so bad. I thought he was going to fall over on that bad hip of his when I got in the dollar cab. I know he didn't want to stay with Nana and have me trudge over here by myself. Which reminds me, I need to call them." She paused as if she was done, and then a new thought emerged. "I didn't raise you to be the selfish bastard you've turned out to be, Courtney."

Courtney looked at her, surprise on his face.

"That's right," she continued, "I called you a bastard. You don't care about what you do or who you cause pain. I spoke to Liza, too, by the way. She told me about this article they got coming out on you. She said Colin was greatly hurt by it, but he tries to blow it off like it's nothing."

"Just like Colin," Courtney cut in, "always blowing shit off like it's nothing. You guys give him a license to roam free and do as he pleases. I'm glad it hurt him."

Lena's voice was burdened by emotion, her eyes blanketed with tears that came like a flash rain. "He's the only brother you have, Courtney. When I'm gone, Nana's gone, and Carl's gone— it'll just be you two. Colin never did anything but try and help you, Courtney."

"You think so?"

"I know so. And instead of being thankful that you have a successful brother that loves you—no—you're jealous. You always was like that, all those years he had you with him like a third arm, all you ever wanted was what he had."

Courtney smirked and moved away from his mother's teary eyes, turned on his side. "Yeah, but he took what I had."

"What?"

Courtney shut his eyes, tight, balled his hands into a fist under the covers. "Nothing."

Lena shook her head and threw her arms up. "You're trying to be like your father?"

Courtney didn't answer.

"He was gonna be a big basketball star, too. Had everyone believing he was gonna get rich throwing that ball through a hoop, too. Grown man with a wife and kids and all he cared about was what the folks at the courts thought about him. Living up to that stupid nickname. Wasn't nothing *prime* about your father, Courtney. You can believe that. He ended up a junkie and with a knife in his back because he touched another man's wife. You headed down the same road, boy."

"You finished?" was all Courtney said.

Lena shook her head. "I'm going to call your Nana and Carl, let 'em know everything is all right. You want anything from the snack machine? Soda or chips or something?"

"Nah."

"You need to think about the course of your life," Lena told him as she prepared to exit. "You only get to travel this road once." She left.

His mother's words were a map to deep thought. Courtney sat in the silent hospital room immersed by the episode earlier in Star's basement. After the humiliation of a beating, Black had whispered something in Courtney's ear that still played in his head like a favorite song. Black had told him, "Peace be still or yah seed and dutty gurl be next, seen?"

Colin was in his loft office, clawing his way through writer's block when Liza entered, out of breath. "Colin, telephone!"

Without taking his eyes off the monitor Colin replied, "Don't take calls when I'm writing, Liza. You know this."

"It's your mother."

"I'll call her back, later. She'll understand."

"It's about Courtney."

Colin slammed his fist on his desk. "Damn it, Liza! I'll call her back later."

"He's in trouble," Liza said.

"Always is," Colin replied, as a thought hit him and he typed an item on his keyboard.

"In the hospital," Liza added.

Colin stopped typing, looked up at Liza. "What?"

"Your mother's calling from the ER, Colin."

Colin's heart pounded in his chest. "Is he . . . ?"

"Pick up the phone and speak with your mother," Liza said.

Colin reached for his phone, took a deep breath, and then picked it up. "Mama, what's happened?"

The phone rang in Courtney's hospital room, startling him. He struggled to reach for it.

A passing nurse heard the phone ringing and stuck her head in the room.

"You want me to get that for you?" she asked Courtney.

He tried to nod. "Please."

"Hello," Courtney said, the phone resting on his shoulder, pressed against his cheek.

"Hey there, Charles Sexton," a soft voice cooed. Charles Sexton was the fake name Courtney's agent assigned him.

"Chante?"

"Yeah, it's me."

"What do you want?"

"Ms. Lena called me. I wanted to see how you were doing. I can't get up to see you until—"

"Don't come up here, Chante," Courtney replied. He thought about Black's whispered threat. *Peace be still or yah seed and dutty gurl be next, seen?* That's all Courtney thought about . . . Black.

"You can't keep pushing me away, Court. It's not right."

"I mean it, Chante. Stay away from me. I'm going now." Courtney let the phone drop from his ear, reached for his call remote, and pressed the red button that alerted the nursing station. Chante's voice called out through the receiver. Courtney shut his eyes to try to chase it away.

After a moment, the nurse from earlier stuck her head in again. "Did you need something?"

"Can you hang this up for me?" Courtney asked. "I'm done with it."

Colin stopped outside his mother's brownstone building and took in a deep breath as he stood on the bottom step of her walk-up. He watched the hustle and bustle of the neighborhood: the little girls playing double-Dutch in the street, pausing only so cars

could pass, the boys walking up the block with radios larger than
their upper bodies supported on their shoulders—an inner city
version of the African transporting a large basket on his head like
you saw them do on the *Discovery Channel.* The sun had made itself comfortable for the day. Painting the backdrop of the neighborhood in a hue that wasn't yellow and not orange. A combination
of the two exuberant colors instead. Colin placed his car keys in
his right pocket and looked back at his car one last time to make
sure it was still parked by the curb. The suburban life in New
Jersey had made him paranoid of the crimes in Brooklyn. He was
no different than any other tourist in that regard, despite having
lived the majority of his life in this borough. When he lived here
he felt as if Brooklyn were its own planet, with its own special fla-
vor, and enough activity to keep the most energetic of individuals
busy. Now, he looked at the planet like a mourner does their
loved one in a casket. Those young girls with their hair beaded
like Venus Williams would be on this street the rest of their lives,
the jump rope soon replaced by a stroller, those hips that now gy-
rated with the twist of the rope would end up helping to balance
toddlers against their sides. Those young boys carrying the radios
would be supporting those same radios until their backs could no
longer bear the weight. Some would grow successful in the hustle—some would end up facedown in the street because they tried
to pass off a bag of dried basil leaves as that potent street spice
marijuana. Few got to be astronauts on this planet Brooklyn.

Colin fished in his pocket for his cell phone, retrieved it and
dialed home.

Liza's mother answered in dramatic fashion, "Hello? Sheffield
residence."

"Ma—Zennifer, let me speak with Liza. Yeah . . . I got here
safely. I'm standing outside my folks' place now. Okay . . . when
she wakes let her know I arrived safely. Tell her to hit me on my
cell when she gets a chance. All right . . . bye." He closed the flip
and tapped the phone against his palm, clinched his lips together
and looked to the street again. He avoided looking next door at
the brownstone that used to belong to the Parker family.

"Hey there, boy, you gone stand out here all day making calls,
or you going to come in the house with your family?"

Colin looked up, smiled. "Unc, what's happening? I just had to
make a quick call."

"Letting the wife know you got here okay, right?"

Colin climbed the steps and met his Uncle Carl. They embraced. "Something like that," Colin said as they loosened their hold on one another. "Just making sure the baby was okay."

Carl raised both his hands in understanding, almost toppled over but managed to grab the side rail. Colin reached for him, but the old man steadied his own self and moved past the almost-accident like it never occurred. "You don't have to defend it with me, young snapper. I been there, yes, suh. When your Aunt Myrtle was still living, she would insist I call her whenever I left the house and got to where I was headed. Yes, suh. I call that loving, young snapper. Nothing more than loving." Carl turned like a man with ankle shackles and moved inside.

The first thing Colin noticed when he entered the foyer was the picture of him and Courtney when they were younger hanging on the wall. He hadn't seen that picture in years. In fact, it had been tucked away somewhere, and yet his mother must have taken it out and hung it on the wall. Her way of trying to force the brothers back to happier times? He studied the picture like a midterm cheat sheet. Carl watched over him for a bit, silently, and then headed toward the kitchen.

Colin followed on Carl's heels. A deep sadness enveloped him as he watched his uncle struggle down the hall. "So, how's he doing?"

"Busted up pretty bad. Broken ribs, sprains, bruises. Whoever did it tried to stab him, too, his hands sliced to damn from him grabbing at the knife blade. Lena said the doctors say he looks worse than he is. They got him in there under some fake name so the press don't get wind of all this. His agent set all that up." Carl stopped at the kitchen's threshold and leaned against the doorway shaking his head. "So much to look forward to—his workout with that team down in Atlanta ain't too far off—and he's hanging with a bunch of thugs. This puts everything in jeopardy. It's like déjà vu all over again. Something your daddy woulda done."

Colin brushed aside any talk of their father. "He still won't say who did it?"

"Nope. Claims he don't know."

"Where's Mama? She at the hospital?"

"Yeah, and your Nana's taking her nap. First sleep she's had in a while."

"How about you, Unc, how you doing? That hip still bothering you, I see."

"It is what it is; I manage. As long as it don't snow or rain."

The two found a seat in the kitchen and continued their conversation while they nursed glasses of orange juice.

"So, who's running the shop while you're here?" Colin asked.

"Nobody," Carl answered. "I shut it down for a couple days, 'til everything gets settled."

"He turned everyone's world upside down."

"Just thankful they didn't kill him."

Colin moved his glass across the table surface like a chess piece. Words had escaped him. The two of them sat through the silence without any attempt to break through. The sunlight came through the window, blinding them, and so Carl struggled to his feet and went to the offensive window. Colin looked up from the table and watched his uncle struggling to reach across the countertop and grab the wand that controlled the Venetian blinds. His instinct was to rise and help his uncle, but he didn't move. After a few aborted attempts, Carl grabbed hold of the wand and closed the slats. When he turned back facing Colin, his face was bathed in victory.

"You gone head down the hospital and go see him?" Carl asked as he reclaimed his seat.

Colin stared at the old man, but didn't answer.

Close to thirty years Armando Sanchez had been shaving, and it still bothered him to no end that the left side of his mustache didn't connect to his goatee. One of his mother's friends—his first crush, a trick named Cinnamon—had pointed it out when he was seventeen.

"Little man is growing up . . . look at him, Cherry," she'd said to his mother one day as he entered the kitchen. His mother smiled and accidentally dropped her lit Newport in her glass of brandy. She cussed her dumb luck and the empty cigarette box on their kitchen table. Armando held his smile, but poked his chest out, and went on checking the empty cupboards for food as if he didn't hear Cinnamon. Then Cinnamon touched up his ego. "When that side grows in like the other one . . . whew, Armando!" She shook her head and sucked her teeth. "You're gonna have tongues wagging. What a cutey, hey, Cherry?"

Cinnamon said that it was cute, but Armando knew better—it was a flaw. It took everything he had to keep from mentioning the dimples on her upper thigh and that the bright polish on her nails was chipping. In that one instant she went from beautiful in his eyes to hideous. Classy women carried their money in a pocketbook, not stuffed in their bra, under a saggy breast. No, Cinnamon wasn't his fantasy anymore. She was a whore, like his mother. Just as he'd stopped pretending he didn't know where his mother vanished to during the night, he stopped pretending with Cinnamon. She was the last female he ever let break his heart. His old man would be proud of him if he was still around.

Now, Armando leaned over the sink in his back office and trimmed his bushy facial hair with his electric razor, then stood and admired the work, frowned as he looked at the left side. The white porcelain sink had brown rust stains around the rim, with the walls carved out in concrete blocks, and the office, a basement cave, more than anything. One light bulb hung in front of the mirror. He didn't want the area, or his office for that matter, too bright, never liked light much. He ran his cement-mixer hands across his scalp to see if the cut was close enough, and satisfied, turned the razor off. When the loud buzz halted, he heard a knocking at his door.

"Hey-yo, easy," he yelled. "I'm coming." He placed the razor back in the bag. The knocking continued, louder and louder. He dropped the bag on the couch and moved to the door. "What!"

He opened the door to the sounds and smells that made the place distinctive—grunts and musk. "Oh, Mr. Armando, I'm sorry," the young Puerto Rican girl he'd just hired said. "This dude is outside, wants to see you . . . he say he your son-in-law."

He eyed the young girl. She had her hair styled in two ponytails; a shade of lavender on her eyelids and lips; and a dark, penciled-in border around those luscious lips. Yet, she spoke like one of the hardened street boys that came to this place for refuge. He'd given her a job keeping the place neat and running his errands so she wouldn't have to sell her only commodity. Sell it like his mother had done. "That a reason for you to break my door down, Carla?"

"I'm sorry, Mr. Armando. You weren't answering."

He shook his head. "And, Carla, if you insist on being polite, it's *Mr. Sanchez*. You want to relax . . . then it's Armando. Comprende?" She nodded her head in understanding. "Now, you said it's my son-in-law?"

"Yes."

"Colin, did he say?"

"Yeah, yeah. Colin."

"Where's he at?"

"Out front watching them spar."

"Lead him back here."

Damn shame, Armando thought as Carla moved back out to the gym floor, a girl so young, blessed with a woman's gift. In a couple of years he might have to unwrap it for her. Hips wider than the Van Wyck Expressway and breasts that grew faster than Carla could bra shop—at least a cup size larger than her current bra.

"Hey there," he greeted Colin as he came through his door, wide-eyed, "you treating my Princess right or what?"

"Trying."

Armando tilted his head toward the door as he found his seat on the edge of his desk. "Close that. Who's sparring out there?"

Colin shut the door, just avoided stepping in a gaping hole in the concrete floor.

"Watch yourself there," Armando said. "I don't need any lawsuits."

Colin moved over by Armando, watching his feet as he stepped through the dim-lit room. "Big Hawaiian-looking guy's fighting—about six-two, two-forty. With a Mohawk."

"Tulaman. Oh, he's a beast," Armando said with envy. "His handlers think he's the next David Tua, only better than the first David Tua. I think they have a Tua obsession. I mean *Tulaman. Tua.* See the connection?" Colin nodded as Armando continued, "Yeah, well he's a beast, though, like I said."

"I caught on to that. I think he hurt the other guy."

"It's a liberating feeling being in that ring, Colin. Good for your heart, too, your cardiovascular system. You should try it, at least try the punching bags. I see Liza's feeding you well, you looking doughy through the middle."

Colin patted his stomach. "No, I don't think so. Fighting isn't for me. I'd be afraid, honestly."

Armando squeezed his nose up, snorted. "Fear is a woman's ally, a man's downfall."

"Maybe."

Armando let the comment pass. "So, Colin, what brings you here to my humble gym?"

"Liza had the baby."

"I got your message. Little girl, correct?"

"Yeah, you have to come down and see her."

"Will do. As soon as I can. Brooklyn won't let me go."

"Yeah," Colin responded. "I've heard that about this place. I sometimes wonder how I got out."

"My ex staying with you guys?"

Colin rolled his eyes and Armando smiled for the first time. "Yeah, Liza's mom is there."

"Bitch ain't she?"

Colin looked away. "No, I wouldn't say that."

"Well, I would. Seven years of marriage to her gives me the right. Now, most women ain't worth shit, but, Zennifer—*damn*. Hell in high heels."

"That's kind of harsh, you think?"

"Harsh, but true." Armando squeezed his eyes into a frown. "Colin, you got to get into something, you not looking all that well. You know I'm into fruit and vegetable smoothies myself. Add a bit of brewer's yeast—stuff they use to ferment beer—as a nutritional supplement. Protein, vitamin B, minerals, and amino acids—brewer's yeast got it all. I can give you this booklet I give all the boxers. Fatherhood is tough, partner. You need your energy. I know you're up until the wee hours of the morning. Babies are something, brother. I remember it with Liza like it was yesterday. Her mother will tell you I didn't do jack, but then—well, that's a different matter."

"Yeah," Colin admitted. "The baby has been a handful. That, and writing, worrying about my family." Colin saw his opening and moved through it. "Speaking of which, that's kind of the reason I came by to see you."

Armando formed a pyramid with his hands. "Go on."

"My brother got himself into something, I don't know what, but it's got my mother all upset. He's beaten pretty badly, had his jewelry stolen. Thug shit, you know?"

" 'Kay."

"I hoped that maybe you've heard something. Maybe you know something. I know your ear is always to the ground."

"The streets are not gonna be too kind to him, Colin. That much I do know. From what I hear, he's about to come into serious cheddar—I'd suggest he move on from this place."

Colin nodded. "So you haven't heard anything, though?"

"Word is he's been hanging with this low-level cat, Star, just got out the pen. Star's up to his neck with trouble. Stole loot from this cat, Black—bad dude. Wouldn't want either one of 'em around a child of mine. You dig? That's all I've heard. I didn't know about any beating. Courtney okay?"

"Okay? I guess. Lucky more than anything, though. I used to think Brooklyn was big, man," Colin said, "but sometimes now I realize how small it is. If you go to the right people they can tell you something about anyone, anything."

Armando smiled. "I'm the right people."

"Appreciate the info, man," Colin said as he prepared to leave. "And make sure you come down and see this baby. Liza would love to see you, too."

"She said that?" Armando said, smiling.

Colin forced a return smile. "Well, not exactly, but in so many words."

Armando nodded. "Soon as *you know who* leaves, I'll make it a point. You dig?"

Colin nodded, even though he knew it was most likely just Armando's talk. "Gotcha."

Chrp, chrp, chrp. Chrp, chrp, chrp. Chrp, chrp . . .

Colin fumbled to pick up his cell phone. The distinctive ring startled him, stopped him from walking into the hospital. "Hello."

"Baby, hey." It was Liza, her voice weighed down by weariness, scratchy as it attempted to wake up with the rest of her. She was back to calling him baby again, had moved past him grabbing her wrist in anger, again.

"What's up sleepyhead? I called you before."

"I know. Mama told me. So you made it safely? How's Courtney?"

"I haven't seen him yet."

"What? It's . . ." He could hear her rustling the sheets in bed, no doubt checking the digital clock on their nightstand. "It's past six, what you been doing for five hours?"

"I—"

"And where are you now?"

"Actually—"

"I would have thought you'd go see your brother first thing." She'd fought off the weariness of just waking up and sounded like her old self again. "I mean, damn, he could have died he was beaten so badly, your uncle said. Where are you?"

Colin sighed. "Liza, you finished? You going to let me speak, maybe answer your questions?"

"Speak."

"I went by the house to see Uncle Carl and Nana. Then I went to see your father. I'm at the hospital now."

"My father? For what?" She tried to keep her tone normal, her emotions in check, but her words came out distorted by her feelings.

"I needed to talk to him about things."

"My father? Things? Like what?"

"He said to tell you hello and that he'll be down to see you as soon—"

"Why are you doing this?"

"What?"

"Avoiding the issue. You go to check on your brother and mother and yet you haven't seen them yet. I ask you simple questions about why you went to see my father and you start with your bullshit instead of answering the questions. It all correlates— you're an avoider. I hate that about you."

"You're an interrupter," Colin replied. "I hate that about you. I'm not avoiding anything. Never have, never will. You ask me questions and you don't let me answer them. And, I told you I'm at the hospital now, so you can't say I'm avoiding Courtney."

"Should have been your first stop," Liza told him.

"Says you, Liza. I needed to do other things, too. Courtney's not going anywhere."

"I think you wish he did, though," Liza said.

Colin had been standing, but Liza's latest accusation made him find a seat, outside the entrance of the hospital, on a bench. "Now why would you say stupid shit like that?"

"I think you wish Courtney would disappear from your life, Colin."

Colin smirked. "News flash for you, smart-ass: Courtney isn't in my life. I live in Jersey, he's in New York, and we barely speak."

"And that's the way you want it. Except you wish he was farther away from you. He's still too close for comfort."

"You're talking a lot of nonsense. I don't think you got enough sleep, or either you're still half asleep."

"You think I don't know, don't you?"

Colin laughed an angry laugh. "Know what?"

"Your dirty secrets."

"Say what . . ."

"Courtney called me once and told me I needed to get away from you."

Colin's heart pulse increased. "What're you talking about? When?"

"Right when we found out I was pregnant with Lyric. Right after Chante had her baby."

Silence.

"What's the matter, Colin? Cat got your tongue?"

"What did he say?"

Now Liza laughed. "You're a trip, you know that?"

"*What . . . did . . . he . . . say?*"

"Now, I know you aren't taking that tone with me, after all this."

"What the hell did he say?" Colin screamed.

"He told me to be careful of you, that you'd done a lot of dirt. He was too much of a gentleman to sully your name, wouldn't give me any specifics. Just told me to have a long conversation with you about things. I was too afraid, never wanted to know the awful truth."

"And you fell for his lies," Colin replied, back to himself now that he realized Courtney hadn't completely dropped the dime on him.

"Colin, I wouldn't try this route if I were you. I would try to give you the benefit of the doubt, but I can't. Courtney was hurting like you wouldn't believe that night he called me. I could hear it in his voice—it still haunts me. I'm not sure what you did to him, but I'm one hundred percent positive *you* did the doing. And it was bad."

"Your support is appreciated," Colin said.

"Don't do the woe-is-me routine either."

"Liza, don't get me started. You're the princess of woe-is-me: 'I'm not beautiful like the other models. I'm fat, so I'll throw my food up.'"

"Colin, please," Liza begged.

He added, "Mama told me to be self-sufficient, not have to depend on a man. So I'll make a life of being a bitch, just like she is."

"Colin, you're taking this too far."

"No, I'm not. Woe-is-me, my ass. No wonder your father bounced."

"Sore spot with me," Liza said, her voice a whisper. "Please don't go there."

Colin couldn't hold himself, couldn't temper his anger. "I'm going there, baby. He was smart, smarter than I've been. He saw that he had a bitch wife and a daughter headed down the road to being fucked up herself. He ran as fast as he could and I don't blame him."

As soon as he said the words he regretted them. He would have given anything to have them back. Life was like that, came down to moments, some we wished to relive, some we wished to erase. Life in all of its stinginess would give us neither.

"Give your mother and Courtney my regards," Liza said. Colin could hear the tears in her voice. "Nana and Uncle Carl, too."

"Look, Liza, I . . ."

Then he heard that awful sound like tires screeching or the computer modem dialup or the noise of a fax machine interrupting what you thought was a voice phone line.

Dial tone.

Liza had hung up.

9

MAY 13

What Colin walked in on surprised him. Had him holding the breath in his chest as an unbearable weight pressed down on him. He reached through the air for something to provide balance and caught hold of the edge of the hospital bed. Courtney was fast asleep. He looked as if he lay in a casket, with his arms by his sides and his bandaged hands crossed over his stomach. Blood soaked through the bandages from the knife wounds Uncle Carl had spoke of. Courtney's left eye was swollen like a small ball, the lid, purplish, looked like a ripe plum. His beloved medallion, the one he'd saved over a year for and wore to bed, had left a scratchy kiss on his cheek. Sleep was supposed to be peaceful, but there was no peace or tranquility in Courtney's appearance. He was beaten and had, by the grace of God, stolen life just as those thugs had stolen his jewelry.

Chilly needles crawled up Colin's spine as he tried to reconcile with what his eyes saw. He'd ridden up on the elevator loaded to bear, prepared for a toe-to-toe with Courtney. But now, as he stood watch over his brother, emotions akin to grief settled in where anger had presided. A grief that sent a burn up through his nostrils that pinched the corners of his eyes until a drop of moisture slipped out.

"Aw, man, li'l brother," was all he could manage. He held fast to the bed with his right hand and covered the entire left side of his face with his left hand. The sound of his voice made Courtney stir and Colin quickly dabbed at his eyes with his fingers.

"Colin?"

"Where's Mama?" was Colin's reply.

Courtney squinted, made a face like he was trying to swallow orange juice down a sore throat, and shifted his position in bed. "Went to call the house and see if you'd been by," he grunted out. "Wasn't sure if you were coming or not. I was hoping you weren't."

Colin let Courtney have his anger. "Where she go, down to the lobby or somewhere on this floor?"

"Don't know."

Colin moved over by the table on the empty side of the room, placed his cell phone and keys down on the top. He picked the cell phone up again, just as quickly, and flipped the lid to check one last time to see if he'd gotten any calls. He hadn't. This would be a day he'd remember for a long time.

Liza and Courtney. What else in the way of turmoil could the day offer?

"You can ask the nurse at the receiving desk where Ma went," Courtney said. "Veronica, I think her name is. She showed her to the phone." The bruised fat of his lips muffled his voice, but Colin was able to make out every word clearly.

Colin turned back to him with a forced smile. "Nah, I'll hang out until she gets back." This moment between them would be a struggle, he realized. A long-time-in-coming struggle, but one he was committed to moving through. "So, are they going to have you back in shape in time for your pre-draft workout? Uncle Carl was telling me Atlanta wanted you to come down in a couple weeks."

"Look at me. What you think?"

The order made Colin do the opposite; he looked away and quickly changed the subject. "You have to see your niece, man. She's beautiful."

"I bet."

Colin bit into his lip. "Look, I uh . . . I spoke with Armando. He told me about this dude Star you been hanging with lately. That's the kid, Antonio Redman, used to live around the corner from us, isn't it? His mother caught you two stealing quarter waters from Bagley's that time and made you return them?"

"Yup," Courtney acknowledged.

"Armando says he's bad news, man. What you doing hanging with him for?"

"Why ask why?"

Colin wouldn't let him off that easy. "Did he have something to do with what happened to you? Or this other dude Armando told me about, dude named Black?"

"Just leave it, Colin. I don't need you being Superman . . . you've done enough for me down through the years, believe me."

Colin nodded. "Just thought I might—"

"Don't think."

Colin leaned his head back for a moment and then returned his gaze to his brother. "At some point, one of us has to be the bigger man here. I mean, I could have come in here acting ignorant. Liza told me you called her once talking shit about me. My own wife told me she doesn't trust me anymore, that I'm basically an asshole in her eyes."

Courtney sniffed a subtle laugh. "So, in other words, you think you're already the bigger man? That what you saying, *big brother*? 'Cause you ain't, but I am."

Again Colin nodded. It was getting to be a habit for him, acknowledging other folks' comments. "Yeah, I know how you've handled this whole thing isn't indicative of how most would— and I can appreciate that. But we all make mistakes. I'm entitled to one."

"One?" Courtney mocked. "Just one mistake you've made, huh?"

Colin frowned, the old animosity coming back to him at Courtney's hinting of a long-past incident. "Look, Courtney, don't start—"

A soft voice bumped Colin off course. "There you are."

Colin turned. "Mama! Hey."

She pawed at his shoulder. "I didn't know what happened to you. I spoke with your Uncle Carl, and he said you'd been by the house over two hours ago. He was surprised you weren't here."

"Sorry about that, Mama," Colin said as he gave her a hug and kiss. "I had to check on a few things before I made it over here."

"You boys, I swear. You're turning me grayer by the day."

"I'm sorry, Mama."

"Yeah, I figured you had business to attend to. Matter of fact, I told Carl you'd be up here when I got back. I could feel my boy's presence." She moved over by the side of the bed next to Courtney. "I see you woke back up. I spoke with the administrator about the phone. She doesn't know how that call came through earlier. Your room phone shouldn't be active."

"Good," Courtney said, thinking of Chante, " 'Cause I don't want any more calls."

"How are you feeling? Doctor said the painkillers would wear off around this time and you'd need more."

"Doctor's right," Courtney told his mother.

"You want me to get a nurse?" Colin asked, a hand pointed at his chest.

"Nope," Courtney said. "I've got the buzzer here. Page her myself when I get to the point I need it."

Lena said, "Courtney, baby, why don't you let Colin get the nurse. You look in pain."

"Like I said, I can do it myself when I need to."

Lena threw her hands up. "Suit yourself. He was just trying to help."

A growl came from Courtney's lips. "Why you do that?"

"What?" Lena asked.

Courtney shook his head. "Kiss this nigga's ass all the time, that's what."

"Whoa, whoa,"—Colin moved to the foot of the bed—"come on now. No need for that, Court."

"Ain't it though, Colin? You come up in here like you rule the world and shit. Like your shit don't stink. We both know that ain't the deal."

"Courtney! Why you talking to your brother like this?" their mother said. Her voice trembled, her hands shook. She was inside her own private earthquake.

Colin raised his arm to steady his mother, to guide her back from the bed. She looked as if she was about to put her hands on her already damaged son and choke sense into him.

"Me and this nigga need to settle this shit out, Ma," Courtney replied. "I've been bottling this up for too long, and seeing this nigga . . ." He dropped his chin to his chest and closed his eyes, tried without success to keep from trembling as his mother did. Lena pressed her head against Colin's shoulder as he wrapped her with one arm and patted her back.

"I want to make this right, Courtney," Colin said. He was the only one in the room not crippled by emotion. "I really do. We can move on past all this."

Courtney looked up. "You want to make this right?"

"Yes."

"Leave. Don't say shit to me. Don't try and change my mind. Don't try and play brother. Just straight up leave. You'll be making this right." Courtney stared at Colin and Colin returned the gaze. No more words would be spoken, none needed to be. The music CDs Colin had converted to tape so Courtney could listen to them in his Walkman, the bookmark Courtney had fashioned out of Christmas wrapping paper and laminated for Colin, none of the good history between them mattered anymore. Only the bad mattered. That night at Chante's. The ordeal with the Parker girl that they had tucked away for years like it never happened until Courtney revisited it today. The blood between them tainted.

Colin released his hold on his mother. She tried to reach for him, but he put his arm and an upraised hand to stop her. He walked over by the table stand as Lena wailed. He closed his eyes for a quick dose of comfort before he scooped up his cell phone and his key chain.

He didn't say shit to Courtney, didn't try and change Courtney's mind, didn't try and play brother. He just straight up left, and made everything right.

The roadways from New York to Colin's home in New Jersey—the NJ Turnpike and then the Garden State Parkway—had been congested with weekend travelers on this evening in their SUVs and station wagons headed back to the quiet suburbs of New Jersey. Colin's journey, however, may have been toward a new life. After comforting his mother, who'd chased him down before he left the hospital, and stopping by the house once more to say good-bye to his Uncle Carl and Nana, Colin turned the front grille of his vehicle toward home. The day had been a dam of heated emotions and, unfortunately, more were on the horizon, threatening to bulge over the lip of the volcano. There was still the issue of Liza. All the horrible things he'd said to her during their heated phone conversation earlier.

No wonder your father bounced.

The words echoed in Colin's head, as did his wife's subdued response, *Sore spot with me*—her voice softer than the silky hair she'd never appreciated—*Please don't go there.*

But he had. Gone there and several notches higher.

He was smart, smarter than I've been. He saw that he had a bitch wife and a daughter headed down the road to being fucked up herself. He ran as fast as he could and I don't blame him.

The tightness that had moved into Colin's chest from the first moment he saw his brother all banged up worsened as he held to the steering wheel and drove with the radio loud enough to drown out everything except the thoughts inside his head. "Words. Can't take 'em back," he offered as he switched lanes. "Can't ever take 'em back." Oh, how he wished he could take his back.

But Colin, of all people, knew that once you offered your words, once they left the shackles of your mind and burst through your mouth to freedom, they could never be taken back. Still, he'd said them and now they hung above him like a threat of blackmail. Like one of his published books they were now a part of his legacy. He hoped in twenty years he wasn't still reflecting on them like high school students reading over the passages of Richard Wright's *Native Son.*

Lyric and Liza were his new family—Courtney his old—neither family solid anymore because of his actions. "Stupid, stupid," he said as he turned the power to the car radio off. He could no longer stand the bass of the drums, the pound of the beat, the lyrics filled with pain the songwriter, Colin surmised, had carved out just for him. Love lost, betrayal—themes that poke at him like an accusing finger.

So much had happened since that first date with Liza six years prior. So many moments that should have forged a stronger foundation between them.

On their first night together as a married couple, they'd gorged on Chinese food from one of the local restaurants.

"I'm stuffed," Colin had said.

Liza agreed, nodding her head. "The ladies' room is calling my name. I think I better answer."

Colin smiled. "You're about to stink it up, aren't you?"

Liza punched at his shoulder. "Mine doesn't stink."

"Sure it doesn't."

She left without a further word and beelined toward the bathroom, shutting the door loudly and tightly behind her. Colin waited patiently for her return and when she didn't come back out after close to fifteen minutes, he rose to go check on her.

He knocked at the door. "You okay?"

"Just a minute," Liza called out. The toilet flushed, though the sink had been running.

Colin reached for the doorknob, tried turning it, it wouldn't budge. "Keeping that stink in with you, that's good," he joked.

"Told you my shit don't stink," Liza told him as she rushed from the bathroom, shutting the door behind her. She brushed past Colin.

Colin reached for her. "Not so fast, Boo. I'm about to go write; I want a kiss first."

"Stop being so greedy; save some for later," Liza said.

"Nope." He pulled her close and placed his lips on hers. An unmistakable scent halted him. Vomit masked with mint Listerine. "You okay, Boo?" he asked, breaking the kiss.

"I'm fine," Liza said. Her eyes were everywhere but on Colin.

"Food made you sick?"

"A little," she admitted.

"Come lie down. I'll get you ginger ale and give you a back massage."

"I'm okay, Colin."

Colin reached for her shoulder. "No, I mean it. Let me take care of you."

Liza pulled away from him, her voice rising. "Will you let me be, Colin?"

"I want to take care of you," he said again.

Tears came to Liza's eyes, sudden and unexpected. "Don't deserve your help, Colin."

He stood there, rooted in place. "Why would you say that?"

"I threw up."

"I know you did."

She shook her head. "I made myself throw up, Colin."

They'd been through so much, and yet they'd survived. Colin remembered the past and contemplated the present and the future as he approached his exit off the Parkway. It was a fourth of a mile to the off-ramp, another mile after that to home. What would he find waiting or not waiting? Would it be as discomforting as walking in on his battered brother? Would it challenge the tear ducts in his eyes like seeing Courtney like that had?

He traveled down the main stretch of road toward home. The lane lit by his headlights and the large light poles on the side of the road. He looked at the maple trees that stood guard a hundred yards or so back from the roadway, watched as the complex of townhouses that came before his own complex moved from a frontal view to his rearview mirror. He'd come a long way since planet Brooklyn. Earlier in the day he would have deemed the journey a triumph, but now, as the uncertainty of his family life pressed on him, he realized it hadn't been the journey that was the triumph—it had been who traveled with him: Liza. He loved her, appreciated her, but didn't tell her or show her. He was a fool.

Colin turned into his complex and passed by the tan-colored homes that looked the same as his own, except his were gray, passed the blue variety of his home, passed the browns. He came to the gray and parked his car. Stuck in reflective mode, he exited his Lexus truck. Thinking of that night five years ago when his wife laid bare the demons of her soul. He'd never done the same in return, never allowed her to help him recover the parts of himself that had been lost. That was the night he should have told her all about his own demons.

He looked around the lot for Liza's car—found it parked a few spaces down. Mama Brashear's Jaguar was nowhere in sight. From the outside, you could see one light on inside his condominium.

He placed his key in the front door lock and turned it. He noticed his pulse throbbing like a migraine headache as he walked through the foyer and stopped and patted his chest as if this action would calm his racing heart.

Liza was in the living room, curled on the couch with the one lamp on, the baby in the bassinet across the room. She was watching television, what appeared to be a video, because she had the VCR remote in her hand. Colin turned on the second lamp. Neither of them said a word to the other. He looked around with his forehead lined, trying to find the source of this loud static sound.

He moved over by the bassinet and found the source of the static noise. The baby monitor plugged in the wall, on the small table they kept magazines on.

"Why you have the monitor on with the baby in here with you?" He leaned down and kissed Lyric on the cheek, trying to appear nonchalant as he prayed that Liza would answer. When she didn't, he rose and walked over by her. "You hear me?"

"Just brought her in here," Liza said. "She was in the other room crying and I brought her in here and got her back to sleep."

"You turned the monitor off at the other end?"

"Ripped it out of the wall," Liza said, calmly.

Colin sat on the small portion of couch Liza left open. "Where's your mother?"

Liza fast forwarded her tape. "She went home to care for her personal affairs. I told her it was all right, that I could handle things here."

Colin stopped and looked at the grainy image on the television screen. An extremely dark man with skin like damaged leather and close-fitting hair that looked as if it needed conditioner was speaking: "Qwah Cu-wah U-fahl-may Nee Wah-co. Nah N-Goo-Voo. Nah U-too-koo-foo. Hah-tah Mee-lay-lay. Ah-Mee-Nah."

The man clasped his hands together. "Okay, let us now administer the twelve symbols of life, each which represents the love and strength that brings these two families together: Wine, wheat, pepper, salt . . ."

"What is this, Liza?"

"A wedding," she replied as she hit the stop button, pressed rewind, and turned to Colin. "Mama catered the function and she let me borrow the tape to see how wonderful it turned out. They married in an African ceremony. The minister just finished saying the Lord's Prayer in Swahili."

"Interesting," Colin said as the tape rewound. Liza was calmer than he thought possible. He'd ease into an apology, maybe consent to talking over their situation, and then he'd never let what happened between them earlier ever happen again.

Liza looked off toward the television screen, unable to keep her eyes on the husband she'd chosen. "You leave hairs all over the bathroom floor," she said. When she was a teenager she started making pro-versus-con lists to help with every decision. She'd spent most of the night searching for Colin's pros, but coming up with cons instead.

"What?"

"You leave hairs all over the bathroom floor," she repeated without turning to face him. "Every time you shave, I see you with the broom and dustpan afterwards, but there's still always hairs left on the floor. I hate that."

Colin didn't know how to respond. "I'll try harder."

Liza shook her head. "It's not like you haven't tried already, you just . . ." She cupped her face in her hands and let out a forced scream, then looked up for the first time. "You just can't get all those hairs, Colin. You never will."

Their eyes met for a brief moment before hers detoured. Colin continued to hold his gaze on her as she shivered. The tape came to the end and she hit eject and took it from the VCR and placed it back in the cardboard packaging. She tossed the tape on the coffee table and sat back against the sofa cushions with her eyes closed, running both hands through her hair, bouncing her knee. Colin continued to watch her, shaken by the fact that she couldn't sit still, that she appeared to be unraveling like cheap rope.

"You okay, Liza?"

She laughed and looked toward the ceiling. "I'm fine."

"You don't seem it."

"I've been thinking, that's all."

Colin hesitated but he knew he had to ask. "About?"

"I think we should divorce, or at least separate."

"What?" His heart started racing again. "What about the baby?"

"Messy situation," Liza said.

"We agreed that we needed something to bond us stronger, a common interest, Liza. You haven't given it enough time to work, to bond us."

"It was foolish of us to think a baby would do the trick. Foolish and selfish. We were—are—broke, Colin."

"I think we can work through it."

"I don't."

"Your focus is screwed up, Liza."

"My focus is rock solid, Colin, and it's in one place."

"The baby, but not the marriage," Colin said.

Liza's lips tightened, but her decision fought through. "Nope. Not the baby either, Colin. And that makes me sad, too. My focus is on getting out of this marriage, Colin. I have to take a shower, keep an eye on the baby."

It all happened so fast, Colin couldn't move his arms to stop her, couldn't reach for her and change her mind with a soft caress.

Instead, he followed the swishing sound of her slippers scraping across the linoleum floor like coarse grade sandpaper breaking through layers of chipping, worn paint. And that tightness in his chest intensified as he dealt with the reality—there would be no easing into an apology.

10

MAY 21 AND 22

Courtney's steps, those tiny footsteps from his hospital bed to the wheelchair that would carry him to release, left a bitter taste in his mouth. Thunderbolt claps of hurt rose from his shins to his knees as he struggled forward. His ankles, which had always been a problem for him, didn't seem capable of handling his weight. Most of his swelling and bruising had gone down, but the aches and pains from day one remained. Breathing was a problem, too. His cracked ribs saw to that. The most minor of his problems, an itchy face, caused him grief nonetheless. He'd practically rubbed the razor bumps that left a jagged trail along his neck raw. Despite the doctor's optimistic prognosis, Courtney knew he was a long way from the level of physical health he had been accustomed to. Every inch of his body had its own woeful tale. Mentally, as well, Courtney needed further healing, since nightmares haunted him daily, and that menacing character—Black—was everywhere Courtney was, around every corner, in every nook.

"What's the date, again?" Courtney asked the volunteer assigned to usher him downstairs.

"May twenty-first," she responded.

Eight days. In a week, the coaching staff in Atlanta would be running Courtney through various drills to see if he could help their team—by checking his vertical leap and comparing it to the ghost of Dominique Wilkins; checking his time in the twenty-yard dash and charting whether he had explosive speed, regular speed, or no speed at all; and seeing how far his lungs could take him, how strong his heart was, and how well he'd mastered the fundamentals of basketball. Shooting, running, dribbling—all the things that had become as second nature to him as breathing—the thought of those simple tasks now caused him as much anxiety as breathing. Courtney slumped in the wheelchair as the volunteer wheeled him through the crowded halls. His posture burdened by the challenges that lay ahead.

His mother was waiting in the lobby, sitting on a bench, tapping the empty place beside her. She was looking outside at the rainy landscape. Staring hard enough to count the raindrops and sleet that fell like chips of ice from the sky. She was dressed in her housekeeping uniform, and, though she sat, Courtney could tell that her feet ached, that the new soles she'd hoped would quench the fire in her heels hadn't worked. The toll of taking care of Nana and working was evident in her thin frame. He hadn't noticed how thin she'd gotten, how the uniform sagged instead of fit her body. He thought of the workout eight days away and made a silent promise that he would be ready.

"Ma," he said, interrupting her thoughts.

His mother turned to him, a smile on her face. "All ready to go?" she said, clasping her hands together. "Let me go wave Deacon Rainier over."

Courtney thanked the volunteer and used the armrests of the wheelchair to push to a standing position. The wince he tried to hold inside leaked out, but he smiled as if it was the glance of a boxing punch that did no damage. Being ready for Atlanta was a bigger mental challenge than a physical one, and he'd started conditioning himself for it the moment he eyed his mother sitting on the bench.

"Dang," he said as he stood next to Lena and watched the burgundy church van pull up in front. "No limo?"

"Be glad we ain't—what's the name of those sneakers you buy?"

"And 1," Courtney answered.

"Be glad we ain't *And 1-ing* our way home." Lena placed her arm around his waist and walked with him. "I'm thankful the Lord pointed me to the church. I'd been racking my brain trying to figure whom I could get to bring us home. Can't afford a taxi back to Brooklyn. Then I remembered the church and called. Told Reverend Kesey the situation, and though you ain't darkened the doorway in a good three years, he was more than willing to do me this favor."

"He should've been," Courtney reasoned. "You're faithful."

The conversations between them always took on a serious note. Never could they talk and enjoy each other's company like when she and Colin got together. "You'd think that no-account agent of yours would have set something up," Lena scowled. "Makes me wonder."

"He didn't want to call a lot of attention to me," Courtney defended. "This whole deal could mess me up if the NBA teams found out about it. Even though I'm okay, they might consider me a liability, might think I'm a street thug that's gonna be getting into problems all the time. The league is extremely PR conscious from what I hear."

"Are you okay? Should they be worried?" His mother asked before they stepped out into the pellets of rain. She continued holding to him as they moved forward, her eyes looking down to make sure he didn't trip, looking down so they didn't have to look at his eyes and possibly find the revelation in his pupils that she prayed nightly would never come to her. "I worry myself to death that you're some street thug now. You are your daddy's child. I can't get over all of this. Hospitals, robberies, Lord knows what else."

Courtney stopped, though his body wanted nothing more than to settle on the cushioned van seat. How could his mother have these worries? "You're worrying yourself about me being a thug? Come on now, Ma. You know me better than that. You raised me."

She harrumphed, "I sure did and if anyone would have told me, a month ago, that I'd be carrying you out the hospital all beat up, I wouldn't have believed them. So what else is there for me to do but wonder?"

Lena released her grip on Courtney as the deacon came around and opened the passenger side door to the van. Grace, calm, and thanksgiving took hold of her as the deacon greeted them. Sadness found Courtney as he processed this latest unhappy interlude with his mother. When would their moment of resolution come? When would his opportunity to let her know the different layers of his character arrive?

"Sister Merkerson you sit on up front," the Deacon said. "Courtney you sit on in the back so you can stretch those long legs of yours."

The ride home was filled with small talk, quotes from the Bible, and questions from the deacon to Courtney about "hoops." Mostly Courtney looked out the window at the passing landscape while his mother and the deacon talked up front. Every so often they'd hit a bump and the deacon would look back and ask Courtney if he were okay. Every time, Courtney smiled through clenched teeth and said he was. The mental challenge was in full gear; he could do Atlanta.

"I'm gonna hafta double-park, Sister Merkerson," the deacon said as he pulled up to their house. "You've got that minivan right in front of your place."

Lena leaned forward and slatted her eyes to try and get a clearer view. "Now who in the devil is that?"

A silver minivan, with rust along the lower part of the body, idled by the curb. Courtney had seen it before, but couldn't remember when or where. He leaned in for a closer look, his heart rate pulsing, jittery when it came to the unknown. Immediately, he recognized the driver, and then the passenger came into full view.

"What is she doing here?" Courtney wondered out loud.

"Who?" Lena wanted to know.

Courtney sighed. "Chante and her cousin Renee."

Chante sat in her cousin's van, her hands on the dashboard, her lip turned up, resting between her teeth. When Courtney and Lena exited the church van, Chante cracked the door to her cousin's, stuck out her leg, and waited until the church van moved up the block. Lena stopped by the curb with the lessening raindrops, now coming down as a faucet drip, tapping her lightly. Courtney dug within for strength and ignored Chante's voice calling for him to stop for a moment.

"Court," she called, "please don't rush in. Can I talk with you a moment?" He climbed the steps, two at a time, and disappeared through the front door as she remained curbside.

It had taken all of her resolve to come here, then a reserve she didn't know she had, as well as a nudge from Renee to get out the van. She didn't have anything left to chase him. She appeared steady enough, but she feared she would fall, and so she moved to Lena and gripped the sleeve of Lena's raincoat. "Why he do that, Ms. Lena? Why does he have to be so cold to me?"

"Hurt," Lena answered as she touched Chante's shoulder with tenderness. The warmth of Lena's caring hand made Chante aware of the frigidness in the air and she trembled. "He doesn't talk to me about it, but you hurt him. A man shouldn't have to question whether a child is his or not—that would hurt anyone come to think of it. This should all be a lesson to you. I know Courtney loved you, still does. I'll never forget the day he told me you were pregnant. Then the look on his face when he said he didn't think it was his. I try not to get involved, but not a day goes by I don't wonder if that beautiful little girl you got is my grand-baby."

Chante looked toward the house with longing. "I wish I could take it back, Ms. Lena. Wish I could do everything all over again." She wiped the tears of her eyes dry, but her skin sparkled from the sparse raindrops that fell from the ever-brightening sky. "Destiny needs y'all in her life."

"Like I said," Lena continued, "Let this all be a lesson to you. I always liked you, Chante, you know that. I don't know what happened between you and my son, but I wish you two could work through it. Courtney is all alone I'm afraid. You and Colin were the two closest people in his life, and you both left it at the same . . ." Lena stopped, held her tongue as her intuition ran free. Her brow furrowed as she looked to the house, piecing together the puzzle on the spot. Then she looked at Chante. The tears were once again coming down the young woman's face, more pronounced. "Oh my Lord, Chante!" Lena said as she removed her hand from Chante's shoulder and stepped back. "Did something happen with you and Colin?"

Chante looked at the grandmother of her little Destiny, and the burden that held her captive announced its strength. "Something," she sobbed. "I'm sorry, Ms. Lena."

It was the eve of Colin's tour for his newest literary creation, *Prophet's Message*, a mystery set in Louisiana. The critics' early response had been positive; more than one reviewer likened the novel to Jervey Tervalon's *Dead Above Ground*. Colin appreciated the comparison. Tervalon was one of the few African American writers he felt had the talent to justify the killing of trees for paper. This might be the breakthrough hit that Colin's stalled career needed, the injection of hope that his first novel seemed to promise, but each release since trampled. The end of the jinx that had lasted into his junior year. All of his novels had been well-written, and all lauded as such, but with this newest venture, Colin noticed more and more references to the "mainstream potential" of his story. Mainstream meant dollars and awareness.

Colin moved about the bedroom laying out a pair of pants and a shirt for Liza to press. Over a week had passed since she'd stated her desire for a divorce, and yet little had changed between them. How she went about her business confused Colin. Her mentioning of the divorce was so filled with purpose and so thought-out. He'd sat stunned that night as she showered and the baby cried from her crib. He had been unable to move and unable to process what had happened to his life. Liza had admonished him when she emerged from the shower and heard the baby screaming. "Too late for shutting down, Colin. You hear the baby crying? What has happened to us doesn't mean you neglect this baby."

Yet, Liza hadn't revisited the divorce talk once in the past eight days. They talked as if nothing were off-kilter and shared the same bed. A few times he'd reached for her, though, and found the flesh of her hips and shoulders, unlike her demeanor, unforgiving. He didn't press, just happy that she lay so near.

As Colin searched under the bed for shoes that matched his outfit, Liza entered the bedroom, then stood inside by the doorway as if she were an outsider and needed an invitation to enter fully. Colin turned to her and flashed a smile.

"You have that book-tour glow to you, Colin."

He pulled out a pair of brown loafers and sat on the edge of the bed to dust them off. "Glow? I wouldn't call it a glow, just happy to start promoting this book. You know that's all that matters nowadays—how well you promote."

Liza nodded. "The craft of writing, second fiddle to marketing," she responded, repeating one of Colin's rants that had become more commonplace than the three words she'd craved to hear most from him. Now it was too late. She contemplated for a moment and then blurted out, "Should I be looking for a new place or are you moving out?"

"Excuse me?" Colin stopped and turned with his full attention on her. He held to the canopy rail of the bed, held tight like a fisherman steadying himself in his canoe for choppy waters. Colin heard her and Liza knew it, so she didn't repeat her question.

"So you haven't changed your mind?" he managed after a while.

She shook her head and held her eyes on him to let him know she was serious.

"This is some timing, springing this on me tonight."

"I checked your tour schedule, figured we might as well settle this while you were doing the Jersey leg—before you head off to Connecticut and the other out-of-state stops."

Colin looked toward the dresser, the pictures of them in happier times that took up most of the surface. "How do we go about doing this?" he asked. "I mean, there's little instruction on how to make a marriage work and less on how to dissolve one."

"You haven't watched television or been to the bookstore in a while," Liza answered. "There's tons of information on both."

"Why is the divorce rate so high, then? And why are so many divorced folks never able to find their center again?"

"Good questions," Liza acknowledged. "Someone should pose them to the authors of all those self-help books." She smiled, tried to lighten the mood. "You authors."

Colin moved to the dresser and sat against the lip so he wouldn't have to keep looking at those pictures. He looked at Liza, instead, and found the somber expression on her face more bearable than the wide-mouth smiles they both carried in the pictures. "I'm good with the questions—it's the answers that throw me."

Liza found his eyes on her discomforting. She looked down at her hyperactive hands instead. "Me too," she offered as her voice trailed off like exhaust from a tailpipe. "Never was good with the answers."

"You sure this is what you want to do?"

Liza considered the nursery, her mind on the swaddled joy they'd both created, the years they'd shared before Lyric, the sketch of Noah's Ark that had taken everything she had to create, the weeks she'd spent trying to get the angles correct, the weeks before the angles became important—when all she had to show for her time was charcoal fingertips and a blank canvas. Her creativity had dried up, and she wanted that to be the beginning and the ending of her dehydration. She didn't want any other part of herself to shrivel away to nothingness. She had worked too hard to get close to a level of normalcy in her life, a level of comfort.

"You sure you want to do this?" Colin repeated, piercing through her thoughts with the question sharper than a needlepoint.

"No," Liza answered with the clarity of truth. She was still having trouble keeping her hands still, bending the fingers in awkward positions, wringing them like a soapy, wet mop. "In fact I wish I had never mentioned divorcing in the first place. My heart tells me that this nausea in the gut of my stomach is a sign that this isn't the right thing. My mind tells me that the nausea is because it is the right thing—that my stomach is so unsettled because I'm sick that we had to bring Lyric into this cruel world and then figure out that we couldn't survive as a family—mixed emotions, to say the least."

"You ever heard that saying, 'Follow your heart'?"

Liza looked up at Colin, nodded her head. "Did that when I married you, followed my heart, though my mind said no."

The revelation wounded him. She hadn't said it in a mean-spirited way, but instead had said it with sincere nonchalance, as if it was common knowledge between the two of them. It wasn't.

"You had reservations about getting married in the first place?"

Liza came in and sat on the far side of the bed. She sat Indian style and held the canopy rail. Carefree, she looked nothing like a woman whose world was turned upside down. "Sure. I was twenty-two, had all kind of emotional issues at the time if you recall. I know you remember—you so poignantly pointed them out to me when you were in Brooklyn last week."

Shame found him as he remembered again the phone conversation that life would never let him forget. "I was being an asshole. I'm sorry about that."

"Yes, you were, but that's okay, Colin. That day was the plug my tear ducts needed. No more crying over you. No more crying over us."

"Guess it's my time to be weak," Colin said, clearing the tickle from his throat with a stern cough. "I don't want to lose you, Liza. I want to be a part of Lyric's life. I want the family I never had."

"I do too," Liza admitted. "But I realize we can't make it happen. We don't recognize the things we do to hurt one another until after the damage is done. After I hung up with you that day—something took over me, my gravity and balance acting crazy. I fell down in the hallway trying to make it to the living room. I felt like the ground under me was moving at warp speed and all I could do was fall and let it carry me forward. Like I was on a treadmill set too high. Thank God, Mama was busy in the nursery with the baby and didn't hear me. I would have been mortified if she'd come out."

Colin visualized the scene as if it were one of Liza's sketches. The way she'd described it more descriptive than the narrative in one of his novels. "I'm sorry I did that to you," he said, his apologies reaching in the high double digits since the phone call over a week ago.

Liza shook her head, brushed aside the apology, tossed it away like lint balls off her dress slacks. "Doesn't matter about that. My point is that we don't recognize the pain we inflict on one another until after the fact. Like with me, I should have known talking to Langston Campbell and answering those questions—however innocent I considered them—would hurt you. I should have hung the phone up as soon as he introduced himself, but I didn't. I stood at the top of the stairs and watched you sitting in your loft, slumped at your desk, and I kept wondering why you were being a punk about the situation. It was days before I put myself in your shoes and thought of how I'd feel if you did something similar. Days, Colin. Something I should have known the moment I picked up the phone and Langston was on the line—took me days to figure."

The irony of it all didn't escape Colin, the fact that their life together had reached this impossible gulf under the weight of two telephone conversations. "Should have cancelled the phone service instead of AOL," he said, lighthearted in tone.

"What?"

"Nothing. Thinking out loud." He leaned forward. "So you feel strongly about this?"

"Like I said," Liza answered. "Mixed feelings, but I want to do what's best for the baby."

"She's not even a month old. How could this be best?"

"You think this would be better done when she's one or two? After she has gotten used to you being around? To have you ripped away from her like that. Trust me it isn't. Been there, done that."

"I wanted to be different from my father," Colin said. "Different from your father."

"And you had the opportunity, but like I've said many times— you made the choice not to be."

Colin climbed on the bed, took Liza's hands and held them by the fingertips. Their eyes converged, the history between them evident in the natural way they looked at each other. Despite everything, a love still existed. "I lost my head during an argument, said things I regret. I don't see why you think that's grounds for a divorce. I've realized things this week that maybe—no—definitely, I didn't realize before. I want more than anything to move past this with you, to do a better job. I know I'm capable."

Liza smiled as Colin held her hands. She didn't appear in any rush to break free, to sever the physical tie that now held them. "Let me ask you a question I've never asked you before," she said, speaking in a friendly tone. "Haven't asked you once, though I've often wondered. And, please, be truthful."

"I never lie to you, Liza, you know that."

"You don't have to. I make it easy for you. Good wives don't prod." She sniffed a laugh. Smirks and laughter had become her tears this past week.

"Ask me anything."

Liza eased her hands away in preparation for the moment to come. "Have you been faithful to me?"

No.

It held in his chest like a prisoner, captive to his desire to move forward, captive to his shame.

No.

He couldn't move his mouth. He didn't need to.

"Did something happen between you and Chante?" she asked, though Colin had yet to answer her first question.

Colin hung his head. Liza sighed, closed her eyes, willed away the tears that wanted desperately to wash her face, wash her pain away.

Lyric . . . another little black girl lost, mired in the greatest and most sorrowful of life's contradictions—with a father and without a father.

Liza . . . another black queen stripped of her crown by the man commissioned to place it upon her head in the first place.

Colin . . . another black man blessed with God's divine rib—a rib, but no backbone.

No, he hadn't been faithful. Yes, something had happened between him and Chante.

Courtney could still hear the rain falling outside. Sweat soaked into his T-shirt as he struggled to do a set of abdominal crunches. In eight days, the biggest moment of his life would be here. The calendar was an enemy, one of many in his life.

Courtney gritted his teeth as he contracted his stomach muscles. The pain shot through his entire upper body.

Chante had serious nerve, showing up unannounced on his doorstep.

Courtney turned over and attempted a few push-ups. The pain made his eyes fill with water. He forced his way through the pain, did twenty before allowing his weight to collapse on the floor.

The biggest day of his life, eight days away, and he couldn't make it through his warm-up paces. He cursed Star. Would have cursed Black, but didn't, for fear that the dreadlocked thug would somehow hear his name called and appear here in the basement beside Courtney, spitting out threats and handing out hurt with the calmness of a man unafraid of anything in the world.

Courtney had that kind of assured calm on the basketball court, but it would do him little good if he couldn't get his limbs to cooperate. He stood from the floor, grabbed a jump rope, tried a few turns. His ankles burned like fire, his knees barely able to support his weight, his sore ribs making the simple act of breathing a dreaded necessity.

Courtney flung the jump rope to the corner of the basement.

"That rope didn't do anything to you."

Courtney's mother stood on the bottom step, with a glass of lemonade in hand.

"Thought you might be thirsty," she said as she descended the step and came to Courtney.

Courtney took the glass, swallowed the lemonade in one gulp. "Thanks."

"How are you feeling, Courtney?"

"Lousy."

"Are you gonna be ready for your thing in Atlanta?"

Courtney handed his mother the empty glass, turned his back and went to sit in a chair in the far corner of the basement.

Lena followed him, not giving up. "You shouldn't have brushed past Chante like that."

"Chante is getting what she deserves," Courtney replied.

Lena nodded. "Maybe," she answered.

"No, maybe, Ma," Courtney said. "I saw y'all were talking. What was said?"

"Told her you loved her," Lena said. "That people take love for granted too much."

Courtney smirked, eyed his mother hard. "People sure do."

Lena held her eyes on Courtney, wouldn't let the judgment in them chase hers away. "Your father was a womanizer, a drug addict, only cared about his basketball, was good for nothing else," she said.

"And you think I'm headed the same way," Courtney said for her.

Lena shook her head. "I hope you and Chante figure this mess out. I hope you and Colin can somehow repair yourselves. And," she paused. "I hope you go to Atlanta and show them folks you made of strong stock, 'cause, son, you've handled yourself well through tough situations. I didn't know the half of it." She thought about her conversation with Chante. "Let me tell you something, son. Ain't nothing prime about you. And I mean prime as in your father, Prime. You're gonna be fine, I know it."

Courtney looked at his mother, surprised. His pre-draft workout was eight days away, his body racked with pain, his head filled with all kind of horror, and yet, all he could think about now was boarding that airplane for Atlanta, Georgia—sweet Georgia, on his mind.

"Welcome to the Holiday Inn, sir. How many are in your party?"

"One," Colin answered.

"And how long will your stay be, sir?"

"Indefinitely," Colin said.

The front desk clerk eyed Colin for a moment, then offered a smile and went to the back to retrieve the sign-in papers. Alone in the lobby, Colin's mind wandered to that place where it had been stuck for days, then drifted to this morning at home.

Colin stood over the crib, staring at a sleeping Lyric. His feet rooted to the carpet, his heart literally causing an ache in his chest.

Liza entered the nursery as tears threatened to well up in Colin's eyes. Colin turned to her, a brave smile on his face.

"Peaceful baby," he said to Liza.

Liza nodded, though she'd never considered Lyric peaceful. "She makes up for a lot," she admitted.

Colin asked, "You need me to explain the situation with Chante? Will that make this any better?"

Liza smirked, shook her head. "No, don't bother."

"You're letting me off too easily," Colin observed.

"Luckily for you, Colin," she said.

"I think there's hope for us, Liza."

"Your fiction continues to improve," Liza said before she abruptly left the room.

Colin turned back to the crib. He stuck his finger in Lyric's grasp. She squeezed his finger tightly, her entire little hand engulfing it as she sucked on her pacifier.

"I love you, Lyric," he whispered.

The baby's eyes fluttered; she released her grip on Colin's finger. He tried, unsuccessfully, to give her his finger again. Lyric cried as he poked at her, and stopped immediately when he withdrew his hand.

Standing above his daughter, his life falling apart, Colin allowed the tears to fall. They were heavy and dropped down with a thud that echoed through his head, a migraine settling in.

He left the nursery, bags in tow, and passed by the kitchen. Liza stood by the dishwasher, loading dirty plates.

"I'm going," he said to her.

She looked over her shoulder, her eyes vacant. "Been gone a long time," she replied.

Colin nodded and left.

II

MAY 28 AND 29

The balance of her proportions measures the beauty of a black woman. Black men are connoisseurs of that magnificent creation known as the curve, and they covet the right blend like a master chef obsessing over his meal preparations. They covet the thickness—the feminine fat—that sets the black woman apart from other creatures in the universe—her hips flared out like a balloon, thighs wider than two arms, ass round like the top of a heart. Hips, thighs, rounded ass, clear markers of a phenomenal woman.

One such phenomenon eased into the seat next to Courtney as his flight boarded for Atlanta. Her fragrance, some floral mixture, touched the base of his nose, and though Courtney preferred women of no fragrance, he found himself drawn to her smell, enraptured by her scent. Their legs touched by accident and her "excuse me" was softer than teddy-bear fur. Courtney imagined her soft moans in his ear, his arms wrapped around her thin waist and then jutting out as they traveled her hips and butt. A strand of her hair found her mouth and she brushed it aside and licked her lips. Lips like two sheaths of butterscotch, sweet, honey-hued. She shared the same dark-maple complexion with Courtney, and, he hoped, at some point they would share much more. Hoped that the opportunity would come for him to kiss those shaded eyelids, stare into those distinctive, large eyes. Who was Chante?

Courtney could feel warmth from this phenomenal woman; the closeness of the seating allowed her body heat to quiet the chill in him like a day sunbathing at the beach. The incessant throb in his ribs, the loud ache in his ankles, the sharpness—like a draw for blood from an extra large needle—that ran through his back whenever he moved, none of it existed in his mind anymore. Now, his thoughts and hopes coalesced with this phenomenal woman beside him.

"Hate planes," she said as she settled in her seat. Her shoulders hunched inward, squeezing the cleavage of her breasts from a minor road to a major expressway. Her hands clasped together on her lap. Her skirt huddled against the back of her leg. She danced, ran track, or did both, her calves told Courtney's stolen glance.

Courtney generated a baritone from his chest, "First time flying?"

She didn't glance in his direction as he waited, watching her for a response. "Second," she said, motioning with two fingers as her left hand continued to hold her right by the wrist. "Years ago made a quick flight to Virginia. It was only about forty-five minutes, I think, but I was petrified the entire flight. Don't know how I'm going to handle this one."

"I'll be right here if you need me."

"I might grab ahold of you," she said as an afterthought as she reached forward and picked up the in-flight magazine to thumb through and try to corral her stray worries.

"Promise," Courtney said as he shifted in his seat, moved his lean in her direction.

She turned to him, flashed the first of what he hoped would be many smiles, realizing finally that Courtney held more than a casual interest in her, and extended her hand. "Dana Cummings." The glimmer of sun that came through the side window made the bronze of her eyes more defined.

"Courtney Sheffield." He waited to see if the name registered. It didn't. He was glad it hadn't.

"Takeoffs and landings are the worst, Courtney Sheffield." She looked away briefly, shivered. "At least, I remember them being the hardest for me. For most people, I believe. I did research on plane crashes and fear of flying on the Internet before I booked my ticket."

"Damn, that's one I never heard."

Dana smiled, the second smile, the smile that solidified her comfort with Courtney. He smiled back. She had now turned at an angle facing him, sitting as if they were sharing a cup of hot chocolate at a late night café, the flicker of a candle challenging their smiles for brightness. "I like to be informed," she offered in defense of the Internet search. "If it's not a bother, since you've been such a gentleman so far, you mind holding my hand during the takeoff and landing?"

"Mr. Cummings not gonna be upset about that, is he?" Courtney asked.

The third smile—the game-set-and-match smile. "No, my *daddy* won't mind. What about Mrs. Sheffield, she gonna pop out the woodwork hollering at me to get my hands off her husband?"

Courtney sighed. "Haven't found her yet, but I'm young, twenty-one . . . You might be the first to know, though, when I do. I'm looking for that soul mate." Who was Chante?

"Really?" Dana hunched forward a degree. "Me, too, Courtney Sheffield. Like TLC said, 'I don't want no scrubs.' Tired of the scrubs. My family says I'm trying to grow up too fast, that I got plenty of time—twenty-three, myself," she said, answering the question before he asked. "I picture myself married, loving someone with all my strength, sharing in the joys and tragedies of life with them. My Grandy mostly raised me; I think I reached back and took her values."

"For real, for real," Courtney agreed. "Someone to share with, a wife, those are my desires, too. I don't care how old I am, I'm ready for it."

Dana looked at him, deeply. "Now, don't take this wrong, but I have to ask. With men you have to be so specific; the brothers have their own language. You said, 'no wife'. I take that to mean no girlfriend either?"

"Nope," Courtney answered. "And you? No boyfriend?"

Dana shook her head. "You might be the first to know when I find one, though."

Courtney nodded, smiled, his even teeth passing Dana's un-spoken inspection. "Nice, nice, Dana Cummings. I like your style."

"What do you do, Courtney? I figured you for a rapper when I sat here, and you've got a fine rap."

He shifted in his seat, the aches and pains that time had yet to completely heal creeping back into his conscience. "Basketball," he said. "I'm headed to Atlanta for a pre-draft workout with the Flames."

Dana's interest increased, her large eyes, becoming a touch larger, "Really? You're going to play in the NBA?"

"Yep, draft's in June. Flames wanna check me out before they sign over them ducats." He knew his own life story though; he wanted to know Dana's. "What about you? What do you do?"

"I sing," she said, pausing, unsure of herself in the confession. "Well, I want to be a singer. I did backing vocals last year for Mary J. Blige—she's from Yonkers, you know, same as me. Her manager hooked me up with this new label down here, and they're flying me down to record a demo. If they like it"—she crossed her fingers—"they might sign me to a deal. I'd be their first female act; they've got a male R&B group, couple of rappers."

"So you're a blossoming celebrity, huh?" Courtney said.

"Not yet," she replied as she tapped the armrest, "but hopefully one day, soon. What about you, Mr. NBA? I bet you've got game."

"Oh, yeah," Courtney agreed, flashing Dana his trademark dimples. "I've got game, Ms. Dana Cummings. I'm not Kobe yet, but—"

Dana surprised him, touched his lips with two of the softest fingers he'd ever felt, made his thought drift like seaweed. "You're handsomer than Kobe, Courtney Sheffield. Now, hold my hand. The flight's about to take off." He took her hand and rubbed the top with his thumb, that intimate gesture that took most couples months of dating to achieve. But that was Courtney, a fast mover. Dana apparently was one, too. Who was Chante?

All Colin could think about was the promise from the ninth of June, close to six years prior. To cherish one another, love one another, whether the dice rolled terminal cancer or fatty mutual funds. Liza, her hair golden-brown that day, dressed in the most beautiful wedding gown, beaming, an absolute angel. Colin had complained about his tuxedo from the moment he put it on until the moment the organist strummed Liza down the aisle. At that point, the uncomfortable tux, the pre-wedding jitters, it all dissipated as a puddle would during the hotness of summer. That day she had been the most beautiful creature in a universe filled with beauty. She had been his life's dream, his biggest blessing. She had been a friend, lover, confidante, supporter, who became his wife. And now, the friendship, the love, the confidence, the support, all of it was gone. Soon she would be his wife no longer. Soon the only thread left between them would be their heavenly present, their Lyric. Lyric was a wonderful consolation, but Colin couldn't stop thinking about the bigger prize that he'd mucked away.

"This is the author," a voice said, marrying Colin to the present. "Colin Sheffield." Clementine Tish, owner of Ebony Scribes bookstore, stood over his signing table, smiling.

Clementine had long dreads that she bunched together and always wore in a ponytail. Her skin had a kind of sepia tone, like the old black-and-white photographs that Colin's mother and Nana had from their days in Method, North Carolina. If not for the sprinkles of white around the crown of her head, Clementine could pass for a woman ten years younger. She'd been supporting Colin for as long as he'd written—asking him to come in and do a writer's workshop before he had a deal—because she'd read one of his short stories in an anthology and could see the "smoke rising off him."

Colin took one of the hardcover copies of *Prophet's Message* in his hand to have something to grip, to steady his hand. The gesture gave him the appearance of a novelist, though he didn't feel like one, didn't feel like anything of worth today. Book signings were never a favorite endeavor, but as his career moved forward, he realized that shyness only befit the author with the eleventh best-selling novel on a list of the top ten best-sellers. With *Prophet's Message* he planned to kick his self-promotion efforts into high gear. Then the thing with Liza happened, and nothing mattered anymore. Just like the arm on one of his uncle's record players, moving back and forth by rote, Colin signed books today, lacking feeling or emotion, robotic.

After a painful week of stops, he considered canceling this event, save himself the lonely drive to Trenton, the drive with his stereo off, his thoughts fogging his view like a dirty windshield. But because of Clementine, he hadn't. He made it a point to frequent the independent black booksellers, to cultivate the special relationship between black author and black entrepreneur. Something inside told him that Baldwin and Ellison, the heroes whose shoulders he stood on, would make the Ebony Scribes of the world their main priority—the mega-bookstores, their minor. In spite of the loss of appetite, the sleeplessness, and the lack of desire, the unpaid debt to his predecessors trumped it all. He had to come today.

"*Prophet's Message* is wonderful, too," Clementine continued, hand-selling Colin's book to this middle-aged couple, while Colin sat pensively watching, forcing a smile to speak the words his mouth wouldn't. "I was up all night reading it. You see these bags under my eyes? Don't think these are because I'm—" Clementine muffled the age with her hand and giggled. "Trust me. I got these bags reading this glorious brother's work. Maggie, Gerald, you know I don't offer my support to any ole garbage. I know you two like your non-fiction, but, if there ever was a novelist worth trying, this is the one." She left the two of them, winked at Colin, and moved off to the front of the store, another wave of folks entering.

"What's the book about?" Gerald asked. He picked up one of the table copies and turned it over to the back. He looked at the author photo and blurbs before handing the book to his wife. She opened it to the inside flap and read the detailed synopsis.

"Sort of a ghost story, mystery," Colin answered—the clarity and purpose for the book no longer apparent to him, though he'd spent close to a year writing it. "Set in Louisiana. It's about a daughter and her father, actually. She's out to prove that her father—he's killed in the first part of the book—She's out to prove that he was murdered by the local authorities. The authorities claim that he robbed a liquor store, that they shot him in self-defense. It's about the strength of the bond between the daughter and her father. . . . She has visions of him after he dies that keep pointing her in directions that aid her in her claim." Colin grinded his teeth and squeezed his eyes as if the lights were too bright.

"Sounds . . . interesting," Gerald said and turned to his wife. "Don't you think so, dear?"

She smiled politely. "Um, yes, go ahead and buy a copy, honey."

Gerald took the book from his wife, conjured a smile, and placed it on the table in front of Colin. "Would love it signed."

"Of course," Colin answered, grateful. "To Gerald and Maggie?"
"No, no," Gerald said. "Just sign it."

Colin nodded. No doubt they'd be returning it. Colin signed the inside title page and handed it to the couple. He could tell by how they moved in sync, by how closely they walked alongside each other, that their history together was richer than his mother's coconut-custard pie. He reached in his shirt pocket and pulled out his cell phone. What was the chance that Liza had left a message saying she'd made a horrible mistake?

Colin moved from the table and went to the back area of the bookstore, stood off to the side, and dialed his voice mail number.

One message waited. Colin punched in his code; his heart beat, exposing his anxious hope.

"Colin, Henry here. I know you're in Trenton today at a signing, planning on heading to Plainfield for tomorrow. Give me a call when you get this message. There's been a slight change in plans—Angelo decided to scale back your tour a few cities—a 'slightly altered focus in marketing for your newest vehicle' is how he put it. Wish he would have informed me sooner, said he tried to reach you at home, but you must've already left. Nothing to get worked up over from what I gathered. Beale Street wants to concentrate on the bigger markets and bypass the smaller cities. Listen . . . I know you're up in arms about Langston Campbell coming over to Beale Street . . . you're probably thinking that this change signifies the reservations you've had about everything. Trust me, Colin, this is nothing to get worked up over. We'll straighten everything out . . . make sure we do what's best for your career. I promise you that much. Give me a call and we can discuss it."

Colin replayed the message. Turned and noticed *Word of Mouth*, Langston's last book, displayed, and the "coming soon" sign in bright, glossy colors for *Strike a Chord*, Langston's newest. Disappointment clutched him as he flipped his cell phone shut.

Liza wasn't calling.

His family was gone from him, and his career appeared to be next.

Courtney and Dana stood at the exit gate in Hartsfield Atlanta International Airport, their fingers still interlocked long after their plane had landed. A relationship had been forged while they were still in the air, and it continued once they touched ground.

"So much I want to do, so little time," Dana said as her arm swung with Courtney's. "I wish you could stay over longer than two days. I wanted to hit Little Five Points—I hear it's like East Village back in the City. There's a boutique—*Junkman's Daughter*—that I found out about on the Internet. You could have bought me something sexy to wear so I could show you my appreciation for helping me fly."

"You spending my loot, already," Courtney teased.

"Don't worry," she responded, "I would take you out, too. Dance your feet sore at *Club Fuel*, experience the *World of Coca Cola* with you. Treat you to a fine meal at one of the restaurants in Buckhead."

"Damn, you got it all mapped out, huh?"

"I've had this tour guide for Atlanta for months." She bit into her lip, batted her eyelashes. "Didn't think I'd find someone I would be so looking forward to checking it all out with."

"You're something, Dana Cummings."

"Ditto, Courtney Sheffield."

Perspiration clung to Courtney, his light gray T-shirt dampened to a dark gray in the area of his armpits. The coolness of the trainer's table reminded him of that horrible night in the emergency room, Black's voice in his ears, wounds covering Courtney from head to toe. However, that day he'd had his dreams deferred, and now, as he sat having his ankles re-taped, he was preparing to collect on those dreams.

"Your ribs tender?" the Atlanta Flames' trainer asked Courtney.

Courtney quickly surveyed the training room, his competition. Most of the other players were off in their own worlds, having their joints taped while mentally preparing for the scrimmage that would soon follow. Courtney turned his attention back to the trainer, admitted the truth. "Little. How could you tell?"

The trainer smiled thoughtfully. "I noticed you kept flinching during the stamina and performance drills. It looked like you could bite through wood when they had you run those wind sprints. I saw you touch your side and clench your jaw. How'd it happen?"

"Pickup game back in New York," Courtney lied.

The trainer, Wayne Peabody, looked at Courtney and frowned. "Rough pickup game, huh?" Peabody's skin cracked from a recent tan, his bluish-green eyes calm as ocean waves. He'd been the Flames' head trainer for close to fifteen years, had taped ankles and patted players on the butt as they prepared to enter a game; he had also stood somberly over players with torn ACLs who would never run and jump again. At some point, between those two contrasting spectrums, Peabody had picked up the concern of a father.

Courtney shrugged off the probe of Peabody's eyes. "New York City b-ball is no joke."

Peabody nodded. "Look, you're pretty beat up, son. I watched you closely out there, as I said. You should let management know about your present physical condition; see about getting a second workout in before the draft. You're all they've been talking about around this place for the past few weeks. I'm sure your agent could finagle you a second look-see."

Courtney shook his head. "Nah, there's no need for that. I rated pretty well on the performance drills—highest vertical leap out of this entire group. I'll be okay."

Again, Peabody nodded. "You did fine, son, true indeed. But I'm betting your ratings would be off the charts if you were a hundred percent. Plus, this scrimmage coming up worries me a bit. None of these other guys are 'can't misses' like you. They're all fighting just to get an invite to training camp. They'll be out for blood out there."

"I'm not worried about any of them," Courtney replied.

Peabody lowered his voice, leaned into Courtney. "They see you flinch on contact, favoring that right ankle the way you've been doing, your knee unsteady every time you cut to your left— they'll exploit you out there."

Courtney smiled. "I've yet to be exploited on the basketball court in my life."

Peabody finished taping Courtney's ankle, pocketed his supplies, patted Courtney's shoulder. "Just might be prudent you let management know you're less than one hundred percent."

Courtney sat up, rested on the edge of the trainer's table. "Fifty percent is about all I need with these guys. As you said, they're all just fighting for an invite to training camp. Me, I'm about to be the Flames' number one pick. In twenty years, my uniform will be hanging from the rafters with Dominique Wilkins'."

Peabody shrugged. "What do I know?"

Courtney tapped Peabody's shoulder. "That's right. I'll handle mine. Leave the balling to me." Courtney smiled. "That sounds like a nice saying to put on the billboard they'll erect for me on I-75."

Twenty minutes later, Peabody's prophesy was becoming a painful reality for Courtney. Rye, a big, country-hick-looking white boy who wouldn't be on the court if he weren't six-ten in his socks, was giving Courtney fits. He'd cut behind Courtney's guard twice to score quick baskets. Rye was only slightly faster than comedienne Mo'Nique was, and yet Courtney struggled to keep pace with him.

Rye shook his head as he backpedaled down the court, his confidence growing with each basket. He smirked at Courtney. "Rookie of the year? I'm not seeing it."

"See this dunk I'm about to put on your head," Courtney said as he cut past Rye.

"I'll put a hog elbow on them ribs," Rye replied. "I see you making faces like you sucking grapes through a straw every time I touch you."

"Suck on this," Courtney said, showing Rye his middle finger.

"Next basket wins," a voice bellowed from the gymnasium's loud speakers.

Courtney frowned. He hadn't shown much thus far and the game was coming to an abrupt ending. He had to make this last basket, and do it in spectacular fashion. He ran to the right wing of the court, Rye shadowing him, and called for the ball.

Courtney turned to catch the pass, turned and eyed Rye, eyed the basket.

He thought about a move he'd seen his father make at the legendary Rucker Tournament. Prime had dribbled between his legs several times as he moved toward the basket. The crowd was on fire that day with anticipation of what was about to happen. Prime smiled at the player attempting to guard him and took off for the basket, turning his body in a 360-degree spin before rattling the rim with an electrifying dunk.

Now, Courtney smiled at Rye. He dribbled between his legs several times as he made a slow move toward the basket. Rye licked his fingertips. You could practically see his heart beating through his soaked jersey. The other players, as well as the management and coaching staff of the Flames, watched Courtney with the same anticipation as that Rucker crowd with their eyes on Prime.

Courtney took off toward the hoop.

Rye stumbled clumsily, but kept close to Courtney.

Courtney jumped, starting his turn in the air.

Rye jumped.

Courtney raised the ball above his head, prepared to dunk it home.

Rye raised his elbows, connected his sharp left one with Courtney's ribs.

The strength seeped from Courtney, the power of his jump slackened by the clap of pain in his side.

Rye blocked Courtney's shot as Courtney fell in a heap on the floor.

Rye caught the errant shot and passed it off to a teammate who ran unmolested up the court to the other end, putting in the winning shot.

Courtney rolled over on his back, closed his eyes as the voice called out over the loud speaker, "Scrimmage over."

Rye stepped over Courtney as he headed back toward the locker room. "Rookie of the Year? I'm not seeing it."

12

MAY 30

"Very pleased to see you in your angelic guise," Angelo Hayes said, beaming at Colin. "Glad to see you haven't forgotten an old comrade." Angelo made a game out of greeting Colin with lines from classic literature.

"Couldn't tell you," Colin answered as Angelo watched him without extending his hand.

Angelo grinned and offered that hand, now that this latest round was his. "Tolstoy. *Father Sergius.*"

Colin nodded. "Good to know. We need to talk."

Angelo stood in the center of the office, two chairs unattended behind his back—one for visitors and a larger leather one for him. The long drive from Trenton left a sharp ache in Colin's heels, but he refused to sit until Angelo did. Call it psychological warfare.

Angelo's long caramel-colored face, his pointy widow's-peak hairline, the muscular jaw, made him look like one of the president's cabinet members. He used his importance, like an onion press, to grind down his authors until they moved as he wanted—at the end of his puppet strings. Colin was the only author signed to Beale Street that matched Angelo, blow for blow. Colin was the only author with enough clout to strike back. That is, until the day Langston Campbell signed on.

"You upset about something?" Angelo asked with a smile of

manufactured warmth, a microwave ray of a smile. "Because you know I try my best to keep you happy."

"Like cutting my tour back, right?"

Angelo squint his eyes. Colin moved over by the window sill overlooking the Manhattan skyline and sat on the hard lip. It presented a rest for his burning soles but it wasn't the soft pillow cushion of a chair. It wasn't a gesture of weakness, which Angelo could exploit in this battle of wills.

Angelo moved to the leather recliner behind his desk and sat back, rocking the chair with his hands in his lap. Colin couldn't help but smile; he'd won this battle of wills.

"Colin, listen," Angelo said thoughtfully. "Cutting your tour was a decision made to benefit you. We want to concentrate your promotions in the larger markets and get you the sales your talent deserves. How many books were you expecting to sell in Plainfield? Come on, now. Here in the city, a couple retailers in Jersey, Philadelphia, maybe one or two in Boston. That's all we need in the Northeast." He looked away from Colin, pulled at a piece of stray lint on the shoulder of his collarless sweater, nudged at the sweater, pulled it between his fingers, and studied it harder than he'd done the literature classics during his undergrad years at NYU.

Colin watched Angelo, let his eyes probe into the mind of this man. Friend or foe? He couldn't say for sure, but his gut told him the latter. "Langston Campbell getting the same *concentrated marketing*?"

Angelo pulled the portion of sweater around his waist out in front of him like an opened newspaper and checked it for lint, checked his other shoulder. Satisfied after a thorough inspection of the sweater, Angelo refocused on Colin, a smirk on his face. "What was that? I'm sorry."

Colin moved from the window sill, came to a screeching halt directly in front of Angelo, hovering over him like an agitated parent. "You plan on using the same marketing strategy with Langston Campbell?"

Angelo grimaced. "Campbell's a different story, Colin; surely you know that. Everywhere we send him, we can expect sales. Plainfield, the moon, shit. . . ."

Colin turned from the hammering punishment of Angelo's voice and then shot back around. The reds of his eyes circled his dark, piercing pupils. A dab of spit formed in the corner of his mouth. "Thanks for meeting with me, Angelo. I'll be in touch."

"Whoa, whoa, Colin, baby, slow your roll. You're upset, I can see that, let's try and figure this out before you go storming out of here."

Colin shook his head, wiped away the spit from his mouth with the back of his hand. "No storming out for me, Angelo. You've made your point perfectly clear, nothing else to discuss." He noticed that the calm and lack of slack in his voice sounded like Liza. "I should be glad I've still got a contract, that I can make a living doing this. Most writers don't. Most writers are working for groceries, insurance, and the mortgage during the day, burning the midnight oil with their pens. Isn't that right, Angelo?"

"Sad reality, but true," Angelo admitted. "You have a career to be thankful of. I know you want the mega-seller. I want it, too, believe me. But there's something to be said for the author who creates acclaimed novels and is able to take care of his family doing it. I'm extremely proud of what we've accomplished together these few short years. You sold your first book to Hollywood for chrissakes." Sold the first one and hadn't sold another since. Colin hated the fact that the majority of income he'd made these past few years had come from that movie. Plus, the movie, even with a strong cast, had flopped miserably at the box office. Fine acting, but a story no one cares about, the critics had said.

"That settles it, then," Colin said, a strangeness taking over his voice and posture. "I'm one lucky *motherfucker.* Peace out, Angelo."

"Colin . . . Colin . . . Colin . . ."

Colin moved through the doors of the office without heeding Angelo's call and passed by June, the Jamaican receptionist who always offered up homemade cookies and homeland pearls of advice, without saying good-bye. Everything suddenly crystal clear to him as he walked on through the building, his scope focused as if he were staring into space, a zombie. His allies, those he could count on to watch his back, were dwindling more and more with each passing day. The reality of it all made his temples hurt and his vision blurry—he was increasingly becoming dangerous, both to himself, and others. Even in his hazy condition he could feel it happening.

* * *

"Touch me. Tease me." Four words, simple words—a directive as to what it would take to release the geyser that hid beneath the wasps of pubic hair between her thighs. Spoken as soon as she entered the hotel room—the overpowering luxury of the Ritz Carlton Buckhead. Spoken moments before she slipped off her dress and let it pool at her ankles, its light lavender material looking so right with the dark purple of the plush carpet.

Courtney dead-bolted the door, walked around her with his thumb on his chin and a finger on his lips, inspecting every inch of her flesh that glistened from body oil. He said nothing, but took the peach she'd handed him at the doorway and plunged two fingers into its soft ripeness, then bent to one knee, the pulpy wetness on those two fingers, and dotted her waist and front thigh with the sticky fingerprints that would connect him to this crime. "Bring it to the bed," he said. "Rest those feet"—he noticed her pumps for the first time—"but leave those on. They're sexy bad." He bit into the peach and smiled.

Dana took his extended finger, held onto the lasso, moved toward the bed, breaststroked through the silky curtain that hung from the canopy rail. The only light in the room came from the cracked bathroom door. Courtney placed Dana on her back, laying her down like fine china. The bathroom's illumination cut him in half, lit the left side of his body, while leaving his right side, dark. He smiled and kissed her, passed the pit of the peach to her with his tongue, so she could suck its sweetness. He moved down below her navel to suck her sweetness in return.

"Softly . . . softly," Dana moaned, as the bristles of Courtney's mustache commingled with the bristles between her thighs.

"Like that?" he asked as he plunged deeper, closer to her core, her juice and peach fuzz on his probing lips. She massaged his shoulders, moaned, the gesture giving him the affirmation he sought.

"Hmm . . . oh, yes, hmm."

She turned her head to the side, let the peach pit tumble from her mouth and rest on the extra fluffy pillow. Her breath held in her chest, words escaping her as if she'd swallowed the pit and it lodged in her throat, the impulses of her body no longer under her control. She wanted to clasp something with her hands, dig her manicured fingernails into Courtney's back, but all she could manage was to ball her hands in a fist and punch the give of the mattress as the give of her new lover sent chills down her spine.

"Oh, you making a brother put in work, huh," Courtney said, adjusting his position. "That was my 'super-duper tongue flexor' right there. Aiight, then . . . 'super-duper-leave-'em-in-a-stupor tongue flexor' coming up."

"Don't talk," Dana shooed him, swatted at him as if flies buzzed around his shoulders.

Courtney answered with more pressure on her ecstasy nub. Then came the rush as bulls charged from the gates of imprisonment.

The tingle surprised Dana, knocked the breath from her lungs—never had her release been so profound, that painful joy so long-winded. She blinked her eyes to regain the colors of the room, covered her chest with one hand to settle her breathing. Courtney was turned over on his back, breathing heavily himself, with Dana's feet draped across his chest like a shower towel. On the ceiling, he could swear he saw stars, saw the moon winking at him.

"Don't be talking that stupid shit when you're doing that," Dana told him. "Superduper whatever the fuck you said. That's serious business, no time for that."

Courtney saluted her. "Yes, ma'am."

"You damn near messed up my flow."

"Really? 'Cause I'm feeling lightheaded. *You* damn near crushed my skull with your thighs."

Dana covered her mouth, embarrassed. "Did I?" Her cheeks pinked. "I don't know what happened."

"My tongue happened," Courtney said as he turned over and looked at her. "Superduper like I said. Glad you enjoyed."

"Enjoyed is an understatement . . . Don't know what you can do to top that."

Courtney slid up next to her and nuzzled the flesh of her cheek. "I got ideas. Yesterday was for shit, least I can end my short little trip down here on a good note."

Dana furrowed her brows. "Yesterday? What, your workout didn't go well?"

"You can say that."

"What happened?"

Courtney touched his sore ribs, looked at his busted ankle. The drama with Chante had taught him painful lessons about opening up and revealing too much. "Just didn't have it," he said. "Picked a good time to tighten up . . . biggest day in my basketball life."

Dana propped herself on an elbow, stared as deeply into his eyes as he'd plunged into her moments earlier. "It couldn't have been that bad. I think you'll be okay. I didn't realize you were so good; you'll be fine." She was babbling. The smile on her face said she was holding a secret, a secret she wanted revealed like the fools who aired their nasty, funky drawers on talk shows.

"What do you mean? What's up with the smile?"

Dana's eyes lit like incense sticks. She sat up in the bed, leaned her back against the headboard and positioned herself as if she was giving testimony before a grand jury. In the blink of an eye she'd gone from coy to as natural with Courtney as she was with her Yonkers' girlfriends. "I mentioned you to one of the admin assistants at the label today and she damn near fell off her chair." Dana reached forward, grabbed Courtney by the arm and squeezed it harder than her thighs had done around his head when he tickled that pearl. "Sherry—the admin girl—damn near bust my eardrum. She screamed, 'What, girl! I was reading about him.' They had a big write-up on you in the sports section of the *Journal Constitution*. The hopes of the Flames' franchise '*reside on your able shoulders*' I think is how the columnist worded it." She released her vice grip on his arm and hit it with a semi-balled fist— a sexual version of boxing. "Why didn't you tell me you were so large? You made it sound as if you were a new jack chasing a rainbow. Like I'm doing. I thought you were *trying out trying out.* The Flames have pretty much already committed to drafting you. You're one of the top-ranked players in all college basketball."

Courtney looked at her, his eyebrows touching at the center of his forehead. "Dang, I am?"

"Funny dude," Dana said. "Yes, Mr. Courtney Sheffield, I've been checking up on you. I read that article twenty times. Also read this piece on you from an old *Sports Illustrated.* And what about your brother? Colin Sheffield. I've seen his books in the stores."

Courtney cringed. The mention of Colin's name still grated

him, but coming off Dana's tongue the lemon was cut with a touch of sugar. He leaned closer to her. "You ever buy 'em? Colin's books."

Dana gave him the pulling-teeth face; let an ashamed "no" slip out like air from a pierced tire.

"Don't feel bad," Courtney assured her. "Me neither."

The cutting remark didn't cause the slightest ripple in Dana; she didn't know the history and only focused on making her own with Courtney. "So why didn't you tell me all of this about yourself?"

Courtney smiled. "I was more interested in your story, baby doll; didn't want to bore you talking about myself."

Dana wrapped him in her arms, kissed the side of his neck, the nape of his neck, and let her tongue slide to his chest where it finally rested on one of his nipples. Sucked and bit at the bulbous flesh. Courtney's eyes shut as she began combing her hand through his hair, breaking the half-done cornrows out into a fullfledged afro. "Damn, you got nice hair—wavy." She pulled back and teased, "Indian in your family tree?"

Courtney now understood what she meant about lovemaking being serious business. He didn't want to speak, wanted only to enjoy the warmth of Dana's mouth. "Lusters—that pink shit," he replied, and then guided her head back to his chest. "Do what you were doing."

Dana caressed his chest a bit more and then moved down to his stomach area—kissed each ripple of muscle like her mother brushing honey on the top of her slightly brown, homemade rolls. Courtney lay back wondering why he hadn't met Dana a few weeks earlier in life, why the kisses that sent a healing surge through his ribcage hadn't occurred before his doomed workout.

"You should be a freaking doctor," he muttered.

"No," Dana corrected as she took his third leg and kissed around the base. "A nurse. Let me give this a sponge down."

"Oh, fugggg me," Courtney slurred.

It wasn't long before the hot liquid of life poured from Courtney and Dana rubbed it into his thigh and stomach like cocoa butter lotion. She moaned while she played with his liquid seeds, the light inside Courtney still burning bright as she twirled a finger in the muck and rubbed it into his flesh.

"You are a bad-ass, sexy sister," Courtney said to her as he tried to calm his choppy breathing.

She smiled, getting so much joy from the compliment it looked as if her face might crack and settle into small pieces on her pillow. "You're a badass, sexy brother," she volleyed back at him.

Courtney shrugged, gave Dana a smile, and smoothed her hair with his fingers as she warmed the spot next to him, their little sexual interludes separated by crumbs of pillow talk so they could replenish themselves for the next act.

"Tell me about your recording session, today. Hope it went better than my workout."

"Was okay," she sighed. "They introduced me to the producer working on my demo; we talked; he played me tracks; I sang for him. We're not going to start actually recording until next week. I wish my family had come, wish I had support. This whole thing is scary for me."

"You have my support. I know you're going to be successful."

Dana sat up again, turned so Courtney couldn't see her face. "I called my mom today—told her all about you and the goings-on at the label."

Dana had barely mentioned family before. Courtney adjusted his attention. "Yeah . . . ?"

"She was all excited about you, told me not to let you get away."

Courtney smiled. "Smart mother you got."

"Said, 'Maybe now you'll give up this stupid fantasy shit, of being *a recording star.*'"

Courtney touched her shoulder. "She's worried about you, that's all—only natural for a mother to worry." He thought of his own mother. Despite all the complications of late, despite her displeasure with his decision, she'd wished him the best, told him she loved him. She'd told him she loved him countless times over the years, but surprisingly, this was the first time she said it with the same conviction as when she told Colin. Courtney had noticed and tucked away the memory like a photograph in his shirt pocket, close to his heart.

"You don't know my mom," Dana said, shaking her head as the tears fell. "That is one bitter, old bitch. She doesn't want me to succeed. And if I do, she wants it to be because of a man. She never believed in herself, never saw her worth outside of a man, and thinks I should be the same way. All my troubles in life have come because I did buy into that—didn't see any good in Dana unless a man was up on me."

"At least you've recognized that and moved on," Courtney said.

"I thought I had," Dana reasoned, "but then I met you. I can feel myself falling into an old pattern. I'm growing so attached to you, Courtney, in a short time. I can't help but think this might turn tragic for me."

"Tragic? How?"

Dana looked him in the eyes, her smeared mascara made her look like a sinister clown with homicidal tendencies. "When you get on that plane and fly back to the city, will I ever hear from you again?"

"Of course," Courtney replied as he started to feel boxed in. It was a shame how many issues people had to deal with in their short lifetimes. Dana, it appeared, had a few lifetimes worth of issues to deal with. The joy that had clung to her from the moment she sat on the plane next to him was now replaced by a heartache he could never have guessed lived anywhere near her. All of this revealed too late, after they'd already done the nasty and he'd dropped his luggage in the pile by her doorstep. *Oh, how terribly sex messes things up*, he thought, as he watched Dana.

"You don't know the half of what I've been through," Dana continued. "I'm looking at you, this music thing, as a new beginning for me, my last hope. You ready for that kind of pressure?"

Courtney wanted to bolt, but instead he offered up a linty smile—a fragment of the happiness she'd given him earlier. The contented feelings from the plane had long left him. This thing was, like most of his life, moving too fast for him to navigate. Here he was with this new woman, covered in the scent held closest to her skin, and the aroma of another woman still hadn't moved to accommodate it. It upset him to realize that he did still have feelings for Chante.

13

May 31

Ugly gray folding chairs with dents in the seats were lined up eight to a row on either side of the center aisle, twenty rows in all, gymnasium lights keeping darkness at bay. The basketball goals at each end of the gym were upraised to a ninety-degree angle. VIP guests were seated under the goal at the south end of the gym. Streamers, handwritten signs, and banners hung from the pushed-in bleachers on each side of the basketball court. A large banner reaching from one sidewall to the other announced BLACK LITERATURE EXPO 2002. The buzz of voices, like bees around an overturned hive, mixed with the soft playing R&B jams that the DJ kept in constant rotation. Four folding tables were placed shoulder to shoulder and covered with white frilly tablecloths on the stage beyond the basketball goal at the south end of the building. An air conditioning unit, on full blast, created a chill that had the women wishing they'd brought sweaters and the few men in attendance insisting they weren't cold as they fidgeted in their seats.

The finger tapping against the main microphone took a moment to register, took a moment before the crowd quieted and gave the voice behind the finger its full attention. The voice was a pleasant brew of beer, full-bodied, but sweet, mannish and womanish at the same time. The woman behind the voice was unmistakably female, though—high-maintenance beautiful, in fact. She spoke each word as precise as a Shakespearean actress did. The few men in attendance took note of how her well-tailored suit clung to the curves she worked out daily to keep firm. The women identified with the strength of her posture, figuring she was a sister on the ball, a proud figure to rest their own hats on. She was a celebrity, a newscaster with NBC here in New York, and her participation in the event gave it as much credibility as the authors that formed the panel behind her.

"Ladies and gentlemen," said the mistress of ceremonies in that distinctive voice, "Welcome to the *Black Literature Expo's Year 2002* symposium on the state of African American fiction. And . . . welcome to my colleagues from NBC who are taping this panel discussion for a segment of my show—*Reflections*—airing Sundays." She paused to allow the audience an opportunity to clap. "Now, without further ado, it is with the greatest pleasure I introduce our dais guests. Starting on my far left: Tami Truss, author of the Blackboard best-seller, *Get Out the Kitchen,* which has been optioned by a major Hollywood studio and hopefully will begin production in the near future." She pointed her arm toward the author. "Tami Truss. Thanks so much for being here, Tami."

The audience clapped as Tami Truss nodded her head and smiled graciously.

"Next to Ms. Truss," the mistress continued, "Deidre June, author of more than twenty romance titles, including her newest release, the sizzling romance thriller *Chocolate Hearts.* Deidre, it's truly a pleasure to have you with us as well."

Deidre June smiled and nodded, as Tami Truss had, as the applause of the audience welcomed her.

"On Mrs. June's right, is one of my personal favorites," the mistress said, in her version of gushing. "The divine, magnificent, queen of letters, Ms. Mary Toney. She is, of course, the author of such notables as *Notes, Mind's Eye,* and the Pulitzer Prize-winning *Trustworthy.* It is indeed an honor to have you here today, Ms. Toney. Mary Toney, ladies and gentlemen."

Mary raised her palms to the sky as the deafening roar of approval greeted her. Every time it appeared that the roars had reached their crescendo, they would move up another notch. Close to a minute and a half of appreciation for Mary Toney's great works.

"Absolutely, absolutely," the mistress of ceremonies said in agreement. "We absolutely love what you've given us, Ms. Toney, and this greeting is a testament to the love you've garnered by penning some of the most memorable novels of the past twenty years. Thanks again for being here." The mistress fanned herself and jumped right back to work. "Ms. Toney is a tough act to follow, but the next author is up to the task. Next to Ms. Toney, the *New York Times* and *Washington Post* best-selling author of *Word of Mouth*. His novels have been translated in over fifteen languages and his Web site receives a staggering twelve hundred hits per day—yes, *per day*. His newest book, *Strike a Chord*, will be available soon, and is one of the most eagerly anticipated releases of the year and destined to be a major seller as well. Ladies and gentlemen, I present to you, the incomparable Langston Campbell."

Whereas the other authors received only hand claps, Langston's applause included a vigorous amount of whistles and foot stomps as well. He soaked it all in, leaning to the side in his chair with his fingers stroking the whisper of a goatee on his face, nodding to the melody of music playing softly in the background. When the applause seemed as if it would never settle, he threw his head back and smiled and then raised his hands imploring the crowd to give him more. Colin sat two seats down from him, his head down, his mouth closed so tightly that a lobster's claws couldn't pry it open. Langston Campbell was actually receiving a greater reception than the great Mary Toney had. Colin himself was doomed.

"Whew!" the mistress of ceremonies cut in after a few aborted attempts. "Now that's what I call a welcome. Langston, you are one of the phenomena of the publishing industry and we are extremely grateful you took the time to be here with us today."

Langston blew the mistress a kiss and pounded his chest with a fist. "My pleasure," he mouthed as the applause started again.

"Well, Eric Dial," the mistress said, continuing down the dais. "I don't know if it's possible to outdo Langston, but, your debut effort, *Margins*, has established you as a writer on the verge, an author that we hope will be around for years to come. Author of the aforementioned, *Margins*, and a second novel entitled, *Too Much*, due later this year. Eric Dial, ladies and gentlemen."

A pleasant amount of applause rose from the audience and Eric nodded, happy to be among such esteemed company on the panel.

Colin's heart pumped half-melted ice to his brain as he waited for his introduction. He'd committed to this event late last year, before the problems with Liza, before Langston made his play to erase Colin's importance with Beale Street. As the event neared, he'd contemplated canceling on a daily basis, but again, the ghosts of James, Ralph, and Richard wouldn't let him back out. As his stomach churned and his early lunch threatened to rise out of him, he wondered if coming was the wise choice. The desire to confront Langston and try to upstage him dimmed as Colin came to the realization that he just didn't have the ammunition, like an aging boxer, to whip this foe.

"Last among our dais guests, but not least, author of 1999's critically acclaimed, *Sincere Milk,* and widely recognized as one of the most lyrically vivid wordsmiths in contemporary black literature. Ladies and gentlemen, I give you Colin Sheffield." *Give,* she'd said. Give, as in, here take him; he's the same price as an AOL upgrade disk—free—free like his books, most readers coming to them by borrowing a copy from the library.

A burst of applause greeted Colin and he nodded in thanks, though disappointment clutched his insides because the applause fell well short of the love given to the mediocre Langston Campbell.

"And," the mistress said as the applause finished, "I am Erica Montgomery, your mistress of ceremonies for the evening. Once again, give these fabulous novelists a hand."

The resulting applause rose to the rafters and shook the oversized banner that split the building in half. All of the authors on the panel appeared overwhelmed by the show of love, except Langston, whose face held the cocky expression of expectance, and Colin, who looked unbalanced, in his seated position.

"Okay," Erica Montgomery said. "The organizers of this wonderful event felt the best way of opening up weighty dialogue about the state of African American literature would be to allow you—the faithful readers—the opportunity to ask these authors your questions. You'll notice the microphone in the center aisle near the front here. In town-meeting fashion, we're going to allow you to come up in an orderly assembly and step to the microphone one at a time and ask your questions. Our screeners—these beautiful people you see at the beginning of the aisle dressed in all blue—will take your questions and then direct you to the microphone. Now, while we prepare for the question-and-answer portion of our program, please give your warm welcome to Ms. Kendra Warrington, the president of the African Dance Association here at City College, as she sings *The Wind Beneath My Wings*."

Kendra stepped to the microphone, her knees touching, and strained her vocal chords to hit the challenging notes of the song. A trickle of talent oozed from her, and it was hard to tell who was happier when she reached the last lines of the song—she or the audience. She finished the song, placed the microphone back in the stand, and scurried off into the crowd. Her rendition of the classic song drew polite applause. A few people in the audience wondered out loud if she would have gotten the opportunity to showcase her ordinary talent if she was the vice president of her club, instead of the president.

"She sung like an angel," someone near the middle of the crowd lied.

"Ain't gel?" her neighbor asked.

"No. Angel."

"Thank you, Ms. Warrington," Erica Montgomery said as she resumed her place behind the microphone. "Give her more enthusiastic applause, please." The crowd sluggishly obliged. "All right ladies and gentlemen, now for the aspect of today's event that has brought you all out, looking fine and distinguished—the question-and-answer session with these wonderful writers. To our first questioner, and all subsequent questioners, I know the screeners have given you all the particulars, but I'll reiterate. Speak clearly and with purpose into the microphone. State your name and to whom your question is directed. And then ask your question. Okay?" Erica Montgomery pointed to the first woman in line, ushering her forward with a smile and a gentle wave of her hand.

A woman, thirtyish with fashionable burgundy glasses, stepped to the microphone. "Gladys," she said. "This question if for Langston. Your novels tend to sell as well as the best-selling white authors, James Patterson, Steven King, and Grisham. What do you think it is about your writing that makes this possible? Few if any other black authors can make this claim."

Erica nodded. "Thanks for the question, Gladys. Langston, the floor is yours."

Langston leaned forward, adjusted his Howard University T-shirt so the collar didn't constrict his neck, and embraced the microphone like a long-lost lover. "Yes, Gladys, thanks for the question. And, thanks for noticing how well my books sell and placing me within that successful group of authors you mentioned. To answer your question, I believe what sets me apart is that the reader knows when they pick up a Langston Campbell book, they are going to experience a story, well told, with unexpected twists and turns that make it impossible to put down. My books are the epitome of the phrase 'page-turner.' They are suspense-filled, oftentimes romantic, chock full of characters that you grow to care about and love or hate, depending on my intentions. At this point, Langston Campbell is a brand, like Coke or Pepsi, that you can trust, and reading my novels is an experience you won't forget. *Strike a Chord*—available June 26—will give you the same ingredients you've grown to love from Langston Campbell. Cop it quickly, too, because they fly off the shelves like hotcakes. Excuse the cliché."

No need to apologize for the clichés, Colin thought. *We're used to them coming from you.*

"Thank you, Langston," Erica Montgomery said. "Next questioner, please step to the microphone."

A young woman with rich, bronze skin and exotic features stepped forward, her eyes on Langston as she sashayed to the podium, her childbearing hips pulling him to her like metal to a magnet. "Myah," she purred. "This question is for Langston, as well. I loved the character, Myah, in *Word of Mouth,* for obvious reasons. Do you plan on bringing her back in any of your future novels?"

Langston smiled. "Well, *Myah,* I hadn't planned on it, but you might see her showing up in my future works. Don't be surprised if you see added dimensions to her character, too. Your beauty and eloquence have inspired me to make your namesake—from this moment forward I consider her *your* namesake—a deeper, more drawn-out character, with more layers than an onion. I might name the book, *Myah,* who knows?" The women in the audience swooned, jealous that they hadn't been the object of Langston's admiration. Myah looked poised for a collapse. Even Erica Montgomery was flustered when she came back to the microphone.

Erica said, "Langston, you are a charming, young, chocolate brother, I tell you. I would love to be one of your computer keyboard keys so you could—let me stop, my boo might be watching." She turned and waved to the camera in sister-girl fashion, placing the stiffness normally associated with her job in her back pocket for a second. "Hi, Boo. Just jokes, just jokes, keep the silk sheets warm for me." The women in the audience laughed as Erica flashed a mischievous smile. Langston laughed, too.

Langston answered a few more questions, the audience obviously devotees of his work.

Deidre June answered a question about her writing schedule. "Write four hours per day, five days per week. Rest on the weekends; maybe do editing of the work during the week."

Tami Truss was asked when she knew she wanted to be a writer. She said since first grade, when she captivated her snotty-nosed, little classmates with an original poem about George Washington Carver. "Nutty for Peanuts," a poem she still had, was framed above her computer at home.

Mary Toney was asked what it felt like to receive the Pulitzer. She said it was a magnificent catharsis that had purged her of all the reckless mishaps she'd undertaken during her wild youth and that it gave her comeuppance as a novelist. The woman who had asked her the question smiled as if she knew what the answer meant. The other women in the audience did the same, thinking Oprah sure did know what she was talking about when she proclaimed Toney a genius.

Eric Dial was asked about the one thing he found most surprising in regards to the publishing industry: He answered that the glamorous and packed book signings represented on TV shows and in the movies were distinctly on point—minus the glamour and packed crowd.

Colin had been shut out.

As Langston finished answering his latest question, he felt impelled to add, "Come on now folks, you've got one of contemporary African American literature's most—how did you put it, Ms. Montgomery?—lyrically gifted wordsmiths, or whatever, in your midst. Don't miss this opportunity to pick his brain. Someone must have a question for my man, Colin Sheffield." Langston smiled and winked at Colin. Colin returned a half-smile and clutched the bottom of the folding table until his fingers felt numb. Suddenly, all eyes were upon him and the glares made his skin itch.

"Actually, I do have a question for Mr. Sheffield," the dark mahogany-colored woman who next came to the microphone stated. She had a bookish, Ivy League university look to her, wearing stylish, brown glasses and carrying a backpack in lieu of a pocketbook. Colin placed aside the embarrassment of being called out by Langston and leaned in to better hear this sister's question. "Regina," she said, turning to the audience to make sure they'd heard her introduction. "Mr. Sheffield, my question is: Your books garner a tremendous amount of acknowledgment for being well written, yet your sales don't seem commensurate with the praise. How does this make you feel, and to what do you attribute this?"

Great! This chick had to be a Langston Campbell plant, Colin thought, *plunked down in the audience like a chess piece to get him to share his true views and further damage his asthmatic career. Because readers are stupid and don't recognize true art,* he wanted to say.

"Well," Colin said carefully. "We all would love to have the sales figures of my comrade Langston Campbell." The two silent combatants eyed each other and volleyed faux smiles. "But then again, life is a tradeoff and it would hurt me to work as hard as I do on my novels, to slave as endlessly as I do on single sentences at times, and receive some of the mean-spirited reviews that Langston gets. I've seen him get reviews that questioned his skill as a writer and labeled him a fluff artist. Critics are tough and they love knocking off the top person. Thank goodness those unfairly aimed reviews haven't hampered Langston's career." He glanced in Langston's direction and pursed his lips. Satisfaction pulsed through his veins as he congratulated himself for the back-handed show of concern. Had he actually said, "questioned his skill as a writer and labeled him a fluff artist?" Damn, that was beautiful. Excited by his slap at Langston, Colin continued, "I figure that eventually I'll have a breakthrough. In fact, *Prophet's Message* is performing admirably in the early going. I hope that answers your question sufficiently, Regina. And thanks for noticing the consensus that my books are well-written." Colin looked toward Langston and winked. Langston smiled and nodded.

"Well," Erica Montgomery said, "That ends the question-and-answer portion of our program. The authors have been so kind as to agree to sign complementary copies of their novels. They'll be set up out in the lobby for your purchase. Do take the time to support these wonderful novelists and take the opportunity to have a word with them, ask them a question you were too shy to bring forth at the podium. Now, if any of the authors have closing comments, I welcome them, and then we'll close the program with another musical selection from the talented Kendra Warrington."

"Actually," Langston Campbell cut in at that point, "I noticed something and wanted to clear it up." He turned, facing Colin. "Your last name is Sheffield with two *F*s, right Colin?"

Colin was slow to answer, unsure of what ambush awaited his answer. "Correct."

Langston threw his hands in the air and smirked. "Maybe that's it then. They misspelled it on your name placard." Colin looked and noticed his name, spelled *Shefield*, on the folded card in front of him. He returned his gaze to Langston and smiled weakly.

Langston leaned into his microphone again. "Y'all make sure you take note of the correct spelling of this brother's name— Sheffield with two *F*s—no excuses, go buy his books, he's wonderful." Langston shook his head, sucked his teeth. "Misspelled the brother's name, hard a time as he's having selling books and the BLE folks go and misspell his name. Ms. Montgomery you need to check into this."

The audience cackled with delight. Langston turned and winked at Colin. Colin didn't wink, smile, or nod.

Courtney couldn't stop thinking about the opportunities that had slipped between his fingers like a trickle of water as he checked his baggage at Atlanta Hartsfield International Airport. Couldn't chase away the devastation of his two days in Hotlanta as he lounged in first class, thirty five thousand miles above land. Couldn't forget how small he'd come up during his workout and how unsettling the situation with Dana was as his plane landed at LaGuardia in New York. Atlanta had begun with so much promise, the workout with the Flames and a double scoop of chocolate named Dana. By the time he left the new black mecca for his return to the city that never sleeps, playing for the Flames seemed like a boyhood fantasy, and Dana wasn't looking anywhere near as good the morning after as she had the night before. The girl had serious issues to sort through, and Courtney knew he didn't have the stamina or desire to help anyone solve their problems; he had too many problems of his own.

The voice-mail message on his cell phone from his agent, "Talked to the Flames' general manager. Obviously, things didn't go well with the workout, but they still are interested in you," did nothing to soothe his anxieties. The text message on his cell phone from Dana, "Glad to have you in my life, CS. Love Dana," made his palms sweat. Chante, waiting for him on his mother's stoop as his car service pulled up to her brownstone in Brooklyn, was just another stroke of his dumb luck.

Courtney watched Chante from behind the safety of the limo's window tints. He shook his head and tossed a weak-hearted punch at the back of the seat in front of him. "Goddamn! This chick won't let me be."

Bass, the young driver—like Courtney, he was learning to talk when Reagan was shot—turned backwards with his arm up on the back of his seat. The two of them had bonded as brothers from different mothers during the drive from LaGuardia. Bass had immediately pulled a half-chewed straw from his shirt pocket and placed it in his mouth as well as turned on the radio to Hot 97 as they left the airport. Bass looked at Courtney now, smiling. "That your girl and seed? Baby mama drama?"

Courtney shook his head, his eyes refusing to budge from Chante and Destiny. "I used to mess with her. Not sure about the baby. Bitch is like glue, dawg."

"You didn't get one of them DNA joints done?"

"Nah," Courtney acknowledged, shaking his head.

Bass's voice rose, signaling how he'd come to get his nickname. "You betta handle that, son. That's the bible there, can keep her hands out your soon-to-be-phat pockets, or—and I hate to say it— can keep her in 'em for a minute. Regardless, though, you need to know for sure."

"She's against it," Courtney lied. "Wants no part of a DNA test."

Bass blew through his mouth. "Well, shit, that settles it, B. You all in then. She won't consent to a DNA that means she's trying to play the player."

"S'what I'm saying."

"Ass has too many hassles assigned to it," Bass philosophized, shaking his head. "I mean, I got drama myself and I'm just a silver caddy pusher. I can't imagine the problems you got, my man."

Bass's words drifted as Courtney sat in a trance. Chante waited on the stoop with the patience of a good kindergarten teacher, rocking Destiny by the handle of her umbrella stroller, her eyes on the vehicle she couldn't see inside of. Hope, and worse yet, determination, covered her face.

"I don't think she's leaving, Court," Bass offered. "Don't let this chick keep you hostage though, B."

"My moms is a trip, man," Courtney said as he rubbed his hands over his just-done corn rows and then over his sleep-deprived eyes. His senses returned with the gesture, Bass's voice back in his ears. "I know she knows Chante is out here. She set this up. I was wondering why she insisted on knowing when I'd be getting in."

"Damn," Bass offered, nodding his head to the music playing at a low level from the stereo. "Wussup? Your moms like this girl?"

"Something like that," Courtney acknowledged.

"Your moms know all about the situation, that the baby might not be yours?"

Courtney turned to Bass, defiance on his breath like cheap liquor. Instead of answering Bass's question, he said, "Unless this bitch can dunk a basketball for herself, she isn't getting any of my cheddar, dawg. Feel me?" Bass smiled and they clasped hands like friends who'd grown up together. "Let me get my bags so you can go do your thing, Bass."

Bass smiled. "In about twenty minutes, my brother, I'm gonna be working that back seat out crazy. Bonin' the shit out that shorty I told you about. You don't gotta be an NBA star when you got one of these. Yeah, baby, this here shiny cad-a-lack is my crossover dribble. The shorties love getting they shit twisted out on that plush cushioning back there. Word up."

Courtney nodded, forced a smile to cross his lips as he looked out the window again. "Just remember to wear a jimmy hat and you'll be aiight, Bass. Save yourself the baby mama drama."

Bass nodded. "Oh, mos definitely." He opened his driver side door and went to retrieve Courtney's bags. Courtney got out of the limo and they clasped hands again. Bass nodded towards the steps where Chante sat. "Good luck with that," he offered.

Courtney stood by the edge of the street as Bass left his trail of exhaust. He held a small suitcase in his left hand, his duffle bag draped over his right shoulder, neither item weighing him down as much as Chante and Destiny. Chante didn't move, continued rocking the stroller, her eyes on Courtney as she hummed softly. Courtney didn't move either, stood holding his bags, his eyes on Chante as he frowned with displeasure. As always, though, Courtney relented first, took a few slow steps toward her and stopped by the base of the steps.

"Your mom felt the best way to keep you from avoiding me would be to get directly in your way," Chante explained.

Courtney looked up at the front door of his house, smirked and nodded.

"Enough is enough," Chante said when she realized Courtney wasn't speaking.

"Meaning?"

"Meaning, I love your ass and I want you in my life, in our lives."

Courtney said, "Come on now, you know that isn't possible."

Chante removed the blanket from Destiny, turned the stroller toward Courtney's view. "Look at her! This is your baby, Courtney. See how she has her head tilted. Look at how she's holding her hands." They were his unique gestures.

"So . . . she does some things I do."

"She does all the things you do." Chante lowered her head, the strong resolve leaving her side for the first time. The tears she'd absolved not to let flow made up for lost time and wet her smooth cheeks. "I can't get you off me because she's a constant reminder, Courtney. I miss you and me so much. I want you to come to the Family Day Block Party, the first of July, with us. It's gonna be nice."

Courtney found a seat on the stoop, next to the stroller and looked off into the distance. "Didn't have to be this way," he mused. Then, before the memories flooded his judgment, he shifted gears. "I can't see myself doing no family outings with you and the baby, Chante. I met someone in Atlanta."

Destiny's umbrella stroller wheels came to a halting stop. "Met someone?" Chante asked.

Courtney turned to Chante. "Yeah. So you see there is no more me and you."

"You fucked this bitch, whoever she is?"

"Don't lower this to that, Chante. You of all people don't need to go there."

"Why? 'Cause I was tricked into having sex with Colin? You think I'm a slut don't you?"

Courtney sniffed a smirk. "How were you tricked, Chante? Colin hid his dick inside an Elmo doll and it jumped out and said 'peek-a-boo, I see you'?"

"No, Colin was hurting just like me. We didn't realize it was a game until it was too late."

Courtney got up to brush past her and walk into the house, but he couldn't end the conversation on this note. "Chante, you are a trip. What are you talking about? Game? What game?"

"Liza."

Courtney's eyes hunched. "What about Liza?"

"She was having problems with Colin. She told him that you two had been together."

"What?" The jolt of the news hit Courtney square in the chest. He regained his seat on the stoop.

"Colin came over to my place. He was drunk, crying, cursing. Talking about he was sick of you. Said, because you were taller and bound for fame didn't mean you had to shit on his life. I started drinking with him, started getting myself worked up. Stuff happened."

"What?"

"He's jealous of you, Courtney. He's insecure about even the things he does well and he hides within himself. You two are alike in that sense. Liza fed into it to hurt him. I got caught up in their little game."

"This is all bullshit," Courtney said, shaking his head.

"You think so?"

"So all it took for you to betray me, to throw away what we had was for my brother to come over with some cockamamy BS?"

"My emotions were all messed up, Courtney. I know I made a mistake. I had so much on my mind, so many things that were worrying me. All those girls around the way saying they'd been with you or wanted to get with you. Saying they'd do stuff with you that I wouldn't do."

"Haters," Courtney replied. "I told you that then. I told you it was about me and you."

"Sonya Raymond said—"

"I don't give a shit what Sonya Raymond said. You should have trusted me as much as I trusted you."

"It was hard."

"Yeah, well look what it got us."

"It wasn't just that stuff either, Courtney. It was a lot of stuff."

"Like what? We were going strong?"

"Like being nineteen and pregnant," Chante said. "Unmarried. Scared to tell my boyfriend because I worried it would mess up his dream to play in the NBA. You were away at college. This baby is yours, Courtney. I knew I was pregnant before Colin and I did what we did. I thought it would be easier on you if you didn't have to think about this, if you got to realize your dreams first. I knew you were so close . . . Well, now you've gone off to Atlanta and your dream is steps away. I'll be damned if some other bitch is coming in and taking what I'm entitled to."

"This is all too much," Courtney said, scratching at his scalp. "I can't believe any of this."

"Call and ask Liza. Talk to your brother."

"Can't do that," he told her.

"You don't want it to be true because of this new chick."

"That's ridiculous."

"So is me letting you get off easy," Chante said, determination back in her tone. "You're stuck with me, like it or not, Courtney. I'm no gold-digging bitch, but you've given me no choice in the matter."

"Which means?"

"I want to get a paternity test done so we can close this chapter and move on to a new one. I want my fair share. It isn't easy caring for this beautiful little girl we created. Why should I have to go at it alone?"

Courtney gave her his eyes, he could see in her held stare that her hands would most definitely be in his pockets soon. Bass had called it, and now it was happening.

As the vision of Dana flashed through his mind, he considered how much trouble his easily swayed heart had gotten him into.

The irony was, though a part of him despised both women, a part of him cared for them as well. Only question: who had the greater pull? Chante represented the familiar and old, Dana, the fresh and new. Should have been an easy decision, but as he looked at the baby that could be his daughter, or his niece, he knew the decision would never be easy.

Plus, that voice was still in his ears—a voice that made it Courtney's desire to keep Chante and Destiny as far from his life as possible.

Peace be still or yah seed and dutty gurl be next, seen?

Black's haunting voice.

14

June 3

The record shop was absent of its usual scent of Phillies Blunt cigar smoke. Instead, the air held the scent of an over-eager burst of floral air freshener. The dilapidated sound system played an old Mahalia Jackson record instead of the usual blues standard. By one of the side walls, milk crates stuffed with records sat neatly, making it easier for customers to mill around. The sturdy shopping bins made of good, strong wood were marked with scuffs and scratches from years of wear, but, the bins had an eye-catching sparkle, courtesy of furniture polish. The gate that led behind the cash register had recently been repaired and no longer hung from its hinge. The frayed, possibly purple curtain that led to the back office had been replaced by a without-a-doubt dark blue curtain with no frays.

The sun kissed the front of the building and gleamed off the new sign with the fancy computer fonts that hung in the store-front window. The trees from outside cast shadows inside that etched the walls. Shadows that eased from one corner of the wall to the next as the day progressed.

Bing, bing, bing, bing, bing.

Colin slowly strolled in, looking around with a wide view, admiring the changes.

"There he is," a voice greeted him. It was Deacon Rainier from Lena's church. The deacon had a bounce to his step that Colin never remembered seeing before. The deacon's wife had died years ago and every time Colin saw the deacon it seemed as if she'd died maybe the day before.

"Deacon, nice to see you again," Colin said as he extended his hand. He looked over the deacon's shoulder in search of his mother. "Where's my mother at?"

The deacon turned back, smiling. "Lena, she's in the back there. Go on back, I was headed up the street to fetch us a couple cups of Joe; you want anything?"

"No, no. I'm fine, thanks," Colin answered.

The deacon patted him on the shoulder, still smiling that Cheshire-Cat grin. "Good to see you again, Colin."

Colin made his way to the back office. Lena was busy looking through a pile of ledgers and didn't look up when Colin moved through the curtain. Colin stood for a moment and then cleared his throat. Lena looked up and simply nodded.

"I bumped into Deacon Rainier on my way in," Colin offered.

Lena sat back in her chair and turned facing Colin. "Yes, Herbert was kind enough to come help me out this week."

"Herbert?"

"That's his name."

Colin let her comment slide. "So how's Uncle Carl taking this forced vacation? Has he been calling you here every ten minutes?"

Lena shook her head. "No, I think Nana is keeping him plenty busy."

Colin found a seat on the radiator across from the desk, looked around the back office at the organized clutter. When he turned back to his mother's gaze, the intensity in her eyes threw him. "What's wrong Mama?"

Lena held her gaze, held her intensity. "Wondering how things could be the way they are is all."

Colin knitted his brows. "Things? What things?"

"With you and Courtney," she said as she finally broke the gaze and looked at the pile of ledgers in front of her. Colin had her more upset than Carl's poor bookkeeping.

"People grow apart sometimes," Colin offered. "I've got my family, my writing. It's only natural we wouldn't be as close as we were, even if he didn't have this unreasonable problem with me."

Lena's intense glare returned. "You've got your family, huh?

And Courtney has an unreasonable problem with you, nothing that you've caused?"

"That's correct," Colin lied. He could feel unspoken tension between them, could feel his mother probing.

"I spoke with Liza yesterday," Lena said.

Colin tried not to appear too eager. He smiled gingerly. "Did you? How was she doing? I've been so bogged down with this tour I didn't get a chance to speak with her yesterday."

"She put up a good front," Lena answered. "Same as you're doing now. Tried to act as if everything was going good, but I could tell the contrary. She slipped up enough times—with little trivial things—enough for me to know that you two ain't to-gether. Not because of no tour either."

Colin sat back against the wall, blew out an air of frustration and looked down to avoid his mother's glare. "How long you two been separated?" Lena asked.

There was no use in lying to his mother. "Thirteen days, Mama," he answered without looking up. He said it with so much sadness it caught Lena off guard. She could feel her heart fluttering, clap-ping like wings against the inside of her blouse. This was no longer the Colin who had disappointed her, had made an anger boil inside that she didn't know could heat up against him. This was her baby boy, that shoulder she'd leaned on when Prime was no longer strong enough to hold up himself, much less a wife and kids.

"When were you planning on telling me?"

Colin shook his head. "I was thinking the week after never."

"How long you two been having problems?"

Colin guessed the unasked intent of the question. *Why would you two have a baby and then do this?* "Since before she got preg-nant. The stress of the baby made it worse I guess."

"Y'all getting divorced?"

Colin moved from the radiator, moved to a far corner of the small office with his back to his mother. "She says that's what she wants, but we haven't settled anything yet. Haven't filed any pa-pers or anything."

"Y'all make sure you think this thing through. Do what's best for my grandbaby. You two ain't kids so don't go acting like chil-dren behind this, you hear?"

"Yes, of course, Mama."

Lena's voice had softened as she talked of Colin's marital problems. The intensity of her eyes had drifted far from the room, but now as she prepared to move on to another thought, the intensity returned and her voice hardened again. "One other thing, Colin," she said in a scolding tone. "You also need to take responsibility for the horrible harm you did your brother."

"Never did him any harm."

"Don't lie to me boy."

"Mama, I—"

"I know about the thing with Chante so don't go playing dumb."

Colin's eyes widened.

"Terrible," his mother said, "just terrible."

Colin moved back to the radiator and took his seat before his equilibrium left him. He could feel her eyes burning a hole in his scalp, could feel the disappointment that ran through her by the way she breathed—slow, steady, each single breath calculated with more precision than the angles in an architect's blueprints. His life of late had been a mix of emotions—all bad—anger, pain, hurt, frustration, disenchantment, bitterness. Nothing, though, could equal the embarrassment and hurt he felt for disappointing his mother. This was it. He officially had nothing left in this world.

Lena noticed the slump of Colin's shoulders. That his neck muscles all of sudden slackened. "I hope you've already asked God for forgiveness," she told her son. "If you haven't, you need to drop to your knees and do it now. But you also need to ask Courtney for forgiveness. You need to try and fix this horrible mess. I'm trying not to judge you on all this . . ."

Back at the brownstone in Brooklyn, Courtney and Uncle Carl were huddled in the hall outside Nana's room fretting over Courtney's romantic entanglements. Uncle Carl was propped in the worn recliner chair he'd had Courtney drag from the living room to outside Nana's door. Uncle Carl looked official, as if he were an FBI agent standing guard over the president of the United States, as he sat in the sagging cushioned chair outside Nana's bedroom door. Courtney was seated on the floor, with his back supported by the paneled wall.

Courtney was more animated than usual, talking with his hands, his voice full of bass and anguish. "Tamika, she was a diversion during the school year, Uncle. She isn't in the picture far as I'm concerned."

"A wild-oats thang?" Uncle Carl noted as if he knew a thing or two about sewing oats.

"Yeah, something like that," Courtney admitted. The admission sent a twinge of shame through him that made it impossible for him to look at his Uncle. He studied the peeling mat of linoleum flooring that ran along the floorboard instead. Tamika was a good girl, had given him plenty of good times to remember, and here he was discrediting her. He wished his heart could embrace her like it did Chante and Dana. Things would be so much easier if that were the case.

"And the young gal, Chante, wants to get a test done to prove you fathered her child?"

"Yup."

"I don't know, young snapper," Uncle Carl said as he shook his head with a wistful look in his eyes. "Your Aunt Myrtle and I never had these problems. Fussing and fighting, deceiving each other. You young folks sure know how to make a mess of things. I'll give it to you, matters of the heart ain't ever easy, but you young folks make it so much harder than it need be." He noticed the preachy tone of his voice, and that hadn't been his intention, so he cleared his throat and spoke from a quieter spot in his diaphragm. "And tell me about this other girl, again. One you met down in Georgia."

Courtney's face took on a look of extra concentration. "Dana. She's a beautiful woman, Unc. Talented—she can sing like a bird. But she's got all kinds of family issues, all kinds of problems with commitment and dependency. She'll tell you straight out that she's a clingy chick when she loves someone. I'm not sure I can deal with all the drama a relationship with her would involve. If you could take away all the different issues surrounding her life she'd be my dream woman, though."

Uncle Carl scratched at the rough patch of hair growing on the underside of his chin. "I remember you saying the same thing about that Chante at one time."

Courtney nodded. Chante had always been special to him, had always held a piece of his heart he didn't think anyone could reach. The betrayal from her still burned like a newly lit match. If he could get past that hurt, if he could truly believe the things she now professed, he knew he could spend the rest of his life with her. "Yeah, that's most definitely true, Unc." He paused with the same wistful look on his face that his Uncle had when he thought of his Myrtle. He had to literally shake himself free from the chains of desire that still bound his heart and mind to Chante. "Again, though, if you could take away the drama, she'd be perfect."

Uncle Carl chewed up his lips as if he had a mouth full of tobacco to spit. He turned his head back against the headrest of the chair and continued scratching at the patch of hair beneath his chin, his eyes closed as he thought all this through. "Your Aunt Myrtle couldn't make a meatloaf to save her soul," Carl began, "but she cooked one every Wednesday for as long as we were married. Her body temperature would change from hot to cold at least four times throughout the night, and she'd wake me up every time to go and reset the thermostat. Yes suh." *Hay, hay, hay.* He coughed. "Oh, and one time she tossed records I had stashed away in the basement because she didn't thank they were any good. First editions—would be worth a mint if I still had them."

"All those faults and you still managed to stay together," Courtney said.

Uncle Carl jutted out a finger as if to say *bingo*. The quick movement sent a wrenching pain through his shoulder, but he wouldn't let the pain overshadow his point. "That's it, young snapper. All those faults and we still managed to stay together. You gotta figure out which one of these ladies—with their many faults—you'd cherish like the Good Lord's fresh air. And believe me, you got faults of your own that they gotta deal with. Ain't no such thang as perfect, young snapper. Cain't be worrying so much about the stuff that you cain't take away from these gals. You gots to concentrate on the things they got going for 'em that you would never take away—the things about them you cain't live without. Whichever one of those gals has the most you cain't live without—that's the one you belong with."

"Hogwash!" Nana's scratchy voice called out from the bedroom. Courtney and Uncle Carl both raised their heads in attention. Courtney moved to his feet and helped Uncle Carl to his. They both went in Nana's room smiling.

"What was that you said, Nana?" Courtney asked.

"Hogwash! S'what I said. Carl, you cover your ears on this one baby, I don't wanna dis'lusion you none. Courtney,"—she directed him to come closer and lean down—" 'chever one of your women friends make your toes curl when you lovin' 'em, that's the one you choose. That'll make it a whole lot easier to swallow nasty meatloaf. You hear me?"

Courtney wrapped his arm around his Nana, shaking his head and smiling; it was all he could do.

The voices came at Colin all at once from every angle of the large bookstore. He couldn't seem to find where one ended and the next began.

*What'sthethemeofthenovel?Howlongdidittakeyoutowrite?Wereyoupleased withthereviewyoureceivedinthe*NewYorkTimes*?Whatareyouworkingon next?Howdidyougetpublished?Who'syouragent?Whatadvicedoyouhavefor aspiringauthors?Whatwouldyoubedoingifyouweren'tanovelist?*

Colin's head burst from the jolt of a tension migraine. The migraines were getting to be commonplace during the course of each day. The smell of freshly printed books wafted from the table in front of him, from the pile of novels at his fingertips, up into his nostrils. When he'd first started his writing career, at his first book signing, the scent had been welcome like a hug from a loved one, but now, it choked him a bit and left a tickle in his throat that he couldn't clear away. Colin reached for the cup of cold water the manager had given him. The cubes of ice had melted in the water and the coolness of the glass tricked him into thinking the water was still cold. It wasn't; it was lukewarm at best. Nothing had been right since his mother's scolding earlier. Seeing her so disappointed, seeing the tears in her eyes at the end nearly broke him. Having her tell him to leave had in fact broken him.

Colin let the warm water settle in his throat and then looked up at the small audience with a smile. He could do this. A thought crossed his mind. "Okay . . . I don't read my work once it's in book format, but I would love to read to you faithful few a passage or two from the novel. How does that sound?" The faithful few clapped and expressed their enthusiasm. Good, Colin thought, at least now the only voice I have to concern myself with will be my own.

"This is from the chapter 'Sweet Dreams are Made of This,'" Colin informed his audience. He placed the book flat on the table, leaned in on his elbows, and began reading.

The whistling didn't get Jeremiah's attention. Nor the white silhouette that danced across his room. And neither did the scratching noises that sounded as if a cat was playing patty-cake baker's man on his bedroom windowsill. The tingling of his skin woke him from his solid sleep. He'd had his eyes closed, but could still feel all the strange goings-on happening right around him. In sleep, he heard the ghosts, saw them even, as he lay unable to wake fully, on his bed. Then the sheets shocked him and made his skin bubble like a bottle of shaken ginger ale. His attention peaked, and he opened his eyes with an accompanying yawn and stretch.

He woke up sweaty, just like in the movies. He had a giant urge to scream, but the air was so dense he was afraid he'd choke to death if he opened his mouth and allowed any of it inside his lungs. The first thing he noticed in the darkness was his desk lamp—his night-light—burned out. He'd just changed the bulb a few days before and, at best, the bulb had burned maybe three hours. Jeremiah pushed aside the aggressive sheets that clung to his damp skin and walked across the room with his arms outstretched as a guide. He touched the bulb, planning on twisting it free from the threads and putting in a replacement, but the heat scorched his fingers and made him jump back. He looked over the top of his desk and found a crumple of paper towels. He wrapped the towels around his fingers as a cushion to loosen the hot bulb. The bulb, however, wouldn't budge from its base. He pressed a bit harder and the bulb cracked into pieces, splattering glass fragments all over his desk. "Great!" he called out.

Colin paused, smiled at a couple in the front row that hung on his every word. He was pleased that they didn't realize how his head ached, heart raced, and that his ears rang. He went back to his book, continued to read, and started to mumble incoherently.

A murmur went through the audience.

Colin loosened the top button of his shirt, massaged his temples, returned to this passage.

Colin looked up at the faces in the crowd. "Who changed this book?" He turned and gestured toward the store manager. She looked over her shoulder warily, then toward the audience, before taking small steps in Colin's direction.

"What's the problem, Mr. Sheffield?" she asked, bent at the waist and whispering into Colin's ear.

"Somebody changed this book," Colin said. "I want another copy."

"Mr. Sheffield, that's the copy you brought with you. You've had it by your side the entire evening." She lowered her voice another notch. "The audience, Mr. Sheffield, they're waiting."

"I don't give a shit about this audience. I want to know who thinks this shit is funny, changing books on me like this."

"I assure you, no one is playing a trick on you."

Colin stood, sweat glistening on his forehead, and with one long sweep of his arm knocked the entire stack of books on the table before him on the floor. The audience gasped. "You going to take me serious now? Are you going to get me the right fucking book?"

The manager took a couple hard steps backward, and once she'd made distance between them, turned and ran off.

Colin turned and faced the audience, all of them wide-eyed, mouths hanging open. He announced to them, "I'm not taking anymore bullshit."

The manager returned, a police officer flanking her. Colin looked down at his hands. They shook violently. The officer approached him with measured steps. Colin took a step backward, tripped over his chair, and fell to the floor. The officer rushed his approach, leaned down, pinned Colin to the ground.

Colin gasped for air, leaned against the officer, said, in the softest of voices. "Take me away from here. Please, take me away from here."

15

June 5

The image of little Destiny in the stroller, head tilted, holding her hands like him, endured in Courtney's mind. Was Dana's angelic voice, the sexy way she moved, the hypnotic smile—was it enough to push aside the deeper feelings he had for Destiny, for Chante? Could he believe Chante? Could he truly embrace the joy of fatherhood? What if he did only to helplessly tumble back to earth once the tests confirmed little Destiny's parentage? Could he ever recover if the DNA ruled in Colin's favor? Even if the child proved to be his and he gave it another go with Chante, could he ever get his mind to forget—*Oh baby, yes. Touch me, baby. Push harder, baby.* The sounds of a woman tricked into sleeping with her boyfriend's brother? He touched his still sore ribs, rubbed his fingers over the cocoa-butter-lessened scars on his hands, thought back on another sleepless night. No, the mind never forgets.

The messages he'd been receiving the past few days from Dana endured in his mind as well. Was the history between him and Chante—that time she fell at Coney Island and scraped her knee and he carried her on his back, the way she always buried her face in his chest when she laughed—was it enough to push aside the new memories he was sure Dana would bring to his life? Damn those messages, the joy in Dana's voice, the singsong buoyancy of her tone. She sounded surprised herself by the positive vibe of each and every syllable of each and every word and was openly celebrating, dragging out the most insignificant thought, making it significant, discovering language as an infant does. How long had it been since happiness clutched her? Did he have the spirit to defuse that happiness, send it back into exile?

He rubbed his hands through his cornrows and thought about Tamika. The easiest of his many decisions, the throw away, and even she had left her mark. How many times had she caressed his scalp with those bony fingers? How many times had she then moved to his shoulders and eased the stress from his life? How many times had she made him smile, laugh, feel loved? September to May wouldn't have been manageable if not for Tamika.

And how had he dealt with it all? For the past two days, he'd ignored Dana's messages on his cell phone. He shook his head and waved his hand every time the phone rang at his mother's and his mother or Uncle Carl looked his way. He knew it was Chante without them having to say so. He never gave Tamika his mother's number in the first place. Purpose was his ally, now, as he sat listening to the phone ringing, waiting for the other end to pick up.

"Hello? Sheffield residence."

He cleared his throat. "Liza."

"Courtney?"

"Yes." He could hear a baby crying in the background. The niece he'd yet to see. The daughter he'd heard his mother painfully telling Nana and Uncle Carl the other day that Colin didn't get to see either. "That Lyric I hear?"

"Yup," Liza said. Her tone was suddenly clipped.

Courtney picked up on the chill in her voice. His mother, Chante, Liza . . . when would the woman's burden be lessened? "How are things going?" was the only thing he could think to say.

"I'm not about to sign a million-dollar NBA contract," she offered, warming, "but I'm managing. Congratulations!"

"Thanks."

"Colin's on tour, right?" he probed.

"Oh, yeah, he sure is. I haven't had a chance to speak with him yet today—he doesn't call in until around noon, but—"

"My mother knows you two aren't together," Courtney said, saving her.

Liza sighed. The baby's cries grew louder. "I figured she might. Has she spoken with Colin?"

"I overheard her talking to my Uncle and Nana. She didn't tell me personally. I think she did speak with Colin. What happened?"

Liza laughed. There was no joy in her laugh. She sounded like Chante, sounded like his mother at times, sounded nothing like Dana did in the messages she'd been leaving him. "I happened. He happened. We happened."

"You guys seemed like a perfect match."

"Yeah, we did seem."

Courtney didn't know how to ask her. Come right out and ask? Beat around the bush and hope she said something, admitted to something she'd had many chances to admit to but never had? *Oh, yeah, by the way, I told Colin once that you and I had slept together to get him upset.* He closed his eyes and tapped the receiver against the side of his face. Opened his eyes and scanned the walls. They offered no answers, provided no wisdom. "Liza, may I ask you something?"

"Of course," Liza said.

"Did you tell Colin once that you and I had slept together?"

The line was quiet for a moment, then Liza's horrible laugh again, even less joyful in this encore. "Remember his friend, Gregory?" she asked.

Courtney furrowed his brows. "Yeah, they stopped talking. Why?"

"Told Colin I slept with Gregory, his other friend Jonesy," she admitted. "He blew me off both times. Said I was bugging. Then I decided to tell him I did something with you."

Courtney couldn't contain his shock. "Why? I don't get it. Why would you do that?"

"He knew I would never do anything with those guys. I could barely stand him being friends with them. We were having problems. 'Emotional warfare' is the best way of describing what we were going through. He was having problems coping with his own doubts. I was having problems thinking I was worthy of love. He couldn't deal with me. When I told him about you, he just knew it was true. It was like his greatest nightmare come true, and since we'd gotten to be so brutal to each other, he was sure I would take it to that level. God, I'll never forget that day. He was in so much pain. I've never seen him like that. I let him wallow in it. It made me feel good, now as I remember."

"I never heard of anything like that," Courtney managed to say.

"Be lucky you've never been through it," Liza said. "We're suffering now because of all that foolishness. Two fractured souls trying to piece together our pieces and make one whole. Remember that time you called and said I should watch out for Colin, that he wasn't what he appeared to be?"

Courtney cringed. Yeah, he remembered. He'd had to drink a pint of E&J to get up the nerve to call her. He wasn't sure what he'd said, just knew it was fueled by the betrayal from Colin and Chante. "Yeah, I remember."

"I've been thinking about that a lot lately. I know what you were trying to tell me. I'm sorry about Chante."

"Colin told you?"

"In a roundabout way, yes," she said. "I'm sorry. I feel responsible."

Courtney sat, silent.

Liza broke the silence. "It's funny, because I wasn't what you thought I was, either. I'm still not what I need to be, but I'm trying to be, trying to learn how to love myself."

"Sad."

"No," Liza said as the baby crying in the background continued. The crying came closer as if she was standing over the bassinet now. "Sad is all the lives we've damaged by our foolishness." Liza had begun to cry herself, but then stopped and regained an impressive calm. "Look, I've got to go, but . . . You should try to talk with Colin if you get a chance. He's been alone for a long time and too ashamed to ask anyone for help. I'm sorry I couldn't be there for him. I am. Give your family my regards."

"Take care, Liza."

"Yup."

She hung up.

So, Chante had been telling the truth, Courtney thought as he placed the phone back in the cradle. He sat there in the bedroom he'd shared with Colin and remembered. The big oak dresser turned at the odd angle in that odd corner of the room because they'd been fooling around and busted a hole through the plaster wall. They'd spent a sweaty hour turning it to cover the gaping hole. The little electric beard clippers that Colin had used back in the day to form the three cuts in his eyebrows like Big Daddy Kane were still on the dresser, rusty blade and all. He wondered if Colin's copy of *Manchild in the Promised Land* still hid in that shoebox in the closet, tucked neatly under the baseball cards in the box. He laughed aloud as he reflected on the fight that had provoked him to hide the book from Colin—because Colin wouldn't let him watch the Dukes of Hazzard in the bedroom. He remembered Colin taking his hand, when Prime ran off for the last time, and telling him, "Don't worry, we can still play basketball."

So much wasted time they could never recover.

Angelo Hayes and Henry Marshall congregated around the small coffee table in Angelo's office. Henry busied himself pretending to read over an article in *New Yorker* magazine. Angelo had his full concentration on the latch of his platinum bracelet, his forehead lined with determination as he examined the workings of the latch. Neither man spoke or acknowledged the deafening silence of the room, the dread the quiet stirred in the pit of their stomachs. When the office door finally opened and June, the receptionist, ushered Colin in, Angelo looked up for a brief moment and then lowered his head, mind on that latch again. Henry tried not to stare, not to appear too sympathetic, too worried, but he couldn't take his eyes off Colin, couldn't keep the smile of pity from crossing his lips.

Colin looked normal enough, a smile on his face as he came to Angelo. Angelo placed his bracelet in a side pocket and stood to greet Colin. Henry slowly rose as well. Colin knew the calling of this meeting couldn't possibly mean anything positive—the three of them after all had never shared the same room at the same time—but he was steadfast in his conviction to remain upbeat. Too many dark moments had gulfed him lately. This, he was determined, wouldn't be another one. "You, young dog," Colin said to his editor, "what fat cheeks you ha' got."

"Excuse me," Angelo said, puzzled, as he looked from Colin to Henry for support.

"Dickens, *Great Expectations*," Colin offered. "Come on now, that's one of your favorites. I looked it up before I came over, memorized it and everything."

Angelo nodded, smiled like a deadbeat dad before a female judge. "Right, Dickens."

"You're not impressed?"

"About as much as Faye Hopkins was when Sean Riggins stepped to her at the Pimp's Cup Lounge," Angelo responded.

Colin furrowed his brow. "Say what?"

Angelo shook his head dismissively. "This new book I'm editing. *Don't Hate The Player, Hate the Game.* It's consuming me now."

Colin crinkled his nose. "Doesn't sound like an Angelo Hayes type of novel to me. What made you pick that up?"

Angelo held his eyes on Colin. "Profits, Colin. I'm looking for profits."

Those words made Colin's collar feel as if it were pressing into his neck. He moved to Henry, patted his back, decided to try his luck with Henry, and see if he were still an ally. "Hey there, partner. Long time no see. How've you been?"

"Good," Henry said.

"What about Dylan and Katie?" Colin poked at Henry's ribs. "And your ex-wife, how are they?"

"They're all doing fine," was Henry's rushed reply.

"Good." Colin sat in one of the chairs circled around the coffee table. Henry and Angelo were slow to follow suit, but eventually they both sat as well.

Angelo broke the awkward silence that had taken over the room. "How are you feeling, Colin?"

Colin leaned back in the chair, his face pleasant enough, his posture overly relaxed. "Me? I'm feeling fine. Thanks for asking."

"Been getting enough rest?" Angelo pressed.

Colin looked to Henry. "Yeah, plenty," he said, smiling. "Someone—and the guilty party shall remain nameless—cut my book tour back." Colin rocked in his seat, moving to a rhythm that Angelo and Henry apparently didn't hear. Both men sat so rigid Colin could feel his determination to keep the situation light, wavering. He looked away from them both and surveyed the office instead, searching around to see if Angelo had any promotional material for Langston's upcoming book lying around. He didn't see anything.

Henry rose from his seat and went to the window for a view of that fabulous New York skyline. Colin's eyes trailed his agent, honed in on his slow walk to the window. He took in the maroon flannel shirt, the stocky shoulders, and the perfectly coifed graying hair. "Are you losing weight, Henry? You're not as broad through the shoulders as last time I saw you."

"I've actually put on a few pounds," Henry confided as he continued peering out the window. He'd hoped the distance would allow him to speak more freely with Colin, open up the floor to the matter at hand, but he couldn't muster the nerve.

"Really . . . ? I would have never known."

Angelo scooted his chair closer to Colin and put a hand on Colin's shoulder. Colin looked at the hand—upset by the invasion of his personal space at first—then to Angelo, and smiled. "Look," Angelo said in a voice more tender than Colin had ever remembered hearing. "Henry and I called you here today because of what happened the other day. We're concerned about your well-being—"

"I'm fine," Colin said, cutting into Angelo's words.

"And we want an explanation, an understanding as to what happened to you the other day and what is going on with you." The sternness that edged Angelo's voice made it clear that he cared for Colin, but business was business.

Colin shrugged his shoulder from Angelo's grip. Henry moved from the window and made his way back to the seat next to Colin. A grave look of worry captured his face as he waited with Angelo for an explanation. Colin looked from one man to the other. "I told you I'm fine, Angelo, Henry. I got a bit confused the other day . . . maybe it was the heat . . . it was awful hot and humid that day. I'm fine, though. One-time incident, never happen again."

Angelo shook his head, unconvinced. "The store manager said you were extremely agitated, that you weren't coherent. She said you started ranting and raving, using profanity. They had to call the police. Had to have you ushered out of the store. If you hadn't calmed by the time the officer arrived, you would have been arrested or something. Colin, there were kids in that bookstore."

"I don't care what she said, Angelo. I acknowledge that I was experiencing some kind of problem. You don't have to go into all the details. I get it."

Angelo placed his hand on Colin's shoulder again with a bit more pressure than the first time, making it evident that he didn't expect the contact between his hand and Colin's shoulder to be broken, until he broke it. "Been in this business for a minute now, Colin," Angelo said, "and until the other day, I've never had any complaints about any of my authors. As painful as the situation must have been, as painful as whatever caused it must be, I can't let you come in here downplaying it, expecting me to casually let it slide." He released his hand and sat back in his seat with his hands crossed in his lap. "Now, you had some kind of psychiatric episode the other day, and if you can't give me a full explanation as to what it was and what caused it, as well as some assurance that it won't happen again . . ." He leaned forward so Colin could see the seriousness in his eyes up close. "Then you leave me no choice but to end our business relationship, effective immediately."

Colin remained defiant. He slanted his head to the side, turned his brows up. "Are you threatening me, Angelo?"

"I'm informing you of the gravity of this situation," Angelo countered. "I'll leave it up to you to assess whether you're threatened by what I've said."

"Colin," Henry chimed in, "You have to understand that this is an atypical situation. As Angelo stated, I've never had an experience that mirrors this either. Make no mistake about it; our most important concern is with your welfare. But, we all have professional reputations to protect as well. If you can't offer us more explanation than you're giving, then I'm afraid I'm with Angelo. I wouldn't feel comfortable continuing our business relationship."

Colin shook his head, stood, and paced the room. "This is bullshit. You mother—" He pounded his right hand into his open left hand, tightened his jaw and took a breath to settle himself. "You guys bring me up in here for this tag-team, gang-up shit."

"I hope you don't feel ganged up on," Angelo soothingly said from his seat. He kept moving his chair angle on the roller wheels to keep contact with Colin's pacing. "Colin, I hope you don't feel this as a gang-up because that truly is neither one of our intentions."

"Blow it out your ass," Colin fumed. "You've been trying to break me, trying to destroy me for as long as I've known you. And, Henry, don't think I don't know how you've been sabotaging my career. Both of you have. You don't want me. You want non-talents like Langston Campbell. You're not ready for what I have to offer. You can't deal with my talent. You're both freaking bozos."

Henry stood and cut off Colin's manic pacing. He gripped Colin by both shoulders and forced him to look him in the eyes. "You can't believe all this," he said. "Just from a selfish viewpoint it wouldn't make sense for either of us to *want* you to fail."

"Sure."

Angelo spoke. "It's now obvious—" But Henry cut him off, gesturing with his hand. "Colin," Henry said, "We've got to get you help. This isn't you."

Colin fought it for a fleeting moment, flailing like a plane with damaged wings. But then the energy seeped from him and he slumped into his agent's arms. "God, Henry, everything is so messed up. What's happening to me? What's happening to me?"

16

June 8

Courtney washed his face in the bathroom sink, rubbed the water into the corners of his eyes and scratched his scalp with the ferociousness of a dog with fleas. He took a breather from the intense scratching and supported himself with a hand on each side of the sink basin, stood staring at his reflection in the mirror. He tried to make his trembling body sit still, but it rebelled. His dream, moments before, had placed him back in Star's basement, catching Black's vicious and unwarranted punishment. Then, he'd walked down a hallway, leaning at an odd angle as he moved because of his beaten body, and walked in on Chante and Colin. In the dream, he fell at that point like a pair of tossed work boots and whimpered like a child. In real life, now, he felt like doing the same. Instead, he decided to bravely give sleep another try and, if that didn't work, he'd watch television until his eyes burned.

He found his cell phone vibrating for a missed message when he emerged from the bathroom. He picked it up and retrieved the text message.

What's going on, CS? Call me. Love Dana.

This situation needed to be dealt with, he had to settle it once and for all. He picked up the hotel phone and dialed her number. His heart raced once the phone rang, but he refused to cower from this. For once he had to take the lead, use his strength as an offensive weapon instead of as a defense.

"Hello?" A sweet voice he wanted to stamp away sung in his ear.

"Dana."

"Courtney? Hey baby, what happened to you? This NBA draft thing has you so busy. I've been trying to get in touch with you. I've been calling and—Hey, your area code came up 770, are you in Georgia?"

Courtney grimaced, cursed the modern technology that made it impossible for him to move quietly from Dana's life. He couldn't escape her any easier than he could escape the nightmares. "Yeah, I had to fly down and meet with my agent. He has a place down here. We've got to go over things before the draft."

"Really!" Her voice had the heft and jittery feel that excitement brings—no doubt from fantasies of the time they'd share together.

"Yeah."

"I hope you'll be around long enough for us to finally hit Club Fuel. How long you here for? And please don't tell me it's another three-day quickie like last time."

Courtney hesitated to answer. "About a week," he said.

Dana in all her joy didn't pick up the hitch in Courtney's voice, didn't sense the low-key tone that peppered his words. "That's wonderful, baby! This trip we can spend time together."

"I'm not gonna be able to see you," Courtney said.

"What?" Disappointment clung to her words like cobwebs in a basement. "Why not?"

Courtney shifted the phone to his right ear, sat back in his chair and casually placed his big, sneakered foot on the flowery hotel bedspread. "Just can't."

"Just can't?"

"Nope, don't have the time, or the desire."

The line was quiet for a moment as she took it all in. Then, the words gushed from her, "Courtney, what kind of shit are you trying to pull? I call you in New York and all you talk about is you can't wait to hook up again, can't wait to get down here. I've practically bankrupted myself buying calling cards so I could keep up with your ass. I was worried sick when I couldn't reach you this past week. And, it's like you sneak into town, and now you're saying you don't have any *desire* to see me. Is this a game to you?"

Courtney sighed. The nightmares were still in his head, but, unlike with most people, his nightmares at one time had been a reality. Was Dana headed to playing a prime role in his nocturnal haunts? "Look, Dana, I like you a lot but you've got a few things you need to figure out first. It's as if you're looking to me to be your savior. I can't chase away all the wrong that has happened in your life. You got my wedding finger itching. I know you've picked out rings already, the way you talk. I don't think I want any of this. We need to chill before we take this thing too far."

Even over the phone line her smirk was as clear to the ear as a picture to the eye. "Before we take this too far? Are you sick?" She stopped, sighed, gathering steam. "It's too late for that shit, Courtney. *Before we take this too far.* I gave myself to you, Courtney. You weren't concerned about taking this too far then."

Courtney laughed a laugh filled with disbelief. "Gave yourself to me? You buggin', girl. I'm sure plenty dudes ran up in your shit. Don't be acting like you hooked me up with the new Jordans or something. Bitches kill me, I swear."

"What did you say?" Dana's shrill tone touched his inner ear drum through the fiber optics.

"Look, Dana, we did our thing and it was cool. I was considering a relationship or something with you, but I've reconsidered. I hope you can accept that."

"You . . . son . . . of . . . a . . . bitch!"

"That mean no?"

"Fuck you!"

"Eloquent, aren't we?"

"Fuck you, Courtney!"

In the sweetest tone he could muster, Courtney said, "I'm hanging up now, okay?"

"You're making a huge mistake, Courtney."

"Already made it," he corrected her. "Now I'm trying to stop from repeating it again. Buh-bye now."

Courtney gently placed the phone receiver in the cradle and hopped on the bed, turned over on the too-firm mattress and laid his head on the pillows that were no thicker than a pack of construction paper. His thoughts were of the abstract variety. *If you opened the top of a jar that held a trapped bee, the bee might fly away. Or it might fly out and sting you.* He liked Dana, but was petrified of getting stung again. No, he couldn't open up the opportunity for her to sink her stinger in him; his flesh and soul was already too black and blue from pokes and prods.

The phone rang.

"Chello," he answered, full of sarcasm and annoyance. He knew it was Dana, and was looking to push her buttons further. Let her know he had no intention of getting stung.

Nothing but dead air met his attempt.

He hung up and, before he could turn over, it rang again.

"Dana, leave it alone. Stop calling, aiight?"

There was a light sniffle in the background, the faint sound like raindrops tapping a metal garbage lid as you listened through a thick glass window. Courtney waited a heartbeat for her to speak. When she didn't, he hung up. Moments later, it rang again.

"You want me to call the cops, Dana? Do you want to get jammed up in unnecessary shit because of this? Go sing your songs; get rich and famous; you'll find plenty of dudes to give the booty to, trust me."

"You're not worthy of me," Dana said, between sniffles. "Whoever made your heart so cold . . . I hope they got you good, you punk bitch."

"Calling me names now, Dana," Courtney mocked her. "Come, come now, you're better than that."

"Rot in hell!"

"You're sinking fast, sistergurl. Don't let yourself drown. Not over me. You said it yourself, 'I'm not worthy of you.' "

"Why are you acting like this?"

"Change of heart, that's all."

"You a faggot or something?"

Courtney laughed. "Nah, nah, don't try that one. I don't want you, Dana. Handle that."

There was a silence, long enough for Courtney to start to hang up, but Dana's voice froze him at the last second. "Your mother didn't love you or something?"

That caught his attention. "What did you say, ho?"

"Oh," Dana sniffled a laugh, mockery now in her tone as well. "That's it, huh? I hit the nail on the head."

"Eff you, I'm hanging up." There was a tremble to Courtney's voice that he hoped she didn't pick up on.

Dana went for the kill, grasping for something to wound him, wounding her own self during the journey as she became more and more the classic woman scorned. "You dog women out because your mammy didn't breastfeed you long enough, that it? You mad because you still want your mammy's tit in your mouth?"

"You're sick, girl."

"Am I? Maybe so, but it's because of punk-ass niggas like you. I hate you."

Courtney forced a laugh out that hurt his chest as it came from his mouth. "You gave me the ass a day after meeting me, and now you're vexed because I'm treating you like the ho you are—that's wild. And hate? Ten minutes ago, you were ready to come suck me off if I'd given you the okay. Now you hate me. Get a grip, sistergurl." His words halted her like a brick to the forehead. "Wussup, Dana? You mighty quiet all of a sudden?"

She was crying again but she dug deep for a reservoir of dignity, determined to set Courtney straight and chase away the depression dogging her trail at the same time. "I slept with you because I thought you could be special."

"Right, that was it."

She ignored him, kept talking. "When we talked, I saw someone holding as much pain inside as I do. You didn't tell me about anything you'd been through in particular. I just . . . I can sense pain. Could see it in your eyes, how you carried yourself, the things you didn't say, spoke volumes about what you must have been through in life. I can relate to that. Hurt is a great silencer."

Courtney stayed quiet on his end.

Dana took in a breath that seemed to start with the sunrise and looked as if it wouldn't release until the sunset. "I also thought I saw a gentleness and compassion in you that most men don't have, a capacity to love hard and deep. Again, I could relate, because when I love, I love deep. I can tell now that I was right about the pain I thought I saw in you, which is the only explanation for the way you're treating me now, lashing out."

"I'm not," was all Courtney could offer.

"I wish I'd been right about the gentleness and the compassion, too—ditto for loving hard and deep. Can't believe you're as cold as this, not to me. I haven't done anything during this short while I've known you except prepare myself for loving hard and deep again, something I swore I'd never ever do. God, I'm so stupid!"

Shame found Courtney, closed him in like a room with four

walls, no windows, no doors. He'd taken this thing farther than it needed to go. He'd hurt her, bad, and that wasn't a natural impulse for him. That was how he'd imagined Colin to be. It saddened him to realize that he'd become the person he thought he despised. Calling women bitches as readily as he blinked his eyes. "Dana, I—"

"Wish you the best, Courtney Sheffield," she cut him off. "And I truly hope the pain and hurt ends for you." Her voice softened, barely above a whisper. "I wouldn't wish pain on my worst enemy. Knock 'em dead in the NBA."

"Dana."

It was too late. The line clicked. Courtney hung up the phone and tried to dial her back immediately, but the busy signal greeted him instead of a ring. Busy signal stone-walled the apology on his tongue and in his heart.

"Damn!" he muttered as he held the phone to his cheek and searched the ceiling for solace.

The parking lot had a fair share of cars for a weekday, but Colin was able to find a spot close enough to Mama Brashear's Jaguar and Liza's car. He positioned his vehicle so he could see them but they couldn't see him when they exited through the back entrance. He turned off his engine and sat waiting, picking his teeth with one of his ragged fingernails. The interior of the car reeked from the bags of half-eaten fast food that he'd been too lazy to discard. A pile of cassettes and CDs littered the passenger's side floor, strewn so carelessly it would take Johnnie Cochran to convince anyone that Colin worshipped his music collection. Colin worked a piece of the KFC's fried chicken that had served as his lunch from between his teeth and spit it out. It landed on his dashboard and he plucked it away. Removing that pesky piece of chicken meat had been his greatest accomplishment of the day thus far.

It wasn't long before Liza emerged from the back door of the store. Colin's posture tensed, he reached to his side and gripped the black, plastic bag with the tie string knotted so tightly that the bag would have to be ripped open to get at the contents. He watched his wife with longing, rage, desire, and contempt, a hodgepodge of feelings. Her hair was up in a tight bun, she wasn't wearing makeup—not even lipstick—and she was dressed down in a velour gray-colored sweat suit that looked too hot for the June day, though the sun was barely shining and there was the nip of a breeze in the air. He missed her more than words could express, missed her as this day missed the sun.

Mama Brashear waltzed out casually behind Liza, pushing Lyric in the stroller, balancing it on its two hind wheels to climb the two or three steps. Colin watched his baby girl, wondered if she was still colicky, if the baby acne that dotted her cheeks had cleared up. No man—no father—should be subjected to this. The urge to grab up his family and drive off with his tires screeching coursed through him. Hadn't he read a scene like that in one of Langston's books? He released his grip on the black plastic bag, considered tossing it in the backseat and doing just that, kidnapping his family and dashing off to wherever it was kidnappers went.

Liza swung her two large Bon Ton shopping bags like a carefree teenager, smiling and stopping every few feet to turn back and gaze at her mother and daughter. Mama Brashear was moving at a diva's pace, pointing out insignificant parts of the landscape to Lyric. Colin clutched his steering wheel now, jealousy on his bones like skin as he spied his daughter being pushed by someone else, his wife happier than he'd ever remembered. At the least, he should have been the fourth member of this little sickening family outing.

He cracked his door and stuck his leg outside as they approached. Mama Brashear's Jaguar was directly across from where he parked, Liza's car next to it. He hoped that Mama Brashear would get in her car first and drive off as Liza loaded the stroller in the trunk of her own car, but he knew the chances of that were slim. He'd have to confront them all. He gripped the black plastic bag again in anticipation.

Liza came to her car, unlocked the doors and tossed her bags on the front seat. The smile that had yet to leave her face was so inviting. It had been so long since he'd seen that smile; he'd forgotten how manipulative it was, the power it held. He desperately wanted to take Liza by the shoulders, face her to himself and cover that smile with his lips. Feel the give of her mouth and the warmth of her tongue.

Mama Brashear stood behind the stroller as Liza detached the carrier car seat from the stroller and placed it in the base inside the car, facing the rear. The simple maneuver rose up a new anger in Colin as he realized he didn't know how to collapse the stroller, didn't know all the intricacies of taking his daughter out into the world. Colin bit into his lip as he remembered the dreams he'd had while Liza was pregnant, the good dreams that had him and his child at Barnes & Noble or Border's, moving down the Fiction & Literature aisle, stopping at the last-name-that-starts-with-an-*S* authors. His jaws tensed and he cursed his wife, mesmerizing smile withstanding, and his poisonous mother-in-law for depriving him of his fatherly rights.

Liza bent over and was showing Mama Brashear—who obviously wasn't interested—which lever on the stroller did what. Then she lifted the collapsed stroller and placed it in the back of the car, closed the back door hatch and rubbed both hands together as if she'd been playing with Lyric in a sandbox and needed to get the granules of sand off her hands. It was at that point that she turned her head and her eyes met Colin. Twenty feet separated them, but Liza's face took such a stricken look that Mama Brashear turned as well, and she, too, adopted the stricken look. Mother and daughter stood paused in fear like a pair of wounded and trapped animals.

Colin looked down and quietly got out of his car, moved toward them without offering any eye contact. Liza and Mama Brashear moved behind the open rear door of Liza's car, glad for the barrier.

"Liza," Colin said as he came upon them. "Mama Brashear."

"What are you doing here, Colin?" Mama Brashear asked. "You a stalker now, too?"

Liza eased her mother behind her before Colin could react. She stepped from behind the door, against her mother's objections, and moved closer to Colin. "Watch the baby, Mama. Colin, you want to go sit and talk?" Her voice had a tremble, but her demeanor, especially her proud chin, stayed steadfast in its calm and confidence.

"Can I see Lyric first? Give her a kiss?" Colin held up the black plastic bag. "Give her this outfit I bought?"

Liza shook her head, reached forward and took the bag from Colin without any trouble. Mama Brashear said a defiant "that's right" that Colin wanted to chase away with a knee to her belly.

"Please, Liza." He held up one finger. "One second, one kiss."

Again, Liza shook her head. "It's too soon. You want to talk in your truck for a minute, let's do it now, otherwise I'm leaving."

"That's right, Liza," Mama Brashear said again.

Liza turned to her mother and shook her head. Mama Brashear watched her for a moment, in a stare-down with her lips pursed in displeasure, and then she nodded and looked away to settle the bitter words hanging on her tongue.

"So, Colin," Liza said, once the business with her mother finished. "You want to have that talk, yes or no?"

Colin tried to grab a glimpse of Lyric through the back windshield of the car, but couldn't. His shoulders slumped and he looked at Liza, looked at Mama Brashear. "Okay," he said in a voice filled with so much sorrow even Mama Brashear took note, and shifted uncomfortably.

"I'm right here if you need me," Mama Brashear told Liza as she moved from behind the door.

Liza said, "Mama, stop, okay?"

Mama Brashear put her hand to her mouth, smiled sheepishly. "Sorry."

Colin had already gotten into the truck and closed his door. Liza moved inside and sat next to him, left her door ajar.

"What's up with this?" she asked, her nose pinched up.

Colin looked around the interior, evidently didn't see what she saw or smell what she smelled. "What do you mean?"

Liza shook her head. "Nothing. Why are you here, Colin?"

"Wanted to see you, see the baby. I stopped by the house. Saw both of your cars were gone. I was praying you and your mother still did your Tuesday shopping, that you two still liked the the Bon Ton." He smiled as he looked at Liza's car, so far away now. "I guess if worse comes to worse I could find work as a PI."

Liza avoided any lighthearted banter. "You shouldn't have come here like this, Colin. Frankly I'm feeling skeezed out by you being here."

She had her eyes on him as he continued staring at her car.

"You don't have to fear me, Liza."

"You look terrible, Colin."

"How so?"

"When's the last time you shaved?"

"Couple days ago."

"Showered?"

"Couple days ago."

Liza sighed. "Make both a priority. Maybe then you won't look so crazed."

"Why won't you let me see my daughter?"

"Like I said, Colin, you're in no shape to see her and it's too soon."

"You're my judge?"

"And jury."

"Dangerous game you're playing, Liza."

"Not a game," she said. "I spoke with Henry. I know about your little episode."

"Wasn't anything," Colin reasoned. "Henry had no business calling you on that."

"Actually, I called him," Liza said. "Wanted to see how you were doing. He's worried about you, Colin. I am, too, despite everything."

Colin turned and looked at her for the first time since they'd gotten in the truck, gave staring at her car a rest. "You called him?"

"Yes."

Tears crossed his mind, but he was able to hold them back. He felt so emotionally unbalanced, had been having fits of crying and laughter for a while. The littlest thing could send him off in either direction. He knew he had to keep this under wraps, though, or he'd never get to see Lyric. "Thanks for your concern," he said, grateful.

Liza nodded. "Henry said they stopped your tour and that your career is in jeopardy. Have you been writing?"

Colin forced a smile. "All I have left is me and the words. If they leave me then I'd just—" He noticed the sudden interest in Liza's eyes and rerouted. This conversation was like an audition and he was on pins and needles trying to say and do the right things. "Yeah, I've been writing. What about you? Sketching?"

"Like my life depended on it," she said. "A friend of mine has been getting me contacts. I might start selling my sketches and paintings to a children's book publisher for covers and illustrations."

Colin wanted to know whom she knew with publishing contacts, but he refrained from asking. He figured he wouldn't get any sleep, stuck wondering, but that was the boat he had to row, for Lyric. He tapped his fingers against the steering column. "How's motherhood treating you?"

Liza sighed. "Even on the days Mama is able to help me, it's the toughest job in the world."

"That rough, huh?"

Now Liza looked toward her car. "Yup. Mama's been a blessing, though. She convinced me to bring Lyric out today, though it's short of her two months."

Colin reached over and touched her leg. Happiness found him when she didn't retreat from his touch. "Let me back in your life, Liza. Can't we give it another shot? Please?"

His words were the prompt his touch hadn't been. Liza moved from him like the tease of a breeze on a hot, muggy day. Without saying a word, she got out of the car as Colin sat cemented in place. She eased the door shut and leaned down in the window so he could see her, so she could say her parting words. "Shave and take that shower, Colin."

"And then what?" he asked, staring at her car again, too angry to give his eyes to her. At least there were a few things he still had control over when it came to the two of them.

"Then we'll discuss you coming by to see Lyric."

She moved to her car and dismissed her mother's barrage of questions with a tired upraised hand. Colin watched her, noticed for the first time she appeared aged, years rapidly piling on her as she attempted to raise their child alone.

Mama Brashear stared toward Colin and turned without responding when he offered her a fake smile and wave. Mama Brashear got in her vehicle, Liza got in hers, and soon they'd driven off and left Colin to himself.

After a moment, he attempted to place his keys in the ignition but dropped them somewhere between the seats. The clumsiness brought about a fit of painful laughter and then a flood of tears.

17

June 26 and 27

The NBA commissioner stepped to the podium as the crowd at Madison Square Garden buzzed with excitement. The commissioner had an odd patch of white-gray, off center of the crown of his head, and a fondness of placing his reading glasses up on his forehead, despite admonishments from his long-time wife. He was a shade over five feet eight inches, had never played the game, but had a shrewdness about him that helped him carve the NBA into a global brand. He'd met with all the invited rookies—the projected Top 15 picks—before the draft and offered up his philosophies. Well-tailored suits in neutral, dark colors were a plus. Baggier suits the color of any fruit except blueberries weren't. Humble recognition of past coaches and influences was fine. Shout-outs to the homies back in the hood, weren't. Not once did the commissioner mention the actual game of basketball in his short speech to the rookies. Marketing and image were the names of the game, he made it perfectly clear to them, and malcontents, prima donnas, and public relations headaches would be excised quick fast and in a hurry. Courtney's stomach, which was already unsettled by his nerves, was doing backflips and handstands after the commissioner finished speaking.

"With the first pick in the 2002 NBA Draft," the commissioner said into the microphone as the crowd quieted enough to hear, "Charlotte selects Wang Yulong from the Beijing Barracudas of the China Basketball Association. The clock is reset to five minutes with Minnesota set to pick next." The commissioner smiled and moved from the microphone and the crowd buzzed once again.

"How come they didn't call your name?" Lena leaned over and whispered into Courtney's ear. She'd been receiving a crash course in the NBA draft from Courtney.

"Atlanta doesn't pick until fifth," Courtney informed his mother, happy she'd consented to come and was by his side.

Lena squinted, looked off into the arena. "Are my eyes . . . Are those people over there blue and orange?"

Courtney looked up into the rafters of the Garden. A row of fans had a large banner with his name on it. "They're city fans," he told his mother. "City colors are blue and orange so they painted themselves to show what big fans they are."

Lena looked in their direction again, focused closer. "Painted? Why?"

"More than just a game," Courtney said. He enjoyed bringing his mother up to speed on the bigness of this night, the importance of this event.

"And these painted people are fans of yours," she said. "Wonderful."

Courtney smiled.

The commissioner returned to the stage and waited a brief moment, a sheet of paper in his hand, a smile on his face as the noise level in the Garden reached its crescendo. He stepped forward like a game-show contestant and leaned into the microphone. "With the second pick, Minnesota selects John Mather from Duke University. Orlando selects next."

When Orlando's turn to pick arrived they selected the seven-foot kid from Wake Forrest University. Denver selected Ed Bridges from Georgetown. The clock was set for five minutes. Atlanta had the next pick.

Lena moved forward in her seat. "You're up next, right? Fifth pick you said. That's next right?"

Courtney looked at his mother as a couple of the other players in the room watched him with smiles of anticipation. "Hopefully," he gulped out in response to his mother's latest question. "As far as we know, Atlanta's taking me."

"You mean it's not certain?" his mother asked, baffled. "Many times as you flew down to Atlanta?"

"Nope," he said.

"I thought it was certain," she repeated.

"Nothing is certain in this life," Courtney told her. "Nothing but heartache, that's certain."

"You're too young to be thinking that way," Lena said.

Courtney shook his head. "I'm glad you're here with me, Ma. Really am. But I got to wonder why you never loved me the way you love Colin." He needed an answer before this great moment that approached. Before his dreams for the future met with realization, he needed to know why so many dreams of the past had met with disappointment.

"Do love you," Lena offered.

"The way you love Colin," Courtney countered.

"Just different," she said. She smiled easily. "Colin could say the same thing about your father. Jeremiah tolerated Colin, but he adored you. You two shared that basketball greatness thing, I guess. Colin played, but you and your father, you *played*. You barely paid me any mind until the day your daddy left. And when he did, you acted as if you hated me, blamed me, I guess. You remember trying to hit me, you were so angry?"

Courtney didn't know how to respond. He did remember lashing out at his mother, angry with her that his father had more desire to raise hell than raise his sons.

"But," Lena continued, "we made it from that place." She looked around at the packed arena before turning her focus back to Courtney. "I worry about you more than I do Colin, but that's because you wear your emotions on your sleeve and he holds it in. You're different people, Courtney, and so I love you differently. Don't love either one of you more than the other, just different. I guess I've been so worried about you being the second coming of Prime, I didn't see what you were."

"Which is?" Courtney dared to ask. He didn't want to interrupt his mother, the warm feelings she'd raised in him, but he had to know what he was in her eyes.

She smiled and said, "My future NBA superstar son. My baby boy, all grown up, doing well. Not perfect, but well."

Courtney smiled. Lena reached forward and touched his

hand. She said, "I'm glad an old lady put aside her fears and came to share this moment with her son."

Courtney was about to say something, but the commissioner returned to the podium, a minute shy of the five-minute allotment that the teams had to decide on their pick. Courtney's heart raced as his dream moment grew closer to reality. There were ten players, besides him, left in the sequestered area. Velvet rope and dark curtains separated them from the five thousand fans in attendance. There were tables set up for each player, his family, professional teams of consultants, agents, and the like. Courtney reached forward and took a sip of his cola, gripped his mother's hand tighter for comfort. Lena looked anxious, too, which surprised Courtney. Courtney's agent and college coach were standing by the foot of the stage. It was Courtney and his mother at their table. Courtney considered the empty seats at his table. Five spots in all—enough seats for Chante, Destiny and Colin. Regret found him as he considered the empty spots. He wondered if they were home watching this on TBS. Chante in her cramped apartment bouncing Destiny on her knee with her fingers crossed, superstitious as she was. Colin, alone in a hotel, a tray with a cold hamburger and French fries nearby, food he was too nervous to touch, though his stomach growled from hunger. Courtney continued to hold to his mother's hand as the commissioner played the crowd. Regardless of the muck of the past year, this moment wasn't Courtney's alone. Those chairs were empty, yes, but they had names attached to them.

"With the fifth pick, the Atlanta Flames select . . . Barry Jeremy from the University of North Carolina. Seattle picks next."

Courtney released his hold on his mother's hand. He could hear her speaking, but couldn't make out her words. He looked to the area where his college coach and agent were standing. Coach had an indescribable look on his face; his agent had popped open the flip of his cell phone and was barking at someone, his hand on his hip, his jacket tail flapping as if he was outside running laps around the Garden. Courtney imagined Chante now, her knee still, mouth agape, fingers still crossed. He pictured Colin, too, talking loudly to the television and then smashing his hand down on the small hotel dinette set, squashing that burger, getting ketchup all over his sleeve, saying "shit" as he jumped up and dabbed at the red on his cuff.

* * *

The parking situation hadn't changed any—too many cars, too few spots. The condo maintenance fee still appeared to be put to good use—the recycle bin wasn't over-cluttered with trash, the lawn had recently been cut, and none of the look-alike housing screamed for paint, or replacement shingles, or any kind of cosmetic touch-up whatsoever. The sun pushed down an orange glare that gave off an eerie feeling, an apocalyptic type of vibe, but the hoodooy feel of the day wasn't bringing Colin down. He smiled at the waving leaves on the maple trees planted symmetrically across the freshly cut lawn. Breezy, that's precisely how he was feeling when he woke up this morning, showered, shaved, and changed into a fresh pair of underclothes. After that day at the Bon Ton, he was sure he'd never experience this moment.

One end of the morning newspaper was leaning against the door of the Sheffield Condo, the other end touching the slight step-up that the condo association folks called a porch. Colin looked at the paper, curiously, wondering if the paperboy had tossed it and it landed that way, or if he'd carefully set it that way. Colin bent and picked up the paper, placed it under his arm, and rang his doorbell. He felt this urge to whistle and tap his foot while he waited for Liza to answer, but, he wasn't much of a whistler, and foot tapping was too out of character for him. So, he stood, newspaper tucked like a football under his arm, waiting for the door to open. A car alarm went off and took Colin's concentration for a brief moment, and when he turned back Liza was standing in the doorway. She yawned as if she'd just woken, stretched, and blinked her eyes a few times. Colin nodded, smiled, and pulled on the screen door. It didn't budge. Liza observed him for a moment, straining her eyes to see him as she'd done that day at the Bon Ton, and then unlocked the latch. She looked unprepared for his visit, though she'd called him. Colin pulled on the door again and stepped in as she turned and made her way up the foyer without giving him the greeting he'd been hoping for on the car ride over here. He closed the screen door, shut the big door, and turned the lock and deadbolt. He walked into his home for the first time in close to a month, observing the hallway as if the walls held expensive paintings.

Liza plopped down on the couch and stretched again. "I brought in the paper," Colin said to her as he moved into the living room area. He fought to give her his attention, but his thoughts and eyes kept drifting down the hall, to that room of pinks and biblical animals climbing to the portal of their love boat. "Tired?"

Liza ran her hands through her hair at first, then down her face. "All the time," she replied.

Colin sat on the arm of the couch, looked around the living room, then toward the baby's room again. "I'm going to go check on the baby."

"No, no . . . she just got to sleep."

"I won't wake her." He rose and stood over Liza, as if her permission counted, though he was prepared to look in on his daughter regardless of what Liza said. It had been too many minutes, too many days, weeks, tears, since he'd seen his precious daughter. He could barely stand the thought of letting another moment lapse. The specialist he'd been seeing, to talk over his problems, had suggested as such. Henry had used her when he went through his own divorce. The agent had called Colin and implored him to do the same. Reluctantly, Colin had gone. It was the best thing he'd done for himself in recent memory.

The specialist, Dr. Samuelson, was warm, professional, and, most importantly, wise.

She felt the chord of discontent in Colin's life wasn't with the publishing industry, wasn't with his brother, wasn't with his wife— it was with his daughter, fatherhood issues. "I have a feeling," the pleasant-enough psychiatrist had told him, "by the inflection in your voice when you speak of your child, that if you're able to resolve that one issue, the other issues will become clearer as well." How could Colin disagree?

All the memories of the past, though, came crashing down on him. He thought of the pressure, pressure he'd put on himself.

His mother . . . Colin had tried so desperately to be more than a son to her. He had tried to fill in that gaping hole that consumed her those first few years after Prime took a knife in the back from another woman's husband. Prime had called her from a payphone outside a clinic over on Fulson Street. Colin had picked up the phone at the same time as his mother and held on, unbeknownst to his parents, when he heard his father's gravy-thick voice. The sounds of accelerating engines in the background made Prime's heavy voice all the more appreciable.

"Lena, I'm in a bit of trouble," his father had said. Lena had said nothing in return, so he went on. "Went and got myself stabbed."

"By who?" Lena wanted to know.

"Street stuff, don't be worrying about the whos of it all."

"Why, then?"

Prime coughed, cleared the mucous from his chest. "Don't be worrying about the whys either."

"Do with some woman?"

"I said don't be questioning me, bitch."

Colin had then quietly placed the phone in the receiver, old enough to know this was one of those grown-folks conversations his Nana warned him about. He went in his mother's bedroom later—it was all hers from that point on—and found her laying in bed, curled up in the fetal position, with the phone dangling off the side of the dresser by its coiled chord. He knew then that his life wouldn't be the same again. And, it hadn't. But he'd done a good job. Her depression was short-lived. She understood that her two boys were the most important things in her life, especially her oldest, who always was "making a fuss over her."

Then there was Courtney: Colin tried to mold and shape Courtney, to lead him down the correct path. After all, Courtney was his father's son, was Prime's only love in the world besides basketball. It was a shock to Courtney's system to look up one day and find Prime gone.

Funny, but Colin never felt like he needed a father himself. But he thought Courtney would suffer without one. Uncle Carl and the rest of the family allowed Colin's influence to be Courtney's main influence. They thought it was great that a big brother would take so much interest in his younger brother. Plus, Courtney had always looked up to Colin so. Colin had willingly doled out his love and earned the admiration and respect of family in the process. It wasn't until Courtney came into his own, receiving recognition because of his basketball skill and innate charisma, that the resentment formed in Colin. He'd created Courtney in his own image, and here the image was poised to surpass everything the original was, and ever would be. That hurt. Colin knew it shouldn't, but it did.

So, at the height of Courtney's popularity outside the house, Colin ran. Ran before the college recruiters started beating down Courtney's door and making the mailbox overflow.

He fell in love with Liza, and before they could build the solid foundation that would serve them well in the years to come, they married. More pressure. He was a published novelist shortly after the union, and so the success or failure of his books meant the success or failure of his family. The one thing he did learn from his father was that a man took care of his family. He learned that lesson in reverse, unfortunately, as he watched his mother struggle on housekeeper wages to support her two boys. Nana had pitched in back then, as well, before her body made her be still like peace, and Uncle Carl had been a surrogate father in many ways. Colin was smart enough to know that wasn't the natural order of things; the man, the father, the husband, those were his responsibilities. When a man shirked those responsibilities, as Prime had done, those left to carry his weight would forever have their lives altered. Colin never wanted to end up like Prime, stripped of his dignity. Never wanted to beg his wife for permission to see his child. But here he was. Still, though, if that kind Dr. Samuelson was correct, this moment could be his moment of reawakening.

Now, away from those thoughts of the past, Colin looked to Liza. "I want to see if she still looks like an angel when she sleeps, Liza." A pained expression crossed his face, darted across like a rabbit on a busy road. Behind the pain was his stony proclamation, "I'm taking care of her today, so if she wakes, she wakes."

"I don't want her waking this early; she cries nonstop when she's awake," Liza snapped. She looked at the unbending expression on Colin's face as he stood over her. "Quick," she offered after a moment. "Please, though . . . try and not to wake her."

Colin's unblinking eyes settled into a blink again, a smile showed. "Thanks," he said.

He moved through the living room toward his daughter's room. Somehow, the house wasn't right to him. He looked at the coffee table as he rounded it, looked at the tables on each side of the couch, looked at the phone stand. He looked at the wall by the entrance to the kitchen. That was it! Liza had taken down all their pictures. Even the picture they'd blown up of the three of them in the hospital during those first few days of Lyric's life. Colin frowned and shook his head. *The lengths we go through to forget the things that cause us the most pain only makes the pain worse.* The place was so bare Liza had to think about it as she moved around the house. How was taking down those pictures making her pain any less?

Lyric was fast asleep on her back, still sucking and puckering her lips, though her pacifier had fallen out of her mouth. Her little chest rose in rhythm and her arms were raised next to her head with her little hands fisted. She was the most wonderful sight in the entire world, so cute and full of innocence, as he'd remembered her, only bigger, a little lady now. Seeing her made Colin aware of his own heartbeat and breathing patterns. All of a sudden, he felt as if he would hyperventilate, as if his heart would burst through his chest and the oxygen in the air would be wasted on him. He gripped the crib sides and forced a deep breath, steadied himself. *I refuse to burden you with an absent daddy. I'm going to make this right.*

He turned from the crib and headed from the room. By the doorway entrance, he noticed the finished sketch of Noah's Ark. He stopped and admired the artistry of the charcoal-black drawing, turned his lips up in an appreciative smile and tapped the picture with his middle three fingers as he left the room.

"You didn't wake her, did you?" Liza wanted to know as Colin reappeared in the living room. She had dozed off that quickly and didn't appear cognizant of how much time had lapsed.

"I told you I wouldn't."

"You've told me many things, made all kinds of promises down through these years that you didn't keep," Liza barked.

Colin moved past the bait. He didn't want to fight with Liza any longer. It was pointless. "I appreciate you calling, Liza." He looked toward the baby's room again. "I'm looking forward to today. Where did you say you had to go again?"

"I didn't say," Liza said. She rose from the couch, stretched and yawned again. Was it possible for one person to be so devoid of energy, to be tired all the time? "I'm going to go take my shower and get ready. If the baby stirs, make sure she has her binky and rock her gently by her shoulder, right there in the crib. Try not to let her wake up until her first feeding, around eleven."

"Binky?" Colin asked.

"Nipple . . . pacifier . . . whatever you want to call it." Liza waved her hand dismissively.

Colin nodded and cleared his throat. He looked to the clock to see how much time before the grand hour of eleven—not even an hour. He could manage that. The angst of a teenager was in his voice as his eyes returned to Liza. "It is good to see the baby, to see you. You look good, too. I didn't realize how much I'd missed admiring you."

"Yeah," Liza said.

"I've stopped having the nightmares. Did you know that? It's like that Babyface song, 'Every Time I Close My Eyes.' Liza, every-time I close my eyes, now, all I see is you and Lyric." As soon as he'd said those words he regretted them. He'd told himself that he had to take this slowly and here he was moving at warp speed before he'd warmed the couch cushions. Last thing he wanted was to upset Liza and have her banish him again. He'd been in the doldrums thinking this moment would never come. If he got a peek back into their lives and then found himself dismissed again, well . . . even Dr. Samuelson's kind, easy voice couldn't get him back in off the ledge. And, the thought of bringing lawyers into this made his stomach churn. Liza paid the comments no mind, though, kept on her way to the shower. Colin grimaced as she disappeared around the corner, tapped a fist against his fore-head, and settled back in his seat on the couch to make a call. *Take it slow.*

He dialed and waited. His mother picked up, absent of the cheer he'd come to expect. "Hey," he said. Maybe he could inject her with the cheer he felt inside; he had plenty to share. "How did it go last night?"

"Not too good," his mother replied. "He didn't get picked by the team he thought was taking him."

"What!" Colin shifted, pressed the phone closer to his ear and mouth. He hadn't expected to hear this. The media had been touting Courtney as a sure thing pick for Atlanta. "Did he go higher or lower? Who picked him?"

"He was picked eighteenth," Lena said.

Colin fell back into the give of the couch. "Eighteenth, that's unbelievable. There aren't seventeen better players in the coun-try than Courtney. Who picked him?"

"By . . . shucks, I forget the team. He's gotta go way out to California."

"California! Not Los Angeles," Colin said.

"No. I know about them, they got that smart coach and that big, big boy."

"Let me see." Colin tapped his temples. "California teams. There's Sacramento? Golden State?"

"That's it . . . Golden State."

"Golden State," Colin informed her. His voice eased down like a cooling engine. "Oakland."

"Yes, Golden State."

"How's he taking it?"

"I don't know. Being picked at all is a blessing, he said. That ol' agent of his wasn't too happy, though. He said something about falling in the draft cost Courtney millions of dollars. I don't get any of it. Not as if I knew what was going on. I didn't know a bit more what was happening when that Atlanta team didn't pick him. I still don't know what this falling in the draft stuff means, and his agent tried to explain it all to me. Was telling me something about Courtney had a poor workout, should have worked out for more teams. Should have done the pre-draft camps—I just nodded my head and smiled."

"Sucks," was all Colin could add.

"I think he's gonna want to talk to you, soon," Lena said. "He mentioned you afterwards. He was kind of in shock, I guess, was just thinking aloud. He said something about you and Chante should have been there and that he was foolish."

"Did he?" Colin said. The possibility made him a bit emotional, as sitting on his own couch again, in his own home, did. "I hope so. I've been thinking about things. Things I need to say to him, things I need to try to explain. I'm going to reach out to him, though, regardless. But he . . . he mentioned me?"

"Sure did. I do hope you two can get beyond this mess; life is too short."

Lena's words sparked Colin. "Guess where I'm at?" Before his mother could venture a guess, he told her. "Back at our house. Liza called me and asked if I wanted to see Lyric. She has something to do today, so I'm going to get to play daddy. I think this might be the start of something good. I'm not saying reconciliation, but . . . well, I'm hopeful for a lot of things."

"That's wonderful, Colin," Lena said, the joy in her voice matching the joy in Colin's. Again, he'd managed to pick his Mama up. "I hope you and Liza work out, too. Lord knows I pray for you young folks so much."

Colin thought about his recent psychotic episodes and contemplated letting his mother know how much the recent turmoil affected him. He almost told her about Dr. Samuelson, and then decided not to. "Listen, I hear Liza coming. I'll talk with you later."

"Tell Liza hello and kiss my grandbaby for me. Maybe if I'm lucky I'll get to see her before she starts walking."

"Soon, Mama, I promise. Love you."

"Love you, too, Colin."

Liza walked in as Colin hung up. She had a large towel wrapped around her body and was rubbing her drippy hair with a smaller towel. The shower looked as if it had done her serious good. She appeared so much more alert and vibrant. "Who were you talking with?"

Colin shook his head, but answered, "My mother. I wanted to know how the draft went for Courtney."

Liza continued scrubbing her hair, took a seat on the arm of the couch as Colin had done before. "Oh, yeah . . . Courtney fell in the draft. Atlanta snubbed him. I heard about it on the news last night. The baby kept me up late."

"I'm the last to find out everything," Colin said.

Liza pursed her lips, prepared to say something, and then decided on another topic altogether. "I wrote out a list of things you have to do for the baby. I put it in there. It's on the kitchen counter. Follow everything according to the note." She bent down to make sure their eyes met. "Make sure you read it, Colin, okay?"

"Ok. Your cell phone battery charged in case I need to get in touch with you?"

"I had it turned off." Liza then bent over and shook her hair out, the curls cascaded down like a waterfall.

"Turned it off," Colin said, amazed. "I thought you couldn't stand life without a cell phone."

She stopped, still bent, and looked up at him. "Times change, okay?" He'd irritated her. "I'm going to go up, put my clothes on, and get ready. The bottles are in the fridge . . . in the kitchen."

Colin reached forward and touched her wrist. She didn't flinch and her eyes set upon him, waiting for his words. He smiled at her, a closed-mouth smile, full of love and appreciation. "Thanks for giving me this chance."

She patted his hand, returned his smile, and left to get ready.

When she got to the foot of the stairway, she turned to him. "Despite everything," she said, "We'll always be in each other's corner. Always look for the best in each other, and let Lyric know it, not poison her against each other. At least I hope that's the case."

Colin smiled her way. "Of course, Liza," he offered.

The words reassured her, brought a sense of comfort to her. "You should start warming the bottle now." She nodded, appreciatively, and climbed the stairs.

The taste of being passed over still sat, bitter, in Courtney's mouth after he'd gargled with Listerine until he gagged. He'd showered until the old plumbing starting crying out in agony, the pipes making noises deep in the walls. His mother's apartment was dark now, his mother in her room, Nana in hers with the television still on, Courtney alone to his thoughts at the kitchen table. He nursed a can of warm ginger ale, too frustrated to bother with a glass and ice. Uncle Carl would have turned his nose up at the soda, asked him why he was drinking "that warm piss." Apparently, each tragedy in life had its own drink: a buddy dying . . . a half can of beer, the second portion of the bottle poured out in their memory; girlfriend cheating . . . a pint of E&J would come as close to numbing the pangs of insecurity and outrage as humanly possible; getting snubbed in the NBA draft . . . warm piss/ginger ale hit the spot.

In front of Courtney, on the table, he had yesterday morning's newspaper, opened to the sports pages. One of the columnists had forecasted the draft and presented his opinions on how it would go down. At number five, the columnist had Atlanta picking Courtney. This guy might as well have been a television weatherman—having folks scurrying for their umbrellas when they could have been unpacking their beach chairs. Off to the side of the picks, though, the columnist had a thin margin of extra information, "the skinny," on each player. By Courtney Sheffield it read: "Stock could slide because of poor workout and failure to participate in any pre-draft camps."

Courtney studied the words like a crib sheet for an exam. He took another swig of the ginger ale, letting it settle in his mouth for a brief moment before he swallowed. He looked like a broken husband at some local bar, shirttail out, tie knotted but loosened, bent in dismay, wife at home eating a meal-for-one without a care if her husband walked through the door or not.

Courtney's thoughts moved to Dana. He could imagine her in Georgia walking around her room singing that Mary J. Blige song from the *Waiting to Exhale* soundtrack. A grin crossed his face; he tapped the spread-eagled newspaper with his soda can.

"One good thing," he said aloud. "I don't have to worry about bumping into Dana's ass and getting stabbed with a screwdriver or some shit."

He took one last gulp of the ginger ale, turned and shot the can toward the sink. It landed on the counter beyond the sink basin, not close to his intended target. Courtney smirked, sighed, and looked down at the flattened newspaper as if it were a road map or building blueprints. He glanced one last time at the draft projections, glanced at his name forecasted by the columnist as the number-five selection.

"So-called expert," he said, disgusted.

He gathered the pages of the paper in a mound at the center of the table and started crumpling them together. He stopped midway through and craned his ear. The phone was ringing. He rose from the table and grabbed the phone hanging on the wall.

"Hello?"

"Hey . . . I thought you weren't there I was about to hang up."

Courtney cradled the phone to his ear and cleared space on the nearby counter so he could sit. "I was doing something, didn't hear it ringing. I'm glad you caught me." He cleared his throat. "You saw the draft?"

"Yup."

"Did you curse the Flames for devaluing my sperm? That is if—"

Chante cut him off. "Courtney, you know it's not about—"

He returned the favor. "I know, I know. I'm sorry . . . being stupid."

"I want you to be successful and happy because that's what you want," she said, starting to boil. "It's not about me. Now, you may think I'm low-down trash because of the mistake I made, but I'm not."

"I know, Chante. I know."

"Don't get it twisted, then." She tried to sound extremely agitated, but her voice flowed with concern and disappointment.

Atlanta hadn't only toppled Courtney, they'd toppled her as well. It had taken her last evening and most of this day to get up the strength to call Courtney. The phone call to Courtney carried the same weight of dread as a call to a relative to inform them that a beloved member of the family had passed.

"No, I'm not getting it twisted, not anymore," Courtney said. "I spoke with Liza."

Chante made an interested noise. "Care to apologize to me?"

"You got that," was Courtney's version of an apology.

"No, though," Chante admitted, "what I did was still wrong. I let all that nonsense make me question the belief I'd built in you."

"You know what I was remembering tonight?"

"What's that?"

"Summer before my last year of high school, how you would get up early and go with me to the park or the rec center and rebound while I shot free throws. You were always telling me to bend my knees more. I shot free throws better senior year than all the other years."

Chante laughed. "Yeah, I didn't know jack about shooting free throws. I told you to bend your knees 'cause that's what they always say in sports—no matter what you're doing—bend your knees, bend your knees."

Courtney smiled. "You're kidding! Here I had you pegged a genius."

"A genius? Nah, I wish. No one would accuse me of being smart."

"Don't be so hard on yourself."

"Look where I'm at."

Courtney thought about her neighborhood, about Destiny. Sadness much deeper than the Flames' surprising decision overtook him. "Is Destiny asleep?"

Pep came in Chante's voice. "Yeah. I took her to the doctor's early yesterday morning for her shots, and then bought her more summer stuff. She grows like a weed, I swear. Doctor said she's going to be tall." She paused and let Courtney swallow that bit of news. "Then I watched videos with her—*Stuart Little*, 'bout the mouse—and she sat up and watched the draft with me. Today, she's been kinda quiet, must feel something. I put her to sleep before I called you."

"Busy day yesterday," Courtney replied.

"All of 'em are."

Courtney twirled the phone cord, considered things. "Listen," he said. "Last time we spoke, you said you wanted to get the paternity test done."

"Yeah, I want to do it, so you'll know for certain; maybe it can erase this cloud that hangs over Destiny's head. I know you've got a lot on your mind, though, so I ain't sweating you to do it right this minute. We waited this long; it can wait until you get yourself situated."

"No, no. I want to get it done, soon. What all we got to do?"

"Holeup a sec, then," Chante told him. She moved from the phone but returned before Courtney's mind could wander. "I've got information on a clinic in Manhattan, uptown."

"How long it take to get the results?"

"Umm,"—Chante quickly scanned the brochure—"the regular program, you get results back in about ten days."

"Damn, that long?"

"Then, they've got a program called the 'Unique' that can get you same-day results, but you've got to go to the lab, and it costs three times as much."

"That's cool; I wanna do that one. Colin would have to go, too?"

"Yeah, but they've got testing centers in Jersey. He could give his sample there and have them ship it here." She paused. "I mean, you and I don't have to go at the same time."

"No, I'd want us to go the same time."

Chante tried, but was unable to hold back a smile. "So you're ready to do this, then?"

"Ready as I'll ever be."

"I'm glad. I hate the way you look at Destiny. Like you want to love her, but . . ."

Courtney let out a soft grunt.

"You want to talk with Colin and see if he'll do it, or you want me to?" Chante asked.

"I'll handle that," Courtney told her. "You go ahead and get the ball rolling tomorrow with the people at the testing place."

"Okay," Chante said. "And, Courtney?"

"Yeah?"

"I am so sorry we have to go through this."

"The worst is already behind us. I'll talk to you soon. Aiight?"

"Okay," she replied, wondering what he meant by "the worst is already behind us."

"Bye."

Getting a crumb of him in her life, even if he was mad at her, always gave her a certain kind of jolt. When it was time for that inevitable separation, her insides always pressed in on her, constricted her lungs, and altered her breathing. "Bye," she said, not wanting to go.

He hung up, looked off somewhere, buried in thought. Was the worst behind them?

18

Back in the Day (Circa 1989)

Dreams of a Wannabe Rap Dude

It started out simply.

Colin and Kim walked through their neighborhood, hands entwined, arms swinging in unison. Passing by brownstone after brownstone and oblivious to anything but each other. Then Kim had mentioned offhand that she was finished with her period—thank goodness!—and stirred an urge in Colin that had been burning for some time, unfulfilled. They stopped at Bagley's corner store so Kim could get an ice-cream pop. Colin stood outside by the curb, scheming a way to get the full benefit of his empty house. His mama was at the hotel where she worked, bent over a toilet, or stuffing those paper-thin sheets under a mattress.

"I'm ready," Kim said as she emerged from Bagley's, her butter soft voice breaking Colin's thoughts. They grasped hands again and walked, Kim offering her ice pop, Colin saying just being with her was enough and he didn't need any ice pop.

After a minute or two of silence Kim asked, "You sure you don't want some of my Popsicle?"

Colin shook his head. "Me? Nah. Told you that shit got pork in it."

"Does not . . . I checked the package." She flipped it over again and looked at the label to be sure.

Colin turned his lips up. "You don't know what you're looking for, Kim." He didn't either, but the boys at school would snicker and call him names if he ever let that fact get out. "Nah, I'm okay." He squeezed Kim's hand.

"Whatchu thinking about?" she asked as they turned the corner.

Colin played dumb. "Nothing," he lied. "Why?"

"You got a big-ass goofy smile on your face."

"Oh. Nah, I was thinking how I would looooove to hit skinz with Salt from Salt-N-Pepa." Kim sucked her teeth and released her fingers from Colin's hand. She licked her rainbow ice pop as they continued to walk up the block. "Or better yet," Colin continued, "That Puerto Rican chick with the squeaky voice that my man rubbed the ice cubes on in *Do the Right Thing.*" Kim bit her Popsicle, tearing off a piece of the white stripe in her teeth and rolling it around on her tongue. Colin smiled and tried to think of another name. "Damn . . . or what's her name? I saw her on Arsenio Hall the other night."

Kim stopped, hands on her hips, waving the mutilated ice pop at Colin like one of her Mama's switches. "You are pissing me the freak—"

Colin covered Kim's mouth with his fingers, her cold lips warmed by his tender touch. "Don't go getting mad. I was playing. I wanted to see if you would get jealous."

"Word is bond," she said, still angry, twisting her head from side to side and waving the headless Popsicle. "I swear to God. You play too much. Ain't nothing funny about that junk. If I said I wanted to do the nasty with LL Cool J or Al B. Sure, would you like that?"

"I wouldn't care to be honest with you," Colin told her. "That's just talk. It ain't like you're going to get a chance to do it. Come on now, you gotta stop being so sensitive. You know you're the only one I want to hit skinz with."

"Hmph." Kim started walking again, left Colin standing alone.

"What's up with that? Why you frontin'?" he asked her as he hurried to catch up.

"You dope and all," Kim offered. "Different from these other guys. Reading your books and whatnot." Colin grimaced. Kim continued, "But I just ain't ready for that move."

Colin eyed the tightness of her body in her bright red spandex jumpsuit. He scanned to the hint of a strawberry-sized birthmark on her neck peeking through the opening of her large door-knocker, gold earrings. She looked to him like some sexy celebrity, and he had plenty of ice cubes at home and an empty house to boot. He wanted to shift this thing in his favor. The locker room during gym class was unbearable, his boys taunting him daily about not getting none from Kim or no other female. He'd already been through the taunts because he used to talk like a white boy and because he actually carried books home. It had taken drastic measures on his part to get the teasing to stop: a backpack that he told them contained "his rhyme books," a serious departure in the way he spoke, and a dedication to learning to play basketball like his father, shoot, like his little brother. He needed to hit skinz with this girl, and soon. His dignity and budding manhood was on the line. Yet, he liked Kim and respected her. She was like him in many ways. Of the neighborhood, but not like her peers. She was soft-spoken and talented, talked constantly of singing her way out of the hood, blushed every time Colin cursed.

Colin sighed. "Aiight, I'm cool with that if you ain't ready. I'm not about to pressure you into doing something you not ready for. You are still coming over though, right?"

Kim eyed Colin suspiciously. "No dumb junk?"

He looked at her and batted his eyes until she smiled. "Word is bond. No dumb shit."

" 'Cause the minute you try touching on me or start talking about skinz, I'm Audi five thousand, Colin."

He pressed his hand to the heart area of his chest. "We can watch TV. *Yo! MTV Raps.* Fab Five Freddy. That's it."

Kim sucked her teeth. "I don't wanna watch that. Can't we listen to your uncle's records?"

Colin shrugged. "Well, whatever then. We'll just lounge and you can sing to me."

Kim smiled, squeezed Colin's hand.

It ended badly.

Colin carefully slid his hands in the long, yellow gloves his mother used to do the dishes. The kitchen was a blanket of darkness around him. He looked next door to the Parker's brownstone. Their house was dark, too, except for that one light that shone from the second floor. But Kim slept with the light on, so Colin wasn't worried. Colin pictured her, under her covers, that round belly growing by the second. Recollection of the episode earlier crashed down on his head like a boulder.

Colin had been walking toward his house with Juno and Pumpkin, two of his boys from school, when Kim came bolting out of her brownstone, the door slamming carelessly behind her, tears welling in her eyes.

"There go your girl, Colin," Juno said. "You gonna see what's up with her?"

"Colin ain't hitting it right. What's wrong," Pumpkin joked. "Ain't hitting it at all, actually." Pumpkin and Juno gave each other high-fives.

Colin ignored them, his eyes meeting Kim's as she caught his and slowed her steps. Colin moved toward her and she back-tracked and crossed the street.

"Oh, shit!" Juno exclaimed. "She's jetting on you, Colin. Damn!"

"Holeup, Kim," Colin called after her, giving chase.

Kim jogged a few steps, then stopped, her shoulders losing all strength. Colin caught up with her. He looked across the street to see Juno and Pumpkin, all eyes on him and Kim. They were clowning, making faces, coughing, and laughing into their fists.

Colin turned his eyes back to Kim. "Wussup, Kim?"

She wiped the tears from her eyes with the sleeve of her over-sized sweatshirt. "I had an argument with my parents. We've been arguing a lot lately."

"That why you've been avoiding me?"

Kim dropped her eyes.

"What all y'all arguing about?"

Kim looked at Colin, her eyes softening. "You're so sweet, Colin. I'm sorry."

"Sorry? Shoot, what you sorry about girl?"

"I'm stupid, Colin. Maybe I need to start reading them books you be reading."

Colin shifted his weight from one foot to the other. "You're not stupid, Kim. You're special."

She sniffed a laugh. "Special."

Colin nodded. "Special."

"I'm knocked up is what I am," she replied.

"What do you mean?" Colin asked, all pretense gone from his speech. The wannabe rapper and homeboy oozed away as his innocence soon would.

Kim lifted her oversized sweatshirt. Her belly, full and round, stared at Colin like a joke gone bad. Juno and Pumpkin made their way closer, in the center of the street, within earshot. Colin didn't care. He eyed her belly, his brow furrowed, his heart started to race. "How could you be pregnant?" Colin asked Kim. "We haven't done anything yet."

Juno and Pumpkin snickered. Kim turned to them, sneered. Colin paid them no mind.

"Kim, answer me," Colin said.

Kim turned back to Colin. "I should have done it with you, Colin. You'd have treated me right. I'm stupid. Listening to my girls on who they thought was cool and stuff."

"Who did you do it with, Kim?" Colin asked. His voice was deep, authoritative, but not deep and powerful enough to chase away Juno and Pumpkin's taunts in the street.

Colin's a buster.

Damn, Colin, yo' girl had some other dude filling her.

"Trevor Wheatley," Kim offered.

Damn, Colin, Trevor Wheatley got game you wish you had.

"Trevor Wheatley dogs girls out," Colin said.

No, Colin, Trevor Wheatley gets pussy.

"I know," Kim replied. She smiled and touched Colin's cheek. "I'm sorry, Colin." And then she walked off, leaving Colin rooted in place, Juno and Pumpkin in the street laughing into their fists and slapping fives.

Run after her Colin, you know you want to.

Oh, damn, Colin! Don't be crying over a female.

I'd burn her house down, that was my girl, Colin.

Now, Colin, his jaw set hard, poured a cupful of his Mama's cooking oil into each of the two empty beer bottles he'd grabbed from the dumpster behind Bagley's corner store. He pocketed a few of the long matches his Mama used to light the broken burner on their rusted oven.

He looked over his shoulder through the blanketing darkness of his kitchen before stepping outside in the backyard. He tiptoed across the cement alley between his house and Kim's, holding a beer bottle of cooking oil in each hand.

He set the bottles at his feet as he reached the Parker's brownstone and peered through their kitchen windows. Their house was black, as his was. He took two matches from his pocket and lit them before he could change his mind, before logic and clear thinking could find him.

He dropped a lit match in each bottle, the oil and lit match causing a flame to shoot up inside.

He broke the back-door window with his elbow and tossed the bottles inside the Parker's brownstone.

The bottles burst when they hit something hard inside the Parker's kitchen.

A roaring fire came to life quicker than Colin anticipated.

The heft of it surprised him, shook the cobwebs from his head. What had he done? He was no different from the other fools who'd been setting fires in the neighborhood, boys his mother said needed to be sent away upstate. Hoodlums.

His heart pounded in his chest. He felt a bit dizzy, all these voices in his head. Kim, apologizing for betraying him, Juno and Pumpkin, laughing and taunting him.

The fire devoured the Parker's table set and ran across the floor, sucked their curtains like soda through a straw. Colin's eyes widened at the orange-and-blue monster before him.

He almost ran back home and hid under his covers, but then he turned back.

He banged loudly several times on the door before darting across the grass to his house.

He shut his kitchen door behind him and leaned against it, his hand against his chest, trying to steady himself.

"What you doing, Colin?" a voice called to him from the darkness.

Colin moved closer to the voice. Courtney stood there, eyes wide.

"What are you doing up, Court?" Colin asked, his heartbeat in his throat, garbling his words.

"I saw you get up," Courtney said. "And I couldn't sleep, so I followed you down."

"Go back to bed, Court."

"You mad at Kim about something, Colin?"

"Go back to bed," Colin repeated, his voice deeper and harder.

"I've got to go get Mama. You slept through all of this, you hear?" He grabbed Courtney by the shoulders, shook him. "You hear me! You slept through all this, didn't see a thing?"

Courtney nodded. He slept through all of this. Colin wasn't angry with Kim, and if Courtney kept to the script—he slept through all of this—Colin wouldn't be angry with him, either. Wouldn't up and leave him one day as Prime had done.

Right, he slept through all of this. . . .

Colin shot up on the couch and fumbled the baby rattle he'd used earlier to entertain Lyric. His heart was racing as if he'd literally run from that horrible day, years ago, to now. He pressed his head back against the couch and stared at the ceiling. Pack rat, he was, had packed so much garbage in twenty-eight years. The future, however long it turned out to be, would be spent cleaning up the litter and making sure he kept things eat-off-the-floor pristine.

He could smell the musk from his armpits. He looked over at his laptop computer on the small table in the corner of the room. He'd brought it to get work done when Lyric fell asleep. That had been for show—he hadn't written one word today, too keyed up. The screensaver flashed the words *Kill Your Darlings*. It was a quote from a long-ago writer about cutting and rewriting.

Colin took a couple breaths. Today, of all days, why would the dreams start again? Setback?

He looked at the computer again, a staring contest with the machine. At least he'd turned it on and thought about writing. Damn, the battery was running down. Colin searched for the digital clock—it was past six P.M. The baby needed feeding. He slumped back against the couch again and blew out a puff of air. Liza would be all over him if she knew he'd missed Lyric's five o'clock bottle.

Liza!

He stood and went to check the caller ID for calls and messages. It wasn't flashing. Liza should have returned hours ago. Now, where was she? He was moving from the phone to go check outside when it rang and startled him. He turned back and moved swiftly to pick up the phone before whoever it was hung up.

"Damn, bet that's Liza." He took a quick look at the caller ID screen. The Brooklyn number of his mother flashed on the screen.

He picked up, smiling. "Mama, hey there. I was thinking it was Liza."

"Colin."

"Courtney?"

"Yeah," his brother said softly. "Wussup? How are you doing?"

Colin took a seat on the arm of the couch. "Good, good. What's up with you?"

They both were surprised to hear the other's voice, angling into the conversation slowly.

"Hanging in there," Courtney offered. "Ma, told me the problems you've been having—sorry to hear about it. But, you're back at the house, huh? I hate to think of you out and about. This is going to be a permanent thing again, I hope."

Colin struggled to find his tongue, still in shock that his brother's voice was in his ear. "No, not for the moment, but hopefully, eventually it'll happen for me. Liza surprised me today. Called me and said I could come over."

Courtney attempted to move beyond the pity he felt for his older brother, his keeper despite what happened in Chante's apartment so many nights ago. "So how is Lyric doing? I can't wait to see my little niece."

"Oh, she's doing wonderfully. How's Des . . ." Colin stopped and let his words trail off into an awkward silence.

"Destiny, you were going to say? She's doing well."

"I'm, I'm glad to hear that." Colin paused, searching for the right words. "About that whole situation, I never apologized to you for—"

"I spoke with Liza," Courtney cut him off. "She told me about how she deceived you and all the issues you two were facing. I have a better understanding of the entire thing now."

"Liza told you, huh?"

"Yes."

"Still, though, I was umm . . . I was wrong for how I reacted. Trust me—that day has haunted me ever since it happened. Wish I could take it back. What's that saying . . . ? Four things that can't come back: the spent arrow, the spoken word, the past, and neglected opportunity. Can't undo what has already been done. As much as I wish I could take what I did back. As much as I wish you hadn't got caught up in me and Liza's foolishness, you did. I'll never forgive myself for that, Courtney. But I hope you can." He took a breath, his lungs pleased that the heavy weight on his chest lessened. "I'm sorry."

"Apology accepted." It was funny. As many times as Courtney craved an apology, as much as he thought about how dramatic it would be, it turned out to be so quick, so devoid of everything he imagined. Yet, still, it felt good to hear.

Colin tried to shift the conversation to more pleasant ground. "So, congratulations on getting drafted. I know you're disappointed by where you were picked, but Golden State got themselves a hell of a player."

"Thanks. I'm happy to get the opportunity. Many want it, but few are chosen."

"Isn't that the truth," Colin said.

"It's been a while since we talked."

Colin thought it through. "That day at the hospital, right?"

"Damn, that's right." The memory still burned inside Courtney like an ulcer, eating away at his pride, his dignity. That beating from Black, in many ways, was the turning point in his life, more so than the situations with Colin and Chante. "I know I was pretty hard-hearted that day," Courtney mused, "but I was glad to see you. Glad to know you cared."

"It was tough seeing you like that, little brother."

"Tough being in that situation; my pride was as bruised as my body was."

"You never told the cops anything?"

"Nah, my agent suggested I let it rest. Didn't want the media getting a hold of it and painting me out as a street thug." He thought about Black's whispered message: *Peace be still or yah seed and dutty gurl be next, seen?* Just this evening Black had called his cell phone, left a message offering his congratulations. Courtney tried to pretend the situation was at a standstill, but the threat of more violence clung to him like a damp basketball jersey.

"Media loves building us up and then bringing us down," Colin added.

Courtney shook away any more thought of Black. "Yeah, my agent thought that would hurt my endorsement opportunities. I don't know. By the same token, if I had spoken on it, let it out in the open, then that would have explained my poor workout with the Flames. Maybe disclosure would have kept me from sliding like I did in the draft. One never knows."

Colin smirked. "Agents."

"Tell me about it. I fired mine right after the draft."

"So, what are you going to do now?"

"Find another one, one more suited to me."

Colin cleared his throat. The nightmare from moments before was still on his mind. "Can I ask you something?"

"Course."

"Why didn't you ever tell Mama I was the one that set that fire at the Parkers', that I wasn't the hero she made me out to be?"

Courtney thought about Prime. "Ma, she needed a hero. And, truthfully, I did, too."

"I found out Kim was pregnant by some other cat, while we were supposed to be going together. Juno and Pumpkin teased the shit out of me. I lost it for a while there."

"That's what that was about?"

"Yeah."

"Romance is truly a nuisance."

Colin sighed. "You're not lying."

"I was confused by it all," Courtney said. "I couldn't figure out why Ma was making you out to be so good in the situation. I couldn't figure out why you did what you did, and why you let Ma talk you up."

Colin nodded. "I'm going to tell her."

"No need for that, Colin. That's old news."

"I've been seeing a specialist, talking things over," Colin admitted. "She thinks I need a total cleansing; it'll do my spirit good. I agree with her. So much stuff I've held inside for so long. It eats away at you like a poison."

"Ma will be disappointed," Courtney warned him.

"She needs to know the true me, Court. I've already brought her opinion of me down a notch. I need to make sure the air is completely clean. Besides, it hasn't been fair to you."

Courtney asked, "How so?" though he knew the answer.

"I was perfect," Colin said, "and you, you were like Prime."

Courtney laughed. "Ma was cool until I learned how to dribble behind my back and between my legs."

Colin laughed in turn. "Isn't that the truth? She didn't worry about me. She knew I only played because . . ." Colin paused. "She knew I was only trying to get Prime's love."

Courtney's voice rose. "Say what?"

"Come on, Court, you were Prime's *boy*. You'd think the man's blood didn't run through me. He wasn't trying to hear me. I gave everything I had to get him to give me a smile, rub my head the way he rubbed yours."

Courtney shook his head. "This is insane. You were seeking Prime's love and I ended up seeking Ma's."

"Ma loves you, Court. Always has. She was different with me because I was the one laying my head on her chest, while Prime took you to the courts and acted as if I didn't exist."

Courtney stayed silent.

"Fatherhood," Colin said.

"What?"

"Fatherhood," Colin repeated, "is a serious responsibility."

"Yes," Courtney agreed. His thoughts ran amok again.

"All right, Court," Colin said as he consulted his watch, "We have to continue this some other time. I have to track down my wife."

"We can get together, soon," Courtney assured him. "Before I head out to Cali, I'd like that."

Colin was pleased. "Good, good."

"One thing I need you to do for me, if you would?"

"Sure. Anything you need."

"I had Chante make a call. We want to get the paternity test done on Destiny. There's a collection lab there in Jersey that can take a sample from you, and ship it to the city. I want to get this thing settled. Would you go and give a sample?"

Colin considered the question. This conversation with Courtney was the smoothest one they'd had in years and he wanted more like it, needed more like it. But what would happen if Destiny were his? What would that mean for the two brothers? What would it mean for Colin? He'd never considered the possibility remote, but it was. He had already mucked up things with Lyric. Destiny would double his failings as a father in an instant. Still, he had to do it, had to lift this weight of burden off his brother. "Sure, I'll give a sample," he said, unconvincingly, but still it was said and it would be done.

"Cool. We were thinking June 30 if that works for you. You can go to Qwest labs right there in town where you are."

"Consider it done. You and Chante trying to work things out, get back together?"

"Taking it a step at a time," Courtney told him. "I want to know if Destiny is mine or not; the rest will work itself out."

"That's good. I hope you get everything you want, man. I do."

Courtney's voice cracked a bit, though he did his best to keep his emotions checked. "I appreciate this, man. I know we've had our differences, but, things are making me realize how small they are in the grand scheme of things."

"What's that book? Don't sweat the small stuff?"

"It's all small stuff," Courtney added. "I saw the book at Barnes & Noble the other day."

Colin let out a fake cough, then laughed. "What, you were in the bookstore. I thought you were allergic to books, that you'd break out in hives if you got within twenty feet of a book."

Courtney's tone turned deadly serious. "I got over that, had to. There was this one book that I've been hearing about that I had to go cop."

Colin swallowed. "Don't tell me . . . Langston Campbell's new book?" He was surprisingly calm about it, his balance steady since this morning when he walked in and saw his beautiful wife and daughter.

"Nah, man," Courtney replied. "This book I picked up is some real literature." He put emphasis on the word literature. "It's called *Prophet's Message*."

Next to tickling Lyric's feet and hearing her giggle, what Courtney said was the sweetest sound Colin could imagine. His voice choked and he didn't care that Courtney could hear it. The both of them were being so emotional. "That means a lot, man, means an awful lot."

"We're brothers," Courtney answered.

Colin nodded, a smile brightening his face, his shoulders bouncy, joy encapsulating him. "Yes, we are. Yes, we are."

19

Approaching Midnight, June 27

I'm in a funk. I'm depressed. My mood swings are horrible. And, worse than anything else, I've been taking it out on my child. I get so upset at her for crying. I know it's wrong, but, I've been shaking her and I can't stop myself. I'm scared of what I might do. Afraid of what I've already done.

When would the ebb and flow of Colin's life end, the dramatic ups, the humbling and defeating downs? One minute he was on the phone having a mending conversation with his brother, the next minute he was finding notes, in a desperate search for the wife who'd not only shut him out, but, apparently all hope as well.

"Hello? Brashear residence."

Colin dropped the note on the couch. His mouth was cotton dry, his hands shaky, and his feet sore from standing and pacing. "Mama Brashear, this is Colin. Liza there?"

There was a brief moment of pause and then surprise and anger fluttered from her tone like a flock of southbound birds before the chill of winter kissed the air. "No she is not, and—"

Colin ignored her. "We've got a problem." He looked over to Lyric. She was lying in the pack-and-carry crib he'd struggled to erect in the center of the living room. She had her eyes closed but was moving her little stray fingers as if she was striking the keys of a piano. His baby girl was enough to keep him from needing a late-night emergency session with Dr. Samuelson, but she wasn't enough to keep him from practically rubbing his scalp raw with his anguished fingers.

Mama Brashear must have picked up on the panic in his voice, because her own softened. "A problem? What's going on, Colin?"

"I'm at our house. Liza called me this morning to come watch the baby. She was supposed to be back hours ago."

"You're back in the house? She called you?"

"Yes, she did. Out of the blue, I didn't think nothing of it at the time, was just happy."

"Where was she going?"

"Don't know, she wouldn't tell me." He moved to the arm of the couch and sat on it, popped back up before he got comfortable, walked the floor again. The indentations from his feet dotted a line across their carpet, a straight line from the couch to the grandfather clock that Mama Brashear had convinced Liza "opened the place up," back to the couch. "God! Why didn't I press her to tell me where she was going?"

Anger replaced Mama Brashear's initial worry. "This is pretty irresponsible on her part."

Colin stopped his pace across the carpet. "Maybe it has something to do with the children's books she's been illustrating. You think?"

"What children's books?"

"Liza told me she's been getting interest in her artwork; she might sell it to children's books publishers. She has a friend that set her up with contacts."

"What?" Mama Brashear said. "She told you that? I've been trying desperately to get Liza drawing again; she hasn't been in her drawing studio since you left." Mama Brashear let out a sigh that sounded like a tire blowout. Worry was closing in on her by the second; the more she found out, the more pressing the worry. Her voice had a drifty effect to it. "Not once, son-in-law. I purposely left the door open, hoping she'd see that easel thing and walk in, but no." There was a need in her tone. In a matter of minutes she'd allowed her heart to try and embrace Colin again. The horrible things Liza had told her about him, about his faults, none of it mattered at this moment.

"Why would she lie about this?" Colin said aloud, more as a

piecing together of this puzzle than as a question. His voice was hollowed out as it came from his nasal passage, an effect from blowing his nose so often the past few hours.

"Did you try her cell phone?" Mama Brashear offered, trying to place the pieces of this puzzle together from her end as well.

"She cancelled the service. I called to check and, sure enough, the service was disconnected."

Mama Brashear tried not to be angry, but failed. "This is one of Liza's jags," she said. Anger was much better than worry. Anger was something you could admonish the person about later. Worry, on the other hand, often ended at funerals. Mama Brashear continued to vent, "She holds this stuff in and then does immature things like this. These, these—jags."

Colin forced himself to sit down on the couch; his bottom barely brushed the edge of the cushion. He looked to the crib again, thinking he heard Lyric shift, but the child was still sleeping, still making that beautiful music on those invisible black-and-white ivories. "I think it's more than that, Mama Brashear. Liza left a note."

"Note?" she responded, drawing that one syllable out as if she was in a spelling bee and it was one of the letters in a word she vaguely knew how to spell.

"Can you get over here?" Colin asked her before she could ask him any specific questions about the note. Just reading it made his stomach hurl. "I know it's late, but . . ."

Worry returned again, displacing Mama Brashear's anger. The last five minutes of her life, an unwanted roller-coaster ride. "I'm on my way," she said. For once, the drama that her tone always carried, fit.

"I have to unpack food from my car," she continued, "and store it so it doesn't spoil. Shouldn't take me more than ten minutes, and then I'll head right out."

"I appreciate it, Mama Brashear."

"Nothing to appreciate, son-in-law," she said, voice full of sadness. "Liza's my little girl."

Mother-in-law and son-in-law bid each other adieu, offering a few last words of comfort. "Everything will be fine," Mama Brashear told him. "I'm sure it will," was Colin's halfhearted response before he pressed the receiver down and dialed the second number that came to his mind.

A gruff voice came on after a few rings. "Gym. Speak."

"Armando, this is Colin."

Armando's battering ram of a voice settled down to backyard barbecue, easygoing. "Colin, how's it swinging, partner? You get a handle on those cats that roughed up your brother? I heard things about the both of them. The cat, Black, messed around with this white girl. The wrong white girl—her people are eye-tal-lions, if you know what I'm saying. He's been lying low. Might be maggot filet by now; no one knows. The other cat, Star, shit"— Armando laughed his breezy, even laugh—"that fool got popped for stealing radios. Did the shit out in broad daylight. What a dummy. He's back in the slammy for one to five and his Mama refused to try to post bail for him this time. Karma. That 'what goes around boomerangs' shit."

Colin hadn't had the energy to cut Armando off, just waited until his father-in-law finished. "That's all good, Armando, but listen. I'm at the house in Jersey. I know this is short notice, but I need you to come out here. Tonight."

"Whoa, partner. I'm locking up late here as it is. Told you I'll come down and see the baby soon, see all of you." He paused like a boxer between rounds. "Put my Princess on the phone. I know she must have pestered you into calling—I'll explain it all to her. I know you stuck in the middle, partner."

Colin tried to keep his voice from shaking, but the more he thought about the situation, the more he talked about it, the more grief and worry touched him. "There's been a problem with Liza. I need you to come down, Armando."

There was a rustling, like Armando had dropped the phone in an empty potato chip bag. Colin figured Armando had changed his position in his chair, took his feet off his desk, and leaned forward. Colin asked, "Armando, you still there?" when his father-in-law didn't initially respond.

"What kind of problem?" Armando tried to sound brave as if the answer, regardless of what it was, wouldn't shake him off his seat. This week he'd had two distant buddies bury three children. He'd become accustomed to the violent way life yanked away what you weren't prepared to relinquish.

Colin shook his head as if Armando could see him. He had to think positive. "I need you to come down; I'll explain then. She was supposed to have been home a while ago and she didn't return. I can't get in touch with her. She turned her cell phone off."

Calmness took over Armando. "Oh, she's out with the girls letting off steam, partner," Armando reasoned. "The women need that, too, every now and then, not like us, but they need it, too."

"We've been separated," Colin said. He felt compelled to share that info.

"Separated?"

"Yeah, for the past month I haven't been living here."

"Damn, partner, what happened? She caught you boning another lovely? You gotta keep your fingers out the cookie jar, partner. Many a problem can be avoided that way, trust me."

"No," Colin replied. "Just been having problems, but, she called me today and said I could come over—"

"Listen," Armando cut him off, "that's my Princess and all, but don't be letting her punk you down and put no skirt on you. You're the man in that house, Colin. You pay the bills."

Colin hid his agitation, decided to get straight to the point. "Armando, something has happened and I'm not sure what. She should have been home, but she hasn't come back. I have no way of getting in touch with her and . . . she left a note."

"A note?"

"Yes, and it isn't good. I don't want to get into it now on the phone, but she revealed scary things in the note. I think she's considering hurting herself. I'm worried like you wouldn't believe."

"But . . ." Armando spoke for a moment and then the words left him. The shock of all this made him mute.

Colin's voice now held the girth that Armando's did. He was about getting the business at hand attended to, didn't want to talk about the battle of the sexes. Didn't want to talk about street thugs. Just wanted his wife home, safe. "So, can you come? And, I need you to go by my folks place and get my mother, too. You remember where the house is?"

Rock hard Armando spoke as if he'd taken a few blows from that big Hawaiian boxer Colin had watched spar when he went to the gym. "Your mother's place is in the teens, right?"

"Sixty three East Fifteenth Street."

"This is something bad, huh?" Armando was able to say.

"Pick up my mother and get here soon as you can," was Colin's answer.

The heft was gone from Armando's voice. "All right, partner. I'm leaving now."

The next call was Colin's most difficult. He needed to gather himself before dialing. He placed the phone on the couch and checked again on Lyric. She was sleeping so soundly, oblivious to the storm swirling around her. Liza had complained about her being a fussy baby, but she'd slept through most of the day. There was something deeper to Liza's complaints, but then, the note proved that. Colin blew his daughter a kiss.

He moved to the kitchen. Only thing in the refrigerator to drink was a two-liter bottle of ginger ale. He pulled the liter from the fridge and held it up to his lips, guzzled down the stomach soothing elixir. It was like Liza had prepared everything down to the most finite detail. Presented this brave front, canceled her cell service, wrote out the detailed note on baby care, wrote the other note—the one Colin kept rereading—and made sure the refrigerator had ginger ale for any stomachs weakened by her plotting. Colin leaned against the countertop, sipping at the ginger ale now, instead of guzzling it. How had life gotten him to this point, like a character in a novel? All he truly wanted was a simple life, a family, and the ability and resources to care for them. Simple things.

He placed the soda bottle in the garbage can, surprised he'd finished it off, and peeked out the kitchen window at the parking lot. No headlights were circling the lot. No tired woman was making a slow stroll up the walkway. He sighed and headed back to the living room, sat on the couch, picked up the phone, and dialed.

"Mama," he said before she could get out the full "hello."

"Colin, hey, baby. You must have good news for me, calling this late. What happened? You and Liza done patched up?"

"No, Mama," he said.

"No. What's going on then?"

"Liza never came home. And, she left a note, a bad note, Mama. She's been going through things. I think she finally reached the point she couldn't take it anymore." Like Mama Brashear and Armando before her, Lena was dumbfounded by his words.

"Armando is coming down to Jersey, tonight. I asked him to swing by and pick you up," Colin continued. "Can you get Uncle Carl to look in on Nana? I need you all around to help me try and figure out what to do next, to help me help Liza if she comes home, to help me prepare things if she doesn't."

"I'll be there, Colin," his mother said. The shock in her tone was palpable over the fiber optics. "You take care of yourself and that grandbaby of mine until I get there. You hear?"

"Hurry, Mama. I don't feel good about this."

"Heard anything?"

Colin looked up from his spot on the couch. He had Lyric in his lap, the television turned down low, the phone close by. He hadn't heard Mama Brashear come in, and as if he'd awakened from a deep sleep, it took him a moment to gather his senses. "What? How'd you get in?"

Mama Brashear placed her pocketbook on the floor next to the big chair, sat on the seat, her bracelets clacking. "Spare key," she said. "And I asked if you'd heard anything. I suppose you haven't."

Colin laid Lyric back against his chest and held the back of her head. She'd started crying for a moment and he'd gone and got her, rocked her back to sleep in a matter of seconds. "No," he said—his mind, an unanchored boat. "Haven't heard a word. I keep calling her cell phone—what for, I don't know."

Mama Brashear leaned back in her seat, took off her famous rhinestone hat and smoothed out her hair, thinking as she performed each task. "Don't know what to do." Then she looked up at Colin as if she'd taken a shot in the back and he didn't hear or see the bullet pierce her. "You said there was a note."

Colin nodded, gestured toward the coffee table with his head. Mama Brashear sighed and then leaned forward and took the two sheets of lined paper. She sat back to read over the note. "Umph, umph, umph," was all the noise she made as she read over the pages, shaking her head. When she finished, she carefully placed them back on the table. She avoided eye contact with Colin.

"What do you think?" Colin prodded.

"Have you called the police, yet?" Mama Brashear asked him, still looking in any direction but his.

"Was waiting on all of you," Colin said.

"Who all else is coming?"

"My mother. Armando . . . he's bringing her."

Mama Brashear looked to Colin again. Her brows were knitted and her bracelets clacked from the quick snap of her head, the momentum of her suddenly active body. "Why would you call that man?" she asked.

"He is her father."

Mama Brashear held her eyes on Colin. "Some father."

Colin shifted Lyric to a more comfortable resting position against his chest. "I'm sorry if I've done something wrong. I don't have any experience in this thing. I made calls to anyone I thought might help."

Mama Brashear considered it all, thought about how she would have reacted to the situation, how she would have handled those first few moments after finding the note. She pressed her lips together, tightly, and ran the fingers of her arm without those clacking bracelets over her eyes. "You're right, son-in-law. I can understand that." She got up from her chair and moved over by Colin, took the baby from his arms and held Lyric against her chest, as Colin had been doing. She sat next to him and scooted over as close as she could get, reached her hand to him. He studied the hand and then took it. They sat holding hands, waiting.

The doorbell, over an hour later, made the both of them jump. Colin looked over to Mama Brashear; she looked to him. Neither of them moved at first, and then they both moved at the same time. Colin stood and wiped his sweaty palms on the front of his pants. Mama Brashear rearranged the bracelets on her arm, smoothed her unwieldy hair once again, and cleared her throat. She turned toward the baby's room. "Go let them in," she said, in the softest of tones. "I'm going to sit the baby in her crib." Lyric was fast asleep.

Colin walked down that long hallway to the front door and flipped the switch by the doorway so the porch light would come on. He struggled to unlatch all the locks, knowing nothing but more grief waited on the other side, and then cracked the door open. Colin's mother looked so small standing there; Armando looked small, too, because of how his shoulders drooped. Colin nodded as a greeting and then opened the screen door and let them in. They walked in quiet as falling snowflakes, looking as if the past hour had been their worst nightmare. Colin scanned the lot before he closed the door behind them all. They all walked down the hall back toward the living room without a proper greeting, all of them stunned by the thick uncertainty of the night.

Lena settled on the couch. Armando looked around the house for a moment, his lips pursed, and then he took a seat in the chair in front of the couch. Colin eased into a spot on the couch by his mother.

"So, what's going on, baby?" Lena asked. "Any update?"

Colin shook his head. "I called the police, spoke with a captain that I knew—I'd used him to help with research on my second book. He said they can't file an official report until twenty-four hours after the person was last seen, but that he'd check around for me."

"That's good to hear," Armando said. His eyes shifted up and everyone turned around to follow them. Mama Brashear entered the room, with Lyric wide awake in her arms.

"She woke up, Colin," Mama Brashear said. "Hello, Lena. Armando." She turned the baby to face everyone. "Lyric, sweetie, this is your other grandmother and your, your grandfather."

They all concentrated on the baby, using her to soak up the dread that had been in the air.

"Blessed be," Lena said, moving to the baby. Mama Brashear handed Lyric to Lena, a smile on her face from watching the smile on Lena's face. Lena moved the edge of the blanket off the baby's face and touched Lyric's brown and pink cheeks. "Look at you. You're more beautiful than they said. Oh, my goodness, look at those eyes."

Armando continued sitting, but he was smiling as he craned his head to see the baby. "Those are Liza's eyes."

"Yeah, they are," Colin responded, warmed by the thought. Lena settled next to him on the couch. Though there wasn't much space, Mama Brashear managed to grab a slice of the couch as well.

"So what do we do? Sit around and wait?" Armando asked as Lyric gurgled noises for her newest admirers.

Colin took his concentration off his ham of a daughter to address Armando's question. "I guess. I'm waiting for that captain I mentioned to call me with something."

Mama Brashear leaned back on the sofa, watching the baby and how well she interacted with family. She looked in Lena's direction and added to what Colin had said. "Colin's police friend told us, in cases like this, a lot of times the person is crying for help and that they go off and try to clear their head and then they resurface. That's what we're hoping for."

Armando huffed and hit the inside of his left hand with the fist of his right. "Hope that's the case," he said, offhandedly. "Hope it's just some drama queen act like that. It'd fit, too, 'cause, Zenny, you all drama queen yourself."

Mama Brashear didn't like the comment. She'd been taut like rope, waiting for him to say something that could set the beast inside her loose. She rose from the couch, came within feet of Armando. She did it with such calm, at first none of them realized she'd taken offense with Armando's perception. "Don't you dare come up in here insulting me you, you—"

Armando leaned back from her barrage, put his hands up. "I'm not your enemy, Zenny," he reasoned. "I was just saying."

"Don't say shit," she barked. Colin's eyebrows arched. He'd never heard anything close to profanity cross his mother-in-law's lips. Lena kept her attention on Lyric. "We don't need your sorry ass coming up in here saying nothing," Mama Brashear finished.

Armando almost let it go, but couldn't hold his tongue. "You never could get over the fact that Liza didn't have this deep-down hate for me like you do, though you tried to poison her against me."

Mama Brashear looked as if she might choke him, or die trying. "I never had to try and poison Liza against you. You did a pretty good job of messing up yourself. She loves you, but she doesn't respect you one iota. All the times you said you would come to see her and didn't. All the times you let her down. It takes great, big balls for you to come up in here today, finally, after promises to visit I don't know how many times. Your granddaughter is a month old and this is the first you're seeing her. And it's not as if you couldn't make it down, like Lena here. I'd have to give you a tour of the place just so you could find the bathroom. Liza would be so happy to know you finally made it down, though. You're right, in a way, she was always extra-forgiving of you. It's a shame she couldn't be here to see you; it would mean so much to her." Mama Brashear collapsed down on the

seat of the couch as Colin and his mother looked at the two war-
ring exes, Mama Brashear and Armando, in silence. When had it
been that love existed between them? How had it come to this?

Armando was openly wounded. "I did the best I could, considering the situation," he defended to no one in particular. "It ain't
like we were on the best of terms, Zenny."

Mama Brashear composed herself, intent on standing up to
her ex-husband. The man that had hardened her as she stood
soaking in the rain begging him to come home, her seven-year-
old daughter in the backseat of their car, trying to avoid looking
at the spectacle as she played with a doll. "Whatever *term* we
were—or are—on has nothing to do with your relationship with
your daughter, Arman."

"It's been hard on me," Armando said, his voice tender, subdued. He shifted in his seat. "Been harder than you'll ever know
or believe. Liza's my Princess. 'Bout the only thing in my life that
turned out right. I know I'm never gonna get nominated for any
father-of-the-year award or anything, but, I love that young lady
with all my heart."

Mama Brashear looked at him, unmoved. "Let's hope it isn't too
late for you to show her all this instead of just always talking it."

20

JUNE 30

Courtney stood over a table of magazines in the lobby outside Cureton Gerard's office. Gerard, through years of grit and success, had carved out a niche as one of the most successful and respected African American sports agents. Johnson Price, a bruising running back who was the NFL's reigning Rookie of the Year, was one of Gerard's clients. So was Frenzy McLain, a fierce boxer on a meteoric rise through the heavyweight ranks, and Ken Edwards, a perennial NBA All-Star. Courtney could have been on that list as well, but he'd chosen a different agent. That decision, Courtney was absolutely sure of now, had cost him millions of dollars. Now, he was here in the outer offices, humbled and wounded, hopeful for a second chance. A chance to salvage his career before it had begun.

Courtney moved to a second table of magazines, bent, flipped through them, and found, as with all the others, no sports-oriented magazines. There were a couple past issues of *Ebony*, a few issues of *Jet*, and a ton of *Black Enterprise* at each stop in the sparse lobby. Courtney thumbed through the small pile of *Ebony* magazines several times, trying to settle on one to read through.

A young, light brown gentleman, attired in a white dress shirt with subtle pink stripes, suspenders, and dark trousers came through the door talking into a headset. He stopped and caught the swinging door with his elbow and motioned for Courtney to come his way. Courtney slid the *Ebony* he'd finally decided to look through back on the table and moved toward the young man. They exchanged quick handshakes at the door, but no words. The headset had this brother's ear.

"Her game isn't on par with Venus or Serena, or anything like that, yet . . ." the light-skinned brother was saying into his headset. "But she's strides ahead of the Kournikova girl."

One week had seen Courtney's stock plummet to this point— second string at best—not worthy of full attention.

The hallway was wider than the outer lobby suggested. The bowels of this building deceptively bigger than an outsider could anticipate. Along the right wall hung pictures of athletes of courage, athletes of wisdom, athletes of merit, more so for their convictions and the lessons their competing had taught, than for their gamesmanship. There was a picture of Jim Abbott, the one-armed major league baseball pitcher, a picture of Lance Armstrong, the champion cyclist who had battled back from cancer, and a few others that Courtney had never heard of. Along the left wall were paintings by famous black artists—at least they were famous according to the gold plates below the paintings, for Courtney had never heard of any of them. The paintings were exquisite, though, and held his attention. He noted the names: Archibald J. Motley Jr., William H. Johnson, Palmer Hayden, and Aaron Douglas. When he got himself settled in California, he would be looking these artists up.

A few of the staff hustled by as Courtney made his way down the hall, and not one of them gave him the slightest attention, busy with their tasks, professional in their approach. Courtney was led through a door at the end of the hallway that ended in a large conference room.

The young brother was still glued to his headset. "This girl's got the goods, believe me. She's beautiful in her own right. Okay, maybe she doesn't have that blond-hair, blue-eyed profile that makes Madison Avenue tongues wag, but, she has gorgeous bronze skin, light brown eyes . . . Trust me. There's a market for her. Yeah . . . but see that's the difference. Unlike Kournikova, this girl's got game." He took a quick moment to tap Courtney on the shoulder, give him a thumbs-up, and disappear back out the door.

Courtney stood for a moment and took in the spacious room.

There was an empty table built for sixteen, an expensive-looking silver bowl with elegant carvings on the side—filled to the brim with prepackaged crackers—empty glasses turned upside down and formed in a tower, and a sizable container of orange juice. Courtney took one of the glasses from the top, filled it with juice, and settled into one of the chairs that was comfortable enough to swallow his long frame.

It was fifteen minutes—ten A.M. on the dot—before the conference door swung open again. Courtney had been humming along to the classical tunes coming through the wall speakers. He sat up in a rush, cleared his throat, hoping he hadn't been heard enjoying Beethoven or whomever it was. Cureton Gerard paused once he entered, smiled, and then came over to greet Courtney, who stood in reverence.

"Cureton Gerard," the agent said. "So nice to meet you, Courtney." Cureton had a shiny, balding head. What little hair he had was cut close on the sides. His short, thick fingers were too small, even for his modest five-feet-seven-inch frame. His light brown skin had a suggestion of Shinnecock, like this Native American girl Courtney had dealt with his first year of college. But it was Cureton's smile that served as his most intriguing characteristic. On a less respected and sincere individual, it would have been deemed a smirk.

"Nice to meet you as well, Mr. Gerard," Courtney said.

Cureton continued to hold Courtney's hand in his clamped, firm grip, those stubby little fingers packing more punch than George Foreman before the grills. He appraised Courtney, from his height, to his posture, to the features and outline of his face. All of that would matter as much as, or more than, his basketball skills—if the agency chose to take him on as a client and package him to the sports marketers. "Tell you what. Call me Cure. All my friends do."

Courtney nodded. "Okay, Cure."

Cure placed his hand on Courtney's shoulder, the heel of his spit-polished shoes breaking contact with the ground as he reached up. "Go ahead and have yourself a seat, Courtney," Cure instructed him. "Mi casa es su casa . . . that's if you're willing to take this outrageously expensive lease agreement off my hands."

Courtney laughed, Cure did as well, and then they both settled into their seats. Cure got comfortable, leaned back in his chair.

He formed a pyramid with his hands and rested his chin on them like so many men of power did. That pose, like the arms-crossed-b-boy poses of the eighties and nineties, was like American Express, accepted the world over. "So tell me, Courtney. My son, Jeremy—he was the one that ushered you in—he tells me that you contacted us right after the draft about possibly representing you."

Courtney nodded. "That's correct, I—"

"If you don't mind my asking," Cure cut in, "but why didn't you contact us before the draft? In other words, why did you pick the agent you chose and not our firm? I know we sent a feeler to your college coach. Butch and I go way back and he was a bit surprised, or so he told me, when you didn't give us more consideration."

Courtney shifted. "Guess I needed more than a feeler," he reasoned. "My former agent came out to meet me. He sold me on the spot. Coach did suggest I go with your agency, but I made a different choice. One I paid for."

"Fair enough," Cure responded. "I have to ask that question, to get a sense of things. I have to admit that many of our black athletes bypass us for white agencies. Somehow they have this notion that a black agent can't get the job done for them." Cure placed his hands on the table so Courtney could get an unobstructed view of the anguish on his face. "It's an unspoken truth of sorts, one that wounds me greatly. Our people have been poisoned against each other for a long time."

"Oh, no," Courtney quickly jumped in, "That didn't play into my decision at all. I made my choice solely because of his eagerness. It was an ego thing, I suppose."

"I can dig that. There's nothing wrong with ego, Courtney." Cure leaned forward to divulge a secret. "In fact, I instructed my son not to press it with you after you didn't originally contact us. Now that was *my ego* speaking, because I'd been watching you for a long time. Only two other guards I ever coveted out of New York slipped through my grip—Kenny Anderson and Mark Jackson. I didn't want you to be the third, but, well, you know." Cure smirk-smiled again, his mind floating through the years of his agency, the many successes and the few failures. "Your coach implored me to make a more impassioned pitch, but I wouldn't hear of it. Guess an old man is losing that eye of a tiger." A gleam sparkled in Cure's eyes. "No, it was an ego thing. I've been around long enough that I thought my name should matter for more, that you should come running to me, instead of me come running to you. You taught me a valuable lesson, Courtney, about not getting too high, not resting on your laurels. Jeremy was upset at me when I told him to let you sign with that other agent. You see, I've been grooming Jeremy to take over the business in about five years."

Courtney hunched his eyes; he wasn't too happy about that prospect at first, and then he thought about it further. Jeremy had bruised his ego by virtually ignoring him, but he was doing it because business was his number-one priority. Who better to guide his career than a pit bull with a headset and clear aims?

"I was afraid I'd burned this bridge," Courtney said. "I'm grateful you agreed to take this meeting with me. I mean, I'm damaged goods at this point."

"Yes, you are," Cure acknowledged.

"So what changed your mind? You could have turned me away."

"Same thing that made you fire your agent, Courtney. I put aside that ego and thought about the bigger picture. How can we give you the best opportunity to showcase your talents and be paid in accordance with your abilities?"

"So you're willing to represent me?"

Cure was still comfortably reclining in his chair. "Willing? Yes, of course." He leaned forward and poured himself a glass of juice, filled Courtney's cup again. "But let me ask you a few questions first. Get to know you, you get to know me. That is important in an agent-client relationship."

"Okay."

"I was reading in the paper about the ordeal with your sister-in-law. How's your family doing? How are you doing?"

Courtney hadn't expected that question; it took him a moment to gather himself and answer. "It's all so unreal, Mr. Gerard, Cure. I haven't gotten down to Jersey yet with my family. I plan on getting there before the week's over. I talk with my mother daily, though; spoke with my brother a few times on the phone—he's pretty much in a daze over the whole thing. We're all hoping that she turns up."

"My thoughts and prayers are with you and your family, young man. You know my wife and I are big fans of your brother's work.

My wife more so than me, but she says he writes clever novels. Reminds her of Jimmy Baldwin. Now that's saying something."

Courtney nodded, taking the appreciation for Colin. "Thanks, I'll be sure and tell him."

"As for business," Cure said as he tapped out the pile of papers in front of him. "Not going to the pre-draft camps in Portsmouth and Chicago hurt you, and your poor workout with Atlanta scared them and the other lottery-pick teams away."

Courtney shook his head, thinking back on all the poor decisions of his past. "Yes, my old agent acknowledged as much."

"Was Atlanta an aberration?"

"You mean is that the best Courtney Sheffield? What I showed them during my workout?"

"I mean is that the *real* Courtney Sheffield, what we can expect on a day-to-day basis. You know, the pre-draft analysts felt you were a can't-miss prospect, but, after your poor workout in Atlanta, and your unwillingness to participate in any of the other camps . . . well, let's just say no one looks at you as a can't-miss anymore. You're a mystery right now." Cure stopped, took a sip of his orange juice. It was clear on the note that he ended that he had more to add, so Courtney sat quiet and waited. Cure swallowed the juice, smiled, and placed his glass back on the table. "So, again, Courtney, what can we expect from you on the court, on a day-to-day basis?"

"Mr. Gerard, no disrespect intended, but you've seen me play, quite a bit, too. You know what I'm capable of and what kind of player I am and will be. You know that Atlanta wasn't my best and that I was passed over because my agent didn't advise me correctly. I would have gladly participated in those camps, Portsmouth and Chicago both, if that had been requested of me." Courtney thought about his ribs at the time, his injuries from Black's beat down, knowing that he couldn't have possibly done more than he did, but his desire would have been there. He turned his mouth up, looked Cure straight in the eyes. "You know I can be an all-star in the NBA."

Cure smiled, nodded, stopped, and took another swig of his orange juice. Courtney kept his eyes on Cure as he lifted the glass, placed it to his lips, and then placed it back on the table. He wanted Cure to know that he was as serious as an IRS audit when it came to his basketball career.

Cure tapped his lips with those midget fingers, then said, "I like the conviction in what you're saying, young man. That's all fine and well, and I agree with you. I do think you can be an all-star in the league. Question is, do you know it? Because hardly any of the so-called experts and analysts hold that kind of expectation for you anymore. Golden State isn't sure of what they're getting with you. You're in the position now of having to prove yourself to everyone all over again. What you did in college doesn't matter anymore. I've checked into your background, young man, and without saying anything too specific, I'd say you have to clear up a lot of things in your life and then maybe you can give basketball your one-hundred-percent effort. Would you agree?"

Courtney looked at Cure. That eye of the tiger the older man said might be gone was roaring loud and clear in his pupils. Cure, Courtney was sure of, could get his career back on track, could get him the success he wanted. Did Courtney have things off the court that he needed to clear up in his life so he could concentrate on basketball with all his might? No doubt. He looked at Cure and nodded.

Cure clasped his hands together and sat forward in his chair. "Okay, then. Let's get to work, young man."

Grief can hang over a person for weeks without making his shoulders slump, without making tears form in his eyes, without making his body tremble, but, inevitably that grief will consume him, and his emotions will pour out in an unsettling burst. On the morning of Liza's third day missing, the morning of Colin's DNA sample collection, that unsettling burst of grief found his shoulders, eyes, and body. In the master bedroom, with the door closed and latched, he sat on the king size poster bed with the colorful linen spreads wrapped around him like a superhero's cape. But if he were Superman, the smell of Liza that still held so strongly to the sheets was his Kryptonite. He'd slept down the hall in the living room the three previous nights, but a stiff back made him use the bedroom last evening. He'd come into the room after midnight and decided to finish writing on his laptop, then fell asleep in the big corner chair with the computer in his lap. Around five in the morning he woke, closed his computer, and lay on the bed. The smell of her caught his nostrils immediately and he hadn't gotten any sleep from that point on. When the sun came through the windows this morning to deliver the message that another day had begun, the tears flowed freely down Colin's face. He realized that with each passing day, the prospect of good news dimmed.

By six A.M. he was still sitting in the same spot, now trembling.

By seven A.M., his shoulders had slouched as if he carried big baskets full of fruit, like the Africans on the Discovery Channel, on each one.

The looming DNA sample collection only added to his tension, worry, and distress. He'd planned to be at the collection site when they first opened, ten thirty according to the woman he spoke with on the phone the other day. Colin glanced at the clock. It was five minutes to eleven and he'd yet to shower or shave, stuck like mud by second thought. Did he want to do this?

He thought back to his call to the lab the other day, to schedule a collection time, and make sure he had clear directions.

"Is this a court-ordered testing or for curiosity purposes?" the receptionist had asked.

"Curiosity," he answered.

"Okay, you can come in anytime. I suggest first thing in the morning, because the lab gets increasingly busy as the day progresses. We're open for collections starting at ten thirty. Now, hold on the line and I'll transfer you to our automated directions line."

Curiosity—curiosity killed the cat. What harm might it inflict, what damage might it do if his blood swam through Destiny's veins instead of Courtney's? Why not continue as they had, Chante's word bonding Courtney as the child's father? Courtney had called him last evening and said he understood if Colin didn't get the testing done in light of the situation with Liza. That had been Colin's out. But he'd said he wouldn't hear of it, that he would do the test.

A light tap at the door broke through his concerns. He wiped his eyes with the backside of his hand.

"Yes?"

"May I come in, Colin?"

"Sure, come in, Mama." She pushed in, but the door didn't budge. "You got this thing locked?"

"Oh, yeah, hold on. I'm coming." He rose and unlocked the

door, turned back, and sat on the bed before she came through the door.

"Why you all locked up in here? You okay?" She had left the door open, but, as she got a good look at him, she turned and closed it behind her.

"I'm doing fine," Colin lied. "Lyric didn't wake up yet, did she?"

"If you were doing fine, you'd know. You haven't stayed shut up in your room like this any of the days since I've been here. Yes, she's still sleeping. Liza's mother is keeping her ears open for her." She moved next to him on the bed, sat, and placed her hands on his knee. The gesture made his eyes start to water again, and so he turned and looked away, forced the tears to reconsider.

"Today's the day you have to go give that sample at the lab, ain't it?" his mother asked.

He nodded, still looking away.

"Having second thoughts?"

"Nervous."

"You do know it's something you've got to do?"

He sighed, nodded.

"Your brother's counting on you, Colin."

"I know, Mama; I'm going."

"Let me ask you something," his mother said. She paused, waiting for Colin to give her permission, but he didn't, so she continued, "I know you didn't want Liza's mother to know about you going to the lab, today. Liza knew about this mess with Chante?"

"It only happened once, and it shouldn't have happened then, so I didn't tell her at first. Recently, before we separated, she figured it out. Why?"

His mother tapped his knee. "Just been wracking my brain trying to figure all this out, what that poor girl is going through."

"Pain," Colin said. "A lot of it."

Lena nodded. "You young folks."

Colin cleared his throat, looked at his mother. "You remember that fire at the Parker's house?"

Lena smiled. "I sure do." She touched Colin's knee again. "You knocked on those folks door and—"

"I set it," Colin cut her off.

Lena stared at him, unable to speak.

"Kim wouldn't have sex with me, but she went and got pregnant by this older boy. We were supposed to be going steady and she did that. My boys, Juno and Pumpkin, were with me when I found out. They were busting on me, as usual, and talking about what they'd do in retaliation if that happened to them. They mentioned burning her house down."

"Oh, my Lord!"

"I just wanted to fit in," Colin admitted. "Always have wanted to fit in, to feel loved, to belong."

Lena sat quiet.

"That girl . . . Kim. She lost her baby because of my foolishness, Mama. I've never gotten over that. Never will. I think I deserve everything that is happening to me."

"Was a terrible thing to do," Lena replied. "But God doesn't punish folks like that. Have you asked Him for forgiveness?"

"I have," Colin told her.

"Move on, then, Colin. Make it your mission to do the right things from this moment forth." She tapped her watch.

Colin looked at his mother, tears in his eyes. "I'm sorry I couldn't be what you needed, Mama. I tried, I really tried."

Lena looked back at him, her eyes moist as well. "You remember what you said to me when your father was gone for good?"

Colin shook his head.

"You said, "It's all on me now, Mama. I'll take care of us.""

Colin smirked. "I couldn't have been further off base."

Lena shook her head, smiled. "You did, though, Colin. You took care of us and that shouldn't have been a weight for you to carry. You were a boy. No matter what mistakes you've made, and will make, I love you for taking that weight. I love you for taking care of us."

Colin looked at her, grateful.

"Liza will return, refreshed, and realizing how lucky she is, Colin. You bet on that."

She rose from the bed, patted Colin's back, and left the room. He appreciated that none of the family talked about Liza in the past tense, though he couldn't do the same.

Figuring life out was in most cases impossible. Understanding the whats and whys of things. Colin might never see Liza again; he'd been trying to prepare himself for that reality, and that was beyond his control. Destiny's paternity, though, he could get the answer to that question. All he had to do was get up, get ready, and go take the test. He pounded his fisted hands together, took a deep breath that rose from his chest, and chased away the sudden grief that had overtaken him this morning. This had to be done.

The lab still hadn't filled by the time he got there, shortly after twelve. They had him show his driver's license for identification purposes, and he had to present his social security card as a second verification. Then they handed him a form that he had to fill out. The form was short, asking for the names of all persons being tested, the date of birth or approximate age of the child whose parentage was in question, the city and state of all persons giving samples, any attorney's involved, and the lab where his sample was to be forwarded to. Courtney had prepared him for the form, so it took just a moment to fill out. He tapped the form with his pen when he finished and took it back to the lady at the counter.

"Finished already?"

"Yes, ma'am," he said, swept up in a sea of easiness. On the ride over, Colin thought about how much hope was in Courtney's voice the past few days as they talked on the phone. God wouldn't dare dash that desire Courtney had to be a father. Would He?

"Come on in, Mr. Sheffield." The decisive moment had arrived.

Colin walked through the door and turned in the first room on the right as instructed.

"This is pretty simple," the woman informed him. She held up what looked like a large Q-tip. "This is a buccal swab, a special applicator with a Dacron tip. I'm going to rub it in your cheek to collect epithelial cells for the DNA testing. Okay?"

"All right."

She moved in close, her hands in white medical gloves. Colin opened his mouth and she rubbed the inside of his cheek as promised. "Okay, Mr. Sheffield, thanks. We'll be sure and get this sent to the lab in New York today."

"That's it?"

She smiled. "Told you it was simple."

Colin uncrossed his fingers and took a breath. He'd done his part, now all he hoped was that God did his.

* * *

"Any news?" Courtney asked his uncle.

Uncle Carl turned and looked at him, those sad, droopy eyes telling more than words could. He shook his head, ran his fingers down the side of his face. The skin on his face, much like his eyes, drooped, forming a puddle of jowls around his jaw. Courtney hadn't noticed them until the past few days. Carl turned from Courtney's glare—none of the family could stand to look at each other much lately, all of them saddened further by the sadness on each other's faces—and leaned against the kitchen countertop for leverage so he could reach up in the cabinet and pull down a juice glass. "I fixed iced tea; you want some?"

"Nah," Courtney said, and pulled out a seat at the kitchen table.

"Your Mama called up here before you got in," Uncle Carl muttered. "Thangs is pretty much stagnant she said. The police don't know anything and they haven't gotten any clue whatsoever as to what might have happened."

Courtney shook his head, taking it all in. "Unbelievable."

Uncle Carl poured his iced tea and hurried a sip before Courtney could question him whether or not it had sugar in it. It did. Carl's diabetes, though, was the least of his worries lately. He pulled out the seat across from Courtney and sat at the table. "Your Nana been sleeping like a rock these past few days; that's got me to worrying, too. You never know what's gonna set old folks back, what's gonna make 'em lose that zest for living. You lose that zest and . . ." He looked away, looked up, could feel Myrtle watching him, and so he rerouted. "Yessuh, young snapper, I tell you. I ain't seen so much drama in my life; you young folks are just a breakin' my heart."

"Hopefully, that'll change," Courtney replied. "I know I want it to. I've had about enough of all this drama."

Uncle Carl tapped two misshapen fingers on the table top. "That young gal of yours called here. She mentioned a Family Day Block Party, and also to tell you that y'all can go meet up with the folks at the medical center on Thursday morning around eleven to do your testing, and then they'll have the results by five. Your Mama also said to let you know that Colin went and did his part today."

Courtney sighed at that bit of news. "Yep, this is it, Unc. We finally get to settle that situation once and for all. I'm glad we're getting this all done."

"Yessuh, you boys got your ways about you, but basically you trying to do right. I talked to Colin the other day about this . . . whatchamacallit?"

"It's a DNA sample," Courtney offered. "They'll be able to tell which one of us is the father by comparing our DNA, everyone's is different."

"Okay, well I talked with him that day and he was hopeful the baby is yours. He was remorseful about the whole thing. He did a lot of talking about the future. I was telling him that once I open the shop back up, he should come in and do one of his book signings there. He said he'd never thought of that."

"That is a good idea," Courtney agreed.

Uncle Carl tapped the side of his head, managed a smile. "That's the entrepreneur in me, yessuh." Hay, hay, hay. He coughed.

"We haven't gotten a chance to see each other, me and Colin," Courtney said, "but I think we are at peace with each other. At least I feel like I am with him. We're going to get together soon. Everything has made me realize where my priorities lie. I'm moving on from all the negative aspects of my life and trying to reach a greater level of happiness and success."

Uncle Carl tapped those two same fingers on the tabletop again. "That's right; you had your meeting with the colored agent today, right? How did that go?"

Courtney smiled. "It went well, Unc. That brother is on the ball. His offices are off the heezy—" Uncle Carl looked at Courtney with a blank expression. "I mean, his offices are big, and he has artwork up by black painters, an entire hall of them. It's like a museum. He's mad-cool . . . down to earth. He told me point-blank where I screwed up, and came up with his plan to get me back on course. After we signed the papers, he got on the phone right away and called out to Oakland to speak with Golden States' general manager."

"Oh, yeah?"

"Yep. Told them he didn't want to play any negotiating games, that he wanted me signed, sealed, and delivered in time for the Summer Pro League."

"What's that? Summer Pro League?"

Courtney leaned forward on his elbows, his enthusiasm bubbling over. "It's like a mini-league for rookies and free agents, some hopefuls. Starts July 10 and runs through July 17—six games and two practices. Games are at this place called the Pyramid, at Cal State Long Beach. We'll be playing a bunch of other NBA summer league teams. I'm looking forward to it."

"So you gonna be an official professional basketball player. I'm proud of you, young snapper, yessuh."

"Yeah, Unc, everything is starting to fall into place for me." He looked off around the kitchen. "I hope it works out for Colin, and hopefully this thing with Destiny goes well."

Both men sat still at that point, reflecting on life. Life was a collage of colors, bright, vivid, loud colors during the high moments, and dark, drab, quiet colors during the frequent lows that life tossed like shells from an angry sea. In a few days Courtney would have the answer to his most nagging question. Was Destiny his child? Also, Colin's life would be settled. Was either man truly ready for the fate mailed to them from that heavenly Postmaster? Time would reveal the answer.

21

JULY 1

Colin was in the baby's room, struggling to adjust the side of the crib, when Mama Brashear walked in. The morning sunlight slid through the venetian blinds, but Colin had been in this room fiddling around with first one item, and then the next, way before light. Sleep, the commodity Liza craved so much, was an afterthought in his life. On the surface, he dealt with its absence well, but just as he'd missed Liza these past few days, this past month in actuality, his body missed rest. His reflexes, the sharpness of his mind—all of it thrown off-kilter by his inability to close his eyes during the night hours.

Mama Brashear came up next to him and placed a hand on his shoulder. He continued pulling at the levers on the crib, trying to get the side to move down. He could only manage to get it to move up. His failed attempts were pushing him farther from his goal, each thrust up moving him farther from the position he'd wanted to achieve when he first moved the side. Mama Brashear eased back to allow him the space to operate, but, when he became frustrated and kicked the leg of the crib, she moved back to him and took him by the elbow.

"Come sit down, son-in-law," she said. "I'll fix you up breakfast. You can work on that later."

He eyed the crib, close to despondent over his failure, not wanting to leave the job unfinished. Mama Brashear gave his arm a slight tug, and this time he moved with her. On his way out the door, the Noah's Ark sketching caught his eyes; he bit his lip and looked away. Four days—was there any point in hoping anymore? In a way, he'd hoped going and doing the DNA sample the other day would gain him favor with God and that Liza would be waiting for him when he returned from the lab. But it hadn't worked out that way.

Mama Brashear pulled out a chair for him at the small kitchen table, tossed him the morning newspaper, and moved to the sink. Colin considered the seat before he eventually sat. Eyed it like a combatant. "Thanks," he said after awhile, and took the seat. Mama Brashear turned back to him, surprised to hear his voice, and smiled a "you're welcome."

"You like your coffee black?" she asked.

"Actually, I'm not much of a pure coffee drinker. I'd prefer it with a lot of cream and sugar, if it isn't too much of a problem."

Mama Brashear shook her head, signaling that any way he wanted it was fine, and pulled down a large coffee cup from the cabinet. She was pouring the coffee out of the pot when she thought about Liza. Liza always drank her coffee the same as Colin. Sickening was how Mama Brashear always described the creamy, sugary sludge. That's how it had been the past few days, the most insignificant things bringing about a flood of memories. The memories made the tears threaten to form in her eyes— though she'd managed to push them back. Other memories made her mouth crease up in a smile.

"You were thinking about how Liza likes her coffee the same way, weren't you?" Colin said, breaking her thoughts.

Mama Brashear turned to him, her brows hunched, a half-smile on her face. "Yes, I was. How did you know?"

Colin smiled, his first of the day. "I was thinking the same thing as soon as I said it. Plus, I saw you smiling. You know Liza's the one that turned me on to drinking my coffee that way?"

"You get sugar diabetes, you can blame her," Mama Brashear offered as she mixed in the condensed milk.

"I hope I get the chance to," Colin sadly replied. The brevity of those words anchored both of them in place. Neither one spoke for the next few minutes.

Colin sipped his coffee in silence, thumbing through the newspaper, looking at the pictures.

"Would you like another one?" Mama Brashear asked him as she stood over his empty coffee cup.

"Yes, please." Colin smiled. "Only about two thirds coffee, though. You have to save room to top it off with that cream and sugar, a bit more this time."

Mama Brashear shook her head. "You're going to be hopping around here like a kangaroo today, for sure."

The phone rang and made both of them jump. They looked from each other to the phone to each other again, both of their faces conveying hope that good news was waiting on the other end, both of them afraid to pick up, in case the opposite held true. Mama Brashear wiped her hands on her apron and moved over to the phone. She moved slowly enough so a telemarketer might get the hint that they were off at work and would stop trying to get through. The phone continued to ring, though.

"Hello?" she said as Colin looked on, his heart waiting for a response before it committed to another beat.

"Oh, Arman, hello." Mama Brashear looked back at Colin and he resumed breathing. "I was fixing Colin breakfast. No, we haven't heard anything yet today. Lena took Lyric out for a walk in her stroller. No, that's fine. Come on over whenever you get the chance. Okay, bye-bye."

Mama Brashear placed the phone back in the cradle. "That was Armando. He's going to head back down here later today."

"That's good."

"He wants to stay involved in all this."

"As he should; Liza's his daughter."

Mama Brashear nodded. After their flare-up the other day, she and Armando had gone outside and walked around the complex, airing their differences as the early evening settled into a stargazing darkness. They didn't come away from it with a renewed love for one another, but they managed to squelch the bitterness that had enclosed them both since the divorce. Armando had opened up about things Mama Brashear never knew. She, in turn, had told him things he never could understand about her. They both came away with a more thorough knowledge of the other, both aware that the one bond between them, their daughter, was more important than a decades-old feud.

The room got silent again as Mama Brashear thought over how to broach the concern that had captivated her mind since she

came the other night and read that note. She whipped the eggs
with her eyes on the parking lot outside. She chopped little por-
tions of ham, onion, and peppers as Colin tried to keep himself
busy scanning over the newspaper. He struggled with the paper.
The sports section's box scores and who Simon Cowell dissed on
American Idol couldn't hold his attention any more than a passage
in one of Langston Campbell's overblown novels.

Mama Brashear was about to pour the whipped egg whites and
the ham and the onions into the frying pan, when she decided to
take a seat by Colin. He put down the newspaper and looked up
in expectation.

"One thing has been on my mind," she said. She pushed the
words out.

"What's that?"

Mama Brashear frowned. "I was thinking about that note Liza
left and, well, she said she'd been shaking the baby and that she
was concerned about that."

Colin looked down at the table surface. Mama Brashear could
see that the same thought had crossed his mind. "Maybe," she
said, "it would be a good idea if you took Lyric in to the doctor
and got her checked out. Just to make sure she's okay. That she
hasn't been damaged in any way." The horror of the thought
made her immobile, her fidgety hands sat still.

"She seems okay," Colin said, his tone defensive, sticking up for
his missing wife.

"Yes, she does," Mama Brashear conceded. "But we're not doctors. I'm sure she's okay. Just as a precaution, like I said."

"I don't want them thinking Liza is an animal, that she would
hurt her own child," Colin answered.

Mama Brashear looked away briefly to compose herself. So
many aspects of this situation were hard to deal with. Her only
child could be in a ditch, bathing every morning in mud and
squirrel urine. Her only grandbaby could be suffering from neurological damage, suffered at the hands of her own mother.

"Liza is the best kind of mother," Mama Brashear said, her tone
one of convincing. "She realized something wasn't right with how
she was handling motherhood, and she tried to come up with a
solution that was best for her child. Nobody can call her an animal, son-in-law."

Colin soaked it all in. How might he have made things different if he'd stayed? If he'd deserved to stay, that is? Fact of the matter was that Liza was overwhelmed with the task of raising this child alone. Who wouldn't be? It was a task meant for two and he'd failed her. Mama Brashear was right; his missing wife was no animal. He gritted his teeth, tapped the table with a balled fist.

"I'll call our physician and see if she has any openings today," Colin said. Immediately, he rose from the table and went in the living room to place the call.

When she heard Colin's voice coming from the living room, him stuttering as he talked to the receptionist at the doctor's office, Mama Brashear slumped down on the table and allowed the tears that she'd held inside for the past few days to flow.

Courtney rifled through the pile of letters, three shoeboxes worth. Chante had been with him when he was still wearing Nike and endured up until he switched over to And 1. There was a lot of history between them, most of it good, he had to admit. But then . . .

Please forgive me, the card he held in his hand read, marked with Chante's neat handwriting. He opened it and read through the inside.

I made a terrible mistake.

Colin means nothing to me.

I can't go on without you.

He slammed the card shut like a heavy book, tossed it in his throwaway pile. He'd decided to do spring-cleaning with his soul. Anything lacking a positive value had to go. The toughest part of the task was the deciding—defining positive, measuring value.

The phone rang.

"Hello?"

"Hey, there," Chante said. "What you up to?"

The deciding—defining positive, measuring value—made Courtney's head hurt. He was filled with frustration that Chante wasn't giving him the space he needed to carry out the task. "Same thing I was doing earlier when you called," he said. "Cleaning up my room, packing things."

"You sound on edge," she observed.

"I am," he admitted.

Chante made an assumption as to the root of his problem.

"You've got to put the draft behind you. The Flames made a mistake. You'll make them regret it. I believe in you."

"I'm not studying the Flames," Courtney shot back. His voice had a bite that he didn't recognize, that he didn't mean to cut into her.

"So, are you coming to the Family Day Block Party later? I'd love to see you. Destiny would, too."

"No. I told you already."

"What's wrong, Court?" she asked. "You worried about the test tomorrow?"

"No," he said. His worries went beyond the short term. He wondered how Chante fit into his future.

"Liza?"

"Of course," he said, "but that's not it."

"Tell me what's wrong then," Chante said.

"What's wrong is you keep calling me every five minutes. I can't breathe, Chante. What's wrong is you aren't allowing me the space or peace to get my mind wrapped around everything that's going on."

"Oh." Her voice was crestfallen, embarrassment and hurt her newest allies. "I guess I read something wrong the past few days. I'll let you go then."

He softened. "I'll be by tomorrow so we can go to the lab, okay?"

"Sure," she struggled to answer.

"All right, then, see you tomorrow."

"Tomorrow it is."

They hung up in unison, though their intentions and thoughts weren't in sync—his on the future, and hers on the devastating present. Would they ever gel?

I'm in a funk. I'm depressed. My mood swings are horrible. And, worse than anything else, I've been taking it out on my child. I get so upset at her for crying. I know it's wrong, but, I've been shaking her and I can't stop myself. I'm scared of what I might do. Afraid of what I've already done.

These words were found on the bottom of the second page of the note Liza had left. It was as if she'd written them as an afterthought, as if it took her getting to those last few lines of the page to work up the courage to admit the demons that controlled her. Colin had crumpled up the second page after he showed it to his mother, mother-in-law, and father-in-law. He crumpled it up that first night as he slept on the couch waiting for his wife to walk through the door. He burned the crumpled note into ash after the twenty-four hour period had passed and he could file an official report with the police. The police only saw the first page of the note. They were looking for her as a missing person, not a criminal. But now Colin had to face the possibility that she had in fact committed a criminal act, that she had harmed the most precious thing God ever gave either of them—Lyric.

He was in the examining room of Lyric's pediatrician, Dr. Shamalan, a pleasant Indian woman with peanut-butter-colored skin and thin, bony fingers that curled over in delight every time a young child came in contact with them. Dr. Shamalan had Lyric in her arms, rocking her as a mother would, but few doctors did. Colin couldn't help but think that Dr. Shamalan was one of the few people in life who knew what it was God had intended for her. She looked as comfortable with a baby in her arms as Zora Neale Hurston with a pen in her hands.

"Shaken Baby Syndrome is still relatively new and there are few statistics, and even fewer facts, about it," the doctor advised Colin as she toyed with Lyric. "We do know the dangers of shaking an infant. Blindness, cerebral palsy . . . death."

Colin swallowed and closed his eyes. What a pitiful trifecta if he ever heard one.

"Here is a pamphlet I pulled out for you," the doctor said. "It lists the neurological symptoms, signs that can possibly point to Shaken Baby Syndrome."

Colin reached for the pamphlet, his hands trembling.

Head turned to one side
Child unable to lift or turn head
Pinpointed or dilated pupils
Blood pooling in the eyes
Lethargy
Difficulty breathing
Pupils unresponsive to light
Seizures or spasms
Swollen head

The pamphlet startled him even more. He looked at Lyric, feeling helpless and small. "All this just from shaking?" he asked.

Dr. Shamalan sat on her roller chair, let Lyric rest against the collar of her lab coat. "From vigorous shaking, yes, Mr. Sheffield. A baby's brain is fragile and, by shaking the baby, the brain slams against the skull. This can cause cerebral hemorrhage, contusion, edema—that's bleeding within the brain, tears in the brain tissue." Colin shivered, threw his head back and moaned the Lord's name. "I know," the doctor said. "It's pretty gruesome stuff."

"I don't know what to say," Colin confided. His eyes were welling with tears.

The doctor rolled over by him, handed him Lyric. "Continue to care for her as you've been doing, and hopefully once Mrs. Sheffield returns—and I'm sure she will—hopefully you can impart upon her how important it is that she handle her child with the gentlest care."

"What about the baby?"

"She's fine," the doctor said, soothingly. "I'm glad you brought her in, and I'm hoping for a happy ending for you and your family. Mrs. Sheffield impressed me with her knowledge and the questions she always asked—she's like a sponge when it comes to child care. She's a worrier, though, and I hope she isn't somewhere beating herself up thinking she harmed her child. Trust me. Lyric is doing wonderfully."

Colin sighed, his eyes shot open wider. "Really!" Next to Liza walking through the door, this was the greatest thing Colin could experience. His daughter was healthy. "Thank you, Dr. Shamalan," he said.

The doctor nodded, smiling. "When Mrs. Sheffield returns, you be sure and give her that card I gave you. I think if she sits and talks with Dr. Knight, she'll find peace with herself. Dr. Knight has been dealing with mothers and the myriad emotions they encounter after childbirth for years. Like I said, I highly recommend her."

Colin rose, holding Lyric in his left arm, and extended his right hand to the doctor. She took it, and covered it with her other hand, forming a sandwich of comfort that Colin would never forget.

* * *

"*Addicted* by Zane. Fifteen dollar."

Courtney eyed the African vendor, smiled. "I thought this was a family-day event, my man."

With the ease and fleetness of a deer's stride, the vendor pressed another book under Courtney's nose. "*Little Bill presents . . . The Honeywood Street Fair.* Six dollar."

Courtney nodded. "Give me this and—" He pointed his chin at a novel sitting on one of the vendor's overturned milk cartons, away from the stacks on the table. "That book there, too."

"Twelve dollar," the vendor replied as he handed Courtney the books.

Courtney frowned. "It's only six dollars for this other book?"

The vendor eyed the novel, *Prophet's Message,* by Colin Sheffield. "He writes not enough push-push in the bush. Sex big in Nigeria. Sex definitely big here in wonderful America."

Courtney ran his fingers over the spine of Colin's novel. "Give me both the copies you have of this, then." He'd gone, in one week, from disparaging his brother's work to having more copies on hand than Barnes and Noble. He'd need the extra copies, though, gifts to those he cared about most.

"Eighteen dollar," the human calculator of a vendor replied.

Courtney paid him, placed the books in his backpack, and moved up the block.

Children ran around in circles, barbecue sauce from chicken and burgers on their cheeks and mouth. Music blared from opened second-floor apartment windows, car trunks, and the performers playing steel drums. The scent of barbecue and roasted nuts was in the air. A bald Latin man with tattoos up and down his chiseled arms walked up the street in a wife-beater T-shirt, a snake, thick as a tree trunk, draped around his neck and across his shoulders. A pack of young girls with women's hips did an impromptu cheer in the middle of the street. Everyone's face held a smile, oblivious to the bullet-shorn car windows and graffiti-marked buildings right in their lap. The festive nature of the Family Day Block Party actually made Courtney comfortable with Chante and Destiny living in this neighborhood.

"Courtney Sheffield."

Courtney turned to the soft voice that had called his name. The young woman attached to that soft voice was bowlegged, sexy, almond-colored, with big eyes shaded with lavender makeup, and wearing Daisy-Duke shorts and a midriff-bearing T-shirt with *Nympho* emblazoned across the front. She had her hair styled in two pony-tails, a look that made something move within Courtney. He fumbled and dropped his cell phone as his heart rate changed and his mouth went dry. Two-ponytailed Ms. Nympho bent and picked the Motorola flip up, held on to it the same way Courtney's eyes held on to her curves.

"Hey," he replied in his deep voice.

She looked up at him from the street, cocked her head side-ways, bit into her lip. "You don't remember me, do you?"

"Vaguely," Courtney admitted.

"I graduated with Chante, two years behind you. Thalia. Thalia Ortiz."

"Thalia," Courtney said, emphasizing the name. "Right. How have you been?" He eyed her as he waited for a response. She'd been drinking lots of milk, he thought, and it had done her body good.

"Y'all two still hooked up?" Thalia asked.

"What's that?"

She moved closer to Courtney. He didn't step back, though he knew he should. "You and Chante still hooked up?" she repeated.

Courtney squint his eyes and looked up the block. Chante's building was only the distance of three basketball courts away from where he now stood. He turned back to sexy Thalia, half smiling, half grimacing. "In a way, I guess," he answered. He couldn't believe those words had come from his mouth with sexy, two-ponytailed Ms. Nympho so close he could smell the Crème of Nature moisturizer in her hair.

"Don't sound too convincing," she replied. She took a hold of his elbow, used it to pull herself up on the curb, closer to him. The look she gave Courtney for the assistance was as if he'd chased down a mugger and returned her pocketbook. "I saw Chante the other day," she continued, "pushing a stroller. Are you her baby's daddy?"

A black Ford Explorer with tinted windows moved past, the music blaring so loud it shook the back windows. Everyone within distance, including Courtney and Thalia, stopped and watched the vehicle slowly pass by. Courtney noticed the Explorer didn't have license plates. They needed to have more of a police presence if they were going to have these block parties, he thought. He shrugged it off, turned his attention back to sexy Thalia.

"You were saying?" Courtney asked Thalia.

"Are you her baby's daddy?"

"Well—" A loud succession of popping noises rang out, halting Courtney's tongue. He looked up. A sea of panicked men, women, and children were drifting toward him from Chante's end of the block.

"They shooting," somebody yelled out as they stormed past.

Two more loud pops echoed.

Courtney thought about the odd, black Ford Explorer with no license plates. He thought about Chante and Destiny out on the stoop in front of Chante's building sharing a grape-flavored shaved ice. Chante loved to sit on that stoop and people-watch.

Peace be still or yah seed and dutty gurl be next, seen?

Black.

Courtney took off toward Chante's, his heart racing. He looked ahead to see the black Explorer lurching around the corner, smoke literally rising up from under its tires. Panic had subsided and now a crowd gathered up ahead, in front of the building next to Chante's building. Courtney slowed a bit, his heart still racing, and waded his way through the crowd. Paranoia gripped him as he steeled himself for what he'd find at the center of everyone's attention.

He made his way to the front. A young woman's screams pierced through him, loud and grief-stricken. Courtney's legs felt unsteady as he moved his last steps forward.

Courtney took a deep breath when he saw a blue-black man lying on the sidewalk. An expanding crimson-colored stain broke out on his bullet-riddled chest, while his girlfriend, wife, or whoever she was, sat over him, screaming bloody murder.

Courtney looked past the crowd and there he saw her.

Chante was on her stoop, as Courtney expected, with Destiny in her stroller at Chante's feet. Chante was visibly shaken up, trembling, hugging herself. Courtney circled the crowd and walked over to her.

Chante's eyes widened and she made a move to hug Courtney.

"Happened so fast," she said. "I was right here. They could have hit Destiny."

"I know," Courtney said.

"I saw the muzzle come out of the side window and I . . ."

"Don't think about it, Chante." It was easy for him to say, though he knew he'd be dreaming about this event for who knew how long to come.

"I'm glad—" Something caught Chante's vision behind Courtney. Her eyes narrowed. Courtney turned back to see sexy Thalia standing by the curb, his cell phone in her manicured, nailed fingers.

"Hey, there, Chante," Thalia said. Then she looked at Courtney. "I got your phone, Court."

Courtney sighed, went and had a word with Thalia, and took his cell phone. Thalia waved at Chante, a devious smile on her face, and disappeared into the throng surrounding the downed blue-black man.

Courtney regained a spot on Chante's stoop at an angle so he could see Destiny in her stroller.

"You want to explain that?" Chante asked him, her voice hard.

"We spoke a bit, up the block. She introduced herself as a friend of yours. I dropped my cell phone and forgot it when I heard the gunshots. She was returning it to me."

"She hung with Sonya Raymond in high school," Chante said. "Another one of those girls always talking smack about what she'd do with you."

"Don't even remember her, Chante."

"Bet you won't forget her now, though." Chante crossed her arms. "Now that she's all grown up, huh?"

"I ain't thinking about that girl, Chante." And now, watching Destiny safe in her stroller, he wasn't. "I heard gunshots and I was afraid something might have happened to you or Destiny."

"Concerned?"

"Of course," Courtney said. Black's voice found his ear again. He shook it off as he'd been doing for some time, as he'd do until his plane touched down safely in California.

Chante shook her head. "You're playing with my emotions, Court. I know you think I'm a slut, but this isn't right. Why are you here? You said you weren't coming."

"Changed my mind," Courtney said. "I decided to hang out with you and Destiny. I don't have much time before I have to report to Cali."

Chante continued shaking her head. "I can't let you do this to me." She looked at little Destiny. "To us. I have a child now, Court. I don't have the option of not caring for this little girl. I don't have the option of running around trying to find myself while my daughter grows without me."

Courtney sniffed. "That's a low blow, Chante. Remember, *you* put us in this situation."

"This isn't a game, Court. But you're playing like it is." Chante rose up, wiped her shorts off.

"What are you doing?" Courtney asked.

"Giving you space, Court. Isn't that what you were hollering for this morning on the phone? You want to chase after bitches like Thalia or your little Atlanta booty call, do your thing. I'll see you when we go for testing, tomorrow."

"Chante, come on."

She ignored his voice, as he'd done with her many times. He kept trying to get her attention as she struggled with the stroller. She continued to ignore him and disappeared into her house, slamming the door behind her.

Courtney flipped his cell phone over in his hand, thinking. Chante accused him of playing a game. Well, in a game you had to choose sides. It was about time he decided who was on his team and who wasn't.

22

JULY 2

It had been a long night, but now it was Thursday morning, DNA day, and Courtney was on Chante's step again. "Can I come in?"

She eyed him, but said nothing. His words from yesterday on the phone still gnawed at her. *What's wrong is you aren't allowing me the space or peace to get my mind wrapped around everything that's going on.* Then he had the nerve to come to the block party, acting as if they were one, big, happy family, even though his mistress, Thalia, was among the crowd. He was blowing hot and cold with her and she wasn't having it. He could have all the space he needed. She'd never crowd him again.

"Can I come in?" Courtney repeated. A smile crossed his face.

What was he doing here so early when they didn't have to be at the lab for another four hours? Chante looked at Courtney, soaked him up with her tired, morning eyes as he stood on her stoop. She looked up to the sky, shielded the sun's blinding stare with her hand. Up behind all that blue and orange, her mother was looking down on her. Her father was up there, too. Ovarian cancer had stolen away her mother, an exotic liver problem had taken her father. Her father was gone her junior year of high school, her mother, shortly after she graduated. In the course of two years, the dinner table had gone from three to one. The only shoulders she had to lean on during those times were her Aunt Tammy, her cousin Renee, and Courtney. Chante glanced again at Courtney as he stood, smiling, waiting to be let in. The roof over her head, even if it wasn't in the best of Brooklyn's neighborhoods, and the welfare of their child would be uncertain if she'd waited on Courtney to provide. Thank goodness for the bit of money she received from her parents' insurance policies. How sad was that—death making the life she was struggling to carve out for her and Destiny possible. She looked to the heavens again. *Can he come in? Can Courtney walk across my doorstep?* A surprising breeze roared down on the muggy, already too-hot day. The breeze scattered the stray pieces of trash that the street sweeper missed and made the few passersby walking down the street stop and look up in appreciation. A sign from the heavens? Chante stepped aside so Courtney could enter.

"Thanks," he said as he moved past her at the threshold. She looked out to the street one last time and then closed the door behind them without reply. "Gonna be a hot one," Courtney said, standing in the small hallway, waiting for Chante to latch all the bolts on the door. Even if he only stayed a few minutes in this neighborhood, the precaution was a necessity.

"That's what they saying," she replied. Her words were softer than the linens that swaddled their child in her crib. She moved down the hall and stopped in the area designated as living room. She settled down on the worn couch, leaning forward and rubbing her eyes. Courtney stood and she didn't offer a seat.

"I caught you sleeping?" he asked.

"It is early," she said.

"I thought you'd be up and a ball of energy today—DNA day."

She looked at him, smirked, and shook her head in disbelief. "Today's no big day to me, I already know the results."

Courtney moved to her windows, opened the blinds, and let the sun come in and flood the room. "Too dark in here," he said.

"I like it like a cave," she said without the slightest bit of sarcasm.

"Nah, you gotta let the light in." He came over and eased next to her on the couch.

The closeness irritated her. What about all this space he supposedly needed? He didn't think it applied to her as well? "Your

Atlanta chick wouldn't be happy if she knew you were up in here huddled on the couch with me."

"Deep-sixed that," Courtney said, sadly. "I'm not going to lie and say she wasn't special, or at least she was headed to being something special—"

Chante shot up off the couch. "What makes you think I care to hear about this shit?"

Courtney sat back, flashing teeth. "You are way too spunky for your own good, Chante. I was just going to say that I realized me and her couldn't work."

"Oh, that's right," Chante said, smirking. "Atlanta dissed you. You're going to California. You can get yourself hooked up out in Hollywood. Hook up with a white girl from *Beverly Hills 90210* or some crap and treat her as a woman is supposed to be treated. Long as she knows I'm here and that I'm going to be getting mines for the next eighteen years, I don't give a damn." It was a lie, but it felt good saying it.

"You still pissed about that Thalia girl yesterday?"

"Screw her."

Courtney looked at Chante, deep, but said nothing. Chante turned in disgust and moved to the window, pulled her blinds closed, but not all the way. When she turned around, Courtney was still looking at her. Looking at her with lust, taking in the form-fitting gray shorts, the snug athletic top that showed off the chest Destiny, unlike most babies, had let her keep. She crossed her arms over her chest. "What are you doing?"

Courtney looked up, surprised. "What?"

She marched toward him, her steps loud on the thin carpet. "You come over here all early. You're looking at me like that? What's up? You think you gone screw me or something and I'll pass go on the DNA?"

"Can you cook meatloaf?" Courtney quickly asked her.

"Look, I don't know what you're selling, but I ain't buying."

"Yes or no. Can you cook a meatloaf?"

Chante huffed. "This is dumb shit, man." Courtney continued to watch her, waiting. She huffed. "I've never tried, so I can't say truthfully if I can cook a meatloaf."

"You like the room temperature hot or cold at night?"

"Oh, my God, you have gone and lost it?" she said, placing her hand on her head. She looked to him, shaking her head. "It depends. Sometimes I like it hot and sometimes I like it cold."

"So if I was lying next to you and you wanted the thermostat turned down or up, would you get up and do it, or ask me to?"

"I'd send your ass!"

Courtney smiled. If it was good enough for his Uncle Carl, it was good enough for him. He played with his hands, wishing he had a basketball to grip and twirl. He reached over and took Chante's hands instead. She hunched her eyes in surprise.

"I've been doing a lot of thinking these past few days, and, after the drama yesterday, I realized something." The shooting still weighed heavily on his mind. He thought about how unbearable life would be if Destiny, or, he might as well admit it, Chante, met harm in any way.

Chante was afraid to ask what he realized, but his touch made her. "What's that?"

"Getting passed over by the Flames hurt," he said. "Having Colin betray me, and me and him not on good terms this past year or so, stung." His eyes bore into her, made her uncomfortable, but she held her gaze on him, not wanting to miss anything. "But nothing, I mean nothing, has caused me as much pain as not having you in my life, and looking at that little girl in there and knowing in my heart she's mine, but, closing her out because I wanted to get back at you."

"Knowing she's yours?"

"Yeah, regardless of what the test says today, she's mine. You know why?"

Chante shook her head.

Courtney moved to a bent-knee position in front of Chante. "Because Chante Warner, for as long as I've known you, I have had nothing but love for you, and what's yours is mine, what's mine is yours. I desperately want to give you and me another try if you'll have me. No bullshit." He kissed her hand.

Chante closed her eyes for a moment as if she was chasing away a headache. She opened her eyes and smiled at him. "What about on the phone yesterday? You acted like you never wanted to speak to me again."

Courtney hunched his eyes in surprise. "What you mean? I told you I needed to think on things, that I needed some space. You mad about that?"

She shook her head, amazed. "No, I'm not mad . . . confused . . . but not mad." She took a breath, still shaking her head as if she couldn't believe what was happening. "Damn, you are full of surprises. For a minute there, I thought you were gonna make this some storybook, movie shit and pull out a velvet box with an engagement ring."

"Ahhh." Courtney pulled one of his hands free and reached down in his pocket. Chante's heart completely stopped. He pulled out a flat envelope. Her blood flowed again. "This is for you."

She took the envelope and fumbled to open it. She cut through the top with one of her fingernails, peered inside and then looked at him. "An airplane ticket?"

"I want you to come to California with me and see how far we can take this thing."

"I don't know what to say."

"Say you'll come."

"Why didn't you wait until after the test results to spring this on me?"

"I wanted you to know that this is my real feelings, that whatever that test says has no bearing on the fact that you're my beacon." He stopped, smiled. "Damn, that was poetic shit I just said . . . sounds like something Colin would write."

Chante wrapped her arms around his neck, squeezing so tightly. "No, Courtney. That sounds like you, like you and only you. I never gave up hoping and praying for you, never."

Courtney wrapped his arms around her in return. "I know you didn't, Chante. I could always feel you pulling me."

"We gonna make it?"

"I don't know," he answered, truthfully. "But we sure are gonna try."

Chante let the guard that she'd been holding up for so long fall. She trembled in his arms. That's all she could ask for, that they try.

Colin clasped hands with Angelo, their grips firm, the duration of the handshake solidifying that they, indeed, had a bond that went beyond book sales. Angelo said nothing, no great work of literature coming to mind that was poignant enough to express how he felt at the moment. Instead, he smiled, took in the resurrection of Colin, standing tall, standing strong. Weeks before, if he'd faced this newest disappointment, a missing wife, Angelo was sure Colin would have toppled over like a pile of uneven-sided blocks.

Colin turned to Henry, clasped hands with him as well, and then they broke the grip and gave each other a full hug. Henry patted Colin's back, batting away the moisture that wanted to visit his eyes.

"Thank you two for agreeing to this," Colin said after their initial greetings. "I know it's highly unconventional, but I wanted to gang up on the both of you." He smiled, letting them know his spirits hadn't been broken. "I wanted to thank you both for reaching out to me when I was at my lowest. Wanted to thank you for making me face my problems, for not allowing me to pawn them off. That last meeting with the both of you, painful as it was, saved my life."

Angelo nodded, Henry as well.

"How are you holding up, now," Henry ventured.

"You mean with Liza?"

Henry nodded. His eyes drooped. "Yes. Any new news?" His discomfort evident by his choice of word phrasing.

Colin moved to take a seat; Angelo and Henry followed, took seats of their own that placed the three of them in a circle around the small coffee table that Angelo had recently added to the office's décor.

"Police have been helpful," Colin said once they'd all gotten comfortable. "But, no clues, no developments, only hope."

"Did you see the ad we took out in the *Times*?" Angelo asked him. It was a full-page ad from the Beale Street family to the Sheffield family, conveying the publisher's thoughts and prayers during one of its most respected author's difficult times.

"Yes, I did. My family was greatly moved by that outpouring of support."

"Just our little way of conveying how much we care."

"Nothing little about it," Colin said. "And, the feeling is mutual. In fact, not only did that ad comfort me, but it also made me realize something, too."

"What's that?" Angelo asked him.

"The words were directed to me and my small family with the potential of reaching the *Times'* substantial circulation. But, whether or not anyone but my family saw it and paid attention is irrelevant. Those words were true and sincere—I'm sure of it— and they reached those they should have reached. That's how I look at my writing. As long as it's true and sincere, it'll reach who it was intended to reach. It wasn't intended to reach everyone, because everyone wouldn't receive the value of the words. I may never do Langston Campbell numbers, and I'm cool with that, but as long as I continue to write, I'm going to write with purpose. Speaking of writing—" Colin leaned down and opened the shopping bag he'd brought in with him. He pulled out two Bon Ton gift boxes. "You'll have to excuse me for this," he said, smiling sheepishly. "I was running a bit late this morning and this was the closest thing at hand." He handed one box to Henry, the other to Angelo. "Again, I know this isn't conventional, but I've been working on this and I just finished it. It's my newest novel, and I wanted you both to read it at the same time. I was on an unbelievable roll putting this together; I'm proud of it."

"Second half of the manuscript you already turned in?" Angelo wanted to know.

Colin shook his head. "No, something different entirely; this is the most personal piece of writing I've ever done. Read it over without thinking about publishing it, and let me know what you think." Colin turned to Henry who was busy removing the top of his gift box. "Henry, I know you might be upset I didn't discuss this with you, but it's something that just materialized."

Henry looked up. "No, no. I understand." Colin was grateful for that. He knew few agents would be that understanding.

"So, what's the title, the premise?" Angelo asked.

Colin smiled. "Don't think publication . . . read it at your leisure."

Angelo and Henry were both scanning the first page, reading over the first paragraph. They both smiled and nodded appreciatively as the words drifted from line to line. When it appeared both of them would read past the initial paragraph, Colin leaned in and pushed down their manuscripts like a minister tucking a reformed sinner below water for baptism. "Not now," he said.

"I wanted to see—"

Colin shooed Angelo. "Later, after I leave if you like."

Angelo looked at the neat stack of papers shielded by Colin's hand. The bit he was reading so far had pulled him in even more than Colin's normal prose. "Okay," he said, reluctantly.

"So," Colin continued, "I wanted to also apologize, to the both of you, for spiraling down like I did. I know this is a business, and the both of you had been counting on *Prophet's Message* being a commercial success."

"Actually," Angelo perked up, rose, and went to his desk. "Henry and I were looking this over before you arrived." He retrieved a single sheet of paper and returned to their circle, handing the sheet to Colin. "Sales have been strong. You'll make the best-seller list for *Essence.*"

Colin quickly glanced over the sheet, placed it on the coffee table. "Well, that's good, unexpected news."

"I'm getting word it might also break Doubleday's book club *Black Expressions.* It's doing well nationally," Angelo added.

"I'm sure the publicity over my missing wife has helped sales," Colin reasoned. Both Henry and Angelo looked away. "But that's okay," Colin continued, "Sales, and the circumstances of those sales, isn't the end-all-be-all for me anymore. All my life I've been struggling to be that one thing I wasn't. When I was a child I acted more like an adult than I should have. When I was nerdy Colin that liked to read, I tried to transform myself into cool Colin." He thought about the Parker girl. "When I was unpublished all I wanted was to be published, and then once I got published I wanted to be a mega-seller. I wanted to be Langston Campbell."

"So what do you want to be now?" Henry asked him.

"Right where I'm at," Colin said, smiling. "With all the good and bad that comes with where I'm at in my life. I figure if I stay still and appreciate the good, then I can evaluate the bad and figure out what to do about it." Colin shifted in his seat. "You know, people pick up books and they think all the answers to the book will be slowly revealed through the chapters, and then on the last page . . . poof . . . everything is clear." Colin shook his head. "You want to know about a book? It's all in the acknowledgments. All the people and events that made the book possible, that's as important, or more so, than the actual book. Me, in the book of my life, I'm still writing the acknowledgments."

"I like how the *Ricki Lake Show* does it," Courtney said. "Ricki just pops open an envelope and pulls out a colorful sheet of paper, then she looks up and shows the paper in big letters, YOU ARE THE FATHER. She does it right during the segment after they talk to the guests, too, none of that waiting to the end of the show garbage."

"Yeah," Chante agreed. "On *Montel* they have an expert come out and talk all that probability of ninety-nine point nine you are excluded or included stuff. Don't nobody care about all that shit."

Courtney held to her hand, looked around the crowded waiting room of the Medical Center. "Some nervous-looking dudes up in here."

"Are you one of them?"

He took her hand, his fingers still wrapped tightly with hers, and kissed it. "Not one bit."

The lobby door that led back to the testing rooms and the conference offices opened. The lab technician stood in the doorway with her clipboard. Courtney dropped Chante's hand and his posture tensed so, he could have balanced a ruler on his head.

"Ariel Sanchez, Virgil Holmes," the technician called out.

Courtney's posture slumped.

"Liar," Chante teased.

"What?"

"You're nervous."

Courtney smiled. "Okay, maybe a bit. Either way, though, like I said, I love you. This isn't going to change anything."

Chante was about to respond that she hoped it changed a lot, when the door opened again. Courtney's eyes shot to the woman by the door, the ruler on his head again, lying flat, balanced perfectly.

"Courtney Sheffield, Chante Warner."

Courtney took a deep breath, rose, and headed toward the woman. He was halfway to the door when he realized he'd forgotten something. Chante wasn't by his side or behind him. He looked toward their seats, she had her head cocked to the side, her hand extended and held in the air waiting to be escorted. Courtney rushed back to get her.

"My bad," he said.

"Don't worry about it," she said. "I'm the woman you love, that's all."

They walked back arm in arm to the technician who held the key to their future pressed against her chest on a clipboard. The technician ushered them into one of the counseling rooms and closed the door behind them. Courtney's pulse was off the charts, pumping harder than it had when he tried out with the Flames. Why did they have to come for a counseling session? Did this mean a good result or a bad result? Then again, hadn't Chante said everyone was counseled when they received their results? Courtney couldn't remember.

"Okay, Mr. Sheffield, Ms. Warner," the technician said, "We—"

Courtney interrupted her normal spiel. "Umm, I know you have to explain everything, but I just want to know if I'm Destiny's father."

"I know you're anxious, Mr. Sheffield, but we like to prepare our clients for every aspect of change that these results will bring about."

"I understand that," Courtney responded, "and I'm interested in knowing as much as I can about all of this, but please . . . I just want to know at this moment if that beautiful, little girl . . . If Destiny is my daughter."

The technician studied Courtney a moment and then looked at Chante with pinched eyes and a pursed mouth. "Did you give this young man a Father's Day gift, a card, or anything this past Father's Day?"

Chante gulped. "No." She could feel Courtney's grip tighten on her hand.

The technician continued to watch her. "And where is Destiny right now?"

"My . . . my . . . my cousin took her after we tested her. We didn't want her to have to sit around here all day."

The technician nodded her head. "And you say you didn't give this young man anything for Father's Day?"

Chante nodded.

The technician smiled. "Well you owe him, then."

"So, I'm the father?" Courtney asked.

"Yes," the technician confirmed, still smiling. "Congratulations."

Courtney let out a whoop.

Chante pointed her finger at the technician, smiling now herself. "You are bad."

Courtney turned and hugged Chante; she let her arms slip around his waist. They sat in their seats, rocking together, both of them crying.

23

JULY 3

Armando walked in the gym. He stopped every few feet to observe the different boxers. At one stop, an Irish bulldog of a pugilist was taking out all his frustrations on a jump rope, swinging the cords quicker than light traveled, landing in between skips with his full weight. At another stop a boxer, newly transplanted from Philly and fresh off a successful pro debut, was doing crunches in sets of ten, his mind focused on the day he'd fight for the title. Then there was Tulaman, the Hawaiian sensation, battering his sparring partner's ribcage with cinderblock blows, testing the lesser man's ribs and courage with each punch. Armando stopped by the ring, fixated by Tulaman's power, intrigued by the bad intentions and lack of mercy that followed each fist.

"You're a beast, Tula," he called out. He balled his own hands into fists, swung them through the air, energized. "Hmm, hmm, crush those ribs, baby."

Tulaman sensed Armando watching, heard him singing his praises, though he'd learned to channel in the ring, to block out everything except his opponent's agony. He punched harder, took liberties with the other boxer's head now. His sparring partner had enough; he dropped to the canvas, hit it headfirst, because his arms were too spent to help break his fall.

"Boo yow!" Armando screamed with delight.

Tulaman wheeled from the fallen boxer with disgust on his face. He ripped the tape that held his gloves in place with his teeth and threw them down on the canvas. He moved through the ropes without waiting to get his trainer's assessment of the workout.

"A beast," Armando repeated to no one in particular.

Carla moved over by Armando. She'd been waiting patiently, knowing better than to disturb him as he watched Tulaman wreak his havoc. She looked like she'd walk barefoot on hot coals if it allowed her the option of not saying what she had to say to Armando.

"What?" Armando snapped, picking up on her reluctance.

"You was gone long, long time."

"Told you I would be. Tomorrow's the Fourth of July; the bank was crowded." Armando bore into her with those intense eyes, but his stare-down did little to her, she wasn't looking, had her focus on the ground. "What is it, Carla? What now?" he asked her.

"You have a visitor."

Armando turned, scanned the gym.

"In your office," Carla confided.

"In my . . ." Armando broke off in a near trot in that direction. "Without me in there? You had better be bullshitting. I'm about to fire your ass behind this, Carla." The young Puerto Rican girl had been following on his heels, but she drifted off to the darkest corner of the gym when he threatened termination.

Armando broke through his office door, cussing. His eyes immediately went to his desk. His leather chair was turned with the back facing the door. The chair turned and froze Armando in his tracks; the knob from the office door swung into his lower back, pushing him inside.

"Hi, Daddy. Surprised to see me?"

Armando didn't know how to respond. Smile, frown? "Liza, everyone's been worried to death wondering what happened with you. What are you doing here?"

"Is that so?" she said. Her hair was mussed, her complexion marred by the dark patch of skin below her eyes. "I've been spending quality time with myself. Today I decided to come see you, spend quality time with my daddy."

Armando moved closer. Something, he couldn't pinpoint what, unnerved him about Liza. It was more than her disheveled appearance, it was her demeanor. His sense told him to move slowly. "Where you been, Princess?"

Liza plucked at the cup of pens and pencils on his desk, knocked the canister over, everything scattering. She looked up, touched her mouth with her fingers. "Oops."

"Princess, you're bothering me. Are you okay? Did someone hurt you?" He took a couple more small steps toward her.

"Hell, no, I'm not okay—and, yes, someone did hurt me. You."

"What can I do to help you now?"

Liza laughed. "When I came in here looking for you, that little, fast-assed puta out there could've told me you were in Jersey, distraught over your missing daughter, instead of at the bank. That would've helped."

Armando raised his hands as if Liza were the police. "I've been out to your place this week, Princess. In fact, I was going back, today, tomorrow at the latest."

Liza pushed back from the desk. "You haven't changed one bit." She moved over to his sink, turned on the light, and eyed herself in the mirror. "Damn, I look straight up tore up."

Armando watched her, stuck in his spot. "Princess—"

"Stop calling me that," Liza barked. "Makes absolutely no sense for you to always feed me that Princess nonsense, and yet . . ." Her voice trailed off, the tears flowed. She had been determined to keep from breaking down, but her emotions were in a weight class above her own. The fight found her overmatched. She bent down and opened the cabinet below the sink, pulled out a tattered cigar box.

Armando's eyes widened. "Liza, baby, what are you doing?"

She ignored him, flipped the cigar-box lid. "Ahh. See I told you that you never changed. Hi, Zennifer." Liza looked at him. "Ain't that what you named it, after my mother? Said you disliked her so much you had more than a bullet with her name on it."

"Princess . . . I mean, Liza, baby, that ain't no toy. Why don't you put that away before one of us gets hurt?"

"One of us already has been hurt," she replied, defiant. "One of us has been suffering a long time. One of us doesn't know which end is up anymore. Love is all I wanted. Nothing but love."

Armando remained calm, kept his eyes on her hands. "Liza, baby, you're obviously upset . . . You shouldn't be handling that right now."

"I'm way cool," she said, mocking him. Those were the words she'd heard him say to her mother, before their divorce, when Mama Brashear had threatened never letting him see Liza again. Armando didn't understand, didn't pick up the significance of the words as Liza said them to him now. They'd just been words, his way of keeping Zennifer from breaking him down. He hadn't meant them.

"Princess—"

"Argh," Liza cried. She swung her arms in the air, made Armando's heart stop as he zoned in on how carelessly she was handling his gun.

"Liza, think about that beautiful, little girl you got at home. Put down the gun and we'll get you help. I promise you, I'll help you."

"How many promises have you made me, Daddy?"

"I know," he said, admitting years of failure with those two simple words. "But like I said, remember that beautiful, little girl you have at home."

"I resent her and I love her," Liza answered. "Isn't that some sad shit? I saw how much it was eating Colin apart, not being around her on a daily basis. There I was, with her twenty-four seven, wishing I could get a break from her. I figured, shit, let him have her then. That's some awful shit, and I know it . . . it must be hereditary. All these days I've been trying to reconcile how I could feel that way, how I could not want my own child. Today it dawned on me. Like I said, it's got to be hereditary. You're responsible."

"Liza, please don't talk like this." He took a step in her direction, feeling as though he'd given the situation enough time to cool. He was wrong. Liza raised the gun and pointed it at him.

"Why not talk this way?" she asked. "It's the truth. You disputing me on this?"

Armando shook his head. "Maybe you're right, but you don't have to give up. We can get you help."

"Too late for that shit, Daddy. My life is fucked."

"No it's not, Liza."

"You know Colin cheated on me, Daddy?"

Armando shook his head.

Liza smiled. "I told him I did the nasty with Courtney. It fucked him up good. I practically gift-wrapped my husband and sent him to another woman's arms. He messed around with Chante."

"Chante?"

"Courtney's girlfriend."

"Oh?"

"Yup." She thought back on that night Courtney called the house, the pain in his voice. "Messed Courtney's life up, too. Telling my lies."

"Don't be so hard on yourself, Princess."

She ground her teeth. "Don't you get it, Daddy? I don't love myself. I'm indifferent to my child. I drove my husband to infidelity. I messed up his brother's life. I'm totally fucked." She sighed long and hard. "Why didn't you love me, Daddy? Why couldn't you stay by Mama and me?"

"I do love you, Princess. Always have. Your mother and I didn't work out. That doesn't have anything to do with you and me."

Liza took turns pointing the gun at her father, at herself. "You . . . Me . . . You. . . Me."

"Princess.".

"You."

"Don't do this—you're breaking my heart."

"Me."

"I want you to put that gun down on the ground right now. Okay, baby?"

"You."

"No matter how bad the situation, there is always an answer."

"Me."

"You have a mother that loves you."

"You."

"A husband that wants you to come home so you two can get your marriage back on track."

"Me."

"A daughter that loves you, that you love. I can't think of what they call it, but a lot of women get this deep depression after they give birth. Your mother had a mild case of it herself."

"You."

"I love you, Liza, you're my Princess."

She squeezed the trigger, released that white heat.

24

JULY 4

"How is she doing?"

Colin took his eyes off the monitor that kept track of Liza's vitals long enough to smile at Courtney, who'd walked in. "Thanks to the ventilator, she's still with me."

Courtney eased next to his brother, placed a hand on Colin's shoulder, the other on Liza. Her chest rose and fell in sync with the pump of the machine. "Man!"

"Congratulations," Colin said to him, his eyes fixed on the monitor. "Mama told me the news about Destiny."

Courtney squeezed Colin's shoulder. "Thanks, again, for giving your sample." He followed Colin's eyes. "What's those numbers mean?"

Colin squinted. "Top one is her heart rate. Normal is seventy-five to one hundred. Hers pretty much stays around ninety. That number nineteen is her breaths per minute. A breath every four seconds, fifteen per minute is normal, so she's okay. That ninety-six is her oxygen level. It should stay at, or close to, one hundred."

Courtney shook his head. It was all so overwhelming. "Man."

Colin let the numbers rest for a moment, turned and looked at Courtney. "It puts things into perspective."

"Yes, yes, it does," Courtney agreed.

"My book is doing wonderful, you and I are talking again, my daughter is becoming more of a little woman with each passing day . . . and my wife is breathing through a tube." Colin smiled—a grimace really—like a track star that pulled a groin muscle around the last turn and came up lame. "Guess you can't have it all."

"She's gonna pull through; she's got to," Courtney said.

Colin shook his head. "No, she doesn't have to."

"I meant—"

"I know," Colin said. "I've been thinking a lot about my life, about the mistakes I've made. At first, I thought of this as punishment. I've done shady things in my life."

"You've done a lot of good, too," Courtney said.

"Kim Parker didn't deserve to have her lungs filled with smoke, to lose her baby." Colin shook his head.

"It was a bad situation."

"You ever hear anything about her?" Colin asked.

Courtney shook his head. He'd heard that she found comfort in drugs, but he didn't want to bring that to Colin, have Colin wondering if that mistake he'd made so many years ago had destroyed her life course.

Colin continued, "So many mistakes, little brother. The thing with Chante—it's easy to feel like this is payback." He pointed his head to Liza. "But, I've moved on from that thinking. This isn't punishment; this is a lesson, Courtney."

Courtney had begun to tremble. A tear came to his eye and he quickly wiped it away. "What's the lesson in this?"

Colin took his free hand and ran it over his chin. "We spend too much of our lives chasing things, reaching for the stars, climbing the highest mountain, trying to realize the impossible dream. We need to spend it being thankful for what we have, while we have it. Liza wouldn't be lying there right now if she'd ever learned to be comfortable with where she was in life, or if I'd done a better job showing her appreciation for what she was. I have this emptiness in the pit of my stomach. I messed so many things up in these few short years of my life. You know?"

More tears came to Courtney's eyes as he looked on his sister-in-law. "I feel so bad for you man. I can't stop thinking about how much time I wasted being jealous of you, hating you."

Colin's eyes turned up. "You were jealous of me? I was jealous of you, Mr. Basketball Superstar. Prime wasn't about shit but I always envied how he responded to you. I wanted that. You had an easier time in school, too. You were cool. I had to pretend to be. I remember the first day I realized that you were taller than I was. I was standing next to you and I noticed your shoulder was higher. I moved from you and sat; couldn't get over that. It shook me up."

Courtney laughed through the tears. "Jealousy is one strange beast, man. Everyone always looked at you differently, expected so much out of you. No matter what I accomplished, I never could match you. Basketball superstar or not . . . I spent most of my years wanting to be you."

Colin looked down at the bed, looked at his brother. "That's another lesson there, little brother. Again, be thankful for who you are, and what you have. If you were me, then that would be your wife lying there, hanging on by a thread."

Courtney sighed. The gravity of Colin's words hit him in the chest; he struggled to clear his lungs as if he'd taken a devastating punch in the solar plexus, and struggled to catch his breath.

Colin noticed his brother's discomfort, placed his hand on Courtney's back and tapped it as if he were burping Lyric. "Come on; let's go down to the cafeteria. Mama and everyone else is down there getting a quick bite. I want to compare notes with you about raising daughters."

Courtney pursed his lips, shook his head up and down. He couldn't think of anything poignant to say, so he remained quiet, kept looking at Liza, so peaceful in her state. Was that how it was when heaven was close enough you could smell and touch it? *Come on,* he thought, *you can pull through this, Liza.* He looked at his brother, Colin. *You have to pull through this, Liza.*

Colin kissed two fingers, pressed them against Liza's forehead. "I'll be back in a while, sweetie, you hold on for me. My little brother and I are going to go down and get food and talk. I know how happy this must make you. You never liked it that we were at odds. I want you to know that me and Courtney, we're going to be okay."

Colin turned and put his arm around Courtney's shoulder and they walked off, supporting each other. Colin, though, had the strength in his legs to carry his own weight.

As they made their way toward the elevator, a smile broke across Colin's face. He looked at his brother, excitement in his voice. "Man, I have to tell you how much you're going to enjoy being a father. I'm so happy for you. It's one of life's greatest thrills."

"I've been tripping off the things that Destiny does," Courtney said. "It's like she has my mannerisms and stuff. It's bugged."

The elevator door opened and the two brothers stepped in. Colin hit the button for the first floor while nodding his head. "Yeah, Lyric does this thing with her mouth while she's asleep. Cutest thing you ever saw."

The doors closed.

PLAYING WITH DESTINY

PHILLIP THOMAS DUCK

ABOUT THIS GUIDE

The questions and discussion topics that follow are
intended to enhance your group's reading of
PLAYING WITH DESTINY by Phillip Thomas Duck. We hope
the novel provided an enjoyable read for all your members.

DISCUSSION QUESTIONS

1. In the novel, Courtney assumes that his mother has a greater love for Colin than she does for him. Do you think Courtney was correct? Is it possible for a parent to love all their children equally?

2. What do you think Colin would say was his greatest desire at the beginning of the novel? Do you think he would still consider this desire his primary hope at the end of the novel?

3. Chante betrayed Courtney and it affected him deeply. Do you think Chante's explanations for the betrayal were valid? Is the kind of betrayal Chante committed ever understandable?

4. Armando's actions had a profound affect on his daughter Liza. Do you think she was correct to harbor the ill feelings she had toward her father?

5. If Liza had a chance to do life over, do you think she would make the same choices? Do you think her choices, in the end, were good ones or poor ones?

6. What do you think would have become of the two brothers if Destiny's paternity had turned out differently? Would they have still reconciled?

7. What kind of relationship do you envision for the two infants at the heart of the novel, Destiny and Lyric, as they grow older?

8. After all the brothers endured, how well do you think they will ultimately perform as fathers? Which brother do you think will be a better father?

9. When the novel ends, Colin and Courtney are in different places in their lives. What do you think the future holds for each brother?

10. No person is all good or all bad. Discuss the good points and bad points of the major characters in the novel.

11. What was the most memorable scene in the novel? What made the scene so memorable?